MASTER OF CROWS
A NOVEL

Grace Draven

Copyright © 2009 by Grace Draven.

All rights reserved. No part of this publication may be reproduced, distributed or transmitted in any form or by any means, including photocopying, recording, or other electronic or mechanical methods, without the prior written permission of the publisher, except in the case of brief quotations embodied in critical reviews and certain other noncommercial uses permitted by copyright law. For permission requests, write to the publisher, addressed "Attention: Permissions Coordinator," at the address below.

Grace Draven
Grace.Draven1@gmail.com
www.gracedraven.com

Publisher's Note: This is a work of fiction. Names, characters, places, and incidents are a product of the author's imagination. Locales and public names are sometimes used for atmospheric purposes. Any resemblance to actual people, living or dead, or to businesses, companies, events, institutions, or locales is completely coincidental.

Book Layout ©2013 BookDesignTemplates.com
Cover Illustration © 2009 by Louisa Gallie
Cover Layout Design by Isis Sousa

Master of Crows/ Grace Draven. – 2nd ed.
ISBN 978-1-5003694-8-4

This book is dedicated to my editors, Lora Gasway and Mel Sanders. Ladies, without your help I would have never been able to write "The End." Thank you for your time, your patience, your suggestions, and most of all for your wonderful friendship.

To my sister, Kim Sayre, who has read nearly everything I've written and been one of my most enthusiastic fans. Thanks, kiddo.

To Isis Sousa, whom it's been a privilege to not only work with but to also call "friend."

Last but definitely not least, an enthusiastic thank you to Louisa Gallie who found the heart of this book and brought it to vivid life in her stunning painting Beyond Neith.

CHAPTER ONE

Yield to me, Master of Crows, and I will make you ruler of kingdoms."

Silhara of Neith groaned and doubled over, clutching his midriff. Blood streamed from his nose and dripped on the balcony's worn stones. The god's voice, familiar and insidious, wrapped around his mind. Transfixed beneath the rays of a jaundiced star, he huddled against the crumbling parapet, fighting an evil the priests assumed long vanquished.

The god seduced him, filled his head with images fantastic and horrific sacrificial blood pooling on a killing stone, armies marching across a sun-scorched desert, a sea of starving people kneeling in adulation. Magic surged through him, a colossal power bred of hate. Unstoppable. Terrifying. He was drunk on the knowledge that the armies moved on his orders, and the people worshipped at his feet. The victims sacrificed were offered to the god, and Silhara reigned over all before him.

The voice sang its malevolent song. "You will be an emperor unchallenged, a sorcerer unequaled."

Silhara ground his teeth against the agony splitting his skull. "And be a thrall to a beggar god?" His lips bled with the question. "I will not yield."

Soft laughter echoed within him. "You will, avatar. You always do."

The god released him suddenly, a wrenching pull that almost sucked the marrow from his bones. He cried out and dropped to his knees. The visions and the voice faded, leaving an unseen foulness in their wake. The saltiness of blood burned his throat; sweat and urine drenched his robes. Poisonous light pulsed from the yellow star above him.

Silhara collapsed on the balcony floor. "Help me," he prayed to no one.

His servant found him hours later as the rising sun set fire to the eastern horizon. Silhara clambered to his feet beneath Gurn's steadying hands. The giant gazed in sympathy, gesturing at the mage's face. Silhara touched his nose, tracing a rough, crusted line from nostril to jaw.

"Blood?"

The servant nodded and nudged him toward his room. Silhara ignored him and gazed at the star suspended like a cats-eye moonstone on an invisible cord. No true illumination flowed from the star's center, only a turbid haze that suffocated the sky.

"Gurn, can you see the star?"

Gurn shook his head, blunt features wary. His hands traced intricate patterns, and Silhara sighed, his suspicions confirmed. While anyone possessing a thread of intuition might sense the god's presence, the Gifted alone saw the physical manifestation. The priests of Conclave were surely running around in their seaside fortress, panicked over the knowledge that their illustrious forbearers had ultimately failed to defeat the god called Corruption.

Suspicious of Silhara's activities and resentful of his refusal to swear allegiance to them, the priests—pretentious clerics who couldn't scratch their backsides without uttering an incantation—would turn a baleful eye on him now. Still, the malevolent force hovering at his back and slithering into his consciousness with promises of untold power and subjugation made Conclave nothing more than a nuisance by comparison.

Silhara picked at his soiled robes, disgusted. Corruption's presence lingered in the smell of his sweat, his clothing, even his hair. He spat twice, ridding himself of its taste. "That parasite has reduced me to a babe," he said. "I pissed myself."

He stripped off the ruined garments, dropping them in a damp pile at his feet. Naked and shivering in the cool, pre-dawn air, he motioned Gurn back and recited a spell. His clothes burst into flame, leaving a circle of blackened ash on the stone pavers.

Gurn's mouth turned down in disapproval. Silhara smiled. He knew that look. Paupers did not destroy good clothing, no matter the justification. "They had Corruption's stench on them, Gurn." Just as he did now. "Power like that defiles whatever it touches."

He strode to his room, grateful for the warmth from the hearth fire blazing in the corner. Gurn had brought wash water and laid a clean, threadbare shirt and breeches across the bed. Silhara went directly to the wash bowl, desperate to scrub Corruption's taint off his skin. He reached for the sponge, hands still trembling from the residual shock of the god's assault.

The subtle voice returned, whispered in his mind. "Welcome me, servant reborn."

Silhara growled low in his throat. He couldn't deny such seduction, more deft than the practiced hand of any painted whore. The visions of empires at his feet and limitless power at his fingertips were the god's bait. Greater men than he had fallen before such temptation, and there were many men greater than he.

Gurn's light touch on his shoulder brought him back to earth, and he banished the enticing thoughts. Blood from his nose trickled onto his hand and ran across his knuckles.

"Peace, Gurn," he said. "I'm not broken yet." The servant's eyes narrowed at his words, but he stepped away and allowed his master his bath.

Water sluiced over Silhara's arms and torso as he issued instructions. "Prepare one of the chambers on the third floor—whichever one doesn't have a hole in the roof." Gurn's eyebrows rose. "I'm inviting a guest to Neith."

The giant servant's eyebrows lifted higher.

Gurn's reaction amused him. No one visited Neith. The manor's reputation as the home of a dark mage—a crow wizard—kept all comers at bay, and Silhara encouraged that reputation, uninterested in entertaining dull aristocrats or killing young sorcerers intent on making names for themselves by challenging the notorious Master of Crows.

Circumstances had changed. As much as Silhara despised the idea, he needed Conclave's help. Nothing was immune to destruction, not even a god. The priests returned his contempt in full measure, but they might each use the other in the common goal of defeating Corruption. Conclave was known to turn a blind eye to crow mages and their forbidden arts if such practices aided them. Silhara wanted one of Conclave's novitiates, a cleric-scribe versed in ancient tomes, one with knowledge of forgotten and arcane languages. Killing a god required magic far older and much darker than a Conclave ritual, and such knowledge was often buried in dead languages or ancient scrolls. Conclave had its strictures, but its scribes were unmatched in their skills for translations. He had little doubt an exception to the ban on reading the black arcana would be granted if necessary.

Morning brought burgeoning sunlight streaming through the open window as he finished his bath. A discordant caw greeted the day, followed by a symphony of like calls. A black mantle of crow wings burst from the orange grove, blotting the sky before veering north to circle the manor.

The mage smiled. He'd send his letter by messenger crow. The priests would cluck, conjecture and wonder why the Master of Crows, who had always rejected their overtures and insistence for allegiance, suddenly asked for aid. They would answer, eager for the chance to place a Conclave spy in his house.

He turned away from the window, from Corruption's star still hovering low on the horizon, and sat at his writing table. The surface lay buried beneath scrolls, inkwells and broken quills. Finding one quill still whole, he pulled a piece of blank parchment from beneath a stack of manuscripts and dipped the quill in a nearby inkwell. For a moment, the tip hovered over the paper. Silhara smirked and wrote.

The old gods are not dead. Your demon has awakened...

CHAPTER TWO

Martise studied the long path leading to Neith manor and considered whether she was an apprentice or a sacrifice. The scent of curse magic streamed from the fog-shrouded road, making her nostrils twitch.

"I still allow you the choice, Martise, but there's no turning away once we take this road."

She gazed at her master, saw the silver chain holding her spirit stone threaded through his fingers. Cut into flawless facets that caught the sunlight and bounced rainbows into her eyes, the azure jewel was the cage for a part of her soul. Memories assailed her. At seven years old, she'd been terrified of the stern, beak-nosed priest who'd assessed her with an icy, measuring eye and bought her from a starving mother with a handful of coins. He'd enslaved her with a magic that had made her scream in agony, one that ensured she would serve the house of Asher until her death or until Cumbria sold her and passed on the secret of the stone to a new master. Or until she won her freedom.

Her resolve strengthened. Desperate people didn't have the luxury of fear. There were things worth dying for, even if the endeavor failed.

"I haven't changed my mind, Your Grace."

She didn't lower her eyes as Cumbria, the High Bishop of Conclave, stared at her, his graven face harsh in the late afternoon light. Whatever he saw in her expression satisfied him. He motioned to his three retainers waiting nearby with the horses. One approached, bearing a large crow on his forearm. The bird hopped to Cumbria's outstretched arm, fluttering dark wings until he ran a gentle finger down the feathered back.

"Micah. My best watcher. He will act as the messenger between us. Silhara's groves are infested with crows. One more won't be noticed. When you have information, call Micah down using the Nanteri lullaby. He will deliver your message."

The crow squawked once in protest as the bishop lifted his arm and sent him skyward. He flew south, over the gnarled Solaris oaks guarding Neith's road, toward Corruption's star.

Cumbria relayed his instructions to the retainer. "Stay here and tend the horses. They won't walk the path willingly. I should return in no more than two hours." He frowned, a spark of anger flitting through his gray eyes. "I doubt Silhara will do anything foolish, but if I don't return at the appointed time, summon my brethren. They'll know what to do."

The servant bowed. Martise might have pitied his lot and those of his comrades. Dressed in the heavy livery robes of the Asher household, they would broil in the merciless summer heat as they waited for their master's return, but the reciprocal pity in the servant's eyes squelched her own. He and the others might sweat like mules, but they remained behind in a far safer place.

Cumbria tapped her shoulder. "Come, Martise. It will be dark soon, and I've no wish to linger here."

A seeping cold penetrated her layered clothing the moment they stepped onto the road, and the scent of dark magic blanketed the air. She peered over her shoulder, half expecting the sun-filled plain behind her to have disappeared, cut off by more of the sinuous mists caressing her ankles.

Bathed in natural light, the sea of swaying grass remained, beckoning her away from the gloom and a dangerous task. She turned her back before temptation took hold.

Cumbria sneered. "Typical of him. Silhara would find a means to scare off visitors or lost travelers who come too near Neith."

They continued on, their steps strangely muffled on the gravel as they passed beneath the thick canopy of Solaris oaks. Martise had always admired the stately giants with their widespread branches and thick foliage. Most wealthy manors had them planted along their grand entrances—avenues preparing guests for even grander homes.

The road to Neith, however, left a different impression. The great oaks offered respite from the heat but cast the surroundings in semi-darkness. Black, crippled limbs arched overhead, twining together in a grappling dance, as if each tree sought to wrench its adversary from the roots.

Not only did the trees quell the light, but so did those smaller things growing beneath them. Weak sunlight pierced the gloom in a few places and faded midway to the ground, snuffed by stunted shrubbery dressed in gray leaves and menacing thorns.

She hugged herself for comfort and warmth. "This is a dark place," she whispered.

As if punctuating her words, a lean phantom shape burst from a stand of bushes, running low and fast before disappearing into the forest depths. Martise gasped and closed the gap between her and the bishop.

"What was that?" She peered into the wood's murk, half afraid of what she might see.

Cumbria's voice, normally forceful and carrying, was stifled. He shrugged. "Who can say? A leopard. A fox." He scowled. "Something more unnatural. Silhara is a dark mage, and his mentor, the first Master of Crows, experimented with…things. Any number of horrors may roam these woods."

He noted her shudder. "The manor will be your greatest protection, Martise. Never seek sanctuary in this wood."

Her skin danced around her body at his words.

They completed their journey without further incident, though she sensed something watched them–either a shadow of the wood or the misshapen trees themselves.

The forest gave way to a treeless courtyard flooded in sunlight and framed by dilapidated metal gates. A hot breeze spun off the plain, dissipating the unnatural chill permeating the forest.

The gates swayed and creaked in the wind like bones hanging from a gallows tree. A rusted chain and lock fastening them struck the metal with a dissonant clang.

Beyond, the remains of a large manor sprawled across a stretch of rocky terrain and withered grass. The structure's western half was reduced to rubble, as if smashed by a giant hand. Broken stones and mortar littered the courtyard, and the skeleton of a winding staircase spiraled into nothingness. Rotting fabric clung to the splintered risers, fluttering in the wind. She was hemmed in by the bleak and the dead.

Martise turned away from the ruins and surveyed the part of the manor still intact. Graceful arches and spires, silhouetted against the setting sun, reflected an age before men reigned supreme, when those who built Neith and laid the path to it had not yet vanished into history.

Her eyes widened when a figure suddenly emerged from the remnants of the west wing, as if rising from the parched ground. No one had lurked in that spot moments ago, and the giant approaching them couldn't have stayed hidden from view long. Dressed in a tunic sporting the Neithian coat of arms, he crossed the courtyard in graceful strides despite his gangly form and size. His bald pate glistened in the afternoon light.

He smiled a greeting and motioned with huge hands that they step aside so he could open the gates. Martise considered his strange sign language and wordless commands. A mute. Somehow that didn't surprise her, here in this eerie place forgotten by the living world.

The chain and lock fell away as the gates swung open on a thin scream. Martise stayed close as Cumbria strode into the courtyard. The bishop ignored the servant, but she smiled shyly and nodded as she passed. He grinned in return.

He overtook the bishop, directing them to the part of the manor still intact. They halted in front of an ornately carved door weathered by the elements. A trickle of nervous sweat slid between her breasts.

She stiffened in self-reproach. Images of her spirit stone in Cumbria's hand flashed in her mind, and she admonished herself So far they had seen shadows in the wood, a ruined estate and a mute servant. Nothing truly frightening. But she couldn't rid herself of the tiny voice that said *"They are all ruled by a crow wizard, and soon he will rule you as well."*

To her relief, nothing attacked them when they entered the house. *Bursin's wings, when did you become such a coward?* She reddened, shamed by her fright. Braver souls were more suited for this work. Again that inner voice taunted her. *But few are as motivated.*

They moved from an empty vestibule into a more spacious room suffused in muted sunlight. Martise blinked until her eyes adjusted, then gasped at the sight before her.

Lost beneath a shroud of dust, the main hall's faded grandeur left her breathless. Blackened timbers soared above her head, their beams crossing in a massive spider's web of support for the lofty ceiling. An enormous fireplace stretched across one wall, the mantel and surround carved into the shapes of mythical beasts entwined in eternal combat. This was once a grand place, far larger than Cumbria's estate–a place built for kings and their fighting champions.

How low the great had sunk. Brittle rushes snapped beneath their feet. The few pieces of furniture stood gray with dirt, and the tapestries bore moth holes. Light filtered through windows caked in layers of grime, creating a false gloaming. Though the walls still stood, the hall was abandoned as surely as the west wing's battered ruins.

The servant bent, patting a cushioned stool in a coaxing gesture. A cloud of dust swirled into the air. Cumbria's lip curled in disgust.

"No, I don't want to sit." He gathered his robes around him and took in his surroundings. "No better than a hovel. Why should have I expected more?"

Martise stared at the bishop, shocked by his rudeness. She glanced at the servant and saw his smile fade to a blank, waiting stare. She knew that look—had used it often with her master.

Cumbria frowned and kicked the stool out of his path. "Well," he snapped. "Get on with it, man. I won't linger at your master's pleasure. Fetch him!"

The servant shrugged before disappearing into a corridor dimly lit by tallow candles in bent sconces. Their flames flickered as he passed.

Cumbria's voice resonated with loathing. "An insolent servant to an insolent carrion mage. See what happens when you elevate street filth?"

He touched her arm. "Guard your words and remain silent unless he addresses you, Martise. Silhara is fond of entrapment. He possesses a sharp tongue and has eviscerated more than one hapless opponent in a conversation. You'd be no match."

Martise lowered her head and hid her smile. Cumbria had chosen her for this endeavor because of her abilities, among them the talents for staying silent and unnoticed. His warning amused her and revealed a hint of his unease in the upcoming meeting. How interesting that a man didn't always admire his own traits in another.

The mute servant reappeared, followed by a slender shadow silhouetted against the hallway's weak light. Cumbria stood rigid next to her as their host emerged from the shadows. Martise sucked in a sharp breath, enthralled by her first sight of the Master of Crows.

A living flame in the begrimed room, he burned with a cold, still fire. Long scarlet robes swirled around his ankles like bloodied smoke. Taller than most men and lean, he wore his black hair in a tight braid that fell over his shoulder. The severe style accentuated a sun-burnished face neither handsome nor kind but carved from the same rock strewn across the courtyard. His black eyes and aquiline nose reminded her of those Kurman nomads she'd sometimes seen in the markets, selling their rugs and weaponry. Her belly tightened in dread as he gazed at her and Cumbria with sloe-eyed malevolence.

"I see you didn't get lost. A pity. To what do I owe the honor of your august presence, Your Grace? I expected a Conclave minion. Instead I get the High Bishop himself."

His deep voice grated against her ears, broken and harsh, as if he forced the words from a ruined throat. Contempt laced his greeting, and a scornful half-smile curved his lips.

Cumbria's face froze. The antipathy between the two men swelled in the room, seeping into the walls and floors.

"Still ruler of your squalid little kingdom, Silhara?" Cumbria's derisive stare raked the servant. "You and your army of one."

Silhara's rough laughter drifted through the room. "King of Filth, Master of Crows. What will be my title tomorrow, Your Grace? As usual, Conclave can never reach a final decision."

The bishop's eyes burned. "'Tis a shame they didn't choke the life out of you all those years ago."

In her years of serving Cumbria and the house of Asher, Martise had never seen the patriarch on the edge of losing control. His counsel for silence made more sense now. Even he found it difficult maintaining a level head around the sorcerer.

Silhara's dark eyes narrowed; his tanned features paled. Cumbria's curious statement had drawn blood.

"'Tis a testimony to the will and longevity of wickedness, Your Grace. It does not go down easily."

Silhara's hard face suddenly relaxed, and Martise's instincts buzzed in warning. Mercurial and shrewd, he'd make a deadly adversary. Suddenly the price of her freedom seemed too high, and she wished herself back in the familiar warmth and comfort of the kitchens at home.

Suspicion glittered in that obsidian gaze as he scrutinized her. He addressed Cumbria without looking away from her, and her burgeoning fear of him transformed to instant dislike.

"Never let it be said this emperor cannot be gracious. You have made a long journey. Gurn will bring tea. You can tell me of your trip and the pet you have brought for my entertainment."

CHAPTER THREE

Silhara admired an accomplished liar. He was one himself. The skill was among the few things he could stomach about Cumbria of Asher. So why did the High Bishop of Conclave, a master at fabrication, weave a tale so poorly constructed?

In the comfort of his study, his guests drank their tea. The woman—a small, drab creature—perched on the edge of her seat. For an apprentice, she was long in the tooth. Nor did she seem interested in her future teacher. Her gaze traveled the room, resting briefly on the table containing his potions then to the scrolls stacked haphazardly in one corner. Cumbria's ward? Not likely. This was no poor relation dependent on Asher generosity. Still, Cumbria had selected her as Silhara's apprentice for a reason, and Silhara never underestimated the wily cleric.

The silence in the room thickened until Cumbria frowned and abandoned any show of enjoying his tea.

"Well? Will she do? You've requested an apprentice. I have brought you one. Martise is a good girl—obedient and intelligent. She will serve you well."

Silhara drummed his fingers on the desk. "I asked for a cleric with a strong back and knowledge of the arcane languages. You bring me your…ward. She has no extended training, no noticeable manifestation of the Gift, no hint of any talent." He flicked a sharpened quill with thumb and forefinger and watched it roll across a stack of parchment. "My dog is obedient and my servant intelligent. What use will this girl be to me?" He'd expected a spy from Conclave, just not an inept one with no magery.

The bishop stiffened in his chair, "If you wanted a farm hand, you shouldn't have applied to Conclave," he snapped. He took a steadying breath. "Martise is a skilled scribe and translator and has the Gift. She was once schooled at Conclave. The magefinders sense her magic. We have put her in a room crowded with Conclave priests, and the dogs seek her first." He paused, his expression souring. "Despite your reputation as a carrion practitioner, you're also a sorcerer of renown. The Luminary believes if anyone can make Martise's Gift manifest, you can."

Silhara studied his new apprentice. She returned his gaze, her plain features placid. Not likely. He'd deal with a Conclave minion, but not one hand-picked and delivered by his most hated adversary.

"An intriguing puzzle, to be sure, but I have little time for indulging in the vagaries of the Gift's blessings. I require an apprentice capable of complex translations and simple enchantments that take more of my time than I can now give. Like Conclave, my first priority is defeating Corruption."

"Is it?" Skepticism peppered Cumbria's question.

Silhara smirked. He'd wagered with Gurn over whether or not the bishop might reveal his suspicions. "Concerned, Your Grace? Even a carrion mage like me can help in some small way. Or do you represent the entire canonry in your doubts?"

Cumbria's voice turned sly. "Surely, the god speaks to you, tempts you with all manner of promises if only you give the loyalty you refuse Conclave?"

Silhara's amusement evaporated. If Cumbria knew what dreams plagued his slumber at night, what whispering evil seduced him even in the light of day, Conclave's unease would turn to outright witch-hunting.

Martise had remained silent since first entering his domain, offering no hint of her character. If he refused her, it would alarm the priests even more.

"Martise of Asher." He smiled when she stiffened. "His Grace has spoken for you during this entire meeting. Have you no words? Or did you suffer as my servant and have your tongue cut out?"

He followed her gaze to Gurn. The servant gave her an encouraging nod. Silhara might have considered her easily intimidated save for that calm demeanor.

"No, sir, I'm no mute. It is rude to speak out of turn, is it not?"

He stilled at her question. Bursin's wings, what generous god blessed this woman with such a voice? Refined and sensual, it possessed a silky quality, as if she physically caressed him.

The contrast between her dulcet tones and bland appearance startled him. Before she spoke, Martise had faded into her surroundings, forgotten. Now she shone, riveting the attention of anyone within hearing distance. He glanced at Cumbria who treated him to a smug smile.

He didn't like being caught off guard and lashed out. "Far be it from me that I compromise the deportment of a lady. I wouldn't tempt a well-trained dog into forgetting the commands of 'Fetch' and 'Sit'."

Her jaw tightened. She dropped her gaze, but not before he saw the sparks of anger in her eyes. Not so docile as one might first believe, yet his new apprentice exercised admirable control over her emotions. Behavior of a long-time servant. Cumbria had indeed brought him a spy.

He rested his elbows on the desk. Negotiations were at hand. "I will take your ward." He paused for effect. "For three months, no more. If I cannot find what Gift lies within her, I will send her back to you. I have no interest in feeding an additional mouth any longer than necessary."

Cumbria frowned. "Six months, and I will pay her keep."

The coins clinked as he placed a small velvet bag atop a stack of parchment. The girl visibly flinched and blushed to the roots of her hair.

"Four," Silhara said. "And I keep the entire amount." He hefted the sack in his palm, ignoring the bishop's derisive smile.

Cumbria stood, brushing imaginary dust from his robes. "A bargain is struck then. Four months." He wasted no time taking his leave, his concern for his ward now a thing of the past.

Martise rose stiffly from her chair and faced Cumbria.

Silhara stood as well and leaned against the edge of his desk. The bishop frowned at his informality. Silhara raised an eyebrow. "You are High Bishop of Conclave. I've sworn no allegiance to Conclave, Your Grace. You are nothing more than a mage like me."

Martise stepped back in alarm at Cumbria's murderous expression. Thin lines of crimson light coiled around his twitching fingers.

"Never compare yourself to me, crow wizard!" His face was skeletal in the fading light, hatred blackening his gray eyes.

Silhara waited, his hands and arms tingling with defensive magic. *Do it, old man,* he thought. *Give me a reason, so I may blast you into oblivion.*

Cumbria took a deep breath and raised his chin in haughty dismissal before turning his back and striding to the door.

Silhara couldn't resist goading him a final time. "Have you no farewell for your beloved ward, Your Grace?"

The question halted the High Bishop. He returned to Martise, grasped her hand in a courtly gesture and bowed stiffly.

"Good fortune favor you, Martise."

The statement's fervor surprised Silhara, but it was Martise's reaction that fascinated him most.

Her hand jerked in the bishop's grip, and her thin smile wavered. "A fair moon above you, Mas . . . Sir."

Her eyes widened at her blunder, and Cumbria winced. Silhara smirked.

Cumbria glared at him. "I take my leave of you. You will keep Conclave abreast of any changes in Corruption's actions? The Luminary feels he can trust you, though I cannot fathom why."

Silhara shrugged. "My honest face perhaps?"

The bishop sneered and stalked out of the room, slamming the door behind him. Gurn tried following, but Silhara stopped him.

"Don't bother. He'll find his way and won't appreciate your guidance. He is, after all, the High Bishop of Conclave. He can take care of himself."

Gurn shrugged and pointed at Martise, who stared longingly at the door. Silhara strolled around the desk, skirting the chairs and a pile of scrolls, until he stood in front of the girl. She met his eyes, her features serene.

Clearly Cumbria had not chosen her as a means of seducing him into revealing some heresy. No beauty by the kindest standard, she reminded him of a peahen, lackluster and brown. Her clothing was good quality but ill-fitting, as if borrowed, and hung on her small body like empty grain sacks. Wisps of dull russet hair framed a pale face. Her eyes were interesting–the color of new copper and framed by dark lashes, but they didn't save her looks. Overall, she was a drab creature, one who went unnoticed and unremarked in a crowd.

Her voice was another matter. Capable of lulling wyverns to sleep and calling men to worship, it bewitched him. The striking disparity between her voice and plain features was intriguing. Did her Gift lie somewhere in the sultry cadence of her words? As soon as he questioned it, he abandoned the notion. Such a talent was too obvious. Martise of Asher—ward, servant, informant—possessed the Gift. What made her magic manifest, no one knew–yet.

"Why are you here?"

"You asked for me, Master."

A coiling heat wrapped around his body, and he fought closing his eyes in the sheer pleasure of hearing those melodic tones.

"Master. That address comes to you easily, as if you have used it your entire life."

His point struck home. A hint of unease drifted across her face before falling behind that passive mask.

"Would you prefer something else?"

"No." He signaled to Gurn. "No need to invoke impropriety here."

He opened the door. "Gurn will see you to your chambers. You'll have your supper there."

What a shame if he were forced to murder her to protect himself. The world would be a lesser place deprived of such a stunning voice. A long-suffering look settled over her face, as if she tolerated him through sheer force of will. He frowned.

"Take your rest early tonight. We rise with the sun. You'll start earning your keep, and I'll introduce you to Cael. I am curious what you will think of our other denizen here." He ignored Gurn's disapproving scowl. "Good evening."

He closed the door and made his way through the shadowed passages that took him deeper into the manor. A stairway, twin to the exposed and shattered one in the west wing, wound upward into darkness. Silhara climbed, surefooted, and gestured once. Witchfire lit the torches and sent shadows scuttling across the walls toward his chambers.

His door swung open on squeaking hinges. Gurn had left the window to the balcony open. A cool evening wind swirled inside and relieved the day's oppressive heat. The bed was made, the pitcher on the bedside table refilled, the *huqqah* prepared for his evening smoke. Silhara lived sparingly but was grateful for the mute servant. The man was worth more than all of Neith.

He shrugged out of the stifling scarlet robes, leaving on the simple white shirt and dark trousers he favored.

A pair of tongs lay on his worktable, and he used them to stir the glowing coals in the brazier near the cold hearth. Tiny sparks flew upward as he selected a coal sliver for the *huqqah* bowl.

Soon, the heady scent of matal tobacco and citrus filled his nostrils. The water bowl's rhythmic bubbling and the whisper of wind through the trees outside were the only disturbances to the room's hush. Smoke swirled in spectral patterns around his head while he stared out the window and drew on the pipe.

The view from his bedroom was vastly different from the one greeting the rare visitor to Neith. Rows of orange trees, heavy with ripened fruit, cut the land in neat tracks, stretching to the confines of a stone fence. Lethal enchantments protected the grove from intruders. More than once he and Gurn had recovered and buried a hapless thief who'd scaled the walls and met his death.

Beyond the grove, the flat plain flowed into an endless twilight, and Corruption's star brightened as the sky darkened.

Bluish smoke streamed from Silhara's mouth as he indulged in the matal and studied the horizon. Though the god drew no closer across the southern borders, he sensed its nearness, an invisible gaze avaricious and feral.

He caught a flicker of movement in the grove. A ghostly shape glided in the dark, vanishing and reappearing as it sped toward the house. A droning sound accompanied the specter, like the swarm of locusts. Silhara dropped the *huqqah* hose and strode to the balcony for a better view. The hairs at his nape rose.

A white dog, or what was once a dog, raised its enormous head and froze him in place with a lambent yellow gaze. The creature dwarfed the largest mage-finder male and sported a misshapen skull and mouth filled with teeth like sword blades. A mottled patchwork of hair and scabrous skin stretched across a skeletal frame.

Silhara drowned in those glowing eyes. Once more the images of fallen kingdoms and worshipping throngs flooded his mind.

Satisfaction ran deep within him at the vision of Conclave Redoubt razed to rubble and drowned in the sea, the priests hunted to extinction. He licked his lips and caught the taste of iron on his tongue. Corruption poured power into him, offering gifts even as it sought his enslavement.

The god didn't whisper to his mind as before but spoke through the white nightmare holding Silhara's gaze. *"Come forth, Avatar. Do you not know me, Son of Lies?"*

The voice, hollow as an empty grave, rose above the insectile buzzing and snapped Silhara out of his stupor.

He spun away from the parapet. Racing into his room, he careened into the bedside table, sending the pitcher crashing to the floor in a shower of water and broken pottery. He skidded in a puddle as he grabbed the crossbow and bolts stashed against one corner.

Rage burned his spirit clean of Corruption's bewitchment. "Neith crawls with unwelcome guests this evening." He nocked a bolt into the quarrel groove and strode to the door. "But I am ever a civil host."

He nearly ran Gurn down on the steps leading to the great hall. The giant teetered on the stair's edge, clutching his oil lamp until Silhara shoved him against the wall and squeezed past, snapping out orders as he leapt the risers two at a time. "Lock the girl's door and stay in the house with Cael."

The first floor corridors were sepulcher-black, but he never slowed, fueled by anger and a fevered compulsion to confront the god on his terms.

He kicked the back door open and found the cadaverous dog awaiting him. It slinked toward him, monstrous and reeking worse than corpses left in the sun. Silhara swallowed back bile and leveled the bow's sights on the creature. "What do you want?"

The aggravating drone ceased abruptly, and Corruption spoke through the dog's rictus of teeth. "What you want, avatar. Homage, respect, power."

"Then you have no need of me. You are the god here, not I."

The dog cocked its head to the side. A stream of worms poured from a rotting ear. They writhed in a slick heap near Silhara's feet. He didn't think the thing capable of smiling. He was wrong. The heavy jowls stretched back in a death head's grimace, exposing curved canines gleaming silver in the dying light.

"Oh, I need you, Master of Crows. Do you not wonder why I call you Avatar?"

The spectral voice changed, turned oily and cajoling. "I know your mind, sorcerer, and your spirit. Your hate burns hot for the priests–these men who spit on a whore's get. Surrender to me, and I will see them destroyed in your name."

Silhara pulled the trigger. The bolt struck the cur in the eye with a hard thunk, and the animal collapsed in a heap. Ashen skin and fur melted away, exposing a jumble of bones and more of the putrid worms. Even those soon dissolved, along with the fired bolt, leaving only a coil of oily smoke in a patch of ruined grass. He waved the smoke away impatiently and spoke to the grove's deepening shadows.

"I hate many things and many people; none are worth subjugating my will. You'll have to coax me with something better than a few dead priests." He spat, a mix of blood and spittle striking the ground. "Until then, stay out of my mind and out of my grove."

The star answered him, pulsing sullenly behind a scatter of slate clouds. He turned to the house and caught Gurn hovering in the doorway, peering into the grove's darkness. "Did I not say stay inside?"

The servant pointed to his feet, demonstrating he hadn't crossed the threshold. Silhara chuckled, despite the evening's events and the burgeoning headache ramming spikes between his eyes.

"You're a piss-poor servant, Gurn. Will you ever learn your place?"

Gurn shrugged, unconcerned, and opened the door wider for his master. Silhara glanced over his shoulder at the grove. "I doubt it will help, but I'll strengthen the wards on the walls tonight." He pointed to the ceiling. "Did she try leaving her room?"

Gurn shook his head and mimicked a sleeping position by resting his cheek against his hand. Silhara rolled his eyes. "Unlock her door, otherwise she'll think we've made her a prisoner."

He sent Gurn to bed after several assurances he was well and unharmed by his encounter with Corruption. A last study of the grove before shutting the door behind him and he returned to his chambers.

Gurn had doused the brazier's coals and put away the *huqqah*. The mess Silhara left when he rushed from the room was swept away. A carafe of sweet wine sat on the uprighted table.

He put the crossbow and bolts back in their place and poured a generous dram of wine into a goblet, draining it in two swallows. It did nothing to kill the pain in his head, so he poured another and strolled to the window. His land was deceptively peaceful outside. Only the rustle of sleeping crows whispered back to him. He recalled Corruption's words.

"Do you not wonder why I call you Avatar?"

Of course he wondered, and his suspicion left an abiding horror in his soul. His neck ached as much as his head, and he rolled his shoulders. Conclave spies, demon dogs and parasitic gods–just what he needed during the harvest season. "I grow tired of this wheel," he murmured.

The star glimmered. Silhara raised his goblet to the god's celestial face in a mocking toast. "To Silhara, master of nothing."

CHAPTER FOUR

Great stinking heaps of refuse surrounded Martise. The rancid odor flooded her nostrils on steaming puffs of air and buffeted her face until she gagged. The smell and the heat beat against her head and shoulders, followed by a cool dampness that nudged her neck. The touch startled her out of a restless sleep. She rolled over and opened her eyes to find a face covered in bristling gray fur and gagged scars filling her vision. Cael, Silhara's mage-finder hound, touched a wet black nose to hers and sniffed.

"Bursin's wings." She scooted back and pulled the covers over her head. "Cael, you smell like the dead. Have you been rolling in the pig sty again?"

The dog whined and shoved his nose into the blankets. Martise scrambled out of the bed, anxious to put some distance between her and his repulsive smell. He padded after her when she hurried to her window and opened the shutters.

Pale morning light embroidered the window's edge and cast the last pre-dawn shadows in sharp relief. The crows sleeping in the orange grove fluttered to life, rocking the drooping branches as they hopped from perch to perch and fought for space in the coveted treetops.

Cael joined her. He stood on his hind legs, resting massive paws on the window ledge. Martise stared at him with trepidation as he towered over her. The mage-finder was a massive animal, bigger than any of the males in the pack she'd seen at Conclave. White-muzzled and past his prime, he was still formidable. She'd watched him hunt on Neith land, easily running the fastest prey to ground with a long, loping stride. His kills were swift, efficient and left Martise rubbing the chills off her arms hours later. Once, long ago, mage-finders had hunted and killed the Gifted in the same fashion.

Her first introduction to the mage hound two weeks earlier had scared ten years off her lifespan. Standing in Gurn's comfortable kitchen her first morning at Neith, she'd stood frozen while Cael slowly circled her. As big as a pony, but with the feline grace of a cat, he'd slinked into the kitchen and made directly for her, black claws tapping on the stone floor. His dark eyes, gone crimson the second he saw her, watched her every move. The gray fur along his curved back rose in a spiny arch; his whip-like tail smacked a warning tattoo against Gurn's work table.

Martise pleaded silently for Gurn to pull the mage-finder back. He signed an apology and clapped his hands in command. Cael reluctantly followed the servant to the door leading to the inner bailey but not without looking back at her several times with those brilliant red eyes.

When Gurn returned, Martise was leaning against the table for support. "You have a mage-finder," she said in a weak voice. He nodded. She took a deep breath and straightened, feeling the first stirrings of anger. "He's the 'denizen' your master spoke of." Gurn inclined his head once more.

Heartless bastard. She echoed Cael, growling under her breath. She didn't expect Silhara to believe Cumbria's assurances.

The animosity between the two men was too great. But, there were many, less extreme ways to verify she was one of the Gifted. Ways that didn't involve a deadly mage-finder sniffing her skirts.

She schooled her expression into a placid mask. "Will he be satisfied now?"

Gurn shrugged, his eyes frosty. Martise sensed his disapproval wasn't directed at her. He motioned for her to sit and served her breakfast.

She'd quickly settled into a new routine since then. Cael, despite his initial wariness, accepted her. He was still curious and followed her about the manor as she performed the numerous chores Gurn assigned her during the day, and she grew used to his silent, if odorous company.

In that time she'd seen nothing of Silhara yet felt his presence in Neith's every crook and crevice. She'd met him only once so far, but his image was burned into her mind. He reminded her of a captured whirlwind, spinning fiercely in place, waiting only for the moment to burst free of its confines and blast the surrounding land. Cumbria had assigned her no easy task. Her freedom would be hard-won.

A brisk breeze swept through her open window, dispelling some of Cael's pungent odor. Dust motes danced in a spiral before coming to rest on his coat in a glittering net. In the early dawn light, Corruption's star shown dull amidst tinted clouds. The star never remained stationary. Yesterday it had washed the southern horizon in murky yellow light. This morning it shown in the eastern sky, nearly obscured by the sun's fiery ascent.

Cael snarled softly. His eyes were red once more as he also watched the star, and his fur bristled. No one knew what drew the hounds to magic, but they sought it in the same way an ordinary dog tracked prey. Cael had first reacted to her with restrained animosity, typical of a trained mage-finder when introduced to one of the Gifted. His reaction to Corruption's manifestation was different. The animal exuded hatred, a bestial hostility at its fiercest. His lips curled back, exposing fangs as long as her fingers. Were the god to take a more earthly form, she had no doubt Cael would leap out the window in an effort to hunt it down and rip it apart.

If he were an ordinary dog instead of a mage-finder, Martise might have patted his back in reassurance. But she was reluctant to touch him, wary of having her hand bitten off for her presumption. And he smelled worse than a privy.

"Come on, boy," she said and left the window. "Gurn will be wondering where I am." Her stomach growled, and she swore Cael's bushy eyebrows wriggled in amusement. "I don't want to miss out on the porridge either."

She made quick work of her ablutions and dressed in one of her borrowed cyrtels, castoffs from Cumbria's wife's ever changing wardrobe. She wrapped her hair in a tight bun and secured it with two wooden hair pins. "Dull and plain as a potato," she murmured and smoothed the front of her cyrtel. She wasn't here to seduce, only betray. Her beauty, or lack of it, played no part in this game. And the game might never begin if she didn't see Silhara more frequently.

Gurn had left a half-full oil lamp for her, a necessary navigation aid in Neith's dark corridors. Martise lit the lamp and motioned Cael out the door. The hallway winding through the manor's second floor was just as dark in the morning. Her lamp provided the only light, a weak luminescence that sent shadows chasing each other across the cracked walls and buckled floor.

Cumbria's comment about Neith being a hovel was rude but not far off the mark. This was truly a poor man's house, despite its size and decrepit grandeur. She hopped over a hole in the floor and rose on her toes as the boards groaned in protest beneath her feet. Dust covered every surface. Remnants of cobwebs fluttered like tattered lace from ceiling beams, caressing her head as she passed beneath them. Her skin crawled, and she tried not to dwell on the possibility of a spider trapped in her hair.

Was Silhara an aristocrat with only bloodlines to give him value? After the droughts and famines swept the far lands when she was a child, many of the aristo families were reduced to begging and selling their possessions just to feed themselves. Had such misfortunes brought his family to ruin?

It was the only thing she could think of to explain his haughtiness. He seemed a man born to rule—if not a country than certainly a fiefdom, a dale. His behavior toward Cumbria was insolent, as if he considered himself not only the bishop's equal but his superior. In her experience, only those born of noble stock and to great wealth displayed that conduct. Martise despised such people.

She'd have to temper her dislike for the crow mage. He was no different from any other landowner or high-ranking clergyman, and so far inflicted nothing more damaging on her than a few snide remarks. Still, there was something inherently dangerous about him. Conclave did not always rule by paranoia; instinct warned her to tread carefully around him, though she itched to box his ears for his arrogance.

He confused her more than anything. She was used to haughty behavior from those of his class and should have felt nothing more than the usual disdain of a servant for those she served. But fire had licked her insides at her first sight of him. Her face heated with what was surely the hottest blush ever gracing a woman no longer a maiden. Such feelings had no place here. She was bound; he was outcast. She resided at Neith to spy on him, and if the promise in his expression was any hint, he'd make her wish she never crossed his threshold.

His scarlet robes, bright and overwhelming in a house painted in shades of gray and faded brown teased her memory. There was a stark beauty about him, a compelling strength in his sharp-boned face with its prominent cheekbones and hooked nose. Like Cumbria, he radiated power in the set of his shoulders, the challenge in his dark eyes. Even Martise, Gifted but failed, sensed it. The mage-finders must have gone wild when they first scented him. He was a renegade and possibly a heretic. If he was as formidable as the canonry believed, and as susceptible to Corruption's seduction as they suspected, then the clerics had a right to their misgivings.

The sight of the rickety wooden stairs descending to the first floor made her forget her annoyance with Neith's master. Martise paused, envious of Cael's surefootedness when he eased passed her and took the steps two at a time. Sagging in spots and broken in others, they were a death trap. But it wasn't her place to complain. Instead, twice a day, she took a deep breath, said a heartfelt prayer and trod the treacherous path.

More groaning and popping sounded beneath her feet. She took comfort in knowing the much larger Gurn had climbed these same stairs countless times and not come to a bad end. Her luck might not be so good. The banister almost splintered beneath her grip. She pictured herself stumbling and pitching head first over the broken railing. She'd be of little use to Cumbria as his watcher if Silhara discovered her splayed dead on the floor of his great hall. Nor did she think he'd be pleased. The hall sported decayed furniture, soot-blackened walls and a cold hearth. Abandoned and eerie, yes, but not littered with corpses as part of the décor. As far she knew. She didn't want to ponder what oddities lurked in this place.

She sighed with relief at the bottom of the stairs. Cael waited for her, growling his disapproval at her slowness. She shrugged. "I'm not half so nimble as you, Cael." She wrinkled her nose at the odor wafting off his fur. "Nor half as smelly." He growled again and led her to the kitchen.

Gurn might not have much interest in tidying the rest of the manor, but he took pride in his kitchen. Pristine and uncluttered, the chamber practically sparkled. No unwashed pots or dishes were stacked in the dry sink; no livestock wandered about; no hunting hounds sprawled at the cooking hearth.

Battered cupboards placed against a far wall held an array of chipped dishes and stacks of pots and bowls. Fans of dried sage and rosemary hung next to chains of garlic from a low beam near the dry sink. A shallow bowl of oranges stacked in a neat tower shared space with loaves of cooling bread on a table by one window. The preparation table, dented and scratched with hard use, held a soft sheen that only came from industrious scrubbing.

Martise's admiration for the mute servant grew by leaps and bounds in her weeks at Neith. Even Bendewin, Asher's cook, had to be reminded to polish her preparation table on a constant basis. No one liked splinters in their food. Unlike most of the manor, not a speck of dust grayed the surfaces, and the entire room was redolent with the rich scent of porridge simmering in an iron cauldron suspended over a low hearth fire. Her mouth watered.

"A fair morning, Gurn," she said in greeting. "Breakfast smells wonderful."

He gave her a pleased smile from where he bent over the pot, stirring their porridge. The smile turned to a disgusted frown when Cael padded past him and flopped down in his customary place under the table.

She didn't wait for Gurn's direction but made her way to the cold cellar in one corner. Recessed into the kitchen floor and accessible by a hatch, the deep space was filled with jars of preserved food, slabs of salted bacon and ham, a bowl of eggs and crocks of butter, cream and milk. She gathered butter and milk and ascended the cellar steps, grateful they, at least, were sturdy.

Gurn had placed two bowls of the steaming porridge on the table by the time she set the crocks down. Martise was relieved not to see a third bowl. It was inevitable she'd deal with Silhara, and often. However, she preferred to delay as long as possible, and she didn't relish the thought of those penetrating black eyes watching her as she ate her breakfast.

This morning her luck ran out. No sooner had Gurn set the bowl of oranges and a pot of tea out for their meal, than the door opened, admitting the Master of Crows. Surprised by his sudden appearance, Martise gaped at him with her spoon halfway to her mouth. Rumpled and scowling, he didn't spare her a glance but shuffled to the table where he collapsed on the bench across from her. He folded his arms and rested his forehead on his hands with a groan.

The proud, stately mage she'd met days earlier was transformed into a man who might have spent the night prowling waterside dives. He didn't reek of spirits. In fact, his scent teased her nostrils—citrus and tobacco smoke. The long black hair, neatly queued when he first greeted her and Cumbria, spread over his shoulders and across the table in a tangled shroud. He looked like he'd slept in his clothes. The simple breeches and white shirt were one massive wrinkle, and his feet were bare.

She glanced at Gurn. Unfazed by Silhara's unexpected and disheveled appearance, he put another cup and an additional pot of tea in front of Silhara and took a seat next to him. Was this the regular morning ritual? One briefly interrupted when she arrived?

She went back to eating and tried not to laugh, imagining the High Bishop here instead of her, and how affronted he'd be. She suspected the outcast mage would make no special allowances for the cleric. He'd be served the same porridge as everyone else in the kitchen with the manor's master and his servant.

"Why are you smiling?"

Silhara's question startled her, and she nearly choked on a sip of tea. She snatched the napkin Gurn handed her to cover her mouth and stifle her coughing. The mage's dark eyes were slitted against the kitchen's bright, morning light. Hints of a beard shadowed his cheeks, emphasizing a strong jaw.

She cleared her throat. "I was thinking of the High Bishop, Master. Nothing of consequence. My apologies."

A black eyebrow rose, and her gaze fell to his mouth, bewitched as his lips curved in a faint smile. Such a hard face.

Such a beautiful mouth. A telltale heat made her ears burn, and she dropped her gaze.

"I imagine Cumbria would take exception to that remark. He has always believed himself to be of great consequence."

She couldn't resist the temptation to look at him again. The open shirt revealed smooth brown skin and something she'd missed at their first meeting—something hidden behind formal robes. A rope of white, pinched flesh circled his neck, cutting across the hollow of his throat and disappearing behind his nape. A garrote scar. She stared, shocked. Sometime in his life Silhara of Neith had survived a strangulation attempt.

He rested his chin in his hand. The hint of humor briefly softening his austere features was gone.

"You are excessively contrite over the mundane, especially for a young woman under the protection of a wealthy household."

The casual suspicion, with its leading questions and observations, threatened her composure, unused as she was to such scrutiny. Cumbria had either placed too much faith in her ability in overcoming a lifetime of servile behavior, or he'd grossly underestimated Silhara's acuity.

A sly intelligence gleamed in his dark eyes. Had he guessed their game before she and the bishop ever sat down with him and discussed her apprenticeship? Did the mage just wait to see what she might reveal before using it against her? She gripped her spoon and took a slow breath. It was disconcerting dining with leopards.

"My family was socially prosperous but poor," she lied. "When I came to live at Asher, I soon learned deference. I am a dependent relation and have no wish to be more of a burden, especially to the bishop and his wife."

He reached for an orange, taking his time in his selection. "Ah, the mistress of Asher. Cumbria's penance for sins unconfessed. I wondered if he was still married to that harridan Dela-fé." His smirk matched his nonchalant tone. "Were he more intelligent and less avaricious, he'd find a way to murder her. Her riches are attractive. Her madness is not."

The statement, so cold-blooded in its matter-of-fact observations, left her speechless. She stared at him as he stripped his orange of its peel with long, nimble fingers. It was true Cumbria's wife was madder than an imprisoned falina bird, but Martise was startled to hear someone acknowledge the fact aloud. She'd wanted to murder the woman herself, usually after Dela-fé delivered an undeserved beating.

She glanced at Gurn who winked and went on placidly eating his breakfast.

"Do you want an orange?"

She eyed the fruit Silhara held out to her, wondering what deadly deception an innocent-looking orange might hold. He watched her with an unrelenting regard.

Bursin's wings, she was becoming as suspicious as Conclave. She clamped down on her paranoia and plucked the orange out of his hand with a murmured "My thanks."

"You don't like oranges?" He sounded more curious and amused than offended. "My grove produces some of the sweetest."

"You don't seem like a farmer," she said, failing to keep the doubt out of her voice. She still found the idea strange—this mage, notorious for snubbing Conclave and delving in the dark arcana, pursuing a livelihood so mundane and laborious.

His eyes widened. Even Gurn paused in drinking his tea.

"It's how I keep us fed and this hulk from crumbling around us." Sarcasm sharpened his tongue. "What? Did you think I lounged on my couch all day, reading tomes and muttering incantations while Gurn fed me grapes?"

She knew better. Twenty-two years of servitude should have kept her silent, made her apologize for her impertinence, but some small demon goaded her to respond in a like manner, despite her upbringing and every instinct warning her otherwise.

"It would explain the dust."

Gurn choked into his cup before setting it down on the table with a thump. His face and bald pate turned an impressive shade of pink, and his eyes brimmed with tears. Martise didn't know if they were tears of laughter or asphyxiation and was too mortified to care. Humiliation scorched a path from her chest to the back of her neck. She bowed her head, staring at her now congealed porridge as if it carried all the secrets of the ancients.

Outside, the screeching cries of crows punctuated the silence in the kitchen. She sat stiffly, waiting for a stinging slap or the vision-blackening pain of a cuff to her head for her insolence. What was wrong with her?

Her heartbeat thundered in her ears. Silhara was a dangerous unknown. He might not touch her at all, just transform her into a fat, juicy worm for the crows nesting in his trees. He did neither. When she braved a glance, she found him eyeing her with a speculative gaze.

"You have done an unwise thing, Martise of Asher," he said softly. "You've caught my interest."

CHAPTER FIVE

She was no more winsome in the morning than at day's end. Silhara's new apprentice looked much as she had when he first met her, dressed in a tunic and skirts too large for her, her hair bound in a tight bun and coiffed with torn spider web. When he stumbled into the kitchen, half-blinded by the morning light, he was startled to see her. And then he remembered. Conclave's answer to his request for help. He didn't know whether to laugh or curse. What in Bursin's name was he supposed to do with a helper who couldn't perform the simplest spell or lift a basket of oranges?

He sipped his tea and regarded her over the rim of his cup. Damned priests. Couldn't they have saddled him with someone pretty? A woman with generous curves and breasts to smother in? Someone he could tup in the hallway while she searched for secrets and schemed of ways to betray him? Instead, they sent this ordinary, diffident, untalented girl. At best, her presence was a nuisance; at worst, a dangerous impediment.

Still, she wasn't as colorless as she first appeared. She'd caught him by surprise with her retort about the dust, revealing a flash of wit followed by an impressive blush. She made him wonder—and smile. That alone gave him pause.

Silhara couldn't remember the last time he'd found something worth smiling about that didn't involve mockery, yet in the last ten minutes Cumbria's little spy almost coaxed a laugh out of him with her comment and the way she eyed him when he offered her the orange. He didn't think her expression could be more suspicious or fearful if he'd held out a live pit viper.

"Are you going to eat it?" He pointed to the orange, untouched next to her bowl.

She stiffened, as if bracing herself for something unpleasant. He noted her hands as she reached reluctantly for the fruit. Her knuckles were red, chafed—like his. Like Gurn's. This was a woman who labored in Cumbria's household. No pampered ward here but one who did menial work.

There was a meticulous grace in the way she peeled the orange and something entrancing in the way she ate it. She bit into the segment slowly, either from caution or enjoyment, and her actions riveted his attention. He shook his head. *Gods, it's been too long since I've had a woman.* He smirked when her eyes widened after the first bite.

"It's so sweet!"

"'Twas no empty boast when I said we harvested the best fruit here. Neith's oranges always sell out at market."

He didn't share in her appreciation. Oranges were a staple of his diet, and he loathed them. He conquered the urge to gag each time he ate one. But eat them he did, always with the thought that some day he might grow to like them and rid himself of the memory tied to them.

Martise finished the orange with more enthusiasm but refused his offer of another. She complimented Gurn on his porridge, and the two shared a warm smile. Their immediate camaraderie puzzled Silhara. This wasn't the mating dance of man and maid, more a recognition of long-separated friends finally reunited. He'd noted Gurn's immediate attachment to the girl. Martise appeared to return the servant's affections. His eyes narrowed. They knew nothing of her save what Cumbria told them. There was more to Martise of Asher than nervous blushes and a melodious voice. She had an agenda or she wouldn't be here. He'd grind her into the dirt before he let her use Gurn to get to him

He was tempted to tell her of Gurn's origins—how Silhara found him rotting in a Prime prison for literally breaking a man in half across his knee—but thought better of it. He didn't relish the idea of an irritated Gurn tearing his head off his shoulders and throwing it across the courtyard for revealing private things to a stranger.

A snide remark on their attachment hovered on his lips, stopped only by a foul scent rising up from beneath the table.

"Bursin's wings! What is that smell?" He raised an eyebrow at Martise. Her eyes widened.

"Not me. I bathed this morning."

Gurn nudged him and pointed in the direction of his feet. He bent to peer under the table and almost gagged. Cael lay stretched out on the floor, reeking worse than the shambling, half rotten dog that invaded Neith at Corruption's command. He shoved Cael with one foot, and the hound growled a warning.

"Out of here, Cael. Now." He shoved harder this time. Cael snapped half-heartedly at his toes before abandoning his spot and slinking out the open door leading to the bailey.

Silhara watched him go before turning his attention back to Martise. "Gurn told me my mage-finder verified Cumbria's story. You are Gifted."

She paled and lowered her eyes to mask their expression. "Yes. Gurn introduced us."

Her extraordinary voice had gone flat, hiding a wealth of emotion in the same way her downcast eyes did. He wasn't fooled. She was angry he'd used Cael in ascertaining the truth.

"Cael is a valued member of my household, Martise. I trust his judgment more than I trust most anyone else's. Regardless of Conclave's wishes and Cumbria's *generosity* in sending me his ward as an apprentice, if Cael didn't approve of you, you wouldn't stay."

She met his gaze, her copper-coin eyes unflinching and resolute. "The bishop paid you for four months of my upkeep."

Anger shot through him, incinerating the last vestiges of drowsiness. She dared to challenge him! He bared his teeth at her, barely placated when she flinched. Still, she refused to lower her eyes.

"Aye, he did," he said. "And when I send his insolent ward back to him, I'll include a note stating the exorbitant cost of porridge and a Neith orange has made it necessary for me to recover my expenses by keeping all his coin."

The tension in the kitchen was thick enough to cut. Silhara's temper rose with it until Martise exhaled a defeated sigh. Her voice was even, her gaze carefully blank and tranquil as she focused on a point over his left shoulder.

"I'm being impertinent. I am sorry, Master."

"Somehow I doubt that." She shot him a surprised look. "But I think we begin to understand each other."

He watched as she toyed with her spoon and traced patterns in her congealing porridge. "You have spider webs in your hair."

She patted her hair, grimacing when her fingers touched the remnants of spider web dangling from her hairpins.

"It's no matter, Martise. Such primping isn't necessary. Your appearance is of no interest here."

A hint of hurt or embarrassment danced across her features before she lowered her gaze. He'd cut her, unintentional though it was. No one at Neith stood on ceremony. He and Gurn dressed no better than the lowest servant in a rich household. He hadn't even bothered to shave his beard or put on shoes before stumbling down to breakfast this morning. His remark about the webs in her hair had been idle chat. She'd interpreted his statement as an insult. He chose not to explain himself.

"Gurn," he said. "You'll have to do without her for a time. I've delayed in teaching my new apprentice her lessons. And I'm curious what Conclave taught her."

The giant glowered at him and rose abruptly from the bench. Silhara wasn't fast enough to stop him from snatching the teapot off the table and the cup out of his hand. The servant stalked to the dry sink and dropped the dishes in with a clatter.

Silhara might have reprimanded him had not Martise sat across from him. She straightened to rigid attention, her pale features even more bloodless as she waited for his instructions.

"Have Gurn take you to the great hall. I'll meet you there. You're Conclave-trained, yet powerless. Let's see what might awaken your magic."

Guilt wormed a path into him. He didn't lie. If she didn't run screaming back to Asher as he hoped, he had every intention of finding her Gift and forcing it to manifest. She just might not like his methods.

He left her with Gurn in the sunlit kitchen and returned to his chamber to dress. A part of him wished to stay, to bask in the morning warmth and savor the smell of rising dough as Gurn prepared his daily baking. The kitchen was a sanctuary of sorts, much like his bedroom once was. With Corruption's rise, his chamber was less a retreat and more a battleground between him and the fallen god. He needed sleep, real sleep; not the brief catnaps in which he half-slumbered, braced for the god's inevitable invasion into his dreams.

Corruption's touch was bewitching and lush, luring him with promises of immeasurable power, of respect, of revenge, even as it made him bleed and convulse. He was no longer the bastard get of a wharf prostitute but a ruler of empires, an immortal mage. With those promises came demands. Complete subjugation to another's will, absolute obeisance to the vilest whoremaster. Could he revile the second enough to resist the temptation of the first?

Silhara closed his door and strode to the open window. The star pulsed in the distance. "Still here?" he asked softly. "Don't you have something better to do? Plagues to cast? Cities to destroy?"

A sharp burst of pain behind his eyes made him wince. Corruption's amusement jittered down his bones. *I only await you, avatar.*

He slammed the shutters closed, plunging the room into darkness. Fragile wood never kept out nightmares, but the illusion hid the god's reality lurking on the horizon.

"Not yet," he muttered and cast a spell that flooded the chamber in witchlight. His fingers fluttered along the scar encircling his neck. Ah, to return to simpler times. At least then his executioner had been a dock council with no mercy for a starving thief. Now he had Conclave in his kitchen and Corruption on his doorstep, each wanting to destroy him in their own unique and horrific way.

He had no time for either annoyance. There were oranges to harvest and get to market, bargains to negotiate with the Kurmans and buildings to repair. An honest man's work was never done—not that he was a particularly honest man.

Martise was waiting for him near the hall's cold hearth, surrounded by the flickering sparkle of dust motes. She looked almost ethereal, standing so regal and poised—a pallid queen adorned in spider web and brown wool.

She bowed. "Master."

Silhara half expected a complaint about his delay, but none was forthcoming, and her face remained serene as he circled her, breathing in her scent—sleep and spring mint. "What is the incantation for levitation?"

"Which one? Mysanthanese or Hourlis?"

He halted in front of her, intrigued. "Both."

Her invocations were flawless, her accents in perfect placement, voice intonation correct. The Mysanthanese levitation should have lifted her above his head; the Hourlis one to the rafters, yet her feet remained planted firmly on the ground. If not for Cael's reaction to her, Silhara wouldn't believe her Gifted, only educated.

She must have seen his doubt. "Maybe your mage-finder was wrong."

"The dogs are never wrong, especially not *my* dog," he snapped.

He continued circling her. She was a small woman, lightly made. Articulate and well-read, she had the hands of a scullery maid and the knowledge of Conclave. What Gift lay hidden in this contradictory creature?

His version of the Hourlis spell, a silent gesture, took her without warning. Her feet swung up, a rush of air spinning her to her back as Silhara raised his arm and sent her flying to the ceiling.

Her frightened screech reverberated through the hall. Martise flailed, suspended high above the floor. He caught a glimpse of slender white legs and tangled linen as she kicked her feet and lunged for one of the roof joists. Her hair tumbled free of its pins, the long braid swinging in the empty air.

"What is the spell to descend, Martise?"

She ceased struggling, though her breathing was loud and labored. "What?" She panted, her voice thinned to a squeak as she hovered high above him.

"What is the spell to descend?"

"I don't remember! Please, let me down."

Her terror washed over him, but he held fast to his intent. "I think not. You disappoint me. A skilled mage knows his spells at every turn, even during times of danger."

"I'm not a mage!"

Silhara tapped a finger against his bottom lip. "But you are Conclave-trained. If you know levitation in two languages, surely you know descent in the same two? Were you not taught to keep your composure?"

He traced a half circle in the air. Martise gasped as she slowly rotated so that she looked down on him. Her face was bright red, her eyes huge. She reached for him, even when he was too far below her to touch.

"Master," she pleaded. "I beg you. Set me down, and I will recite every spell ever written in the Hourlis Arcana."

She squeezed her eyes closed, a faint, shuddering sigh escaping her lips. Guilt curdled his stomach. He suppressed it with ruthless determination. If she discovered the truth of Corruption's hold on him, Conclave would strap him to the nearest stake and cheerfully set him ablaze—only after hours or days of torture.

"Think, Martise. What is descent?"

He ended the levitation spell, and she plummeted to the floor. The whistling flutter of her skirts accompanied her screaming attempt to invoke a life-saving counter spell. He invoked levitation an instant before she smashed against the stones.

Only her stuttering breaths broke the silence in the great hall. Silhara bent close to look in her eyes. They were black with terror, the pupils swallowing the copper color.

"That should have worked. You've a stubborn Gift."

His palm hovered over her midriff. He gently lowered her to the ground until she lay in a sea of skirts and coiling braid.

Martise rolled on her side, away from him, and hid her face behind one hand. Hard shudders wracked her. She pulled her knees to her chest and sucked in great gulps of air. Sickened by what he'd done, Silhara looked away. Bursin have mercy on them both; let this be enough to frighten her away.

He waited for her to calm, taking a cautious step back when she staggered to her feet and stood before him. Her head was bowed as if in prayer. Did she pray? He thought she might—for his untimely and painful demise, no doubt. He blinked when she raised her head.

In that moment she reminded him of the Astris statues he'd seen a dozen years earlier. His mentor had taken him east to the Quay province, a land ruled by women. They had sailed through the narrow straits to the main port, passing the Five Queens who guarded the water gates. Silhara had stared, spellbound, at the ancient rulers, their proud, resolute faces worn by neither time nor weather. Theirs was a silent strength, bred of powerful souls never broken. Martise, with that bleak, imperious stare, reminded him of the Queens.

"I remembered the spell."

Disgust for him crossed her still features. Good enough for now. He hadn't succeeded in scaring her into leaving, but he might coax her to it through hatred—if she didn't bury a knife in his back first. She was stronger than he anticipated, and far more stubborn than he'd first guessed. Cumbria must have offered her a small fortune to suffer months at Neith. Silhara intended she earn every coin.

"Aye, you did, apprentice. And it was all for nothing, wasn't it? We try again tomorrow." He smirked at her involuntary shiver. "I understand you've been helping Gurn. A comfort to know that while you can't work a simple spell, you can at least milk a goat"

Her hands twitched before relaxing at her sides. He was curious to see if she'd conquer that urge to slam her fist into his jaw. It seemed so as she laced her fingers together until her knuckles turned white.

"Yes, Master. I've worked among livestock all my life, including cows, pigs, goats...and asses."

CHAPTER SIX

Another morning, another lesson—this one worse than all the others combined. The Master of Crows was a hateful, contemptible pig. If he'd tried to terrorize her with his malicious sorcery, the tactic worked. Her heart still thundered in her chest from the fright he'd given her. Of the many lessons he'd subjected her to so far, this one was the pinnacle of nightmares. If he meant to scare her away, his effort failed. Whatever guilt plagued Martise regarding her mission had evaporated. She swore she'd find some evidence to mark Silhara as a heretic. When the priests built his execution pyre, she'd volunteer to lay the first torch. If they chose to behead him, she'd offer to sharpen the axe.

Bile laced with lingering terror burned the back of her throat. She stumbled into the kitchen, tripping over the scruffy magefinder where he lay by the door. The dog growled a warning and snapped at her heels. Martise hardly noticed. Bastard! Arrogant, pitiless louse with his mocking smile! Bursin's wings, what she wouldn't give to have her Gift manifest and see how he'd like it if she set a shrieking, blood mad demon on him. Such a thing would never happen, but she took comfort in imagining the scenario.

Gurn leaned across the table, scrubbing away the last remnants of breakfast. He stopped when he saw her, slung his wet towel over his shoulder and guided her to one of the benches. She waved him off. It was bad enough Silhara witnessed her screeching in terror. She didn't want Gurn thinking she was some delicate invalid. At least her skirts hid her wobbling knees.

He hovered over her until she sat and gave him a weak smile. "A Woman's Bane demon this time. He banished her just before she leapt on me."

Gurn's blue eyes were dark with sympathy. He patted her on the shoulder before striding to one of the cupboards to rummage through its contents. He came back, holding a small cup filled with a pale green liquid. He motioned for her to drink.

Martise eyed the draught and took a cautious sniff. She coughed as the powerful and familiar fumes of Peleta's Fire scorched her nose. Guaranteed to blister the drinker's entrails and addle his mind by the second cup, its admirers fondly referred to the Fire by its more vulgar name, Dragon Piss. She thought the description apt. Her first and only taste had almost made her retch, and she'd avoided it since. Now, with her composure shattered, she welcomed the drink.

She took a breath, closed her eyes and downed the cup's contents in a single gulp. Gurn's shocked expression blurred before her eyes as the Fire seared a white-hot path down her throat and into her belly. She wheezed and bent forward until her forehead touched her knees, the latest fright forgotten. She concentrated solely on inhaling and exhaling.

Just when she thought her belly would burst into flame, the heat died to a radiant warmth. A pleasant euphoria washed over her, and the floor tilted in her vision. Martise straightened slowly and came face to face with Cael. This close, his large head, with its blunted muzzle and bushy eyebrows, looked enormous. He eyed her in the intense, predatory way mage-finders displayed around the Gifted. Martise, caught in a Fire-induced torpor, forgot her caution and breathed gently into his nostrils. Cael backed away, snorting and shaking his head in protest. She giggled. She didn't blame him. The astringent fumes, whether in the cup or on a person's breath, were enough to curdle milk.

Cael whined, retreating even more when Martise held out a hand. "Come on, my big lad," she crooned. "I won't hurt you." She grinned at Gurn's laugh.

She stood slowly and hiccupped. The room spun on a sloping axis. She grabbed for the table's edge to support herself. "The master sent me back to you, Gurn. You're supposed to give me shears and a satchel."

Her voice slurred the words. They rolled off a tongue swollen and thick. The Fire spiraled through her, heating her blood. Gurn made her sit and brought her a piece of bread to eat. She blinked, certain for one moment there were two pieces in front of her. Her hand hovered over them before Gurn pushed the bread closer, where it became one piece again. She ate slowly, still full from breakfast and drunker than a wine merchant at the end of market day.

The door from the hall to the kitchen opened, admitting a scowling Silhara. He stopped short at seeing her. She tried to stand, but Gurn's large hand on her shoulder held her in place.

The mage had braided his hair and tied a kerchief around his head. He wore work clothes shabbier than anything she owned, and she was a slave. Martise smiled at him in drunken admiration, despite her murderous thoughts about him moments earlier. Even dressed in his worn clothing, he cut an appealing figure standing there in Gurn's sunlit kitchen. Too ascetic to be handsome, there was something striking about his face and the confident way he held himself, as if he ruled a kingdom instead of this wretched excuse for a manor.

Her smile faded. He had just set a demon on her and stood by, amusement curving his lips, while she recited empty spells in a futile effort to stop the gibbering abomination from pouncing on her. Oh yes, not only would she lay the first torch, she'd bring a cart full of extras to share with the spectators.

Annoyance drew his features into tight lines. "What are you doing? Don't you have work to attend to? We don't live to serve you, Martise, no matter the bishop's generous contribution for your care."

Oh, how she wanted to give him a tongue lashing, something that would pin his ears back and silence the scorn he generously doled out to anyone within hearing, but she was far too inebriated to catch a coherent thought much less verbally spar with Silhara. Gurn came to her rescue, his hands moving in agitated gestures too fast for her to follow.

Silhara's eyes widened at Gurn's silent conversation. "She swilled the entire thing?" Exasperation joined the scorn in his voice. "What were you thinking, you foolish girl?" he admonished. "There was likely enough in that cup to drop a plow horse." He was equally sharp with his servant. "What were you thinking to give her that much?"

Martise shrugged. Peleta's Fire also made liars honest. "I was too frightened to think," she mumbled. "Gurn was only trying to help calm me down."

A haunted expression passed through Silhara's eyes, so quick she thought it merely a hallucination brought on by the Fire's effect on her befuddled senses. He frowned at Gurn who frowned in return and made another sweeping gesture with his hands.

"Leave off, Gurn," he snapped. "I'm not in the mood."

Martise stared at the two men in confusion. The unspoken conversation between them was charged with tension. She wondered at the servant's assured, almost berating manner and her volatile master's patience for such behavior. Cumbria would have had her stripped and beaten in the courtyard for that kind of insolence.

Silhara strode back the way he came, giving orders over his shoulder as he left. "Make her finish the bread. It'll keep her from retching up her insides. I'll be back." He paused long enough to level a disgusted look at her. "You're more trouble than you're worth." He punctuated the statement by slamming the door behind him hard enough to rattle the plates and cups in Gurn's dry sink.

Focused on keeping her stomach calm, Martise sat quietly on the bench and chewed her bread. Gurn's tall figure wavered in her vision while he worked in the kitchen. So far, she failed miserably as a spy. Her bid to insinuate herself into Silhara's household as seamlessly as possible was a catastrophe. A little more than a fortnight, and she'd done nothing more than act as Gurn's assistant and subject herself to Silhara's daily tests. She was no closer to revealing some damning information about him than the first day she arrived. Cumbria's messenger crow would languish in the trees, waiting for her summons, until his feathers turned white.

Martise took another bite of the bread and blanched at the threatening roil in her belly. Cumbria might be angered, but he wasn't the one fighting off demons, being set on fire or tossed toward the manor's roof with no means to save herself except a wizard of questionable mercy.

The door leading to the great hall crashed open once more. Silhara had returned. He thrust a goblet under her nose. "Drink this," he ordered.

The cup, finely wrought of silver engraved with Kurman knotwork, felt cool in her palm. She tipped the goblet to her mouth then hesitated. Over the rim of her cup, she met Silhara's gaze, wondering if what he gave her was truly a restorative. His black eyes gleamed with annoyance and a touch of challenge.

Spiteful wretch. Martise half-regretted her growing knowledge of his character. After the torture sessions in the great hall, she knew he wouldn't bother poisoning her. There was no entertainment value in that. She narrowed her eyes at him, the Fire's intoxicating effects giving her a temporary courage, and tossed back the goblet's contents.

Cold on the throat and bitter on the tongue, the draught doused the coals burning hot in her belly and even managed to quell the nausea and clear her head in a single swallow. She stared at the cup and then at Silhara, amazed at the speed with which his potion worked. "What is in this drink?"

His gaze derided her. "All manner of small evils, apprentice. Do you really want to know?"

"No."

He snatched the cup from her. "You've recovered enough to work." He addressed Gurn. "When she's finished her tasks, bring her out to the grove." He left without a backward glance.

The bailey looked no better than the rest of the manor. The wall enclosing it crumbled in one corner; other sections were repaired with a mixture of broken brick and bits of timber. Like the rest of the region, Neith suffered from the summer drought, and the bare patches of earth, once churned to a quagmire by grazing livestock, spread across the yard in cracked, rippling patterns of dried mud. A line of wash fluttered in the breeze, partially concealing a large draft horse feeding at a nearby hay rack and a black goat chewing enthusiastically on the hem of a drying shirt. A sow and three piglets, evicted from their sty by an even dirtier Cael, rooted along the bailey's perimeter, accompanied by a squawking entourage of chickens.

For all its ramshackle appearance, the bailey made Martise smile. Like Gurn, it was a spot of normalcy in this strange, forgotten place.

She spent the remainder of the morning completing her assigned tasks. She milked the goat, fed the chickens and gathered eggs, lugged buckets of water from the well for washing and helped Gurn fold the clean linens on the line. Only when Gurn signaled a pause, and indicated she was to follow him to the grove, did she recall the nature of her mission, and her mouth went dry.

They returned to the house, navigating the maze of dim hallways until they reached the back of the manor and a richly carved door aged to a black patina. Martise squinted against the bright sunlight when Gurn opened the door and gently urged her outside. From this vantage point, she could turn around and see the manor's back façade. Windows faced south with shuttered eyes, and she located her room at the far end of the building. Only one window remained open, in the chamber below hers. Curtains of faded lapis and rust fluttered outward, snapping in the wind like a Kurman dancer's skirts.

She faced the grove again. Orange trees covered the field in an orderly pattern, their leafy branches bowed with ripe fruit. Dark green leaves camouflaged the birds nesting in the branches, revealing the occasional glint of sunlight on a black beak. Somewhere, within that rustle of wings, Cumbria's messenger crow waited for a sign from her.

This was the first time she'd walked the grove. Until now, her forays had been limited to the manor's interior and bailey. She'd only seen the grove from her window each morning and evening, admiring the ordered rows of trees and breathing in the scent of orange blossom lingering in the balmy air.

Gurn led her into the grove, his steps sure as he navigated the orchard's maze. Martise stayed close to him. Each shaded path looked as the other did. Even the manor could no longer be seen as a landmark.

They rounded a corner and stopped before a line of crates filled with oranges and a tall ladder leaning against a tree's yielding branches. The top of the ladder disappeared into the leaves, but Martise saw a pair of shoes balanced on one of the rungs. Gurn whistled low, and the shoes moved. Silhara descended the ladder partway and faced them. She swallowed a gasp, silently admonishing herself for her gut reaction to his appearance.

Working in the morning heat had left a sheen of perspiration on him, and his swarthy skin glistened in the light.

His shirt was plastered to his back and chest, giving her a clear view of lean, sinewy muscle and shoulders rippling with the strength built by hard labor. A pink flush graced his prominent cheekbones, and a bead of sweat trickled down his neck, sliding in a meandering path across the white ligature scar before disappearing beneath the shirt's open neckline.

He swiped his sleeve across his forehead and adjusted the sack, half filled with oranges, across his shoulder. The ladder creaked under his weight as he climbed down to the last rung. Martise looked down, hoping her face didn't reveal her fascination. What was the matter with her, desiring the man who had nearly killed her with fright only hours before?

"Was she a help or a hindrance?"

Her head snapped up. Hindrance? Her fingernails dug into her palms. There were many things she could be rightfully accused of—plainness, shyness, sometimes cowardice—but never laziness or incompetence. She clenched her hands into fists, stopping short of lashing out at him. She was slave-bound and had mastered the art of submissive behavior at an early age, yet there was something about the Master of Crows that made her forget all her training, her low place in the world. He was no more imperious or overbearing than any other landed noble, but he struck an angry chord in her every time he spoke.

Gurn motioned with his hands, his bald head nodding in time with his enthusiastic gestures. Martise felt vindicated. At least one person here was pleased with her performance so far.

The mage grunted and walked away to rummage through an empty crate. Whether he accepted Gurn's silent assessment of her morning's work or not, no compliment was forthcoming. She stiffened when he returned.

"Are you afraid of heights?"

"No," she said softly, schooling her features into a placid expression. "I'm not."

"Good. You can help me in the grove while Gurn prepares our midday meal. Put on your satchel." He waited while she adjusted the bag on her shoulder. "If I remember correctly, the bishop grows olives on his land."

When had Silhara ever had occasion to visit Cumbria at Asher? She'd never seen him there, and she had served the manor and its master since she was seven years old. But he was correct. The olive groves at Asher were many times the size of Silhara's small orchard.

"Does he still bring Conclave novitiates to harvest as unpaid labor?" His mouth turned up in a faint sneer, which changed to a grudging smile. "He's a skinflint, but a shrewd one. If I employed the same technique, Gurn would be able to feed me grapes all day."

Martise clenched her teeth harder, this time to suppress a laugh. Whatever his faults, the Master of Crows knew much about the High Bishop's miserly ways. Each harvest season Cumbria brought novitiates to his groves to help harvest the crops. He used the excuse they could practice their motion spells to shake the trees free of their fruit and gather them in the waiting cloths.

"That custom remains."

He snorted. "I thought so." His expression darkened. "I don't hold with the practice. Magery has its place in the world, but not as a means to an easy life. And whether Cumbria acknowledges it or not, those spells damage his trees. I'll have none of that here. We do it the hard way—as the nongifted do—with ladders, bags and sore backs." He raked her with a glance. "There isn't much to you, apprentice. I doubt you'll be any help."

She stiffened, indignant at his assumption. "I'm stronger than I look, Master, and I take direction well."

He didn't look convinced. "We'll see." He slapped Gurn on the shoulder and walked away to retrieve another ladder lying on the ground near the crates. "I'll take her now, Gurn. Signal when lunch is ready."

Gurn patted Martise on the arm and strode back to the house. She froze at Silhara's forbidding stare.

"You've gained my servant's trust. Don't abuse it."

Apprehension ran cold in her veins. The warning was a thinly veiled threat, ominous in its promise of deadly retribution if she took advantage of Gurn. Whether Silhara felt some affection for his servant or demanded his loyalty at all costs, she knew her interaction with Gurn was crucial to her survival here at Neith.

"I am not an unkind woman. I like Gurn as well."

His cold gaze didn't warm. "Keep that in mind, and any sense of self-preservation you may harbor."

She swallowed and hurried after him as he took the second ladder and carried it to another tree farther down the row. He leaned the ladder against the drooping branches, and a fluster of crows bolted upward, cawing in protest at being chased from their shaded haven.

"You'll find a pair of gloves in your satchel." He raised his hands, displaying well-worn gloves with thinning patches and stains on the palms. "Orange trees sport thorns as long as your fingers, and they're wicked sharp."

She reached into the satchel and found an equally worn pair. They were too big, but not so large that they made her clumsy. Silhara came to stand in front of her, and Martise almost forgot to breathe. This close to him she was bombarded by a multitude of sensations—the scent of citrus and orange blossom laced with the musky heat of perspiration, the quiet rhythm of his breathing as he helped her adjust the gloves, and above all, the tingling flow of his Gift, pouring off him like water from a fast-running stream.

Silhara tightened the leather straps that held the gloves in place at her wrists. His motions slowed when Martise ran the tip of her tongue over dry lips. She blushed at his arrested expression, one which turned calculating.

"I make you nervous." The rasping voice was quiet, almost caressing.

She had no reason to lie except pride, and that was a poor reason indeed. "Yes, Master." She lowered her gaze to stare at his scar. "It's said you are a dangerous and powerful mage."

A faint huff of laughter whispered above her. "It's also said I raise the dead, talk to the dead and eat the dead." He tilted her chin with a fingertip so she had to look at him. He was so close she saw the fine lines fanning out from his black eyes and the hollows beneath his cheeks. His sensual mouth curved into a mocking smile. "What do you believe?"

"I believe in learning for myself instead of relying on the hearsay of others."

A glimmer of approval darted through his eyes before he lowered his hand and stepped away from her. Martise sighed, relieved. The Master of Crows was an overwhelming presence, frightening, annoying and fascinating. Being so close to him, with her senses inundated by the force of his Gift, and his very maleness, made thinking difficult.

She stiffened at his touch on her elbow, then followed him to the ladder and her assigned tree. The spark of warmth from moments earlier was gone. His voice was dispassionate, instructive—that of the teacher imparting the lesson to the student.

Silhara cupped one of the oranges hanging in clusters from a low branch and reached into an outside pocket on his satchel. He withdrew a pair of small clippers. "Clip the fruit gently. If you prefer to use your hands instead of the clippers, pick like this." He demonstrated by carefully twisting and pulling the orange from the limb, leaving a scrap of stem and the button of the fruit. "You still need to use the clippers to cut the stems down or they'll pierce the fruit you've left and cause them to spoil." He snapped the remaining stem off with the clippers. "Now you."

The oranges were cool to the touch, and she did as instructed, twisting and pulling one orange off with a careful tug.

He gave her the shears. "You can use these. I've an extra pair."

When she demonstrated her competency to his satisfaction, he moved onto her next lesson, lifting her satchel so she could see the drawstring ties at the bottom. "When your bag gets too heavy, release this cord. The bottom will open, and your fruit will roll out. I'd prefer you take them to the crates to drop them, but you'll lose a lot of time walking the rows, so just come down the ladder and make a pile by the tree." His eyes narrowed. "Don't open the bag when you're high on the ladder. You'll bruise the fruit if you let them drop that far."

"Where should I start on the tree?"

Once more that derisive smile graced his mouth. "As close to the top as you can reach. Are you certain you aren't afraid of heights?"

He was goading her again. His morning lessons had given her gray hairs, but even if they had instilled a sudden fear of heights in her, Martise wouldn't give him the satisfaction of letting him see it. There were some things her pride commanded she do, slave or not.

She gripped the clippers with tense fingers. "Very certain."

"Good. Then there's no reason to delay. Get up the ladder—that is if you can climb in those skirts."

She wordlessly handed him the clippers and dropped her orange into her bag. In moments she had her skirts twisted around her legs like makeshift breeches, with the ends tucked securely into her cyrtel.

This time his small smile was genuine. "I admire a practical woman." He returned the clippers to her and walked away. "Remember my instructions," he said over one shoulder. "Twist and pull carefully; cut the stems; don't drop the fruit."

Or what? She was tempted to ask in a rare moment of rebellion.

Silhara kept walking. "Or I'll add a special twist to tomorrow's incantation lesson, apprentice."

Her fallen clippers almost pinned her foot to the earth.

CHAPTER SEVEN

A crow landed on the window ledge and eyed Silhara as he dressed for the morning. The light streaming into the room silhouetted the bird in shadow, creating a spot of darkness against the backdrop of orange trees and summer sky.

He ignored his visitor and scrubbed away blood and the last vestiges of sleep. The light hurt his eyes but kept him from falling back to the bed in the hope of catching a few hours of nightmare-free slumber. Corruption had tortured him through the night with sinister dreams of a world burdened by the god's dominance. In those visions, he lived a life of decadent privilege. Wealth untold, armies to do his bidding, women to fulfill any carnal whim, every luxury and desire satisfied with a snap of his fingers. All possible for the price of his humanity. Most tempting of all was limitless magic. The ability to move mountains, divert rivers, attain a near immortal life—this was the greatest gift the god offered, and it poured a tantalizing stream of such power into the sleeping mage.

A taste, avatar, of what I can give you if you yield to me.

The voice waned, replaced by a new dream—a nightmare that still made Silhara shudder. He stood on an endless beach made of ash instead of sand. Above him, a night sky devoid of stars and moon bled into an equally black ocean. Only the dull light of Corruption's star provided any illumination, and its reflection danced across the rolling water in nacreous paths. A steady wind, smelling not of spindrift or fish, but of burnt bone, fluttered his hair, and sent the ash swirling softly over his feet, a caress of cool, dead fingers across his toes.

Before him, the ocean stretched into a limitless horizon. No gulls flew overhead; no fish leapt from the water; no ships sailed the waves. He knew, with the certainty of all dreams that, if he stepped off the beach and into the water, there would be no bottom to touch, only a vast well of liquid blackness into which he'd drown.

The waves pitched and receded, unceasing in their hollow lullaby. Their music was broken abruptly by a curve of darkness rising out of the depths. The shape sank beneath the water only to rise again. Whales didn't swim these lifeless seas. He knew what rode the waves and stalked these dead shores. A leviathan, immortal and pitiless, with a gaping maw that swallowed souls. The steady break of the waves kept time to the wind's rhythms as the creature swam closer.

Terror rooted him to the spot, and he waited. Waited on a beach whose ash was the cremated remains of creatures that traversed a once-living world. Waited for the monster to surface, stretch wide a black mouth and suck him down into an eternal nothingness.

Corruption whispered in his dreams once more. *A taste if you do not.*

He'd awakened to a bloodied pillow and hands that tingled from the god's touch. He'd been tempted to stumble down to the kitchen and filch some of Gurn's Dragon Piss. Only the thought of his servant's expression and his apprentice's watchful gaze kept him from it. He had no wish to explain the blood on his face or why his hands shook so badly he'd be challenged to hold a goblet steady.

He finished his ablutions and stared at the crow that still watched him. A large bird. Larger than those normally nesting in the grove's shady canopy.

"Come," he said, and gestured. Lightning sizzled down his arm. The crow's eyes bulged, and it screeched a final caw before bursting into a scattered pile of smoking feathers and charred bones.

Cradling his burning hand to his chest, Silhara stared at the smoldering mound on the ledge. Corruption had left its mark on him from the previous night. The spell, a gentle summons which should have coaxed instead of coerced, had gone horribly wrong. He held up his hand. Blemished by nothing more than hard calluses and ink stains, his fingers and palm now held a warped power, one that made his magic unpredictable. He growled. This wasn't good. Power uncontrolled and unknown was useless. For the moment, unless he chose to cast any spell regardless of consequence, the god had rendered his magery impotent.

Still, he didn't deny the surge of euphoria coursing through his blood. His fingers twitched, and points of light shot off their tips. Such power was more seductive than a beautiful, willing woman. Silhara knew his weaknesses. So did the god.

He lowered his hand and approached the window. The warm morning breeze sent scorched black feathers whirling out over the grove. "My apologies, friend. Killing you wasn't my…"

The scent of magic, neither his nor Corruption's, teased his nostrils. He knew that scent, both familiar and loathed. The bird reeked of Conclave. He swiped his hand against the remains in a sharp gesture, clearing the ledge. They fell in a thin black rain to the ground below.

Another spy for the priests. His apprentice might well have brought the bird with her, or it might have lived amongst his crows for months, flying home occasionally to tattle to its masters. His regret at destroying the bird vanished.

He finished dressing and left for the kitchen. As usual, tea and oranges awaited him on the table. Gurn and Martise sat across from one another carrying on a conversation made up of hand signals and Martise's lyrical voice. Silhara paused in the doorway, content to observe unnoticed.

For all that he disliked having her entrenched in his household, he'd grown to admire Cumbria's spy. Tenacious and resolute, she'd suffered through his morning lessons without faltering. Her Gift had yet to manifest, but she hadn't fled in terror. Silhara despised admitting failure, but he considered abandoning the morning exercises. They'd accomplished nothing so far besides giving him a sick feeling in his gut.

Most surprising of all, Martise was a good harvester. What she lacked in strength, she made up for in speed and thoroughness. He only had to instruct her once on the proper technique of harvesting the fruit. Heat, ant bites, and the occasional sting from a wasp drunk on fermented oranges didn't deter her. After a week, she was almost as quick as Gurn and ruined fewer oranges.

He admired the play of sunlight on her russet hair and the timbre of her amazing voice. She rarely smiled, and never for him, but he was often amused by the brief flashes of wit she revealed. The dull servant who had faded into the shadows of his study was slowly vanishing. The woman emerging in her place fascinated him a little more each day.

Cumbria was more subtle and shrewd than he first credited him. There was more to this woman than her plain façade indicated. On the surface, she was dismal in her role as spy, but he never trusted surface appearances. Martise possessed something unique, something Cumbria could use for the purpose of bringing his most hated adversary down. The trick was to find it before she successfully cornered him with some damning treason that would bring about Conclave's brand of justice.

Cael, stretched out under the table, saw him first. He wuffled a greeting but didn't rise, content to lie beneath Martise's foot as she methodically rubbed the length of his belly with her heel.

"Lazy mutt," he muttered as he took his place next to Gurn at the table. He eyed Martise who greeted him with a bland look and softly spoken "Master."

"You've ruined my dog."

Cael's protesting snort revealed Martise had halted her massage. She gave Silhara a wary look. "Forgive me, I don't understand."

The oranges in the bowl looked bright, lush and unappetizing this morning. He took one and leisurely peeled the skin in a continuous spiral. "If I hear another apology from you, I think I'll drown you in the well." He swallowed a laugh when she paled. "Martise, you must bear a terrible burden of guilt over past sins. I don't think I've ever heard a person say 'sorry' as often as you do with so little provocation." He popped an orange segment into his mouth and conquered the urge to retch as the juice burst on his tongue.

Martise went crimson but said nothing. Silhara swallowed the bite of orange and sipped his tea to cleanse his mouth. He peered under the table and frowned at Cael. The hound ignored him and rolled under Martise's foot in an obvious request to resume her caress.

"You spoil him. I now have a mage-finder who spends his days lolling with the swine and begging caresses from a woman." Gurn snorted into his tea cup, and Silhara raised an eyebrow. "Not that I blame him for the last."

"I'm confused, Master. Do you speak of the failures of men or dogs?"

He almost choked on the second piece of orange and spat it onto the floor. Martise's face blurred as his eyes watered. Gurn chuckled. His apprentice watched him, her copper gaze steady. For a moment Silhara caught a gleam of teasing humor in her eyes before it vanished.

"Does it matter? We're often one and the same." He let her finish her porridge while he and Gurn made plans for market day in Eastern Prime.

"We'll take what we have now and deliver it to Fors the day before market opens. He'll try and charge a storage fee." Silhara poured another cup of tea. "You'd think he'd learn after all these years of trade that I'm not an easy mark."

Gurn's hands sketched patterns in the air while Silhara watched and answered.

"Martise will be traveling with us. The two of you can buy supplies while I negotiate with our greedy little merchant. The sooner we're done, the better. There's more to harvest, and I don't want my fruit rotting on the trees before we can pick it."

He waited for Martise to eat her last spoonful of breakfast. "Have you ever been to Eastern Prime?"

"Not since I was a child. It's too far from Asher to bother. The High Bishop sends his factor to Calderes, though it's a smaller town and market."

"But well known for its luxury goods and rich patrons." He traced a Calderan trade symbol on the scarred tabletop. "You'll accompany us when we travel to Eastern Prime in ten days. Be prepared. You may not remember, but Prime is a port city. Bigger and far less genteel than Calderes. They run the slave markets there, and the whoremasters are ever on the prowl for young women. When we're there, stay close to Gurn."

Silhara frowned, puzzled by her sudden somber cast. "It's not a wish, Martise. It's a command."

She rose to clear her place, flinching as her free hand held the table edge in a white-knuckled grip. She shuffled to the sink, moving more like a half-dead crone than a healthy young woman. A gray pallor washed her skin, and she couldn't hide a wince when she faced him.

"Should I await you in the hall for our lesson?"

The image of the destroyed crow played across his memory. Silhara had set Martise on fire once during their lessons. Brutal both in purpose and execution, the spell had been one he'd controlled through its entirety. His apprentice had come away from the experience reeling with shock but no injuries save a burnt hem. While he felt it fading, the god's touch still lingered in his hands, made his fingers spasm in short intervals. Despite his wariness of her, Silhara had no wish to mete out the same end, or something worse, to his apprentice. If he had to kill her, he'd do it on his terms with his magic firmly under control.

She stood patiently before him, awaiting his answer. He raked her with his gaze. Martise always carried herself erect, with a quiet dignity he'd grown to admire. This morning she slouched, right shoulder sloped a little lower than the left.

"I think we'll forego the lessons today." Surprise widened her eyes. Even Gurn stared at him, puzzled. "You walk like an old woman. Why didn't you tell Gurn you're sore from harvesting?"

The flush rising from her neck to her cheeks chased away the gray. She glanced at Gurn who frowned his disapproval at her secrecy. "I didn't think it important. My work hasn't suffered for it."

Silhara rose to stand before her. She stiffened and winced. He liked her scent, redolent of sunshine and Gurn's rosewater soap. "No, not yet. But it will. You aren't much good to me on a ladder when you can hardly walk or hold yourself upright."

"I can work well enough..." she argued before snapping her mouth closed in mutinous silence. "What would you have me do, Master?" she finally asked.

"You can look at me instead of my feet."

She met his eyes, her expression blank. Silhara shook his head. "That might fool others, but not me." He addressed Gurn over his shoulder. "I need her in the library today anyway. We'll harvest tomorrow. Are there candles in the stillroom?"

The servant nodded and began clearing the breakfast remains from the table. He waved a hand at Martise, frowning even harder. Silhara sighed and looked back at her. "Gurn believes you're a fragile thing, deserving of my delicacy." He smiled faintly when she held up her palms, revealing a wealth of calluses, blisters and a scar or two.

"These are not a delicate woman's hands. I need no special treatment." She peeked around him to wink at Gurn. "Though I appreciate Gurn's concern."

Silhara stared at Gurn. His servant shrugged, unapologetic over his obvious friendship with Conclave's puppet. Martise's expression mirrored Gurn's, a flicker of rebellion dancing in her eyes for a moment, as if she dared him to forbid such a relationship.

He stepped around her and strode to the door that opened to the bailey. "No one at Neith receives special treatment, but I do need you to work to your best ability. You aren't there today." He waved her to him. "Come. I've something to ease your aches."

Dread and curiosity played across her features, but she followed, keeping a distance behind him as they crossed the bailey yard and wove through rows of Gurn's rose bushes before reaching a small outbuilding attached to the south side of the manor.

It took a few moments for his eyes to adjust to the stillroom's darkness. He found candles in a box by the door and lit four. Martise put two in the holders he pointed out at the long table in the center of the room. He set his own candles in place and waited while she surveyed her surroundings.

The stillroom, smothered in the smells of orange flower and olive oil, was his true money maker. He and Gurn broke their backs each season harvesting cart loads of oranges for sale at Eastern Prime's busy marketplace. It made enough to keep them both fed. But it was the neroli oil and petitgrain he distilled which brought him the greatest profits. Luxury items made in small batches and sought after by the wealthy aristos, they fetched a high price at market.

His apprentice, fascinated by the rows of bottles and decanters filling every space on the tables and shelves built against the walls, strolled around the room, occasionally touching an empty distillation vat or a decorative perfume bottle made to catch a woman's eye. The table held an array of candlesticks, bowls, strainers, mortars and pestles. Dried herbs hung in decimated strings from the low beams, and the scatter of dried orange flowers crunched under foot.

"You make perfumes." A faint yearning colored her statement.

"Among other things. We harvest flowers from a set number of trees in late spring, along with leaves and young twigs. The oils and petitgrains go for a higher price than the syrups and elixirs, but the last two do well enough. We'll harvest again in autumn. The yield isn't as good or as high-quality, but people still buy."

"Madam Dela-fé always wore orange flower scent. I disliked the woman but loved the way she smelled."

Silhara lifted a staying hand when she tensed and parted her lips for the inevitable apology. "You've brightened my morning with that bit of knowledge, Martise, but the apologies are tiresome." He didn't expound on the pleasure he took in knowing Cumbria's deranged wife bought his products.

A large, weathered cabinet stood in one corner. The doors were removed, revealing shelves lined with small jars and crocks. He took one and set it on the table near where Martise stood.

"Remove your clothing," he said.

He scowled at the burgeoning horror in her gaze. He'd earned his notoriety, done many things in his lifetime that had made him outcast amongst his neighbors, acquaintances and the powerful priesthood who sought to control him. But he'd never raped a woman and had no intention of doing so now.

Her wondrous voice was reduced to a mouse's squeak as she pleaded with him and backed against the table. "Please," she whispered, holding up one hand to ward him off. "I beg you..."

"Martise." He kept his own voice devoid of inflection and pointed to the jar he'd taken from the shelf. "I've a liniment to ease the pain in your back." He waited, unmoving as his words seeped into her panic-ridden mind. "Don't you think if I wanted to force you, I would have done so by now? Even Gurn, despite your friendship with him, wouldn't stop me. Nor could he."

She stared at him, eyes still huge with fright, but her breathing had slowed at his words. Silhara noted that while she cowered before him, the hand not holding him symbolically at bay was searching the table behind her for a weapon. He inclined his head in approval. Terrified she might be, but not beaten. She'd fight him, despite overwhelming odds.

"Whether you accept my help or not means little to me. You can continue picking oranges in all your noble suffering, just as long as you pick. Make up your mind. The day is wasting."

Several tense moments passed in silence while he waited. Martise took a deep breath and relaxed, one knotted muscle at a time. "My back and shoulder hurt."

"I imagine they do." He motioned for her to present her back and pulled the cork stopper from the jar. "Gurn makes this liniment, not I. If I didn't know better, I'd think he uses spellwork in the making. It's that effective." He kept up a steady stream of conversation as she presented her back to him and began unlacing her tunic and leine. "He's a cagey bastard with the recipe. Refuses to reveal his secrets. I suppose I'll have to torture it out of him one of these days."

Martise lowered her garments to rest against the crook of her arms. Her voice was prim. "That should be enough."

He might have laughed were he not so distracted by the sight before him. Her nape, darkened to a honey color from working outside, contrasted sharply with the ivory skin of her shoulders. Shrouded in her castoff woolens, she presented a shape with all the allure of a potato. Not so when the clothes came off. The graceful line of her back flowed into a slender waist and the gentle curve of her hips. Two shallow dimples marked her lower back, tempting him to press a finger into their indentations. Silhara was no sculptor, but he suddenly understood why men with such talent were inspired to carve beauty in stone.

That flawless back was currently marred by a misshapen ripple of muscle curving below her right shoulder blade. Another lump swelled where her neck met her shoulder.

Martise, still as a marble pillar, tensed even more beneath his silent perusal. She hissed in pain for her troubles and reached automatically to massage the top of her shoulder with the opposite hand. Silhara caught a brief glimpse of the curve of one breast before she remembered her position and pulled her hand back in place. He chuckled at the blush reddening her nape.

"Your modesty is wasted on me." He slapped a dollop of cool liniment on her back, ignoring her gasp. "I've seen more bare tits in my lifetime than a guild of wet nurses." His fingers worked steady circles on her back and shoulder, massaging in the healing salve. The frozen muscle below her shoulder blade was unyielding at first, and he wondered how she'd managed days of harvesting without uttering a word of complaint.

"Before my mother contracted the pox, she worked in a brothel catering to aristos. I earned a coin or two running errands or delivering messages for the other *hourin*. It was common practice for a *houri* to bare herself an easy and effective way to display her wares to a potential customer."

She turned her head a fraction. Her sidelong gaze was curious. "How old were you?"

"Six or seven. It was much the same when I was older, and my mother worked the docks." He continued kneading her back, moving up to the tight ridge along the top of her shoulder. He smiled as she slowly relaxed under his hands. "And I had my fair share of novitiates at Conclave Redoubt." He pressed the heel of his hand into a tight band of muscle and Martise yelped. "Now, if you had three breasts, I might be curious enough to ogle you."

Her laughter echoed in the small room before she cloaked it in a cough. That, more than the silky glide of her skin under his palms, bewitched him. He'd never heard her laugh before. As lyrical as her voice, her laughter transformed her from peahen to swan. Standing behind her, he had only a view of her tightly bound hair and supple back. He could look over her shoulder and see the press of her cleavage against her folded arms, but he couldn't see her face. The urge to turn her around so that he might watch her laugh again was almost overwhelming.

His slippery hands slid to her waist, fingers pressed against her sides as his thumbs came to rest in the dimples that had teased him when she first revealed her back. A surge of heat suffused his limbs. Martise, smooth-skinned, smelling of flowers and warm woman, stood close enough that her heartbeat skated vibrations across his chest when he leaned into her back. She didn't move, but her stillness was that of trapped prey. She breathed in shallow pants, and a rosy flush dusted her neck and shoulders.

He backed away, snapped out of his stupor by the awareness of her fear. He wiped his hands on his shirt hem and stoppered the liniment jar. "We're finished here. Get dressed." He congratulated himself on the coldness in his voice.

She yanked tunic and leine up in one tug, retying her laces without looking at him. He slid the jar toward her. "Here. I suspect your legs feel as your back did, but you can tend those yourself, lest we forget who is master here and who isn't."

He poured a wealth of scorn into his words, angered by his brief lapse of control. Martise faced him, her face expressionless, eyes gleaming in the stillroom's shadows. She clutched the jar. "Thank you, Master."

He strode to the door. "Take it to your room, then meet me in the library. Gurn will show you where it is if you don't already know. It's time I used you for the purpose that keeps you under my roof."

He stalked out of the stillroom and headed for the house, muttering the entire way about lazy dogs, insolent servants, interfering gods and the evils of womankind.

CHAPTER EIGHT

Martise reached between branches bristling with thorns and snipped a cluster of oranges. They fell into her palm hard enough to press her hand down onto a nearby thorn so that it pierced her glove and jabbed her middle knuckle.

"Ouch!" She jerked away from the evil-looking spike protruding from its branch. The thorn broke, leaving a sharp ache radiating into her fingers. She dropped the oranges into her satchel and pulled off her glove to check her injury. Nothing more than a red pinprick, it felt as if Cael had sank one of his canines into her. She glared at the tree. Harvesting oranges was dirty, painful work—very different from harvesting olives. So far she'd been poked, stung, and bitten by the various insects crawling on or flying about the trees and by the trees themselves. The crows were another pestilence. A day rarely went by that she wasn't cleaning droppings off her hat.

Thank merciful Bursin for Silhara's library. She looked forward to lunch and the hours following it. Spending the latter part of the day and evening among musty-smelling tomes and translating dead languages was preferable to this, even if she battled the occasional spider over a manuscript.

A wet splat struck the brim of her hat. Above her, a crow perched on a branch and eyed her with a beady black stare. She shooed it with her loose glove. The bird fluttered its wings and hopped out of range but refused to give up its place.

"Master of Crows," she muttered. "More like Master of Ants, or Master of Wasps or Master of Bird Droppings." She yanked her glove back over her sore hand and glared at the crow. Silhara might disapprove of Cumbria's use of magic to harvest his olive crop, but from where she stood, balanced on a rickety ladder and wedged between branches spiked with thorns, the idea had real merit.

She stared at the crow. Time had flown at Neith. More than a month had gone by, and she was no closer to finding evidence of Silhara's suspected crimes than when she first arrived. Cumbria would have grown impatient for news. Martise had none to give him other than the Corruption star seemed to hover over the manor these days, and the mage studiously ignored its presence. The bishop might be interested in knowing she now had access to the library, but there was little to tell other than she'd been set the task of finding a kill ritual that could destroy the god. It was better than nothing.

With the hundreds, if not thousands, of crows residing in the grove, there was no telling if Cumbria's messenger crow was nearby, waiting for her to summon him. If only he'd had chosen another way for her to call Micah to her. Though she'd been graced with a speaking voice that mesmerized crowds, she couldn't sing a single note. The servants of Asher had begged her not to chant with them as they walked wool, pressed olives, or performed the endless chores that kept Asher running smoothly. And the hunting hounds never failed to set up a chorus of howls if they heard her.

She shrugged. It was Cumbria's idea that she sing to the bird to summon him, and she was an obedient slave. She descended two rungs of the ladder and peered under the branches. The grove around her was quiet, empty. Silhara harvested the trees in another corner of the orchard, and Gurn was in the house preparing their lunch. She was alone here except for the crow who'd graciously decorated her hat. Martise hoped it stayed long enough to hear the first strains of her lullaby. A fitting revenge.

She ascended into the tree again, grateful for its cover this time. Braced on the ladder, she cleared her throat and sang the first chorus of the Nanteri lullaby. As she predicted, the crow quickly abandoned its perch and flew away. No bird returned to replace it. Martise finished the lullaby, wincing at the off-key notes warbling from her lips, and waited. Micah didn't come. She tried again, a little louder. Still no messenger crow. She tried a third time, almost shouting the words so the bird would hear. In the distance, Cael howled in response.

Far into the second chorus and almost hoarse with her efforts, she didn't hear her visitor until the branches around her shook. She screeched in surprise when her ladder thumped against its supporting branch. Leaves rustled and parted, revealing Silhara's sharp, dusty features. His eyes were wide with astonished horror. He'd climbed her tree and balanced on a thick limb just below her. His height put him at eye-level with her, and she blushed at the appalled look on his face.

"What in Bursin's holy name is that?" he snarled.

If it were possible to die of embarrassment, Martise was sure she wouldn't survive the next few minutes. "I was singing."

His eyebrows rose almost to his hairline. "Singing. Is that what you call it? It sounded like someone was torturing a cat."

"I thought I might work faster if I sang." She wiped the perspiration from her forehead with a gloved hand and regretted the action. The swipe of citrus oil she'd left on her skin burned. Cael continued to howl, and a door shut with a bang.

"That will be Gurn coming to rescue us from whatever demon he thinks is attacking." The branch supporting Silhara creaked as he adjusted his stance and leaned closer to her. "Tell me something, Martise." A leaf slapped him in the eye, and he ripped it off its twig with an irritated snap. "How is it that a woman blessed with a voice that could make a man come, sings badly enough to frighten the dead?"

She was saved from having to answer the outlandish question by the quick thud of running footsteps. Silhara disappeared briefly from view when he bent to greet their visitor. Unfortunately, his answers to Gurn's unspoken questions were loud and clear.

"That was Martise you heard. She was…singing.

"Trust me, I'm not jesting. You can unload your bow."

His next indignant response made her smile. "No, I wasn't beating her! She's the one tormenting me with that hideous wailing!"

Martise hid her smile when he reappeared before her. His scowl was ferocious. "Don't sing." He pointed a finger at her for emphasis. "You've scared my dog, my birds, and my servant with your yowling." He paused. "You've even managed to scare me."

"I'm sorry, Mast…." She halted when the scowl deepened.

"Don't sing," he repeated.

She nodded. He eyed her one last time in warning before dropping from the branch and climbing nimbly down the tree.

Well, Martise thought. That ended in utter failure and humiliation. She didn't know how Cumbria expected her to send him messages when his messenger wouldn't respond to her calls. Then again, if Micah had any sense, he'd flown away with the rest of the crows at her first shrill note.

Her thoughts caught on Silhara's coarse comment regarding her voice. The most left-handed compliment she'd ever received, it still managed to send a pleasant heat through her. Most often, she dreaded such remarks from people, even the more refined ones. They were usually accompanied by the callous observation of what a pity it was her face didn't match her voice.

She had never held any illusions concerning her appearance. She'd been fooled once into thinking it didn't matter to someone else and had come away with a bruised heart for her mistake. The small cuts about her plainness, whether purposeful or inadvertent, hurt less after so many years, but the pain never truly faded. She was grateful that Silhara, as abrupt and snide as he could be at times, had only once commented on her looks. Even then, she wasn't sure if she'd misunderstood his offhand remark about not bothering to primp for them. If he thought her as drab as others did, he kept his opinions to himself.

She paused in reaching for another cluster of oranges and shook her head to rid herself of the memory of her time with him in the stillroom. Rape didn't require beauty. Silhara's blunt command that she undress had nearly driven her into a blind panic. Only the obvious disinterest in his eyes and the half bored, half irritated note in his rough voice calmed her. He'd massaged the liniment into her back with strong fingers, kneading tight, aching muscles until she almost fell in a boneless heap on the floor.

He had good hands. Graceful, adept. They were the hands of a scholar except for the rough calluses that covered the pads of his fingers and toughened his palms. He'd eased the pain in muscles still unused to the rigors of orange harvesting, all the while entertaining her with anecdotes of his past. He'd suffered a harsh childhood, yet he spoke of it and his mother in a matter-of-fact tone, as if every six-year old lived in a brothel and acted as messenger to *hourin* and the men they serviced. He'd even surprised a laugh out of her. His was an irreverent humor, dry and often sarcastic.

Martise frowned and cut the cluster of oranges from their branch with more force than necessary. He fascinated her, drew her in ways no man ever had before him. Not even her old lover Balian, whom she once thought she loved. The sensation of Silhara close behind her, smoothing her skin with rough hands, had mesmerized her. Her first fear had evaporated, making her aware that she stood alone with him in the dark, fragrant stillroom.

That awareness had changed to a humming tension which danced along her spine when his hands lowered to her waist, fingers flexing gently against her skin. He'd curved his tall frame into hers, and she'd drowned in a myriad of sensations—the smoky sweetness of tobacco and orange flower, a whisper of cloth, the puff of air tickling her ear as he drew closer. Thank Bursin he'd stepped away when he did, or she might have been tempted to lean back into his warmth, forgetting her purpose at Neith and the many reasons why she should despise him.

He was an enigma. To anyone except maybe Gurn. Son of a prostitute, poor landowner, Conclave-trained, a mage of notoriety instead of renown, he was a strange combination of opposing roles. Eloquent and vulgar by turn, he was quick with a quip or an insult. His methods for making her Gift manifest were terrifying and extreme. Martise had been relieved when he pronounced them useless and halted them. He was a strict taskmaster, chiding her when she did something wrong but just as willing to show her the proper way of completing the task. He worked her and Gurn from dawn to dusk and even later, when she toiled away at translations and research in the candlelit library. No one questioned who ruled here, but Silhara worked as hard, if not harder, than they did and never put himself above any chore.

Even now, he was ensconced in an orange tree nearby, probably swatting wasps and dodging bird droppings as he picked fruit and cursed her name for bludgeoning his ears with her lullaby. The image made her grin and chased away the seductive heat pooling in her belly.

She was saved from further introspection by a loud clang. Gurn called them to lunch. Her stomach rumbled in response, and she made quick work leaving the orchard, stripping off the hat and cleaning her face and hands at the well pump.

The servant's blue eyes glinted at her as he signed from the kitchen door. Martise, used to his particular language now, blushed and raised her chin. "You're exaggerating. My singing wasn't that bad." He snorted in disagreement and nudged her toward the table.

She was seated and pouring tea for everyone when Silhara came through the door. His face, still damp from a quick wash, was grim. He sat in his customary spot across from her. Martise expected additional acidic commentary about her singing, but he only addressed Gurn.

"We need rain. This drought's lasted too long. Some of the younger trees are dropping leaves. If this keeps up, we'll have little flowering come autumn."

Gurn's normally amiable features went as dark as Silhara's. He finished laying out the rest of their lunch and sat down. The kitchen was dead quiet until Martise, eaten with curiosity, spoke.

"What will this mean for your orchard?"

Silhara filled his plate with cheese, bread, slices of smoked pork and small tomatoes from Gurn's garden. "A poor harvest for next year." He slid the ever-present bowl of oranges toward Gurn. "Too much leaf-drop means fewer flowers. Fewer flowers mean less fruit. Less fruit to sell, less money made. We starve." He wore that familiar, derisive half-smile. "Good thing I'm a crow mage. We sell our magic like hourin sell their bodies."

Martise didn't answer. Everyone knew of Conclave's distaste for the mages who sold the labors of their Gifts for money. Silhara's given title of Master of Crows was no compliment.

She was content to sip tea and listen to him converse with Gurn and plan their trip to Eastern Prime. She no longer watched in astonishment while he ate. The first time he had sat down to lunch with her and Gurn, she'd gawked as he consumed a loaf of bread, half a small wheel of cheese, an entire chicken, five boiled eggs and a bowl of olives.

She'd expected him to eat more at lunch than he did at breakfast, but he amazed her. After working hours in the grove, she was starving by lunchtime, and that was with Gurn's porridge sticking to her ribs. She didn't know how Silhara managed to work on so little breakfast. His scant meal of tea and two oranges in the morning wouldn't hold a child until midday. He made up for it at lunch. It was no wonder the servant baked enough bread for an army and kept a coop full of nesting hens.

"Have you found anything on god rituals?" He popped a tomato in his mouth and chewed.

She paused in buttering a slice of bread. "Only a few things and none that speak of defeating one through magery. The Dalatian chronicles mention a god destroyed by disbelief. But that took generations to accomplish and the introduction of a new god."

Silhara stabbed a slice of pork with his knife. "Generations? That's a luxury of time we don't have. I doubt Corruption will be content to wait another few hundred years before seizing control."

She nodded. "Before I came to Neith, there were rumors of strange plagues in the southern provinces. Crops dying for no apparent cause and famine in the outlying areas."

He scowled. "An impatient god is a dangerous one." He steepled his hands together and peered at her over the tops of his fingers. "Try harder. My library is extensive. There must be something."

A growl of frustration rose in her throat, and she swallowed it down. He'd assigned her no easy task. His library was extraordinary. A room of shelves stretching from floor to ceiling, filled to overflowing with tomes, scrolls and sheaves of loose-leaf manuscripts. Some looked almost new, while others crumbled under her fingers, so ancient their ink had faded to mere shadows on the yellowed parchment. She had no doubt some jewel of information lay hidden in that mountain of knowledge, but the search proved to be monumental and overwhelming. She possessed a unique talent for remembering every detail she'd read, every conversation she heard. But she was one woman amongst thousands of documents.

Silhara helped her at night, when his work in the grove was done for the evening. They sometimes took supper in the library, with Gurn retrieving books from the high shelves while she and Silhara pored over pages of archaic words, looking for that one ceremony that might aid them. For all the power of his Gift, he neither possessed her skill with translation nor her memory. He deciphered text much slower than she did. There were times when he'd pin her with a speculative stare when she directed him to a specific page of a specific grimoir for more information. So far their best efforts had been fruitless, and Martise was as frustrated as he over their lack of progress. *Try harder.* She glared at her plate.

"Martise, lower your knife. There are more than a few people eager to carve out my heart. You'll have to take your place in line."

She glanced up, startled. Amusement lightened his dark eyes. She looked at her hand fisted around her eating knife in a death grip. The knife struck the table with a clatter. She cleared her throat and stopped just short of apologizing when his eyes narrowed. "I wasn't..."

"Wasn't what? Dreaming of ways to skin my hide and nail it to my chamber door?" He laughed, a rough grating sound. "You're better than most at concealing your thoughts." He paused, and his gaze lowered. The timbre of his voice changed, smoothed and deepened. "But you have an expressive mouth. What you hide in your eyes is revealed there."

Her stomach somersaulted against her ribs. She licked her bottom lip. His eyes went blacker than the most forbidden arcana spell. She took a breath, as unnerved by her reaction to his words as the words themselves. "I'll try harder."

"I'm certain you will." He dragged his gaze to Gurn. "Pull out the large chest in the corner by the south window and unlock it. She can search the grimoires."

He looked back. His voice was raspy again. "We'll try something new tonight. I've books taken from Iwehvenn Keep. Old tomes with writings about the Wastelands and their ancient magic. There may be nothing of use to us, but it's worth a look."

The sip of tea she'd taken soured in her mouth. She swallowed hard. "Iwehvenn Keep? The lich's stronghold?"

He nodded. "The very one. The Eater of Souls is far more interested in feasting on the spirit of the unlucky traveler than he is in reading. He won't miss what I took."

Martise struggled to keep from gaping at him. She'd grown up listening to the horror stories of the Soul Eater of Iwehvenn and the hapless victims who'd fallen prey to its ravenous appetite. That Silhara had willingly breached the lich's fortress and come away unscathed was extraordinary and a testament to his cunning and the strength of his Gift.

No wonder the priesthood feared him. A mage that young, who commanded such power, was formidable and not easily matched nor defeated.

Silhara drained his cup and rose. "I've wasted enough time." He eyed Martise. "Gurn will show you where I keep those tomes.

Your fingers may pain you. The lich's taint still lingers on the pages."

He left her with a warning reminder. "No singing in the library. No singing anywhere. If I hear you, I'll see to it you're as mute as Gurn for the rest of your stay at Neith."

She held up her hands in surrender. "No singing. I swear."

The rest of lunch was quick and uneventful. Martise helped Gurn clear away the food and wash dishes.

"Gurn," she said. He paused in straightening the larder. "The grove is more than a source of income, isn't it? Silhara loves those trees."

Mute but adept at expressing his thoughts and opinions, he draped long arms over the larder's door and stared at her in somber approval. Even had he not nodded and confirmed her supposition, she knew she was right. Silhara treasured his small orange grove in the way another man would treasure a beloved wife or child. Martise frowned, oddly troubled by her observation. She had yet to discover his heresy, but she'd found his vulnerability.

The disturbing thought stayed with her as she made her way to the library and the tomes awaiting her perusal. Her long-suffering sigh echoed in the cavernous room, a far cry from her reaction at seeing the library for the first time. Cumbria's library at Asher was extensive, but nothing compared to the one at Neith. Only Conclave's equaled it in scope and variety, and that library served hundreds of priests and novitiates.

Narrow windows, flanked by bookshelves, filtered light in from the south and east. At night, she was often distracted from her reading by the glimmer of stars and moon as they hung jewel-like in the window's frame of the night sky—and relieved that she didn't see Corruption's star from this vantage point.

The chamber wasn't as dusty as most of the manor, but it was far from neat. Grimoires and scrolls lay scattered across the floor and stacked in haphazard fashion on the shelves. The two tables placed in the center almost sagged under the weight of more. Open chests spilled loose pages onto the floor. It had taken her two days to figure out an orderly way to conduct her research and not drown in a sea of parchment.

Gurn arrived and pointed to a small chest tucked in a corner near the south windows. He unlocked it with a rusted key, and a cloud of dust rose from the chest's interior. Martise choked, and Gurn covered his mouth with the hem of his tunic while he pulled the stack of grimoires out and piled them on the floor.

She stared at the cover of the first tome, captivated by the curving symbols etched into the cracked leather. She recognized the writing, an extinct script of the far northern countries that bordered the outland Waste. One of her Conclave mentors, an ancient priestess and scribe from those distant lands, had taught her how to read early Helenese.

"Remember it always, Martise," she'd commanded in a reedy voice. "There are few left alive who can read the old Northern tongue. Too much knowledge is already lost."

Gurn hovered at her side, eyeing the books with more revulsion than fascination. She waved him off. "Go on, Gurn. Silhara is probably wondering what's taking you so long." She sank to her knees before the books. "I'll be fine here."

She didn't hear him leave, too entranced by the knowledge revealed within the books. Her hands tingled unpleasantly each time she touched the pages. Mild nausea made her stomach roil, but it wasn't enough make her abandon the trove of information before her. She took a more comfortable seat on the floor and began reading.

The dying sun cast long shadows across her lap. Martise raised her head for the first time in hours, aware of an ache in her neck and the beginnings of a headache. The library had taken on a surreal cast, silvering with the moon's rise and the last sparkle of dust motes.

"A woman garbed in moonlight is a fair sight indeed."

Silhara stood over her, his approach silent as always. Shadows hollowed the spaces beneath his cheekbones and highlighted the arch of his nose. He stared at her, eyes glittering. "Did you try harder, Martise?" His voice, too damaged ever to caress, stroked her skin.

She raised the book she held to him. "I did, Master. And I think I've found your god-killer."

CHAPTER NINE

"What do you mean half the ritual is missing?"

Silhara scowled at the scatter of loose papers Martise had spread before him. Candlelight danced with the moon's glow as it streamed through the library windows. Martise, sitting next to him, pinched the bridge of her nose. The action gave him pause. His apprentice, normally so diligent at hiding her emotions, had twice today revealed her frustration with him. First, the knife clutched in her hand at lunch and now this. He didn't know whether to laugh or reprimand her. But he couldn't resist the chance to goad her.

"Did you lose the additional pages? I don't like carelessness, Martise."

He heard her teeth snap together. "No, Master. There were no additional pages to lose." She rubbed her temples. It was past midnight, and the two of them had been studying this particular tome since he'd returned to the library and found her sitting on the floor with the lich's books spread around her. "As you can see, the pages are falling out of the book." She waved a hand at the individual pieces. "The binding is old and the threads rotted. I'm surprised it held together this long." Her sidelong look was hesitant. "Is it possible some pages fell and were left behind when you stole...I mean took the books?"

He leaned back against his chair and cursed. "Not possible. Probable. I had no wish to linger and taste the soul eater's brand of hospitality. Those pages, and others, are likely gathering dust in Iwehvenn's library." He smirked at her. "And I'm usually such a careful thief."

Martise blushed and lowered her eyes. "I meant no offense."

"Ah, another way to apologize. You have an impressive arsenal of conciliatory statements. I've known slaves less contrite than you." Her expressive mouth tightened to a thin line. She had a finely curved jaw and a long neck revealed by her upswept hair. Silhara hadn't noticed either before. A trick of the moonlight, he thought. Graced by a sliver of silvery radiance piercing the window, she reminded him of a moth—colorless in the daylight but ethereal at night.

He cast a baleful glare at the papers with their rows of archaic script. He'd done passably well with transcription and translation during his years at Conclave, but his skills were nowhere near Martise's expertise. He'd been too busy brawling with fellow novitiates in the shadowed corridors, terrorizing his teachers with the unpredictable strength of his Gift and causing general mayhem at Conclave Redoubt.

"Read it again. There must be enough there to build upon."

Her faint sigh carried a wealth of grudging acquiescence. Silhara promised himself he'd listen closely and not become ensorcelled by her voice as she read the passage for a third time.

"In the spring of the black moon, before the Waste seized the lands between the Kor Mountains and the ice sea, thirteen kings gathered on Gladia's Knoll to destroy the false god Amunsa. Of these thirteen, only one was from the lands of the sun. Birdixan. Bound by blood and light, they swore to..."

Silhara groaned and held up a hand to stop her. "The gods save us from bards with runaway quills. We'll still be here at dawn before this dead scribe gets to the point." Martise's slight smile lessened the tiredness in her features. "You've a fine voice, Martise, but I want to go to bed soon. Let's summarize."

He began ticking off relevant points with his fingers. "A few thousand years ago a dozen mage-kings gather to kill off one false god who sounds like Corruption's sibling. They invoke blood-bonding, the strongest and deadliest of ritual magic. One of the kings, Birdixan, chooses to act as martyr and sacrifices himself in the ritual. But how?"

She shrugged. "We need the missing pages."

"Tell me something I don't know." He drummed his fingers on his chair arm and cursed under his breath. He'd have to go back to Iwehvenn and find those pages. If he was lucky, they'd still be where he dropped them, in the lich's ruin of a library. If his luck held, he'd make it out of the stronghold for the second time, alive.

Along with his apprentice.

She massaged her lower back. "Whatever ritual the kings used, they were successful. There is no Amunsa listed in the later histories, no ruins of temples built to him, not even in the North."

Silhara caught her stifling a yawn behind her hand. Dark circles ringed her eyes, and her lids drooped to half-mast despite her best efforts to look alert. He'd worked her hard the past two weeks, adding more and more responsibilities, expecting more out of her. She was still here, and making a significant contribution to the running of his household. He was both pleased and annoyed.

"We'll travel to Iwehvenn." An incredulous stare met his declaration.

"We?" she squeaked.

"Yes, we." He arched an eyebrow. "I don't read ancient Helenese, and there are several pages missing from that book. There are likely more gone from the other books I took from Iwehvenn. I need you to make sure we're gathering the right pages. I don't fancy making a trip to the soul eater's lair a second time. I damn well won't do it a third."

A convulsive swallow worked the muscles in her smooth throat. "How does one sneak past the Eater of Souls?"

He rose from his chair. Martise hastily followed suit. "I can cloak us both with concealment spells—incantations that will fool the lich."

"I've heard he has great power and can sense a living man like a wolf smells blooded prey."

"You've heard rightly. If ever a more deadly predator existed, I've yet to know of it." He was tempted to touch her, graze his fingers over the gooseflesh rising on her arms.

"What if he attacks us?"

"Then we'll fight our way clear."

She spread her hands. "I'm neither warrior nor mage. I'd be of little use in a battle."

His gruff laugh was roughened by weariness. "I don't need a brute fighter, and my magery is stronger than a gaggle of priests combined. If you can read Helenese and read it fast, you'll be of great use to me."

"What if your magery isn't enough?" Horror edged her voice, darkened her eyes.

Her reaction was justified. All Conclave acolytes were taught about those rare but vastly powerful and malevolent forces called liches or soul eaters. She knew what would happen if the Iwehvenn lich trapped them. Silhara was thankful she had such knowledge. He wouldn't have to explain the danger or impress upon her the risks involved.

He held her gaze. "I'll kill you before he ever touches you." The blunt declaration made her flinch. For some inexplicable reason, he wanted to soften his words. "There are worse fates than a clean death."

"I don't suppose I can respectfully decline?" She gave him a weak smile.

"You can, but you'd have to leave Neith." This, more than any brutal lesson he might mete out to her, would measure her determination. "If I have nothing for you to translate, I've no need of you and will send you back to the bishop."

Myriad emotions passed in her eyes; fear, acceptance, a touch of anger and most of all, resolve. "When do we leave?"

His respect for her grew. She was terrified but willing to accompany him. A brave woman and one wise enough to accept her fear. It would keep her alive. "Tomorrow."

"So soon?"

"I want to get my hands on those pages as soon as possible. And I have a harvest to bring in to market next week. Playing cat and mouse with a soul eater wasn't in my plans."

He extinguished three of the four lit candles on the table. The remaining one cast a nimbus of feeble light around him and

Martise. "Put the books and papers away. We'll deal with them when we return."

Once in the corridor, he handed her the candle. The only point of radiance in the black hallway, the flame flickered and danced, lending Martise's face a ghostly aspect dominated by her wide copper eyes.

"Get what rest you can," he said. "And pack lightly. A change of clothes, no more. I'll see you in the bailey an hour before dawn."

She held the candle out to him. "Don't you need this?"

Blackness hid his amusement. "I'm used to traveling dark paths, Martise. You need the candle more than I do."

She nodded her thanks and ascended the stairs. He heard the floor boards creak above him as she made her way to her chamber. The candle was truly more use to her than to him. He could light his way with witchfire, but even that wasn't necessary. He'd lived at Neith for almost twenty years and could navigate its winding corridors, with their buckled, broken floors, blindfolded.

The drowsiness plaguing him in the library had vanished by the time he reached his bedroom. The bright moon, suspended high in the sky, plated the balcony and chamber in silver. Corruption's star hovered below it, casting its own baleful light over the grove and the flat plains beyond. Silhara sensed the god's nearness, its predatory regard. Best not to sleep. He could only imagine the horrors awaiting him in what should be peaceful slumber.

"Do you have nothing better to do besides vex me in my sleep and sully my magic?" He recalled Martise's words. "You know, pestilences to create? Villages to destroy? Dead hounds to resurrect?"

He prepared his *huqqah* for his delayed evening smoke and tried to ignore the empty laughter filling his mind.

Sully? I thought you would appreciate that small taste of power. My offering is limitless if you accept me.

Silhara puffed on the hose tip, watching as a trail of smoke floated out the window in ghostly swirls. "Your little 'taste' rendered my Gift worthless for a day. I'm not interested in what I cannot control."

Again, the god's amusement scraped the inside of his skull. *We are much alike, sorcerer. Yield and you will have supremacy over all magery. Your Gift will seem a child's toy compared to a sword, and you will wield that sword with the might of a god.*

The matal tobacco, sweet when it first filled his mouth, burned acrid now. So tempting. He could not deny the persuasion of Corruption's words. His Gift, the one thing that made him whole, made him equal to those who might otherwise spit on him in the streets, was a blessing. Manifesting while he gasped for air and writhed against his executioner's grip, the power of the Gift had changed his life, given him a place above the teeming filth and violence of Eastern Prime's docks.

Conclave, already wary of his Gift's potency and the skill with which he wielded it, would panic were he to accept Corruption's offer. Both priesthood and sorcerer knew Conclave would be the first casualty of Silhara's newly acquired godhood. His eyes closed. The pleasurable images of the famed Redoubt nothing more than rubble and the priests, especially the Bishop of Asher, imprisoned or executed, played across his mind's eye.

Do you not see? This is nothing for you with my help. No more effort than crushing a bothersome gnat.

Corruption's voice caressed and cajoled, and Silhara swayed in its embrace. The memory of a dream replaced the fantasy of Conclave's destruction. A moonless sky over a black ocean and the leviathan traversing its dead waters. He opened his eyes, suddenly desperate to reassure himself the moon and her attendant stars still reigned over the night. Below him, the grove slept undisturbed. Alive and growing, the trees were testaments of his will to survive and conquer.

His lip curled into a sneer as the god's star flickered. "Gods who are poets." He exhaled tendrils of smoke in the star's direction. "As if we aren't already overrun with such useless men. You speak of sword-wielding, of kings and wealth and power unmeasured. But your price..." He shook his head. "They call me a carrion mage now. To yield to you will make me nothing more than a foul tick swollen on the blood of the world."

Who knew you to be so noble?

Silhara laughed, his humor as insincere as the god's. "What nobility is there in being a false god's puppet?" His laughter died abruptly. "I will destroy you."

Corruption mocked him. *Will you? At what sacrifice? Are you willing to act as assassin to do it? Or martyr? What will you do, Silhara of Neith, to remain poor, reviled...and free?*

Silhara put aside the *huqqah* and closed the shutters. His chamber, pitched into sudden blackness, became a crypt. "You ask the wrong question," he said into the unbroken darkness. "Better to ask, what will I not do?"

CHAPTER TEN

If she managed to survive this journey, Martise intended to kill her former master the moment she was free. She paced past Gurn who waited with her in the bailey. Until recently, her dislike had been reserved for Silhara and his unorthodox teaching methods, but the Master of Crows had yet to deceive her. She'd known from the start he'd be a merciless teacher and had expected the worst.

Unlike Silhara, Cumbria had misled her. He'd warned her of Silhara's mercurial nature and sharp tongue, of his power and his reputation. But he'd downplayed her role as spy. Adventuring had never been part of the plan.

"You need only do what you are unequaled at. Observe his actions, hear his words and remember every detail. He will betray himself. No man, not even Silhara, can hide all secrets forever."

"Ha!" she snapped, ignoring Gurn's perplexed look. So far, the Master of Crows had done a fine job of concealing anything that might bring Conclave justice down on his head. She'd seen no evidence of Corruption's influence on him nor any interest in the god's celestial presence. If Conclave ever outlawed orange-harvesting and book-stealing, Silhara was a dead man. Otherwise, she had nothing.

Nothing except a knotted stomach and the burn of fear in her throat at the thought of sneaking around a lich's stronghold. The risks she took in coming here were worth regaining her spirit stone. But a lich? Cumbria didn't mention Silhara's fearless sense of purpose or that he had a soul eater as a neighbor.

His draft horse stood next to her and fluttered her shawl with a soft exhalation. Martise patted his neck and scratched a spot behind the bridle strap. The horse, a gentle dun gelding, was a far cry from Cumbria's high-strung mounts. Saddled and loaded with supplies including Silhara's crossbow and a pair of long knives, he too awaited Silhara's arrival.

Martise looked at Gurn. "Do you think he's still asleep?"

"I never went to sleep, apprentice. You should learn a little patience."

With her back to the kitchen door, she'd missed his arrival. As usual, he moved on soundless feet. She bowed to hide her startlement. "Good morning, Master."

His gaze skimmed over her shawl, long tunic and makeshift trousers. He wasn't the only one who hadn't slept. Martise had spent the remaining hours before dawn cutting down a skirt and sewing it into something resembling trews suitable for riding.

Silhara wore his usual raiment of worn shirt, faded black breeches, and boots. His hair, free of its customary braid, fell straight and silky over his wide shoulders, framing a face sharpened by fatigue. Despite his shabby appearance and the weariness in his eyes, he had the air of an aristo—powerful, arrogant, sure of his place in the world. Martise sometimes found it hard to believe he was the son of a lowly *houri*.

She looked away, unsettled by the pleasant prickle dancing up her legs and across her lower back. She'd found him attractive upon first meeting, and even after, when he'd done his best to frighten her into abandoning her purpose here. Now, more accustomed to his ways and witness to his fair dealings with his dependents, she was even more drawn to him. She crossed her arms and silently admonished herself for such feelings. She had a role to play, an objective to achieve. The price of her freedom grew higher each day.

"What grim thoughts plague you so early in the morning, Martise?" His raspy voice snapped her out of her musings, and she straightened. "Have you fallen asleep standing there? I've asked you twice if you're ready to leave."

Her apology hovered on the tip of her tongue. "I'm ready, Master. I only wondered how long our trip might be."

"Most of the day. We'll camp about three miles outside Iwehvenn and reach the stronghold an hour or two before sunset. We'll return to Neith in the morning."

Alone with him for a day and night. More if she counted the return trip. Nervousness warred with a disquieting eagerness. "Then we shouldn't delay."

His lips quirked, but he didn't reply. The gelding held still when he took the reins, swung nimbly onto the horse's wide back and patted its withers. "You've grown fat on plains grass, Gnat. This journey will do you good."

Martise's eyes widened. "Gnat? His name is Gnat?" She stared at the mountain of horseflesh, heavily muscled and big-boned, with a girth that would make riding astride a challenge, and he stood at least seventeen hands high.

Gnat swung his large head in her direction, as if questioning her incredulity. Silhara stared down his nose, the expression made even more imperious by his high seat on the horse's back. "I didn't think 'Butterfly' suitable."

A betraying flutter rose in her throat. "No," she said, eyes tearing with the effort to hold in her laughter. "I suppose not."

A flicker passed through Silhara's eyes—so quick, Martise almost didn't see it. She grinned and passed a gentle hand over Gnat's soft nose. "Your name, big lad...no one would ever guess."

Next to her, Gurn gave a short bark of laughter and signaled he'd lift her onto Gnat's back. His hands were wrapped around her waist when Silhara stopped him.

"Put her down, Gurn. You're not going with us. She needs to do this without your help." He leaned down and held out his hand. "Take my forearm, Martise. Use it as a brace to mount."

She stared at the graceful hand for a moment. Her fingers tingled in anticipation of the hint of power transferred from his touch—the presence of his Gift, so strong it leached through his fingers. She clutched his arm, gasping softly at that lightning contact, and swung herself up behind him. She landed solidly on Gnat's back only to slide toward the other side. Her hands clawed at Silhara's shirt and arm to keep from falling off.

"Foolish woman," he snapped. "Find your seat before you yank us both off this nag."

"I'm trying." She managed to pull herself upright. He grunted when she wrapped her arms around his waist and squeezed. Legs splayed wide over the horse's broad back, she didn't even think of what she did, too intent on staying in place and not hitting the ground that looked so far below her.

"For someone so small, you've a grip surpassing Gurn's. You're crushing my ribs." He shrugged against her hold.

She let him go, almost falling off Gnat a second time.

Silhara's low growl of frustration echoed in the bailey. "Hang on to me. Just not like a strangler serpent."

"Sorry."

"Of course you are." He frowned at her over his shoulder. "Now are you ready?"

"Yes." She swiped at the damp tendrils of hair stuck to her forehead. Even in the chill morning air, she'd managed to break a sweat with her efforts. This time her hands rested lightly against his sides, feeling the flex of muscle as he guided Gnat through the bailey. Gurn kept pace beside them, nodding as Silhara gave instructions.

"Check the southwest corner of the grove. I think one of the trees is diseased. If it can't be saved, cut it down and burn it." They waited until Gurn unlocked the bailey gate. "We'll return tomorrow. If we don't, send Cael to track us."

Gurn frowned at the last. So did Martise. If their luck held, they'd return to the safety of Neith and find Cael in his customary place beneath the kitchen table. She smiled, despite her trepidation. When did she start thinking of Neith as safe?

She bid Gurn goodbye, squeezing his outstretched hand as they passed through the gate. Before them, Neith's lands lay shrouded in a ghostly cloak of ground fog. Only the tips of the tall plains grasses rose above the murk, fluttering like fireflies as they caught the bright edge of the rising sun. Silhara guided Gnat down a gradually sloping path that curved around the manor in a half-circle and brought them to the gated courtyard with its cemetery of broken stone. At the gates, he spoke a few brief words. The lock snapped free and slipped on its anchoring chain until it clanged against the metal. Hinges sang their anguish as the gates swung open. Another cited spell, and Martise watched the gates slam shut. The chain took on serpentine life, twisting and looping itself around the bars before the lock closed with a loud click.

More undulating fog obscured the main avenue, rolling across the path in wispy tides that broke against the Solaris oaks lining the way. Droplets of dew hung from the trees' gnarled branches like jewels, falling occasionally to splash on Gnat's coat or Silhara's shoulders. Unlike the bishop's more skittish mounts, the draft horse plodded down the road, his hooves clopping a steady rhythm.

"Master," she whispered. "May I ask you something?"

"Why are you whispering?" Silhara's voice, never strident, seemed to thunder in the hushed gloom.

The question brought her up short. Why was she whispering? They weren't slipping out of Neith like thieves. Not that there was anything in that tumble-down wreck worth stealing. Still, the peculiar silence hanging over the woods almost demanded a more subdued tone. And she couldn't shake the feeling of being watched.

She tried for a more normal volume. "Why is Gnat unafraid to take this road? The bishop and I had to walk to the manor because his mounts balked at the entrance."

His huff of scorn was almost lost in the weighted silence. "I could remark on the over-breeding of horse and owner, but that's an old whine and doesn't answer your question." He leaned forward and patted Gnat on the neck. "He's used to it. The first time I brought him here as a yearling, I had to use a calming spell on him to enter Neith territory. Curse magic is a strong deterrent."

He didn't exaggerate. Even now, accompanied by the mage who worked such magic on these woods, Martise couldn't shake her unease. The scent of dark spells, the kind that brought forth demons and invoked force-bondings, hung in the air.

Silhara chuckled at her relieved huff when they left the shadowed avenue for the open plain. Bathed in pale morning light, the ocean of grass emerged from the thinning fog. The plain spread out before them, giving way to sloping hills and plateaus dotted with olive and orange groves. Silhara halted Gnat and breathed deep. His waist shifted beneath her hands, warm to the touch.

"When Conclave banished me to Neith, I thought I'd miss the sea. But it's here as well, only the waves are made of grass."

"The sea was the only thing I missed when I left Conclave Redoubt," she said. The rhythm of the tide had given her comfort in the interminable years of her training.

He glanced at her over his shoulder. "Its proximity to the sea was the Redoubt's one saving grace."

He kicked Gnat into motion, guiding him eastward, toward the rising sun and the soul eater's sanctuary. They didn't speak after that. Martise, suffering from lost sleep, swayed in her seat. Lulled by Gnat's rolling gait, she soon drifted off, cheek resting against Silhara's back. The sun warmed her shoulders while another heat warmed her chest. She nestled closer, breathing in the spicy scent of matal tobacco and reveling in the nearly forgotten sensation of a man's body against hers.

She thought she'd only closed her eyes for a moment when a shrug and a sharply spoken "Martise!" startled her awake. Bleary-eyed, she squinted at the expanse of white shirt and blew away a long strand of Silhara's black hair that stuck to her lower lip. Above her, the sun shone hot and bright. No hint of the morning's coolness remained. She scrubbed at her hot cheek, damp from where she'd pressed her face against his back.

"How long have I been asleep?" Her voice was almost as hoarse as his.

"Three hours. Maybe a little more." He opened one of the packs tied across Gnat's back and handed her a water skin. "Here. Drink your fill. There's a stream not far from here. We'll stop, water Gnat and refill the skins."

The water was tepid and flat but tasted better than wine on her parched tongue. Silhara waved the skin away when she offered it to him. "Thank you for letting me sleep. I was more tired than I thought."

"Altering a wardrobe at the last minute will do that to a person."

She laughed and looked down at her makeshift breeches. His humor never failed to surprise her. Good thing she sacrificed a night of slumber. Trying to ride Gnat while wearing skirts would have been impossible.

"Your singing can be used as a torture method, but you've a fine laugh." His voice smoothed to a silky rumble. "You should laugh more often."

Martise blushed at the unexpected compliment. "Thank you. You sometimes make me laugh." She hastily corrected herself in case he misconstrued her comment. "Not at you, of course."

"No, of course not." Amusement threaded his voice.

She fell silent, content to rock with Gnat's easy gait and survey her surroundings. Silhara's back blocked most of her frontal view, but she still marveled at the plains surrounding them, heard the whispering brush of grass as the horse waded through the sea of blue stem and dropseed. The plain soon gave way to a more rolling landscape, where the grasses thinned and olive trees stood in sentinel rows on the low hills. Sheep and goats dotted the slopes, their far-off bleating carried by the hot breeze drifting across the land.

Silhara pointed to a spot shaded by a copse of trees. "A stream runs there. If the drought hasn't dried it up, we'll stop."

Their luck held. The stream, a bubbling flow of icy water that poured from the melted snows off the Dramorin Mountains, tracked a meandering path past a stand of plum trees before veering south. Gnat picked up his pace without Silhara's urging, eager to drink and graze on the lush grass growing by the water's edge.

Silhara uttered a sharp command. The horse halted, stamping his hooves in impatience as he waited for them to dismount and relieve him of supplies. Silhara looped the reins across the animal's neck and gave him a slap on the hindquarters. "Go on, lad," he said. "Enjoy it while you can. We won't stay long."

Martise found a comfortable spot beneath the ample shade of a young plum and began emptying the packs. Concentrated on unwrapping and setting out the food Gurn packed for their journey, she didn't note Silhara's actions until the sound of splashing, followed by a colorful string of curse words, reached her ears. The sight greeting her made her breath catch.

He'd followed Gnat to the stream. Crouched at the banks, he'd stripped off his shirt and sluiced water across his shoulders and arms. Rivulets traced glistening paths over skin darkened to a smooth nut brown from days spent toiling beneath the southern sun. His hair lay plastered against his broad back and curved along his ribs. A few wet strands fell forward to twine around his upper arms. He was a lean man, with a slim waist and long, ropy muscles, but there was strength aplenty in that tall, wiry frame. She'd watched him heave heavy crates of oranges into Gurn's wagon with ease. He cast spells that would bring a lesser mage to his knees, and he could outwork both her and his servant during a day's labor.

She swallowed, mouth dry as dust, as he cupped water in his hands and poured it over his head. Shivers wracked his body, but he did it twice more before wiping his face with his discarded shirt. He was beautiful—a study in lithe grace and barely restrained power.

When he rose, she pretended to rummage through the empty packs.

"What did Gurn pack? And most important, is there wine?"

She'd composed her features into a bland expression when she faced him, hoping he didn't notice the effect of seeing him burnished with water and sun had on her senses. Her efforts were almost wasted. He'd left the shirt off and sat down close enough that she noted every delineation of hard muscle in his shoulders and chest. Dappled shade danced across his face and arms, shadowing the planes of his stark features. His hair hung down his back, wet and sleek as a seal's pelt.

"Martise? You're staring."

He looked first at her and then at the wine skin crushed in her hand. Mortified that he'd noticed her bewitchment, she thrust the wine at him and searched frantically for something to say.

His scar. She'd been too busy ogling him to give the white collar of puckered skin circling his throat more than a cursory glance. But now, with his inquisitive gaze nailing her in place, she found a ready excuse, rude though it might seem.

She touched her own throat. "What scarred you?"

He took a swallow of wine, then draped his arms over his splayed knees. The wine skin dangled from his fingers. "I'm impressed. You lasted weeks before your curiosity got the best of you."

That wasn't quite true. She was curious, but far better he thought her nosy than admit she'd been unable to tear her gaze away from the sight of him bathing at the stream. And he wasn't making it any easier by sitting there bare-chested. She scooted away from him to sort through the towel-wrapped packages Gurn had prepared. Their meal was simple. Bread, boiled eggs, olives and the ever present oranges. His upper lip curled as the last rolled toward him.

"I was eleven when I got this." He ran his finger over the rucked scar. "Punishment for the crime of stealing."

Martise gasped. "You were a mere child!"

"I was also a thief, and a good one. Most days. But hunger weakens you, slows you down. I wasn't quick enough that day and they caught me."

He handed her the wine and reached for an egg. Martise watched, her heart aching in her chest as the lines deepened around his mouth in a grimace.

"What did you steal?" Surely something valuable. A rich man's purse, a vain woman's jeweled mirror, a length of priceless silk from a fat merchant's stall.

"An orange."

The wine skin fell from her nerveless fingers. A ribbon of wine spilled out, trickling like blood over the grass. Silhara snatched up the skin and corked it before more spilled. "Watch what you're doing, girl. That didn't come easily or cheap."

His chastisement lacked its customary sharpness. Aghast at his words, she gawked. "Someone garroted you over an orange?" She felt sick. Such merciless retribution, and toward a starving child wishing only to eat. Her own childhood circumstances paled in comparison. She'd been sold, but to a master who had treated her fairly enough. As a slave, she'd had felt the razor cut of contempt, but never starvation. Her stomach churned.

Silhara tore a piece of bread from the loaf she'd unwrapped and took a bite. His gaze never left her face while he chewed. He washed the food down with another swallow of wine before speaking. "Save your pity for a more deserving victim. I survived because my Gift is far more accommodating than yours. It manifested while my executioner strangled me, and I pissed myself before a betting crowd of sailors, whores and a Conclave priest or two." He uttered the last with withering scorn.

"What happened?"

He shrugged. "I don't remember much, except fighting to breathe. Suddenly, I felt as if someone had put a torch to my blood. Only I was the torch. I knew nothing after that until I awakened in the household of a Conclave priest. It seems my Gift created a column of holy fire. I came away alive and unharmed save for this pretty necklace I wear and a voice that can still sing better than yours. But the executioner was immolated and part of the wharf burned."

Martise's jaw sagged. "Bursin's wings, no wonder Conclave fears you. Only a Gift nurtured by years of teaching and practice is so powerful."

"Is that why you're here?"

She blinked. "What?"

Silhara's lip curled again, only this time the sneer wasn't reserved for the reviled oranges. "Is that why you're here?" he repeated. "At Neith? Because Conclave fears me?" The breeze caught wisps of his drying hair, blowing it around his face. A few strands fluttered toward her, caressing her cheek.

She stiffened and busied herself with cracking and peeling one of the eggs. She met his gaze, refusing to quail before the penetrating stare that demanded she reveal all her secrets. "I'm here because you asked for an apprentice, Master."

He snorted. "Oh yes. And Conclave, ever obliging, sent me a failed novitiate."

She bristled at his mockery. Were it not for her, he'd still be closeted in his library, sorting through stacks of incomprehensive tomes in a useless bid to find his precious ritual. She bit into the egg so hard her teeth clicked.

Wry amusement softened his derisive gaze. His lips twitched. "Say it, Martise. I don't want to watch my back for the remainder of this trip because you're angry enough to plant a knife between my shoulders."

No longer caring if he thought her insolent, Martise snatched the wine skin out of his hand, uncorked it and drank. Sweet and potent, the wine gave her additional courage to vent her frustration. "You asked for a novitiate, one who could perform minor enchantments and translate old languages." She pointed her half-eaten egg at him. "The enchantments are beyond my abilities, but not yours. You don't really need me for that. But reading ancient text? I am better than most of the high priests at deciphering. And that is no idle boast." She scowled, daring him to scoff at her once more.

"No idle boast," he repeated. A measuring gleam entered his black eyes. "Then prove it. Help me find those pages. Translate them and give me the means to destroy Corruption."

"Why do you think I'm here, Master?" She contemplated how he might react if she threw her egg at him.

One eyebrow arched. "Don't insult me. Whatever motivation sends you willingly into a soul eater's lair, it has little to do with a need to prove your talent—especially to me."

He motioned for her to pass the wine skin. "Finish your lunch. We've rested long enough."

She didn't protest, torn between relief that he hadn't dug deeper into her reasons for being at Neith and disappointed at the loss of the brief camaraderie that had briefly blossomed between them. She remained undecided if it was relief or disappointment she felt when he shrugged on his shirt.

They made short work of the meal and repacked their supplies. Martise rinsed her hands in the stream and splashed her face. The shock of icy water banished the lethargy that tempted her to stretch out on the cool grass and nap the day away. When she returned to their lunch spot, Silhara had tied the packs and weaponry to the saddle.

He leapt onto Gnat's back and again offered his arm. "Not so enthusiastic this time, Martise. I don't want to land on my ass in the dirt."

Her second attempt at mounting Gnat was far more successful than the first, and they set off for Iwehvenn at a steady clip. As they traveled, Silhara kept her occupied by pointing out the various farms and to whom they belonged. He was knowledgeable of the surrounding area—its agriculture and weather patterns, the best hunting grounds and the most treacherous streams, who grew the sweeter oranges—none as sweet as his—and the richest olives. He was especially well versed in the activities and proclivities of the landowners. For a man who actively shunned visitors and practically lived the life of a hermit, he knew a great deal about his neighbors.

She listened, enjoying the conversation and the rough timbre of his voice. She almost forgot about their destination until they topped a small rise and surveyed the dale below them.

Silhara pointed to a graceful structure in the middle of the dale. "Iwehvenn Keep."

Caught in the red rays of the late afternoon sun, Iwehvenn glowed like a gem on a pillow of green velvet. The keep, a modest structure with tall, delicate spires and curving arches carved of pearlescent rock, shimmered in a rainbow of color. Trees, heavy with all manner of fruit, lined the garden walks. Flowers bloomed in lush clusters of vibrant hues watered by cascading fountains. The grass in the dale grew verdant and full, untouched by the drought baking the land behind her.

She gaped at the scene before them, her fingers digging into Silhara's sides. "So beautiful! It can't be real."

"It isn't. But those not Gifted see it that way. Such is the power of the trap. Look closer."

As he guided Gnat down the slope, she squinted and blinked. The jeweled keep and gardens wavered in her vision like a mirage in the noon heat. Picturesque and enticing at first glance, the illusion disintegrated, revealing a black, twisted landscape. Like Neith, Iwehvenn was a ruin. Unlike Silhara's home, it reeked of death. The fruit trees and flowers, luxuriant beneath the illusion's power, were nothing more than stands of misshapen, rotted limbs and tangled weeds. Jagged scorch marks scarred the northern face of the keep, as if it had been struck repeatedly by lightning and burned. The roof was collapsed in one section. What remained clung like ancient skin to the skeleton of warped rafters. Swathes of grass faded to cracked earth and split rock.

More than its appearance, the dale's oppressive silence made her skin crawl. Even drought-stricken and bleached by the sun, Neith sang a chorus of life. The drone of insects, the incessant caws of the ubiquitous crows, the bleats and snorts of farm stock—all these things made Neith vibrant. Even the wood, blanketed by curse magic, had its own manner of living things. This was different. Iwehvenn, devoid of life, sat like a diseased pustule that drained the land around it until there was nothing left but flat sky and an evil that never slept.

"Peace, apprentice. I've been here before and came out untouched. We'll do the same this time."

He kept a tight hand on a suddenly nervous Gnat's reins. Martise peeled her fingers out of Silhara's ribs and breathed deep. She didn't want to suffer some ghastly death at the hands of a soul eater. These pages they risked their very souls for had best be worth the danger.

They rode Gnat ever slower down the hillside until his ears laid flat against his head, and he refused to take another step.

"We walk from here." Silhara held still as Martise slid off Gnat's back then followed after her. "I won't force an animal into Iwehvenn. Gnat will stay close by."

He untied and loaded his crossbow, strapped the quiver of bolts across his back and slid the two sheathed long knives into his belt. Martise rubbed her damp palms on her trousers. No treasure hunt had ever been so deadly. She eyed Silhara standing before her, bristling with weaponry. Despite his confident words, he was taking no chances. Strong magic was his greatest protection, but a sharp knife or two never hurt.

He hefted the crossbow. "These are useless against a lich, but the bandits he lures to his web are alive enough. We may well have more than one adversary at Iwehvenn."

"As if one isn't enough." Her voice sounded shrill to her ears.

His fearless smile lent her courage. "Consider it a challenge." He touched one of the knives. "Do you know how to wield one of these?"

She shook her head, desperately wishing she did. "Only for slaughter. Not for fighting."

He shrugged. "They're often one and the same. Still, you're more of a danger to me and yourself if I give one to you." She watched as he bent and drew out a small dagger concealed in his boot. "Here. "Find a place to tuck it. You're better off armed with something." He tilted his head, and his smirk widened. "If all else fails, you can always sing."

Any other time, Martise might have laughed at his quip, but she only offered him a weak smile. She took the knife and empty harvesting bag he gave her. "I thought we just came for papers?"

He looped the trailing reins over Gnat's neck and sent the horse back up the hill to wait. "We did. And pray to whatever gods comfort you that those papers are still in the lich's library and not used by some now-dead thief to wipe his ass." He motioned for her to follow him down into the dale. "There may be other books, tomes you can quickly decipher as useful. It will be easier for you to carry them in the satchel."

Once they reached the ruins of the gardens, Silhara stopped her. "Give me your hand." He sighed his impatience at her hesitation. "I need to touch you in order for this cloak spell to work."

She placed her hand in his and gasped. The vibrations of power in his fingers shot up her arm and centered in her chest. Martise almost jerked her hand free. A tightening in her ribs made her grasp her side. Something awakened—an awareness within her yet independent of her control. The sensation surged through her body, seeking and grasping for the spell that bound her to Silhara. Before she could question its presence, the feeling winked out, as if someone had slammed and locked a door.

A speculative gleam lit the mage's dark eyes. "Well, well. What secret did you almost reveal just now?" His fingers gripped hers, warm and imprisoning.

"I don't know." She rubbed the place above her breasts with her free hand. "I've never felt anything like it." A near dead hope rose within her. "Could it be my Gift?" She squeezed his fingers, her trepidation at entering the lich's stronghold replaced by a burgeoning excitement.

He shrugged. "Possibly. And it couldn't have picked a worse time to show itself." He released her hand, leaving behind a prickling sensation in her arm and a halo of golden light on her fingertips. "Keep your focus on those papers. There's time enough to discover what just greeted my spell when we get to Neith."

They tracked a winding path through the gardens, avoiding thorny black vines littering the walkways. Martise's nostrils twitched. The scent of old death lingered here. Not the reek of a decaying corpse, but the dry, choking scent of a violated sepulcher and only the dust of the dead to greet the intruder. She shuddered when they passed a man reclined against a broken fountain. Wasted to nothing more than a scarecrow of brittle bones clothed in wool tatters, the skeleton stared at them from empty eye sockets. The jaw hung open, hands clutched to a skull, as if still in mid scream.

Silhara gripped her arm. His whisper flowed warm against her ear. "Prepare yourself, Martise. There are more like him scattered about Iwchvenn."

She shadowed him after that, treading his heels a few times until he warned her off with a threatening scowl. Her jaw ached from clenching her teeth so they wouldn't chatter. Cloaked in a protective spell and accompanied by a powerful and heavily armed mage, Martise still had to squelch the urge to run away. Gnat, safely grazing on the hillside, had more sense than they did.

Darkness spilled like blood out of the entrance to the keep. The large doors, still bearing remnants of a carved beauty beneath their split surface, hung askew on buckled hinge straps. Silhara blew on his fingers. Three points of green witchfire rose from his hands and floated in the air before him. They expanded and coalesced, creating a vaporous torch.

He paused at the doorway. "I suspect I don't need to tell you to stay close." He didn't look at her when he spoke, but the amusement in his voice reminded her she was practically embracing him. Martise's face heated and she backed away. "If we're separated, I may never find you, and you may never find your way out. The halls and chambers of this keep lead to more than just other rooms."

Despite the summer heat, chills rose on her arms. They entered the keep's interior, guided by Silhara's floating torch and his memory of his first foray into Iwehvenn. Martise wanted to gag as the touch and rancid scent of blackest magic oozed over her skin. The witchlight didn't chase darkness away so much as hold it at bay. This part of the keep still had its roof intact, and she saw little beyond the green luminescence hovering before them. As they moved forward, she caught glimpses of a richly tiled floor coated in dust and littered with a puzzling assortment of items—water skins, rolled blankets, a spent torch, weaponry of every kind. Supplies abandoned by long-vanished travelers.

They passed a trio of those travelers near the stairs. Like their unfortunate counterpart outside, the three sprawled on the floor in a tangle of bones and decayed clothing. Broken toys discarded by a vicious child. Protected from the elements, their bodies still bore hints of mummified flesh that stretched parchment-thin over skulls surrounded by matted hair. The shadow of a dying scream was stamped on each withered face.

From outside, the keep was modestly sized, but like the gardens and dale itself, all was an illusion. Inside, it expanded into an endless maze. She lost count of the number of corridors they walked or the stairs they climbed. They passed through spaces either drowning in shadow or bathed in the red light of a setting sun. Silhara never paused, never stopped to check his bearings. He seemed as familiar with Iwehvenn's labyrinth as he was with Neith's. Martise was on the verge of asking him how much farther they had to go when he stopped at a partially open door.

She almost barreled into his back. At some point in their wanderings, she had grasped the back of his shirt so as not to lose him. He tugged until she released the death grip she had on his clothing.

"The library," he whispered. "If our luck holds, the papers are there, and we can leave before nightfall."

She almost shoved him aside then. Wandering through this cursed crypt during daylight was bad enough. She had no intention of being anywhere near the keep once the sun went down.

Silhara arched an eyebrow. "My apologies, apprentice. I'm in your way." He bowed in mock apology and gestured that she precede him into the library.

Eager though she was to find the papers and escape Iwehvenn, Martise stepped cautiously over the threshold. The witchfire torch hovering beside her cast an emerald haze on a chamber of dust-covered opulence. She drew in a breath, awed by the sight of towering bookcases crammed with what was surely thousands of years of knowledge.

"Don't just stand there and gawk, woman. Unless you've a mind to spend the night here?"

Silhara's soft admonishment ended her bewitchment, and she began searching the room. The library was a shambles, with furniture overturned and scrolls spilled onto the floor. Parchment lay scattered in haphazard patterns, tucked into corners, caught between chairs and tables. Surely someone other than Silhara had been here. She didn't think he'd be so careless with such works. Martise glanced at him, puzzled. He shrugged.

"I'm unlike many of the thieves who've ransacked this place. First, I've lived through the experience, and second, I know wealth isn't always measured by coin. Those who usually brave Iwehvenn are only interested in books as a source for their campfire fuel. This was not my doing."

He set the crossbow against a table, within easy reach, and crouched beside her to shift through the papers. "Just gather them all. I'm certain I left them in here, and from the way this room looks, whoever came after me wasn't interested in a good book."

Martise stacked parchments together, her bare hands burning with the taint of the lich's magic. As soon as they made it back to the stream by the plum trees, she was going to bathe and burn the garments she currently wore. Silhara's instructions that she bring extra clothing made sense now.

Her satchel was almost full and growing heavy on her shoulder. Silhara stood and helped her rise. "The light fails outside. We need to leave."

She was on the verge of telling him he'd get no argument from her when an icy fear suddenly poured over her skin, rendering her immobile. The library swam before her eyes, its walls warping and splitting with fissures. Something waited outside. Something malevolent. Ravenous. Martise grasped Silhara's arm. His austere features, bathed in the green witchlight, were strained. "Something comes," she whispered.

His nostrils flared, sensual mouth flattening back against his bared teeth. "We're being hunted." He hefted the crossbow, grabbed her wrist and raced for the door.

Terror gave her feet wings, and she easily matched his long stride. They stumbled to a halt on the landing. At the far end of the black cloister a phantom mist raced toward them, roiling white and blood-flecked as it climbed the stairs.

Silhara cursed and reversed direction, wrenching Martise's arm as he ran across the landing to the other stairway. He skidded to a halt as the risers suddenly crumbled, sending a cascade of rotting boards falling to the first floor. Martise, in full charge behind him, twisted sideways at the last moment in a failed bid to keep from hitting him. She lost her balance. A burst of pain radiated along her hip when she struck the floor.

"No!" Silhara bellowed, crashing to the floor with her. Her momentum catapulted her over the balcony's jagged edge, and her scream echoed in the cavernous dark below. Her knife and Silhara's crossbow fell, the bow glancing off her shoulder before striking the ground with a clatter.

The ache in her hip was a twinge compared to the agony bursting across her shoulder and back. She dangled midair, tethered only by Silhara's iron grip on her arm. He sat on the floor, one foot braced against a broken pilaster to keep her from dragging him off the landing with her.

"You don't look like you weigh this much," he grunted through clenched teeth.

Martise barely heard him. The darkness below gaped like an open mouth, waiting to swallow her. The ghostly cloud paused on the landing, rolling and turning back on itself. It picked up speed as if sensing its prey's helplessness. She could feel its hunger, a craving for the very essence of life. Her life and Silhara's.

Her wrist and forearm burned, chafed by Silhara's rough palm as she slipped slowly from his grasp. "Let go," she whispered. "You promised me a clean death." Shattered bones on the stones below were preferable to what the soul eater planned.

He tightened his grip, hard enough to numb her fingers. "Don't be tiresome," he snarled. "You're holding the papers and the knowledge to translate them."

Were she not hanging midair and facing imminent death by either a long fall or a lich's avaricious appetite, she might have laughed. Her rescuer was quick to assert his own motivations for saving her, and they had little to do with nobility.

The lich drew closer, carrying with it the fetid scent of evil. Behind its vaporous form, the walls and landing warped and melted. Silhara cursed and recited a familiar spell, one Martise hoped he'd never use on her again. The incantation flung her upward, hard enough that her stomach dropped to her feet. She flailed in the air. He immediately invoked a descent spell, and she fell toward him in a flutter of tunic, satchel and hair. He caught her neatly, and just as quickly tipped her out of his arms.

His hands skimmed her sides. "The satchel. You have the satchel." Relief hoarsened his already raspy voice.

Who cares about this bag of papers? She wanted to scream at him. They weren't going to make it out of Iwehvenn. The soul eater was almost upon them, shrouding them in a mist of cold, putrid air. She yelped when Silhara pulled her close, his arm a tight band around her waist.

"Hang on, and don't fight me."

He gave her no time to question him. Agony ripped through her body, and her vision blackened. She arched against him, her fingers clawing his arms as he almost broke her ribs in a crushing vise. Her surroundings faded, going gray and nebulous. An enraged shriek buffeted her ears. When she regained her bearings, it was to find herself still clasped in Silhara's suffocating embrace but in another chamber.

"What…" she asked before he cut her off.

"Not safe yet. The lich is right behind us."

Alerted by a peculiar tone in his voice, Martise looked up. He was ashen beneath the bronze skin, lips leached almost white. Blood trickled in a thin line from his left nostril to bisect his upper lip.

"Again," he said.

This time she was more prepared, though the pain and crushing weight of the spell was just as torturous. They emerged in an antechamber, surrounded by the husks of dead men. More blood streamed from Silhara's nose, dripping off his chin. He stumbled, holding onto Martise as much for balance as to bring her with him through the spell's bonding.

"Stop this." She wiped her sleeve under his nose in an attempt to staunch the crimson flow. Her efforts left a smear across his cheek and a red stain on her shirt. "You're killing yourself."

She'd read of the spell he used. Half-Death they called it, part of the black arcana and outlawed by Conclave. Complex and very handy in tight spots like these, it was known to kill the mages who used it.

His eyes were sunken in his pale face. "Better dead than enslaved."

The remark struck her harder than if he'd balled his fist and punched her. Martise knew he referred to the lich, but his short statement encapsulated every motivation, every reason and every justification for why she was here with him in the first place.

He took a long breath that gurgled with blood. "Once more. I can do this once more."

Martise doubted it, but even weakened by his own incantations, he was far stronger than she. The most she could do was hang on and hold him up when he fell after the third time. For fall he would. Few mages had ever withstood Half-Death multiple times, and none had done so still standing.

The third time made her scream. She might as well have fallen from the keep's second story, the pain was so sharp. They emerged in the outer courtyard, under a twilight sky. Silhara collapsed against her. Reeling from the shock of the spell, Martise staggered beneath his weight but managed to lower them both to their knees. The mage slid lifeless in her arms, awash in blood and colder than a day-old corpse.

Her own pain forgotten, she laid him gently on the dusty ground. Her fingers traced a palsied pattern over his stained mouth and came away wet when she pressed them to his chest and the scarlet ruin of his shirt. "Don't you dare die yet, you bastard."

Her voice trembled as much as her hand. Only the ensorcelled silence answered her.

Shadows swayed and slithered across the courtyard as the sun fell below the hills surrounding the dale. Instinct warred with compassion. An inner voice howled at her to run. Run hard, run fast. Gnat waited on the hillside, and Silhara's sacrifice had bought her time to escape. Again, Martise touched his face, gaunt and lifeless in the eldritch moonlight. He might be dead, but she couldn't leave him. Not here in this bleak pit where time and wind would reduce his body to a desiccated shell, rejected by the very earth on which it lay.

Muscles already bludgeoned by the Half-Death spell burned in protest when she rose and slipped her hands under his arms to lift him. She dragged him past the withered gardens, keeping a wary eye on the lich's tumbled-down lair. Silhara had said the creature was right behind them after the first time they escaped through the spell's spectral doorway. The memory of its shrieking fury when they escaped made her shudder. She prayed it still lurked within the keep, searching for its elusive prey.

Her prayers went unanswered. Intent on getting Silhara out of the courtyard and to the relative safety of the hillside, she didn't see the soul eater's ghostly haze until too late. The creature struck, hurling Martise across the path with unseen hands. She slammed into one of the dead trees, hard enough that black spots danced before her eyes. Rough bark tore her tunic and scraped her back with a serrated caress.

She shook her head and tried to stand, staggering as the courtyard tilted and whirled around her. The mist encircling her transformed, patterning itself into a grotesque shape both human and arachnid. Tendrils of icy cloud spun out from the shadow of a bloated abdomen and wrapped around Martise's ankles and wrists. She yanked on her tethers, clawing at the gossamer ropes that curled around her arms and held fast.

Images of the last victims to fall before the lich's hunger loomed in her mind. Martise understood why their decayed faces wore such tortured expressions. She wanted to scream as well, over and over until the effort warmed her freezing blood and reminded her she still lived and breathed and held on to her life essence. Wisps of mists trailed along her arms—fine hairs on a spider's legs as it skittered closer to its entrapped prey. Her cries hung in her closed mouth, and she twisted her head away from the snaking line curling toward her nostrils. Her efforts were futile. The lich invaded her, pouring into her body and spirit with malevolent purpose.

She screamed, a thin wail lost in the miasma permeating every pore. A draining sensation weakened her limbs. Were she not bound upright in the lich's web, she would have fallen. The coldness flowed through her veins, replacing warm blood as the lich fed on her. Her heartbeat quieted, drowned out by a high-pitched keening that seemed to come from hundreds of voices. Gray, wavering shades fluttered before her vision, beating their fists against invisible walls—memories and remnants of men sucked dry of their souls, forever lingering in an eternal despair.

"Not like this," she thought. "Not like this." All she had risked coming here—a chance at freedom, a life lived unbound, even possible death, but a clean death—scattered before her, lost to an immortal parasite.

The mist around her thickened, fed on the force of her spirit and the rise of her desolation. Martise thought of Cumbria, his smug features when he held her spirit stone before her eyes, the ultimate bait to lure her into doing his bidding. The lich wouldn't have all of her. The High Bishop of Conclave possessed a part of her spirit. An invisible and binding chain, broken only by her death or the sacrifice of the Master of Crows.

Through the opaque shroud enveloping her, she saw Silhara sprawled on the parched ground, bloodied by his own spell. The lich hadn't touched him, and an inexplicable grief melded with hopelessness. He was dead, brought down by his attempts to rescue them from this monstrous feeding to which she was subjected. Anger and the will to remain unbound had saved him.

"Better dead than enslaved."

Those words echoed in her frozen thoughts, acting as a catalyst to free her from the lich's strangle-hold. She didn't want to die, but this horror was far worse. A white fire burned away the numbing cold pulling her into the lich's bottomless well. She wouldn't die. Not like this.

"NOT LIKE THIS!"

The protest, bellowed from a throat clogged with foul smoke, wasn't hers. Deeper, broader, it surged from some hidden cache of strength, carrying with it the strange sentient force that had awakened at the touch of Silhara's cloaking spell. She screamed again, this time in triumph as her Gift burst from every pore. It flowed in waves of amber light, encircling the pallid mist. She felt the lich's shock, its surprise at being confronted by this unknown force. It ceased to drain her, sliding out of her nose and mouth on icy puffs of breath.

Martise huddled before the fierce power surging out of her. Her fury fueled its frenzy, and she rode the tide, instinctively sensing that whatever she'd called forth in a last cry of desperation worked its own will. It attacked the soul eater, seizing the sinuous mist in an unyielding grip. Imprisoned souls fluttered like moths within a crumbling cage as her Gift struck and struck again at the lich, ripping at it with all the viciousness of a wolf pack on a ewe. The cage finally broke, split apart beneath her magery's uncontrolled vengeance. Wraiths, trapped for centuries uncounted, flew past her, through her. She gasped as the touch of each left trace impressions and memories. Thieves and lost travelers, wandering nomads, even prisoners brought to Iwehvenn to suffer a merciless penalty for their crimes—all gave brief flashes of their identities, glimpses into windows of lives cut horrifically short.

A last thin screech signaled the lich's final destruction before the mist roiled in on itself and burst into a rain of dust that cascaded over her hair and shoulders. No longer half-blinded by its possession, Martise had a clear view of the courtyard. She shook off the dust, quaking in revulsion. Within her, her newly awakened Gift pulsed. Stunned by the aggressive power she'd wielded, she fell to her knees and raised her hand cautiously, staring at it as if it were a new appendage. The amber light encasing her faded. She was half afraid her Gift would disappear again and half afraid it might turn on her. Many untrained Gifted had died due to the uncontrolled potency of their talent.

Faint sounds reached her ears, moans more than words. Martise struggled to her feet and limped to Silhara's supine body. She knelt beside him, groaning from the ache in her bones. The faintest breath caressed her face when she leaned close. Elation raced through her, followed by terror when he didn't breathe again.

His head lolled when she lifted him in her arms. Ribbons of blood slid toward his ears from his nose. Martise brushed a lock of gore-soaked hair away from his cheek. "Master," she said softly. "Stay with me." She leaned closer, her nose bumping his. Her awareness shrank and sharpened, centered on his half-opened mouth, the fragile rise and fall of his chest against her breasts. Her Gift stirred, pulsed with her heartbeat. His lips were soft, tasting of salt and iron. "Stay," she whispered into his mouth and closed her eyes.

Unlike the turbulent river that rushed forth and swallowed the lich in its wrath, her Gift now flowed in a lazy stream, connecting her to Silhara in the brush of a kiss and the press of her hands on his cool skin. A faint heartbeat thudded in her ears, growing louder and stronger as she held him. Her senses were swamped—blood and heat, hate and loneliness, and above all, a Gift more powerful than hers, leashed by an implacable will. She fell into him, breathed with him, grasped his hard-edged spirit standing on the brink of an abyss and embraced him.

"Stay with me," she repeated, her plea echoing in the hallowed places of his soul.

A rushing kaleidoscope of gray light spun around her, slinging her back into the reality of dirt, tortured muscle and the scent of blood. She opened her eyes and immediately sought Silhara. His features were no longer so pale or shrunken, and his chest rose in slow, even breaths. Feeling as if a herd of galloping horses thundered through her skull, Martise winced. A tickling below her nose made her look down. Blood dripped, splashing onto Silhara. Her blood this time. She wiped her nose on her dusty sleeve and cleaned him as best she could.

He opened his eyes, obsidian pools that caught the starlight and drowned it in their depths. "What are you?" he rasped.

Uncaring that they huddled in a cursed dale or that he would likely flay her alive for the action, Martise hugged him and laughed in joyous relief.

CHAPTER ELEVEN

She smelled different. Standing next to her, loading orange crates onto the rickety wagon, Silhara caught Martise's scent on the dry breeze circling the grove. The tang of citrus oil mixed with soap and the faint musk of warm female teased his nostrils. A slow heat centered in his groin. Months had passed since he'd brought a woman beneath him and taken his pleasure. None he'd ever bedded smelled as tantalizing as the small woman working beside him. The scent of sorcery, sharp and clean, like the air before a thunderstorm clung to her hair and skin.

All the Gifted smelled of it when their birthright first manifested. He leaned toward her and sniffed audibly. She stopped, hands hovering over the oranges in the crate closest to her and eyed him askance. A thin trickle of sweat slid down her jaw from the hair plastered to her temple. The imagined taste of salt tickled his tongue.

"You smell like the newly Gifted now."

She straightened abruptly. He jerked away just before the top of her head clipped his chin. Her copper eyes glinted in the sun, a wary hope flickering in their depths. She brought her palms to her nose and breathed. "Are you sure? I only smell oranges. The corners of her mouth turned down. "And Cael."

"I'm certain. The scent's unmistakable. I reeked of it for months after my Gift manifested."

Neither unpleasant nor overpowering, it was a signature mark that had once alerted every priest of his whereabouts in the Redoubt and made the Conclave mage-finders go berserk in their pens every time he passed. The scent on Martise wasn't as strong, but Cael had clung to her more tenaciously than lichen since their return from Iwehvenn, his eyes glowing crimson the moment she stepped into the same room with him. Even now, he lay by the wagon, tongue lolling as he panted in the afternoon heat.

"A lot of good such perfume does me now. I no longer feel the Gift as I did at the lich's keep."

Silhara wasn't so pessimistic. Her power might choose to hide behind the shadow of her soul or slumber to regain its strength, but it hadn't deserted her. The effects of her Gift's touch remained with him, along with the essence of the woman. A warmth like silk and water bathed him from the inside, gave him strength and replenished his Gift. He'd nearly died at Iwehvenn Keep, saved only by his apprentice's mercy and untested talent.

He bent to heave another full crate into the wagon, only to have Gurn almost yank it out of his hands. Silhara snarled at his servant, keeping a tight grip on the hand-holds as Gurn tugged. "Do you mind?" He wrested the crate away and slung it into the wagon bed. Oranges fell out of boxes and rolled across the beaten boards. Martise reached out a solicitous hand toward him but snatched it back at his warning glare. "Leave off. I'm not a damned invalid!"

Invoking Half-Death had been an act of desperation, the surest and fastest way to escape the lich's clutches. Such powerful magic took its toll.

They'd managed to find their way back to Neith where he'd collapsed on his doorstep, feverish and delirious. Two days of painful muscle spasms and vomiting blood into a chipped basin had kept him bedridden. Only now, after a full week, did he feel strong enough to resume his work in the grove and prepare for their delayed trip to market. Unfortunately, his servant had yet to abandon his role as nursemaid.

He ignored Gurn's short, precise hand motions. "Horse's ass" didn't take much translating. Martise's stifled giggle faded when Silhara smiled thinly.

"Come with me. We've a lesson to conduct."

He didn't wait to see if she followed but snapped out instructions to Gurn as he walked back to the manor. "Since I'm still too fragile to work, you can finish loading the wagon. My apprentice and I have some unfinished business." Cael rose to follow and stopped when Silhara pointed a finger at him. "Keep him here. He smells foul." The mage-finder bared his teeth and slinked under the wagon to sulk.

He led her to the library. Precious papers, brought out of Iwehvenn with deadly spell work and sheer luck, were neatly stacked on one table. He had yet to look at them, but Martise had already begun her translations. A sheet of notes, written in her precise hand, lay next to the ancient papers.

"We're not having the lesson in the great hall?"

Her voice warbled. Silhara cocked his head, puzzled. The same woman who'd grappled with a soul eater and snuffed it out like a candle flame still feared his lessons. Regret surfaced, annoying and unwelcome. He'd had his reasons for subjecting her to harsh treatment when she first arrived. She'd withstood everything he'd thrown at her.

Brave and surprising. That abject passivity was an act. Martise might be afraid of her lessons, but she had grown comfortable enough in Neith now to reveal glimpses of a more forceful personality.

She stiffened when he approached her. Silhara stood close enough that the brim of her hat folded against his chest. He removed the hat and tossed it to the floor, leaving fly-away bits of hair sticking out from her head in an auburn halo. Rumpled and sun-burnt from working beside him in the grove, she was almost pretty.

"The light isn't good enough in the hall. I want to see what happens when we do this, and I prefer this room."

"Please, Master." He frowned at the plaintive tone in her voice. "Don't summon another demon."

Her eyes were downcast, hidden by the curve of her dark lashes. Silhara tipped her face up to his with a forefinger. Her gaze implored him, the first time she'd asked his mercy in any way. His stomach twisted.

"Martise," he said, stroking the underside of her chin with a fingertip. Finer than costly velvet and just as warm, her skin heated to his touch. "What I want to summon resides within you. It destroys demons." *And saves mages.* "Do you not want to feel your Gift once more?"

Excitement replaced dread in her eyes. "Can you do this?" She worried her lower lip against her teeth. The other lessons didn't work." Her jaw tightened against his finger.

"I used the wrong bait to coax your Gift to manifest." His finger drifted lower, hovering over the hollow at the base of her throat before coming to rest against the fragile line of her collarbone peeking out from the top of her tunic. "A good thing I think. I may not have witnessed what your power did to the lich, but anything that can destroy a soul eater is formidable. I'd rather avoid the same fate."

He'd danced with death while the soul eater fed on her. Her Gift, hostile, sentient and determined to destroy what endangered its host, had made quick work of the lich. By contrast, that same violent power had saved him, gentling as it poured into his body and soul like cool water over parched earth, shimmering with life and fertility, green things and sun on the grove. All laced with the fascinating quintessence of the woman who wielded such power. She had drawn him back when he teetered on the edge of darkness, restored his spirit by giving him the strength to help her bring them both home.

More than a sorcerer's curiosity drove him to seek her Gift a second time. He craved its touch, its clean brilliance. So different from the tainted shadow left by Corruption's rape of his dreams.

"What will you do?"

He met her gaze. Her heartbeat thrummed beneath his fingers, quick and erratic.

"I want to coax your Gift, but I'll need your cooperation. Have you ever seer-bonded?"

She tried to back away. "No! I'd be less vulnerable if I stood before you naked."

Silhara's eyebrows rose. He halted her, hand resting on her waist in a light, warning clasp. Visions of her bared back and his dark hands against her paler skin played in his mind. "If you're suggesting both, I'm more than agreeable."

She blushed. A faint smile lifted the corners of her mouth despite her protests. He understood her reticence. Seer-bonding was invasive, a lesser form of what the lich had done to her and what her Gift had done to him. But he felt certain nothing else would make her talent emerge once more. At least nothing it wouldn't try and attack.

He dropped his hand and stepped back. "Your choice, apprentice. I gain nothing from the effort. *My* magic will not suffer either way." He headed for the door. "We've a harvest to get to market. You're wasting my time." He was almost in the hall when she called out to him.

"Wait. Please." A wary acceptance flickered in her eyes. "I want to try."

As he suspected, she might not trust him enough to initially agree to his proposal, but she couldn't resist the allure of her Gift. She'd risk a harsh spell to bring her magic forth once more.

He moved close and breathed in her scent. "I once seer-bonded with the High Bishop." An old anger made his blood burn. "I'd been a year at Conclave. Two priests bound me to a chair and gagged me."

Martise's features blurred before ugly memories. He recalled the agonizing fire raging in his skull as Cumbria strove to tear down his emotions and thoughts. He still felt the blow of the bishop's fist against the side of his head when the bonding finished, the darkness that followed and the taste of dirt in his mouth when he awakened on the cold floor with a rat scrabbling through the tangles in his hair.

"They forced you." Compassion, laced with revulsion, deepened her seductive voice.

He traced an invisible line over her collarbone. "Are you so innocent to believe the priests are above such things? You were a novitiate. Surely, you saw or experienced them?"

"Not like that. Mockery, lashings, fasting, yes. But never a forced bonding." She cocked her head, questions in her gaze. "Why? The high priests don't usually bother acknowledging the lower orders."

She had small bones, and the exposed skin of her neck glistened with a thin film of perspiration. Silhara ran his tongue over his lower lip. "Cumbria and I have a unique and long-standing relationship. We hated each other even before we met."

"What is unique about hatred?"

His fingers pressed into her flesh, the first layer of the spell silently invoked. Faint vibrations of power swirled up his arm. "So sayeth his servant."

She paled. "His ward. And I meant no disrespect, Master." She glanced down at his fingers. "You've begun the bonding." She closed her eyes briefly. "It doesn't feel like the lich's touch"

"How did the lich's touch feel?"

"Cold, empty. Like falling down a dry well."

Silhara sensed a stirring, a tendril of awareness calling to his own Gift in recognition. "Seer-bonding is different. Wielded harshly, it's agonizing. There's no need for such measures here." He liked her smile.

"You're kind in your way." Her voice slurred as the spell's effects took hold, potent as Peleta's Fire.

He placed his other hand at her waist to hold her upright. "No. I am merely cautious. Your Gift responds to a caress, not a beating. I don't want to end up like the lich."

Nearly drunk on the bonding, she swayed in his arms, held by the hand at her waist and the one touching her neck. Her eyelids drooped, and her lips parted. Silhara pulled her closer, wrapping an arm around her back. He wanted to sway with her, to sink in the pool of heat enveloping him as he sank into her essence. He thrust against her skirts, aroused by the mating of spirit and will as she opened to him. His vision blurred, his surroundings transforming to a sea of amber and ruby. His heart matched with the beat of hers until a single pulse echoed in his head.

Power flooded his soul.

His magic surged in a wave, fed by the well of Martise's Gift. He groaned, drowning in the intense sensation of pure life, laced with a woman's grace, pouring into him.

Had Corruption used such seduction from the first, he would have hosted the god and done his bidding with a smile. Instead, the lure it used made him flinch away despite the promises of revenge and unlimited dominance. Martise's Gift, however, offered no such promise, only strengthened his Gift and asked nothing in return.

"Open for me, Martise. Bring me deeper." He wasn't sure if he spoke the words or only thought them. His hunger for more of her overrode his coherency. She obeyed, opening wide the ethereal door that sheltered her Gift and allowed his spirit full access.

He took her, fed on her, sucked in the force of her power until his head swam. The faintest whimper reached his ears, almost smothered beneath his craving for more of her life force. He fought his way to consciousness, breathing hard. What met his gaze made his heart stutter.

Martise slumped in his arms like a broken doll. Her head lolled, and blood trickled from her nostrils, bisecting her wan cheeks. The whites of her eyes peeked beneath her lashes. A jeweled light enveloped them both, burnishing his skin.

Horror washed through him, banishing the consuming sense of well-being. The sharp burst of pain behind his eyes made him wince as he broke the bond between them. Martise convulsed in his grasp. The light faded, leaving traces of a crimson shimmer on his clothes.

"Martise!" He shook her hard, uncaring that her head snapped forward then back. The pain behind his eyes grew when he recited a simple awakening spell to revive her. She moaned and raised a weak hand to swipe at the blood on her face. Silhara gave silent thanks to gods who'd never before heard him invoke their names in prayer.

"What happened?" Her reedy voice caressed his ear.

He lifted her in his arms. "You're more generous with your Gift than a *houri* shown a full purse," he snapped. She'd rattled him. Bleeding and nearly insensate from their bonding, she awakened more of the unwelcome guilt within him. He'd done much in his lifetime others might consider abhorrent and never suffered a twinge of conscience. But this was no way to repay the woman who'd saved his life.

He left the library and climbed the stairs to the third floor. Weak light filtering up from the hole in the floor illuminated the corridor leading to her room. Silhara kicked the door open and paused. Spare and meticulously clean, the bedchamber was an aberration in the manor house's dusty warren. Even Gurn's kitchen didn't compare.

The small bed pushed against one wall was neatly made, not a wrinkle marring the smooth surface of blankets. No dust motes danced in the sunlight filling the space. Her personal effects were hidden away. No combs, jewelry or other feminine trifles lay on the table near the bed or the chest at its foot.

Martise opened her eyes when Silhara laid her on the bed. Despite her ordeal, her gaze was delighted. "I can still feel the Gift, but I'm very tired."

He peered into the pitcher near her wash basin. Empty. "You should be. Your Gift might lash out if forced to manifest, but it is very accommodating when coaxed. At least with me." Residual power from the bonding still flowed through him. Her Gift strengthened his. His fingers tingled and sparked shards of white light against whatever he touched. Any spell he might conjure would be ten times more potent than usual. Unlike Corruption's offering, Martise's Gift still allowed him control over his increased magery.

Silhara frowned when she wiped at her cheeks a second time. "You're making it worse. I'll send Gurn with water and an elixir to restore your strength and help you sleep."

She struggled to rise but gave up when he placed a staying hand on her shoulder. Her essence inundated his senses, carried by the flow of her Gift into his very being. He smelled her on his clothes, tasted her on his palate. His desire for her power swelled to include the woman as well. He hardened at the thought of stripping her and taking her on the pristine bed with her heat and her Gift running fast in his blood and over his body.

His eyes narrowed. Martise shrank back against the bedding at his expression.

"What about the harvest?"

Still fighting the arousal she engendered, he put distance between him and her bed. "Weak as you are right now, you'll only be in the way. Besides, we've managed well enough without you in past years. You'll be good as new at first light. I expect you to be dressed and ready to leave with us for Eastern Prime in the morning."

Martise rolled onto her side, hinting at the graceful curves she'd revealed when he'd soothed her sore back. Silhara reached out and just as quickly dropped his hand. If he didn't leave now, he wouldn't leave at all. Lust and magic roared through him, escalating every moment he lingered in this room. He strode to the door, wrenching it open. Halfway into the shadowed corridor, he heard her call to him.

"Will you teach me how to use my Gift?"

He paused, pinching the bridge of his nose between thumb and forefinger. "Yes." She'd found a way to exact revenge for his lessons. "You've not been much of an apprentice until now. At least we have something to work with."

Her soft thanks followed him down the hall. She might regret that gratitude. His willingness to teach her was as much motivated by self-serving curiosity as generosity. Fierce yet gentle, almost independent of Martise in how it reacted, her Gift fascinated him. He'd hazard a guess no priest or novitiate of Conclave had ever possessed or encountered its like, and any knowledge he might gain over the priesthood pleased him.

"Do you truly know what you have sent me, Cumbria?" Only the creak of floorboards beneath his feet answered him.

CHAPTER TWELVE

Martise awakened before dawn, alerted by an inner voice that cried "Wake up!" She huddled on the bed for a moment, eyes wide as she peered into the room's darkness, looking for any movement. All was still save the band of moonlight outlining her open window. She rose, careful not to make any loud noise. The night air hung cold and damp with a hint of dew. She wrapped her shawl around her shoulders and padded to the window, drawn by an insistent voice that demanded she look outside.

Neith was still, slumbering in the darkest hours. The orange trees, nothing more than silhouettes edged in silver, were still beneath a night sky arrayed in glittering stars. Only the sickly Corruption star hovering on the southern horizon marred the view. The star pulsed bright once, twice and finally a third time. She looked away and scratched at the crawling tingle on her arms. A glimpse of movement beneath the orange trees' canopy made her freeze.

A black smoke undulated over the ground, rolling fast and sure as it swept through the line of trees toward the house.

Lich!

Horror screamed through her veins. Her Gift burst upward, making her stagger as it consumed her senses. Light shot out her fingertips and bounced off the walls, chasing away the shadows lurking in the corners. Just as quickly, the light died, but the Gift did not, and she struggled to bring her power under control as it sought to destroy a perceived enemy.

Hinges squealed in protest as she banged the shutters closed, plunging the bedchamber into confining darkness. She panted. The tingling sharpened at the certainty she was no longer alone in the room.

"Who are you?" she snapped.

Hissing laughter slithered over her. Her Gift raged within, struggling to break free.

A voice, devoid of any humanity, answered. "The more interesting question is who are you?"

Martise leapt for the window, scrabbling to open the shutters once more. Moonlight painted her visitor in a phantasmal corona. She screamed, a thin, high sound that carried to every corner of the manor and sent startled crows bursting from the trees in fright.

A man—no, a man-shaped atrocity—stood before her. Tall and emaciated, it had slick grub-like skin, white and mottled. Long arms swung low so that its hands brushed its knees. Black nails tipped three misshapen fingers, curving into lethal claws. The splayed toes sported the same claws. They clicked on the floor as the thing crept closer.

Martise's gaze locked on the monster's most hideous aspect. No face. Only a blank canvas of discolored skin split by an impossibly wide mouth. The lips were thin and gray, and they bled each time the thing grinned at her, exposing double rows of jagged teeth.

Corruption—the god assuming physical form. The stuff of nightmares, its presence fouled her room. She raised a shaking hand and sketched a protective ward in the air. Nothing happened, though her Gift writhed in response.

Corruption laughed, a weird chattering noise. "Foolish creature. Why bother? You cannot fight a god." It stalked her across the room. "You weren't here before, and now you are. Your essence mingles with his. Different yet matched." The faceless head tilted in a puzzled gesture. "What are you that you have enthralled the Master of Crows?"

She backed away, breathing hard. She mewled at the feel of the stone wall against her back. Trapped. With a thousands-year old abomination. Nearly frozen with terror, she surrendered control of her Gift. It rushed out of her, a turbulent river of chaotic magic. The air around her warped. Her ears popped, and the shutters slammed together before snapping back against the walls with a resounding crack. The bedroom door flew open, and she caught a glimpse of Silhara, shirtless and wild-eyed, before she turned her attention back to the god.

Startled by the power saturating the room, Corruption paused a second before it was hurled into the opposite wall hard enough to send a shower of broken stone flying through the air. The quasi-human form dissolved back into the sinuous black vapor that had rushed toward her from the trees.

Silhara stood between Martise and the god. She came away from the wall and inched closer. The mage's voice was fearless, caustic as he addressed Corruption. "I've always thought the gods fickle, unworthy of even a sacrificial chicken." He raised his palm in question. "Why are you here?"

Corruption floated toward him. Martise wanted to retch at the sight of ghostly hands sliding up his legs, stroking him with a poisoned caress. "I'm not so easily swayed, sorcerer." The god's voice echoed now, coming from every corner of the room. "But I am curious. Your strength is greater now, if no longer pure. This creature is a source from which you've fed. I approve."

Sarcasm painted each of Silhara's words. "How that gladdens my heart."

"I await you, sorcerer, and I am patient."

The mist unwrapped itself from his legs, sliding back toward the window until it slipped over the edge. Martise and Silhara watched from the window as the haze thinned to a gray ribbon that spun upward and disappeared.

"Congratulations. You've been noticed by a god."

Still reeling from the effects of the god's visit, she breathed deep and succumbed to a long shudder. "I've no interest in such notoriety. That was Corruption?"

"One face of it, yes. I'm guessing he was drawn to your Gift. Were you trying out your newfound powers?"

Martise turned to him. Moonglow outlined his profile, highlighting the prominent nose and a sharp cheekbone. His hair gleamed almost blue, flowing over his bare shoulders in a black waterfall. The breeches he wore hung low on his narrow hips, revealing a lean, muscled torso. Even fighting down her fear, she couldn't help but admire him. He was beautiful. Forbidden.

She tore her gaze away, focusing instead on the murders of crows returning to their roosts. "No. I was sleeping and awakened by a sense of…otherness."

"Now you know. The exiled god who once crushed the world and was imprisoned by Conclave is more than a light in the sky, and he has decided to take up residence here."

"Why? What does Neith possess that he lingers here? And why does he await you?" She had her suspicions.

His sly gaze challenged her to look deeper. "Even gods are limited, especially the lesser ones. They may despise the weak mortals who worship them, but they need a sycophant or two."

Martise couldn't imagine Silhara of Neith acting as anyone's subordinate. Not even a god's.

He faced her, skating his fingers across the air. Sparks followed in their wake. "Ah, I thought so. Your Gift is still alert and ready to do battle."

Martise didn't deny his observation. Once unleashed, her Gift fought against her control. She'd memorized every spell Conclave had taught her, but had not yet adequately harnessed her power. Sheer luck had blessed her the few times she'd managed to do so. "It feels separate sometimes. A thing onto itself."

"I suspect it is. Did you wield the spell that threw Corruption across the room?"

"Not intentionally. I just didn't want that hideous thing touching me, and my Gift reacted."

"That's putting it mildly." He tilted his head, his gaze puzzled. "Yours is a peculiar talent."

He gestured once, a silent invocation. Luminescence flowed from his palm in an ethereal river. She embraced the now familiar heat rising within as her Gift responded to his overture. Amber light met silver, entwined in a lover's embrace. Her light passed his hand, traveled up his arm until his shoulders and face were suffused in a gentle radiance.

Martise sucked in a breath, rocked by the images passing across her mind's eye. Vivid scenes of smooth brown limbs wrapped around hers, the scent of aroused male in her nostrils, a lithe body pressed against hers. Thrusting. Possessing. Overlaying those provocative visions, a deeper awareness of the man. A strong, damaged soul filled with equal measures of hate, passion and a near-dead hope. To these, her Gift strove to meld, yearned to reach and touch. She shared in that yearning.

His eyes closed, his face taut with ecstasy. As in the library, she suffered a slow drain of power, an exhaustion born of her connection to the mage. She wanted to collapse on the floor, curl into a ball and sleep for days.

Silhara's sudden lunge for her and his bruising grip on her arms snapped her out of the sorcery-induced torpor. His black eyes glittered with anger and a hint of desperation.

"Control it, Martise, or I'll take it and you and leave nothing behind."

The threat acted as a bucket of icy water tossed on her head. She concentrated, grappling with her stubborn Gift until it finally yielded to her will and broke the connection between her and Silhara. The effort made her head swim, and she held onto him for balance.

She stilled when he leaned into her. Her head tipped back, lips parting as he drew closer, tickling her cheeks with a whisper of breath. If he kissed her, she'd surrender. Her desire for him, amplified by her Gift's overt attachment, would overpower her common sense. Martise knew she'd help him hitch her skirts, let him take her as he pleased. Standing at the window, lying on the bed. Whatever he wished as long as he gave her a full measure of the passion he hid beneath layers of cold mockery and disdain.

His bottom lip touched hers, soft, tantalizing. "Why are you here?" He spoke the words into her mouth, his tongue flicking briefly across her upper lip.

She smothered a moan. "Because you wanted me."

Lean hips pressed into hers, the bulge of his erection nestling against her thin leine, coaxing her to widen her stance. She obeyed, sighing her pleasure at the feel of him between her legs.

"No truer words." The harsh voice was a broken whisper. His tongue slid across her lip. She met it with the tip of hers, tasting him for the first time. Like his scent, he tasted of oranges and the spice of matal tobacco.

"Please," she implored.

Her entreaty acted as a catalyst. Silhara crushed her to him. His tongue thrust between her lips, took her mouth in a hard kiss. Martise met his ardor with equal fire, taking him deeper to suck on his tongue and slide hers across his teeth and the roof of his mouth.

Her Gift writhed within her, desperate for freedom. Equally desperate to feel and taste more of the Master of Crows, Martise ignored it. His bare back heated her palms, tempted her with smooth skin, muscular slopes and valleys.

He made love to her mouth, stroking and sucking, thrusting with his tongue and mimicking the action with his hips. She slid her thigh over his, whimpering into his mouth when a rough palm hiked her leine and glided across her leg to her hip.

She burned for him. The danger of spying, the questionable ethics of betraying one life to free another, and the motivations of a power-hungry mage all those things be damned. For a single, scorching moment, Martise wanted only this—the feel and taste of Silhara of Neith on her and within her.

His arm slid beneath her buttocks to hoist her against him. She threaded her hands through his hair and tightened her leg on his, moaning in protest when he suddenly stiffened and ended the kiss.

His lips were swollen, his face thin with unquenched desire, but his eyes were as cold and hard as black ice. Martise blinked, knocked off kilter by his abrupt withdrawal.

"I've underestimated the High Bishop. He knew me better than I ever imagined when he brought you to Neith."

He dropped her and stepped back. Startled, Martise stumbled. She gaped at him, stunned by the sudden reversal of events. "Master, I..."

He ignored her and strode to the door, as coolly collected as if they'd just discussed the weather. She stared after him, flabbergasted.

He paused at the threshold. "You need training. And that talent of yours needs a firm hand. We'll start when we return from Eastern Prime." His voice, flat and distant, revealed nothing.

Almost sick with embarrassment, Martise smoothed her leine and wrapped her shawl more securely around her. If he chose to ignore what they just shared, she'd do the same. "Thank you for coming to my rescue."

A fleeting frown marred his brow before disappearing. "You've a screech to raise the dead. I'm surprised Gurn and Cael haven't yet arrived."

As if on cue, servant and dog burst through the open door. Silhara leapt out of their way to keep from being flattened. "Took you long enough," he drawled.

Gurn surveyed the room, brandishing a small ax in his hand. The weapon resembled a child's toy in his massive palm. Cael patrolled the chamber's perimeter, his eyes a bright crimson as he snuffled and growled his disapproval.

"Corruption," Silhara informed his servant. "I think he got the wrong room this time." He glanced at Martise. "You don't have to sleep here tonight. There are other chambers."

She shook her head, feeling as she did when she first arrived at Neith, awkward in his presence. "I'm all right." She smiled at Gurn. "Gurn, you are ever the hero. Were I Corruption, I might have leapt out the window at the sight of you charging through the door."

He smiled and signed to her.

"That won't be necessary," she said. "I'd feel guilty knowing I slept in my comfortable bed while you were stretched out on the floor outside my door." She watched as Cael sniffed the floor and corners. She didn't want to be alone. For a few minutes, in Silhara's embrace, she forgot the flesh-crawling experience of meeting Corruption face to face. Now, the memory brought back a surge of fear. "I'd like Cael to stay with me if you don't mind."

Silhara's eyebrows rose, and his nose wrinkled in disgust. "Can you withstand the stench?"

Martise smiled, despite her mortification over his rejection of her. "Far more than being alone with Corruption lurking outside."

He returned to the center of the room. She and Gurn watched as he created a green sphere of witchlight and sent it rolling to a corner of the room where it illuminated the interior in an eerie emerald glow. He then closed the window's shutters and warded them.

"Should Corruption pay another visit, I'll know it. These wards should protect you until morning."

She bowed. "Thank you, Master."

He snorted. "Go back to bed. Dawn will be here soon enough." His gaze was enigmatic before he left the room.

Gurn smiled and patted her on the shoulder then followed Silhara, shutting the door behind him.

Martise placed her shawl on the chest and sat on the edge of the bed with a dejected sigh. Cael, eyes still glowing red, padded over to her and plopped down on the floor. She leaned down to scratch behind his ears.

"Bursin's wings, you smell foul, but I'm glad you're here."

She lay down and counted the cracks in the ceiling. Her eyes stung with unshed tears. Idiot. None to blame for her foolishness save her. Swayed by her treacherous Gift, she'd believed Silhara desired her as she did him. At least he was honest in his rejection, unlike her last lover. That thought didn't lessen the pain or the humiliation.

She touched her face, running her fingers over her nose, her mouth, the curve of her chin. She thought of Cumbria. "You chose well. He'd never suspect seduction from a woman like me." She laughed, the sound bitter in the green half-dark.

She woke again at dawn, bleary-eyed and sluggish, and rolled out of bed. Cael left her to complete her morning ablutions. When Gurn met her in the kitchen and signed they'd breakfast on the way to Eastern Prime, she barely managed a muttered "Good morning."

They found Silhara in the grove hooking Gnat to his traces. The back of the wagon was stacked with crates of oranges, leaving only a small space for a person to sit behind the seat.

He caught her gaze. The hot blush rising up her neck and face made her cringe. One eyebrow rose, but he didn't mock her. "When we arrive, you'll stay with Gurn while I bargain with the merchants." He patted Gnat and walked around the side of the cart to where she stood. "Don't wander off alone. We'll be away from the docks, but whoremasters don't confine their hunting to the wharves. Don't assume you'll be overlooked. I'd notice you, Martise. Others will too."

A small flame of hope flickered to life then died as his gaze raked her. "Those clothes are nothing more than rags now. When we're there, I'll give you a few coins. You can buy cloth to make yourself something that doesn't look like the crows have been at it."

She curled her hands into fists at his scathing tone. The snide bastard who'd greeted her and Cumbria when they first arrived at Neith had returned in all his full, arrogant glory. Even Gurn paused in loading their meal onto the wagon seat to frown at Silhara.

She clenched her teeth and forgot all caution. "Is it not better to blend into your surroundings?" She swept a hand toward the manor house.

Gurn snorted, and Silhara's eyes narrowed. For one moment a gleam of admiration shown in his gaze. It vanished just as quickly as it appeared, replaced by the familiar mocking smile.

"I will enjoy returning you to Cumbria. I think the High Bishop will be...surprised by his beloved ward."

He said nothing more to her, only ordered Cael back to the house. Gurn helped her onto the wagon seat then took his place beside her as driver. The wagon rocked when Silhara leapt into the back and found a seat in the clear space surrounded by orange crates.

He draped his arms over his bent knees and leaned his head back against the side boards. A ripple of air surrounded him before disappearing. He closed his eyes, cushioned by a spell that protected him from the wagon's rough ride. Martise watched him from the corner of her eye. She turned away when he opened one eye and cast a baleful glare on Gurn. "Don't think I don't know you're planning to hit every rut and hole in the road just to vex me."

Gurn looked skyward, whistling. Martise, despite her melancholy, hid a chuckle behind her hand.

They kept to well-traveled paths, following the roads leading to the coast and the sprawling city of Eastern Prime. Gurn pointed out markers of interest. An outcropping of black rock that erupted from the plain in jagged tips, a circle of standing stones with the remnants of a fresh fire pit in its center, the steep, grass-covered slope of Ferrin's Tor—holy ground where an ancient Conclave gathered and defeated Corruption more than a thousand years earlier. The hill, now peaceful grazing land for sheep, slumbered in the rising heat. Martise suspected no one outside the priesthood remembered the great event that once took place there.

Gurn pointed north and tapped himself on the chest. A faint homesickness darkened his blue eyes.

"You grew up in the north?"

He nodded.

Interesting. Gurn had been friendly with her from the moment she'd passed through the courtyard gates, but she knew nothing of his past; if he had a family somewhere, how he'd ended up at Neith, even his age.

"You're far from home, Gurn. How long have you served at Neith?"

He wrapped the reins in one hand and held up the other, showing five fingers first and then three. Eight years. In terms of servitude, eight years wasn't a long span. How two such different individuals met and managed to live together in relative harmony baffled her. Silhara, often taciturn and unfriendly, wasn't the type to seek company. Gurn, while helpful and solicitous of Silhara, never exhibited subservient behavior. The two men acted as friends and equals more than master and servant. Were Silhara not snoring lightly behind them, she might be tempted to ask how Gurn came to serve at Neith.

Gurn glanced over his shoulder at the sleeping mage. Martise did the same. Silhara's snoring halted, and this time he opened both eyes.

"Gurn and I shared a prison cell once." His lips twitched. "For crimes best left undisclosed. I went free with the help of a few threats and well-placed bribes to the local magistrate. Gurn awaited execution. I needed a servant. He needed to live. I bought him from his slaver and set him free. He's been with me ever since."

Stunned by his revelation, Martise stared at him and then at Gurn. The giant winked and flicked the reins to coax Gnat into a faster clip.

Silhara had saved Gurn, freed him for no other reason than he could. Her thoughts reeled. Every sense of morality, of redemption and fairness, railed within her. How could she sacrifice this man to gain her own freedom? How could she not?

She sat quietly, lost in thought until Gurn handed her one of the honey cakes he prepared for their breakfast. Though he no longer had a tongue, he could still hum. She recognized the tune from her childhood, a tribal chant Asher's Kurman cook sang when she kneaded dough. The memory made her smile.

Bendewin's sunlit kitchen was much like Gurn's but swarming with undercooks. Scents of baking bread and bubbling stews, servants arguing or laughing, and above the din, Bendewin's singsong chanting as she worked.

Her lids grew heavy. Lulled by the repetitive tune and Gnat's steady gait, she leaned against Gurn's arm and dozed.

A hard lurch woke her, and she straightened. Gurn smiled and patted her on the shoulder before leaping down from the seat.

"What's wrong? Why are we stopping?"

"Because Gurn has had his bollocks knocked around for hours now and needs to piss." Silhara vaulted onto the vacated seat.

Less startled by his blunt remark than by his sudden appearance next to her, she flushed. "Oh."

"You might want to do the same. We'll wait for you."

She took his advice and clambered down from the wagon seat. When she returned, Silhara still sat in Gurn's spot. The servant smiled and passed her to crawl into the back of the wagon.

"Are you intending to grow roots standing there, or are you climbing up?" Silhara gestured impatiently, and she climbed onto the seat. He snapped the reins and clucked at Gnat.

The silence between them grew awkward, unlike the silence between her and Gurn. Martise perched at the far edge of the seat, keeping a death grip on the hand-hold so she didn't fall off. Silhara's gaze mocked her.

"Is it much farther?" She wanted to ask Gurn if she might join him in the back of the wagon.

"Another hour or so." He was far calmer around her than she was around him, especially after last night's disastrous escapade. "Any more visits from our celestial friend last night?"

This was something she could discuss without overheating from another blush. "Thank Bursin, no. And I hope to never have such a visit in my lifetime again. The lich was more than enough."

"Corruption is, in some ways, like the lich."

A lock of hair tore free of her braid and blew across her face. She tucked it behind her ear. "We studied Corruption during my second year at Conclave. The Great Deceiver. A lesser god yoked to the world by his dependence on mankind for ultimate power. It's written he awaited the rebirth of the avatar, even during his imprisonment."

He didn't show it, but she sensed the sudden tension in his posture. "The avatar has been born numerous times. And died never knowing his or her role in Corruption's plan."

Conclave had always hunted the avatar. Of the many generations that passed since Corruption's banishment, the priests had located the avatar four times, and dispatched each with merciless efficiency. Any others born as a vessel to the god had escaped the priesthood's death sentence. None had risen to a fabled seat of power with the god's help.

Circumstances had changed. Corruption, free of the sorcerous bonds place on him so long ago, sought the avatar with the same zeal as Conclave. The High Bishop suspected Silhara fit the role. Martise had her own suspicions and understood why Cumbria felt as he did. Powerful, outcast, and intractable, Silhara bore a deep-seated personal hatred for Cumbria and a more general one for Conclave. He'd made no secret of it. If he was the avatar, then Corruption didn't have far to search and Conclave had a disaster on its hands.

"Do you think the avatar is reborn?" She regretted the question when he turned a malevolent stare on her.

His rough voice softened, quiet menace in each word. "No. Did you find anything in those papers we took to indicate otherwise?"

She thanked the gods she didn't have to lie, especially when the mage bore holes into her head with that black gaze. "Nothing beyond more description of the ritual." Her voice remained even. "The southern king Birdixan, sacrificed himself to destroy Amunsa. He was the strongest of the mage-kings gathered there. He had a pivotal role."

"I'll look at your notes when we return to Neith." He frowned and turned his attention back to the road. She swallowed, relieved. "If you translated correctly, those writings are troubling. The southern provinces were barely civilized during that age, and none were ruled by kings. Unless you were taught from books I never saw, Conclave has no record of a Birdixan ruling any of the far lands. Even if they knew nothing of ancient Amunsa and his destruction, there would have been a record of a southern king who met his death in the north."

They reached Eastern Prime, still trying to decipher the meaning behind the translation of the early Helenese writings. Martise stretched, rubbing at the nagging pain in her lower back. The air smelled of the sea, and she heard the beat of the surf against the shore in the distance.

Sprawled over the tops of windswept cliffs and scattered down to the harbor, Eastern Prime bustled and stank in the morning sun. Ships of every size and make festooned the water, some moored at the quays, others riding the waves with their sails partially unfurled as they sailed sedately into the bay. Ramshackle huts clung to the cliff face and lined the serpentine alleyways that snaked away from the docks. Temples and mansions of rose marble shone like polished jewels from their perches atop the highest cliffs, surrounded by sculpted gardens and pristine lawns.

Silhara guided Gnat through the narrow streets with expert ease. People leapt out of their way, intimidated by his grim expression and Gurn's imposing height as he stood in the back of the wagon. The main road descended gradually toward the shore and dead-ended at an open field covered from boundary to boundary by tents, stalls, and milling crowds.

Silhara had to shout so Gurn could hear him over the din in the marketplace. "Get down. Take Martise and secure a room at an inn where I won't have to battle rats to get some sleep. I'll drive the wagon to Fors' stall. He'll be waiting to skive me for this harvest. I'll meet you in the common area."

He dug in the pouch at his waist and passed Gurn a handful of coins. Martise climbed down from the wagon and waited next to Gurn. She hoped the inn he chose had a stable. She could sleep in a protected corner where no one noticed or accosted her.

As if he read her thoughts, Silhara leaned across the seat. "You'll share the room with me and Gurn, Martise."

Any lingering embarrassment was forgotten, born away by gratitude. Martise grinned at him, uncaring that he drew back from her as if her happiness might be contagious. "Thank you, Master."

He frowned. "Don't leave Gurn's side. I won't fight a pack of whoremongers to save one careless woman if you go off on your own." He slapped the reins against Gnat's haunches. "And buy some decent cloth." The wagon rolled past them, wheels creaking as they rolled on the rutted paths toward the market.

In short order, she and Gurn secured a room, a meal and three pallets for the night. Just as quickly, they returned to the market. By the time they reached the outskirts, Martise was tired, sweaty and thirsty from jogging after Gurn. She promptly forgot such small annoyances amidst the controlled chaos and color of Eastern Prime's thriving market.

Everything from grain and weaponry to birds and fruit were hawked in the various stalls. One merchant nearly deafened her with his enthusiastic pitch about the exquisiteness of his silks and cottons imported from the Glimmer lands. Colorful parrots squawked in cages hung on poles while food merchants roasted mutton over open pits behind their stalls and sold it by the slice with a stack of warm flatbread. The mouthwatering smell of charred meat mixed with the pungent odor of unwashed bodies and fish. Cutpurses flitted like shadow through the crowds along with scrawny, nimble-fingered pickpockets. Beggars shared muddy paths with scantily garbed *hourin*, each hoping to earn a coin through pity or lust.

Gurn kept a firm grip on her arm. Martise hoped he knew their end destination because she was soon lost, unable to see or navigate a way to the market's boundaries. Luckily, his size cleared a path wherever they went, and they soon emerged into a quieter part of the market.

The giant grinned at her and signed *"Thank the gods!"* He mimicked the act of drinking from a flask.

Parched from the long trip and just happy to stand in a spot where the crowd didn't crush her, Martise accepted his offer with gusto. "Oh yes. Anything, Gurn. I have a mouth full of sand."

He led her to a canopied stall selling melons and fruit drinks. The vendor recognized Gurn and welcomed him with a smile. "Gurn, I wondered what happened to you. I expected to see you last week." He winked at Martise and bowed.

She took the lead from Gurn. "Might we purchase two of your drinks?"

The merchant jumped to fulfill their order, crushing the melon in a bowl until it resembled nothing more than a pink slurry. He added honey and wine to the concoction and poured it into wooden goblets. Sweet and refreshing, the beverage cooled her parched throat.

As Gurn led her back toward the chaos of the market's central hub, she caught a brief glimpse of scarlet robes. The crowd parted just enough for her to see Silhara standing at the edge of a stall that sold brightly colored silks, stacks of woven carpets and crossbows. Engrossed in conversation with two men, he didn't notice her. Kurman tribesmen, from their clothing and stance. Black-haired and shorter than the coastal peoples, they wore the full trousers, vests and pointed shoes typical of the mountain nomads. Too far away to hear their conversation, she watched them converse with Silhara in a mix of dramatic hand motions and sharp exclamations.

She lost sight of them when Gurn pulled her through the throng toward another stall displaying crocks and jars of various sizes. He released her once they were inside the booth and motioned to the merchant. Martise stood by and watched, fascinated, as Gurn haggled in a combination of hand signals, grunts and verbal prompts from the seller.

A tap on her shoulder made her jump. She whirled, nearly colliding with the person standing so close to her.

"Martise! We meet again."

If the ground suddenly opened up at her feet, she would have stepped willingly into the chasm. The man smiling at her was breathtaking, handsome enough to stop women and men in their tracks for a second look. Thick blond hair grazed his muscular shoulders. The eyes gazing back at her were heavily lashed—bluer than a mountain lake and shallower than a rain puddle. He had a sculpted face of unlined perfection, as if the deities who created him chose one moment to bless a human with godlike beauty.

Eight years earlier, he'd been a dream come to life, a surprising gift to a young woman whose station and appearance barred her from the chance at such things as love and the companionship of a mate. But dreams faded before reality. She'd aged since then, grown wiser and discovered the vain, hollow man behind the stunning visage.

"Hello, Balian."

Her cool greeting became a squeak when he lifted her and crushed her in an enthusiastic embrace. Still reeling from the unexpected clasp, she squeaked again when Gurn almost broke both of Balian's arms wresting her from him.

Flustered by the sudden attack, Balian mouthed a foul insult, then paled when he got a good look at Martise's rescuer. "Ah, forgive me. I didn't realize you were here with your man."

She was tempted to let his assumption stand. Faced with Gurn's obvious protective stance and warning glare, Balian would make short work of reacquainting himself with her and disappear into the crowd. Handsome, yes. Brave, no.

Still, curiosity trumped practicality. The man who'd introduced her to the carnal pleasures of the flesh and spouted lies of faith and adoration in her ear had not risen much from his original station. Once a stable hand at Asher, Balian had big dreams of setting out and making his fortune. His clothing, as worn as hers, revealed he hadn't succeeded in that quest.

"Gurn is a friend." She touched the giant's arm. "It's all right, Gurn. I know him."

Gurn hesitated, then slowly backed away, just enough to give her privacy but still close enough defend her if necessary.

Balian eyed Gurn, wary and braced to dart into the throng in case the giant suddenly turned on him. When Gurn ignored him, he gave Martise a wide, flirtatious smile. "You haven't changed, Martise. Still serving Asher?"

"Yes, though I serve another house for the summer."

He peered over her shoulder and around her in a false show of inquiry. "No husband or children hanging on your skirts? Ah, wait. You aren't allowed to marry."

Martise stared at him, unmoved. Balian always had a talent for conversational barbs.

"And you, Balian? You left Asher to make your fortune in the world." He flushed under her derisive gaze, one she knew Silhara would appreciate. What had she ever seen in this dim, arrogant peacock? "Has the world been unkind?"

His fair features turned ugly. "Kinder than it's been to you. I'm still a free man." He paused, treating her to the same scornful gaze she'd bestowed on him. "Sometimes I don't understand why I ever bedded you."

Such words from him might have cut her at one time. Now she felt nothing more than a mild annoyance at his blustering. "You bedded me because 'I had a body more beautiful than the costliest houri and a voice that made you come.' At least I think those were your words. You bragged to your friends while deep in your cups. You weren't very coherent at the time."

Her blunt response and lack of reaction rendered him speechless. He soon recovered and with an offer that made a lie of his insult. "You always did conceal your finest assets." He leered, peering at her long skirts and layered tunic as if he saw the body beneath them. "And you never found me lacking. Come with me. I've a room nearby and wine smuggled out of Karanset. We can renew old friendships."

She imagined such a scene. A dive near the wharf where the rooms were separated by parchment-thin walls and crawling with rats. He'd take her quick at first, as he always preferred. Against the wall or on a lice-infested pallet stained with the evidence of his previous couplings. Martise's lip curled in revulsion, and she wished for a stiff shot of Peleta's Fire to cleanse the sudden sour taste off her palate.

"No thank you," she said and walked away. The outraged growl behind her made her smile.

"A woman like you shouldn't be so choosy, Martise."

She turned back to him. "A man like you shouldn't aim so high, Balian."

"Bitch," he snapped, loud enough for Gurn to hear. Gurn lunged, almost knocking Martise down in his zeal to reach Balian. Her erstwhile lover yelped in fear and fled into the teeming sea of people. She grabbed the back of Gurn's tunic before he followed his quarry.

"Let him go, Gurn." He stared at her, his silent anger palpable. She took his hand and squeezed. "Such words only hurt when the person saying them means something to you."

He signed to her. She caught the basics of his question and shook her head.

"He was important to me once. No longer." She squeezed his hand again. "Come. Don't you have supplies to buy? I don't want to be held over the coals by your master for distracting you from your tasks."

Balian faded from her thoughts as she followed Gurn through the marketplace and watched him bargain with vendors over prices and quantities of goods with nothing more than a shake or nod of his head and a raised eyebrow. By the time they made their way to the common area to meet Silhara and break for a meal, he'd purchased bags of milled flour, jars of olives and honey, a barrel of salted fish, two small barrels of wine, a pair of nanny goats and new clippers—all to be loaded into the wagon at the end of the day. He'd even bargained down the price of the wool cloth and skein of thread she'd selected.

The common area was an open-air pub. Tables and benches covered the grassy area, unprotected from the sun. Stalls selling all manner of food, ale and wine surrounded the perimeter, and many of the merchants and alewives stalked the tables hawking their goods directly to the patrons.

Tantalizing scents of roasted mutton and pork mixed with the yeasty smell of bread teased her nostrils. Her stomach growled and was echoed by Gurn's.

"I'm starved." She scanned the long rows of tables, searching for a tall, forbidding man in a scarlet robe. "I hope the master won't make us wait until evening to eat."

After looking over the crowd, Gurn pointed to a table near the perimeter of the common area. His unmistakable and irreverent sign for "horse's ass" let her know he'd spotted Silhara. She laughed and nudged him toward the food stalls. "Please get us some food. I'm ready to gnaw on one of these tables." He hesitated, and she reassured him. "I'll be fine. The common area is safer than the market itself. There are even families with small children here."

Gurn surveyed the crowd, this time with a more eagle eye and finally nodded. Martise watched him head for a stall selling chicken and racks of skewered mutton.

She aimed for the tell-tale scarlet robe several tables away and wove through the clusters of people eating and drinking. The sight she came upon made the air freeze in her lungs. Darting behind a large man doing his best to coax a young alewife out of her bodice, Martise hid in his shadow and prayed those at Silhara's table hadn't seen her.

The sorcerer sat alone on one side, peeling an apple with his boot dagger. Across from him, Balian sat with a friend, drinking from a tankard and laughing raucously at something his companion said. Martise grumbled under her breath. Of all the rotten luck. She didn't care if Balian hurled insults at her directly. She did mind if he did so in front of Silhara. Beyond the humiliation of having an old lover regale the mage with her many physical shortcomings, he could expose Cumbria's lie of her being his ward. She knew Silhara didn't believe a word Cumbria told him. No one accused the sorcerer of being too trusting, but unless he confronted her directly or heard the truth from someone else, Martise intended to cling doggedly to the story the bishop concocted.

She circled around the courting couple and slinked past a knot of women until she found a corner bench out of view but close enough to hear what they said.

Mothers often admonished their children not to listen at doors or windows because they might hear something they didn't like. That wisdom sat hard on Martise's shoulders as she caught the middle of Balian's conversation.

He quaffed the wine, wiping away the dribble from the corner of his mouth. "Plain as a stick and shy around people. Until you got her in the stable or on a pallet. She could suck a man dry with a tongue that made you see heaven. And fuck all night. Beautiful body too. If I hadn't seen virgin blood on my cock that first time, I might have thought her a priest whore."

Martise closed her eyes for a moment and hoped she didn't retch. She'd long ago abandoned the illusion that Balian had cared for her. But to hear him tear her down to his friend and in front of Silhara—lessen her until she was nothing more than a bitch in heat—sickened her.

Silhara straddled the bench, silent, his profile to his table mates. As intent as a supplicant at prayer, he pared the apple until the long spiral of peel fell to the ground. His dour features gave no hint of his thoughts.

Balian's companion refilled their tankards from a nearby pitcher. "A lot of women can fuck like weasels, mate. Prettier women. And you've a face to lure 'em in."

Balian puffed up at the compliment, reminding Martise of a bullfrog in mating season. "True, but they didn't have her voice. My cock got hard just hearing her talk. And when she moaned..." His eyes rolled back in ecstasy. "Good gods, I just about shot my seed every time."

Bile rose in her throat. The friend replied but too softly for her to hear. Balian, on the other hand, bellowed his opinion. "Just fuck 'em in the dark, mate. You can put any face you want on them when you do that."

Martise prayed Silhara's lack of reaction meant he didn't recognize whom Balian insulted. She doubted it. Balian had waxed rhapsodic about her voice, and for all she knew, had mentioned her name in earlier conversation. Silhara was no fool.

He cupped the apple in his hand. Paring it into slices, he placed it on the table. He cleaned the knife on his trousers, turned and, quick as a striking serpent, buried the lethal tip in the back of her ex-lover's hand where it rested on the table.

Balian's shocked bellow of pain ripped through the common area, halting all conversation. He bolted to his feet and bellowed again as the movement pulled on his arm. He stared at his bloodied hand and then at Silhara, wild-eyed.

"Bursin's bollocks! You stupid bastard!"

Silhara rose as well, grasped Balian's wrist and yanked the knife out with merciless efficiency. Another agonized shriek rent the air. Silhara swiped the bloodied blade clean on a stunned bystander's shirtsleeve.

"Forgive me," he said in that calm, raspy voice. "I didn't see your hand there."

His icy expression belied his sincerity. Martise, shocked by what she'd just witnessed, shoved her way through the growing crowd surrounding the table. Balian had stripped off his shirt. Despite the blood dripping from his fingers, he presented a sight that had many a female in the mob sighing. His friend tore a strip of cloth from the shirt and bandaged Balian's injured hand.

Balian pulled a wicked knife from the sheath at his waist, brandishing it in front of Silhara with his good hand. "Fuck your apologies. I'm going to geld you."

Silhara smiled, and the crowd sucked in a collective breath. "Are you now?"

A voice behind Martise yelled to Balian. "Leave it be, lad. That's the Master of Crows you just challenged."

Balian paled but didn't back down. "I don't care if you're lord of a dung heap." He spat at Silhara's feet. "And you're a coward if you have to use magic to win a fight."

Silhara laughed in genuine amusement. He shrugged out of his robe and dropped it on the table. Balian tracked him from the other side as he walked to a clear space just outside the common area's periphery. The crowd followed, closing around the two combatants until they formed a makeshift arena. Smashed between a sweating fishwife and a man almost as big as Gurn, Martise jostled for a clear view of the impending fight.

Sunlight flashed on metal as Silhara flipped his dagger expertly in his hand. "You should listen to the wise man who spoke up, *boy*. Take my apology for what it's worth and walk away. I don't need magic to gut you from gullet to bollocks."

He turned his back on Balian in clear dismissal. Martise joined the chorus of warning cries as Balian bellowed and rushed him, dagger raised. Silhara turned at the last minute, neatly side-stepped his opponent's charge and smashed his hand between his shoulder blades. Balian crashed into the crowd, miraculously avoiding stabbing anyone. The spectators cheered. Excited by a growing bloodlust, they thrust him back into the temporary arena.

Silhara shook his head in disgust. "Colossal stupidity hidden by a fair face. At least the gods are sometimes just."

Once again, the mage courted death by turning his back. Once again Balian rushed him. Instead of side-stepping, Silhara turned and met him full-on, throwing a round house punch that snapped Balian's head back and lifted him off his feet. He struck the ground in a cloud of dust.

Silhara stood over him. "You're beginning to annoy me."

Balian rolled to his feet and spat out a gobbet of blood. A split lip and swelling jaw didn't stop him, and he struggled to his feet. Three more rushes, with Silhara dodging and defeating every attack with kicks, slaps and punches—but never his knife—and

Balian staggered. Bloody and bruised, he glared at Silhara from the one eye not yet blackened.

"I'm gonna cut you good, sorcerer." His words were more slurred than a drunkard's.

Silhara looked heavenward, as if imploring the gods. "So you keep saying, pretty boy."

Balian charged him again, and Martise shouted another warning. Silhara, grim-faced and obviously tired of baiting his opponent, kicked his feet out from under him. Balian skidded on his back in the dirt. Before he gasped a breath, Silhara jerked his knife from his hand and pinned him to the ground with his knees pressed to Balian's shoulders. Martise's ex-lover whimpered as the mage straddled him. Armed with both knives, Silhara pressed his blade to Balian's jugular and held the confiscated blade against his cheek.

"The crowd almost got it right, *boy*. You challenged the Master of Crows, but you fought a dock whore's bastard. I was fighting in the muck while you were still tethered to your mother's lead strings."

Martise held her breath as he pressed the knife edge harder against Balian's neck. A line of blood swelled above the blade. For all that she detested Balian, she didn't want to see him die. Not over this and not by the hand of the man who represented the greatest threat to her heart.

"Please, Master. Don't do this."

Her voice, soft and imploring, carried over the noise of the crowd. Silhara met her gaze, his black eyes flat. The knife cut deeper. Balian moaned in terror. The pungent odor of urine suddenly filled the air. Silhara continued to stare at her.

"Please," she repeated. "He isn't worth it."

A shadow of humanity returned to his gaze. He blinked and focused his attention on his fallen rival. "Pissed yourself, did you? Now you know the taste of true fear." He flipped Balian's dagger in his palm so that the tip pointed down, creating a depression in the fallen man's cheek. "These marks and cuts will heal in no time, and you'll once again be a wench's fantasy come to life." His smile thinned.

Whatever Balian saw in Silhara's eyes made him twist and writhe, despite the threat of death. He whined when Silhara deepened the bloody cut on his neck.

"A momento, I think. So the ugliness within isn't masked by the beauty without."

Martise cried out at the same time Balian did. "No!"

He ignored her and addressed Balian. "One move and I'll slit your throat. Die handsome or live honest. What will it be?"

As one the crowd hissed and groaned when Silhara slowly carved a half-moon design in Balian's right cheek. The man, beaten, humiliated and scarred, fainted.

When he was done, the Master of Crows stood and tossed Balian's knife so that it stuck in the ground near his head. No mercy softened his voice. No remorse colored his tone. "Don't fret, boy," he said. "No one will notice it if you fuck in the dark."

CHAPTER THIRTEEN

Neith needed rain. The grove baked in the descending sun's dry heat, with trees losing leaves, shedding the raiment that demanded more water. If the weather didn't cooperate soon and provide some relief, his harvest next year would suffer, possibly fail.

Silhara stood at the entrance to his balcony and puffed on the hose attached to the *huqqah* at his feet. The habit soothed him, kept him from kicking furniture or throwing breakables against the wall in frustration. He should be thankful the well hadn't dried up. Instead he spent hours at night wondering if there was a way to manipulate the unseen rivers below ground to swell and rise and water the roots of his thirsty trees.

If it would only rain.

If Corruption would only pack up its star and leave.

If Conclave would only come and retrieve their spy before she completely destroyed his equilibrium and caused him to make the one mistake that would condemn him to death.

She was in the library now, scribbling at her notes, waiting for him to meet her so they could ruminate over what a gaggle of long-dead kings did to destroy a long-dead god, and how it might help him or the priesthood destroy Corruption.

He blew a stream of smoke into the air, manipulating it with a fingertip until it resembled the spiral insignia of Conclave. The vortex of life to the center of eternity, a symbol of benevolence for a pitiless, avaricious canonry who had forgotten the true magic of the Gift bestowed on them. The symbol disintegrated, shredded by the ceaseless summer winds.

Silhara had little faith Conclave would succeed in its endeavor to destroy Corruption. Birdixan and his fellow kings were described in the brittle parchment as men of great position and nobility. Save for the Luminary, leader of Conclave, he could think of no priest who came close to fulfilling the role of Birdixan and his brethren: none with the power and skill to battle the god and win.

Birdixan. The name vexed him. He'd seen or heard it before but didn't remember where. Martise, for all her learning and talent for recall, was unfamiliar with it. He might not trust her completely, but he had great faith in her abilities. If she didn't recognize the name, few would.

Conclave's spy was proving more helpful than he anticipated and more alluring than he liked.

He'd caught glimpses of her in Eastern Prime's marketplace as she followed Gurn from stall to stall. She might slip unnoticed in most crowds, but he'd spotted her easily enough numerous times. He'd never seen her so lighthearted or at ease as when she shopped with his servant and surveyed the pandemonium around her—at least until she entered the common area and overheard her erstwhile lover vilify her in the crudest terms.

He watched from the corner of one eye as she crept toward his table, her eyes dark with some unnamed dread. He'd been peeling an apple, waiting patiently for her and Gurn to meet him. He hadn't paid any attention to the two men sitting across from him, having no interest in the ramblings of drunken braggarts. It was Martise's fixed gaze on them that made him take notice.

Balian's remarks and the sight of Martise's face, white with shame, had set his temper soaring. For a moment it felt as if the dolt was insulting him instead of his apprentice. Anger, mixed with no small amount of jealousy and possessiveness, roared through him. Stabbing that knife point into the vulgar bastard's hand went a long way to cooling him off. Scarring and beating him bloody had made Silhara almost cheery.

Martise, visibly shaken by what she witnessed, remained mostly silent the rest of the day, occasionally tossing him complicated looks. Gurn was not so quiet. He'd seen the fight as well and signed rapidly, wanting to know what happened. Silhara's clipped "He insulted my household," satisfied him.

That night in the inn, while Gurn slept near the door of their room and Martise slumbered on her pallet nearby, Silhara prepared one of his hand pipes and took a calming smoke by the window. Below him, Eastern Prime slowly darkened, lamps winking out as pubs closed and households went to bed. Beyond the town, the bay sang its tidal lullaby, rocking ships to sleep.

He'd congratulated himself on the deal he'd struck with Fors. For all his blustering, the man knew the quality of Silhara's product and the demand for it. Even with the generous payment he'd given the mage, he'd still make a hefty profit off sales to the city's population.

The heavy weight of the coin purse tied at his waist reassured him. He'd done well, and though the purse would be significantly lighter once he paid the vendors Gurn had bartered with, they were set for another season. His reputation had its uses, his Gift its reward, but neither made food appear on the table. Only hard labor, stealing, or the blessing of aristo birthright did that. Silhara was intimately acquainted with the first two and scornful of the third.

A rustle of blankets made him look to where Martise slept. She sat up, saw him at the window and rose. A stray beam of moonlight revealed the shadow of slender thighs and the curve of a breast beneath her leine before she wrapped her long shawl around her and padded to him. Her bare feet shone ivory in the dark. He thought them pretty. She smelled good too—of sleep and warm female.

He pointed to Corruption's star, now hovering over the bay. His voice was soft. "The Kurman no longer guide their flocks to the Brecken Falls. Corruption has left its mark. The rivers are salted, and the falls themselves fouled. Crops are dying; trees are dying, and livestock as well. The towns are emptying of people seeking food and refuge in the greater cities."

She shook her head. "I don't understand. Corruption hopes to rule the world again. What is there to rule if all are dead and the lands laid waste?"

"It's called siege, apprentice. Starve your enemies; bring them so low that the promise of the simplest necessity will seem a gift from the gods. With enough patience, you can break a man to the point he will do anything you command." He puffed on his pipe. "Effective if unoriginal."

"Do you think Conclave will find a way to stop the god?"

"I doubt it. The priesthood's greatest weakness is its vanity. They'll scour their libraries looking for the one spell that will kill the god, but they can't use what their forbears used. Corruption has had more than a thousand years to consider how he'll defeat his adversaries if they try again. The priests won't look beyond their own walls for a solution. They are Conclave, keepers of all the knowledge and arcane worth having." His smile was mocking. "At least those things *they* consider important."

She rubbed the end of her braid with her fingers. Silhara imagined what all that red-hued hair would look like flowing free over her shoulders and down her back. "Will you tell them what you found at Iwehvenn?"

"Yes, but will they listen? I am no admirer of the priests, nor they of me. To listen, you have to trust, or at least respect."

He puffed on the pipe, waiting for the real reason she'd joined him at the window.

Her eyes, their copper color darkened to obsidian in the moon's cold light, reflected gratitude and the remnants of shame. "Today, at the market..."

Silhara held up a hand, and she fell silent. "When I was nine, my mother serviced a wealthy merchant every week." His lip curled into a sneer. "He'd deign to descend into the wharf filth and pay for an hour of her time, sometimes a full night. She always sent me away when he came to our room." He pointed the pipe stem at Martise. "Understand, I was born to a *houri*, raised around other *hourin* and almost became one myself." Martise's expression showed no contempt at his revelation.

"I wasn't an innocent about the nature of her profession. She wasn't protecting my childhood." An old revulsion, mixed with rage, burned within. "The merchant was an odd sort and sought my mother out repeatedly. The last time she pushed me out the door, I waited in an alcove, then sneaked back into the room."

The pipe stem threatened to snap in his fingers. "He had her crawling on her hands and knees naked, following him around and kissing the floor where he stepped." Martise gasped and covered her mouth, her eyes shining with pity and horror. "He didn't take her, didn't touch her, and didn't let her touch him. He gained his pleasure by hearing her call herself names, tell him what undeserving scum she was and how lucky she was to breathe the same air he did."

Silhara paused, caught between the need to purge the vile image from his system and trying not to retch from reliving the memory. A butterfly touch on his arm settled his seething emotions. Martise's fingers rested against his sleeve, a whisper of comfort. His stomach calmed.

"He came on the floor and made her lick it up, then pissed on her before he left."

Martise's hand clenched his arm. "No child should have to witness that," she hissed in the dark. "No woman should suffer it. That was a monster, not a man."

The past couldn't be changed, but Silhara felt as if a suffocating weight slid off his chest. He'd exacted his revenge decades earlier, dealt street justice that gave no quarter. But only now did he feel as if the hideous shadow of that memory had lessened. He didn't question why, after so much time, he chose to unburden himself to a woman whose purpose was ruled by Conclave. He had used it to make a point. It had transformed into something else. He trusted her to listen and not judge. She repaid him with a reassuring clasp. It was enough.

"Monsters are as vulnerable as men. I followed the merchant when he left." He filled his mouth with pipe smoke and blew it out the window, watching it float, serpentine, in the air before dissipating. "Taking a life leaves its mark on the soul. I bear no scar from taking his."

Martise removed her hand from his arm, and Silhara instantly missed her touch. "He deserved it, whatever you did to him. And more."

He remained silent, watching the ships rock in the bay.

"You knew Balian spoke of me."

"I guessed. Men are not prone to wax poetic over a woman's voice when they can talk about her breasts instead. She'd have to be exceptional for such to be remarked. Your voice is exceptional."

"You didn't have to do that."

"What? Make him bleed?" Silhara shrugged. "I enjoy a good brawl, though he wasn't much of a challenge. Your lover could learn a thing or two about knife fighting."

Her shadowed eyes flashed. "He isn't my lover."

For reasons he refused to consider, he was glad the detestable Balian had been relegated to her past. "Gained a little wisdom, did you?"

"Age and experience do that for a person."

"True. There should be some reward for creaking bones and gray hair."

He chuckled and she laughed softly. They stayed by the window for almost an hour after that, quiet, until Martise hid a yawn behind her hand and bid him goodnight.

Now, the view at Neith was of plains and trees instead of sea, and he indulged in his smoke alone. Once, he welcomed such solitude, but things had changed. He missed those moments of camaraderie, the sense of companionship not even Gurn, despite his affable nature, could provide.

The events at the market place continued to play in his memory. Silhara had rammed his dagger into Balian's hand with relish, hoping he broke bone and severed tendons. While he despised the man for his insults, he couldn't banish the images that rose in his mind—of him in Balian's place, with Martise clothed only in sun and the loose fall of her hair, on her knees before him, her mouth taking him in a deep caress. He pressed a palm against his growing erection.

She continually surprised him. Unremarkable on the surface, she was a study in contrasts. She jumped at her own shadow but faced down a lich to save him. He'd raced to her rescue when she'd screamed loud enough to bring the roof down, only to see her Gift hurl Corruption across the room. He no longer believed her naturally submissive. Quiet, yes, and good at hiding her emotions when she wished. But that lowered gaze had far less to do with acknowledging him as superior and more to do with hiding the fact she sometimes wanted to knock his teeth down his throat.

And she served at Neith. Even knowing his reputation and the fact she'd be left alone with two men in an isolated redoubt with no hope of rescue should they decide to harm her, she'd come to him as his false apprentice. Cumbria must have promised her great rewards to risk so much. He'd first assumed money, but weeks spent in her company proved him wrong. Martise was motivated to act as the bishop's eyes and ears, but the promise of coin wasn't the lure.

That pleased him. Such a woman, untroubled by his penury and the back-breaking labor of maintaining their survival, would do well here at Neith. The thought ran like melted snow through him. He tossed the *huqqah* hose aside in disgust.

One kiss, powerful enough to incinerate every last scrap of his reason and fire his blood, had him mooning over a future neither possible nor wanted. Neith was crowded enough with him, Gurn and Cael in residence. The occasional *houri*, bought for a night, was enough feminine companionship.

His eyes closed. He told himself the residual effects of her Gift sliding over him—through him—brought on that embrace. But he didn't believe his own lies. He kissed her because he wanted her, because he admired her. Because he wanted more than just the ethereal essence of her lingering on his tongue once her Gift withdrew. He'd kissed her on impulse, lured by the tempting curve of her lips and the slight feel of her in his arms. He'd expected her to retreat from his onslaught. Gentleness was not in his nature, and he was desperate to taste her. But she hadn't recoiled from his rough embrace, responding instead with a passion to equal his own. Only a small inner voice stopped him from taking her to the bed, lowering his breeches and climbing atop her.

Spy. Cumbria's means to trap you.

Silhara put out the coals in the *huqqah*. He always listened to that voice. It had saved him countless times. A quiet woman who missed nothing and remembered everything might well catch him in a heresy guaranteed to get him hauled before a Conclave tribunal, especially if she took on the role of lover as well as apprentice. So far, he'd been lucky his clashes with Corruption had been confined to his bedchamber—a room Martise had not yet entered. He'd seen the lurking suspicion in her eyes when she asked if he thought the avatar reborn. If she ever witnessed Corruption's brief possessions of him, he was damned. He'd have to kill her to protect himself, and he now recoiled at the possibility.

Outside, the sun still bathed the west in streaks of red and orange, but Neith's hallways were already swallowed in darkness. Silhara passed through their shadows as he strode to the library.

Silhouetted in the light of candles, Martise bent over a page of notes, scratching away furiously with her quill. She glanced up when he entered and offered him a tentative smile.

She held up a sheaf of parchment. "I've found more on the ritual, what fed its power. The hill where they trapped Amunsa was sacred ground, a pocket of Old Magic still existing outside the Waste."

He dragged a stool next to hers and sat down. His nostrils twitched. Orange flower and mint. Gurn had filched his perfume stores again and given a fragrance to Martise. His lips curved. His servant could be quite the charmer.

He took the paper and scanned the writing. "Ferrin's Tor is such a place. The shepherds who graze their sheep there swear the ewes that eat the grass growing on the hill bear the healthiest lambs with the best wool. Anything more on Birdixan?"

"A little, though I can't decipher the meaning." She handed him two more sheets from her stack. "Each time Birdixan is described as invoking power against Amunsa, this symbol is included next to his name. None of the other mage-kings have that symbol—or any symbol for that matter—by their names. Near the end, when Birdixan dies, the symbol no longer appears."

Silhara read the translated text and frowned. Like Birdixan's name, the symbol, an interlocking pair of cubes bisected with lines, was familiar.

"I've seen this somewhere. On a temple wall or tattooed on a priest. You don't recognize it?"

She shook her head. "No. I can only guess it isn't Helenese. They favor more curving designs. This is square and very angular. The script of the Glimmer peoples is a series of squares and lines. I can read and speak four dialects of Glimming and have never come across anything like this, so I hesitate to make a comparison."

Silhara stared at the symbol. "Birdixan here is described as a southern king. I think it's more than a coincidence the symbol and this unsung king are reminiscent of the far lands." He read more. One passage caught his eye, a sentence almost unnoticed in the ritual's florid descriptions. Birdixan "swallowed" the god before the ritual even began. Unease crawled across his soul on spider legs.

He rose from his seat. "I have some Glimming tomes. Mostly obscure poetry." He winced. "Horrible stuff, but my mentor liked it and collected every bit he could get his hands on. Maybe it will help."

They worked in silence for the next three hours. Martise's lamp dimmed, and Silhara, nauseated from reading several pages of saccharine odes to whiny, over-pampered women, put aside his books and rubbed his eyes. Martise still hunched over the table, scribbling. She paused, lowered her quill and shook the stiffness out of her hand.

"Anything else?" he asked.

"Nothing worthwhile unless you're interested in family lines. I've translated at least twenty generations of ancestors for three of the kings." She gave him a tired smile. "They were a prolific group."

Silhara stretched in his chair and stood. "When you have a dozen wives and a few hundred concubines, you can expect to sire herds of children." He came to stand before her. "We'll work again tomorrow. Are you ready for your lesson?"

Her expression was far less enthusiastic than when they first started to work with her Gift. She sighed. "Yes, though I'm afraid it will be a waste of your time. What good is a Gift if you can't use it for spells?"

He understood her frustration. They'd worked on her control of her Gift since their return from Eastern Prime. She'd been successful in summoning it and directing its emergence. However, he remained puzzled that none of the spells she attempted worked. Her recitation was flawless, her execution as good as his, but nothing happened. They'd tried every type of spell. Movement. She still couldn't levitate. Fire and water invocations. The fire burning cheerily in the library's hearth didn't even flicker when she tried summoning the flames. And the water remained in the goblet. Silhara even encouraged her to sing, bracing himself for the inevitable abuse on his ears, just in case her voice had improved and her Gift was spell singing. After a few notes, he stopped her, certain that whatever magic her Gift controlled, spell song wasn't it.

She stood up to face him, her shoulders slumped with weariness.

"Don't sulk," he said. "It doesn't flatter you."

His caustic remark worked to snap her out of her melancholy. Her gaze dropped to the floor, but her shoulders were stiff, as if she restrained the urge to slap him.

Silhara smiled. "We'll try something different tonight."

She gaped at him when he pulled out his boot dagger and ran the blade's sharp edge over his palm. Blood ran in trickling paths over his hand, sliding between his fingers to drip on the floor. He held out his stained hand to her.

"Heal this."

Untroubled by the blood, she took his hand, holding it between hers. Her callused palms were warm on his skin, stroking. He listened as she recited one healing spell after another. Her eyes closed in concentration. So focused on trying to invoke something that might heal his wound, she lost control of her Gift. Instant heat suffused Silhara's body. Undiluted magery seeped into his pores, his spirit, even as his hand ached and blood dripped from his fingers. His Gift swelled within him, feeding off her power.

Martise, beguiled by her Gift as much as Silhara, raised his hand and placed it on her chest above her breast. The heartbeat against his bloodied palm echoed the one thudding in his head. Though he'd distance himself from the allure of her Gift, he was bewitched by how it transformed her. Her appearance didn't change. The same pointed chin and small nose, russet hair and pale mouth. But all were enhanced, embellished and made beautiful by her magery.

He almost succumbed to temptation, to slide his hand over her tunic until he cupped her small breast. Luckily, the sting in his palm kept him clear-headed enough to fight down his desire and pull his hand away, leaving a red smear on her skin and a broken bond between them. Her moan, strained and stuttered, worked its own magic on him. She might as well have reached out and stroked his cock.

She opened her eyes, saw his hand still bleeding. Her shoulders slumped. "It didn't work."

"No. For all that your Gift can swat gods and liches like they're mice in a cat's paw, it doesn't work with spells."

He stared at the blood on his palm and the smear across her skin. A marking of territory, a claiming, no matter that she'd placed his hand there in the first place. And while focused on healing him. A powerful need took hold—to proclaim that this pale woman, with her prosaic features and extraordinary spirit, was his.

Terrified by his feelings, Silhara spun away and strode to the door. "We're done here," he said over his shoulder.

Her tone was plaintive. "But your hand..."

He paused but kept his back to her. "Is still bleeding. You can't heal it. Go to bed, Martise."

He left, slamming the door behind him. The occasional plop of blood droplets striking the floor accompanied him as he pounded downstairs. The door connecting the great hall to the kitchen crashed against the opposite wall. Gurn's domain was blacker than a crypt, but Silhara found his way unerringly to the cupboard housing the servant's bottle of Peleta's Fire. He swept cups off the shelves until he found a large goblet and poured himself a generous portion of spirits. His curse was loud and vicious when he banged his knee on the bench against the worktable and sat down.

The Fire lived up to its name, scorching a path from his mouth to his gut. Silhara's eyes watered. "Bursin's balls," he wheezed and tipped the goblet back for another molten swallow. He drained and refilled the cup to the brim, uncaring that the morning would see him trying to claw his eyes out from the pain.

A shuffle of movement at the door warned him he had a visitor. He raised his drink in his injured hand, the goblet stem slippery against his fingers. "Hello, Gurn." He struggled to shape the words around a swollen tongue. "Care for a drink?"

The clink of cups rolling against each other on the floor and the hiss of fatwood lit at the hearth broke the answering silence. A wavering light cast a corona over the table where Silhara sat. He shielded his eyes from the candlelight and cursed. "You couldn't just sit in the dark with me, could you?"

Once his eyes adjusted, he lowered his hand to glare at Gurn seated across from him. The servant gestured to his wounded hand and the blood on the table and goblet.

Silhara swiped at the table's surface with his sleeve. "A test for my apprentice. She failed." He raised the goblet and toasted the woman upstairs. Gurn started to rise but was stopped by Silhara's sharp command.

"Don't bother. I'll take care of it in my chamber. I want you to do something else for me."

He finished the dram and reached for the bottle again, only to have Gurn snatch it away and put it back into the cupboard.

"I wasn't finished," he snapped. Gurn's expression was eloquent. Yes he was.

Silhara tossed him the goblet. "Fine. I bow to territorial rights." He rose slowly, relieved the room spun only once before stopping. Gurn watched him, a mixture of concern and mild amusement creasing his blunt features.

"I want you to go to Eastern Prime. Bring back a girl from the Temple of the Moon. I don't care what she looks like, just make sure she's small-boned, of a certain height." He measured with his hand. The height was similar to Martise's.

Any trace of humor fled Gurn's expression. His eyes narrowed, their brilliant blue flattening to gray. He shook his head, hands slashing angry patterns in the air as he signed his refusal in no uncertain terms.

His own anger rising above his inebriation, Silhara crossed his arms. "I'm not asking you, Gurn. I'm telling you."

The two men glared at each for a long moment. Finally, Gurn growled low in his throat, kicked cups out of his way and pinched out the candle flame for good measure. The door's slam was thunderous in the unrelenting dark as he stomped out of the kitchen.

"And a good night to you too, you sanctimonious bastard," Silhara called after him.

It wasn't his fault that Cumbria's little spy had him tied up in knots. Better that he use the bishop's money to purchase a *houri's* time for an evening. No promises of the heart, no tangled emotions or vulnerability. Only a business transaction in which a whore's purchased favors would ease the consuming desire for the woman sent to betray him.

The Fire had taken full effect by the time he staggered to the door. Disoriented by drink and the spinning dark, he walked once into a cupboard and then into the wall before managing to stumble into the great hall. "Gurn, you prick," he muttered, holding on to the stair's rickety railing. "I'll kill you when I see you next. With that candle you snuffed."

Drunk and still bleeding, he managed to mumble the spell for witchlight, stagger up the stairs to his room without breaking his neck and collapse on his bed. He yanked off his clothes, tangling his hand in his sleeve until he ripped the shirt to free himself. The ceiling undulated, and he closed his eyes to keep from being sick. Sleep swiftly overtook him, followed by powerful dreams tainted with Corruption's presence.

Martise, naked and vulnerable before him. Images of him taking her in a myriad of ways, his cock sliding into her mouth, her cunnus, between her buttocks. He moaned in his sleep, his uninjured hand moving beneath the covers to grip the base of his erect penis and stroke.

The god's voice flickered over him like a serpent's tongue. *"She will be yours. Use her in whatever manner pleases you. Throw her away when you tire of her. Countless more will be yours to command and use. I can do this for you."*

The images intensified, coldly seductive. She was servile and silent, never meeting his gaze while he took her, never returning a caress or begging a kiss. Memory intruded on the god's manipulation of his desires. His mother, abject before a toad of a man. The emptiness in her eyes. The smell of urine.

The last broke Corruption's hold on his dreams. He froze, hand still curved around his cock.

His stomach roiled from a combination of the god's invasive touch and too much Peleta's Fire. Blood clogged his nostrils. He laughed, the sound slurred and thick.

"A common whoremonger now, Corruption? Truly, you are the embodiment of divine wonder."

An agonizing pain struck him between the eyes, as if someone drove a spear point into his skull. He curled in on himself, panting and holding his head. Sweat poured off his body as the pain traveled downward, raking his limbs.

"I tire of your mockery, mage. And your rebukes. If you will not yield, no matter. There are other ways."

His pain disappeared abruptly. Silhara lay shivering and wondering if he was dead. For a moment the image of Iwehvenn and Martise's features, thin with shock and compassion, passed behind his closed eyes. *Stay with me.*

He fell asleep again and awakened well past dawn with a mouth full of wool, a head full of splinters and an aching hand. Blood stained the bed linens. Squinting against the merciless morning light, he rolled out of bed and stumbled to the chamber pot to empty his bladder. Afterward, he washed with the cold water in his basin and dressed, plagued by foggy memories of arguing with Gurn and swiving Martise in his dreams.

Despite the pounding between his ears, he cast a healing spell on his injured hand. Expecting only to lessen the ache and prevent infection, he was surprised to see the wound close and disappear. Remnants of Martise's Gift still resided within him. He'd never before possessed the particular skill to fully heal with magic. A suspicion took root and grew.

When he traipsed downstairs he discovered Martise and Cael in the kitchen. Dropping onto the bench, he groaned and clenched his teeth at the smell of porridge and butter. Martise rose from her place at the table and brought him a warmed kettle of tea. The loathed bowl of oranges appeared before him next to the kettle. His stomach heaved, and he shoved the bowl aside.

"Get those away from me before I vomit."

He blessed her silently when she replaced them with a cup.

"Do you want something else?" Her voice was sympathetic.

Tea sloshed over the cup's rim as he poured from the kettle with a shaking hand. "Only if you can offer me a new head along with the tea. Mine is about to burst."

She smiled, then winced when Cael began barking at the rooster's morning crowing in the bailey. Silhara almost dropped the cup to cover his ears.

"Out!" he snarled at the mage-finder, silencing him instantly. The dog slinked toward the door and lay down, staring at his master with an injured expression.

Martise touched his arm. "I found the cups on the floor this morning and the Fire on a different shelf. Do you still have some of that draught you gave me?"

Silhara nodded and wished he hadn't. "As soon as I finish this tea and can walk straight, I'm headed to the stillroom."

He answered her unvoiced question. "I sent Gurn to Eastern Prime. He'll be back this afternoon. In the meantime, you'll have to take over his duties. I'll work in the grove alone. And I need you to prepare a room on the second floor. We're having a guest tonight." His stomach roiled even more at the thought of her discovering his visitor's purpose.

Her eyebrows rose, but she didn't pry. "I'll have it ready when they arrive."

Gurn's condemning expression flashed before him, followed by a surge of remorse. Silhara growled into his cup. She was only a servant here, and a minion of Conclave. He owed her neither faith nor explanation.

A visit to the stillroom for a dose of a revitalizing elixir restored his humanity. Work in the grove offered a peaceful respite. Harvesting and maintaining the trees was difficult, unending work, but he embraced it. The grove validated him, reflected how far he'd risen and what he had overcome.

He picked the trees nearest the house. All the windows were open, allowing a breeze to flow through the rooms, and he sometimes heard Martise admonish Cael for some minor indiscretion as he followed her while she completed her many tasks. He paused. There was a sense of rightness in hearing her voice, knowing she moved through his manor as its temporary keeper. He imagined what it might be like if she lived here permanently, became his lover.

He'd interrupt her work and his, take her hand and lead her to the chamber they'd share and make love to her throughout the afternoon. She'd look upon him with a smile, touch him with loving hands and caress him with that bewitching voice.

Silhara cursed and clipped off a cluster of oranges, almost snipping his fingers in the process. Such domestic contentment didn't suit him. He did well enough at Neith with only Gurn and Cael for company. However, when Martise called him for their midday meal, he joined her eagerly.

The bowl of soup she set in front of him was fragrant with vegetables and herbs. Busy placing bread, butter and the tea kettle on the table, she missed his appreciative sigh.

She handed him a spoon. "I thought you might prefer this today. There's also wine if you want to risk it."

His stomach balked at the thought of the wine, but he managed to consume half the pot of soup and a loaf of bread. Martise no longer stared at him in wide-eyed astonishment. She was used to his appetite and sipped her bowl of soup while he devoured his.

She refilled his tea cup. "I've prepared the room two doors down from yours. It's the only one with a bed still usable. There's water in the pitcher and cloths if your guest wishes to clean up when they arrive. I also cleaned the mirror, though there's nothing to be done about the crack."

He scowled into his teacup at the persistent sense of guilt. She was neither his wife nor his mistress. Just another servant in his household. Like Gurn. Would she be so accommodating if she knew his guest was a *houri* brought to entertain him for an evening?

She was in the midst of clearing away the table while he finished off the pot of tea when Cael suddenly let loose another round of barking.

"I'm going to kill that damn dog."

The creak of wagon wheels announced Gurn's return. Silhara braced himself for more of Gurn's disapproval and wasn't disappointed. The giant entered the kitchen, a thundercloud of condemnation on his normally affable face.

"Gurn, welcome back!" Martise's cheerful greeting only served to darken his visage even more. "Why didn't you come through the front door?"

Silhara heard the puzzlement in her voice. His eyes widened when the servant ushered his companion into the kitchen. A soft gasp from Martise punctuated his own surprise.

Gurn didn't bring home just any *houri*. Silhara gaped at the most beautiful woman he'd ever seen. Long, black hair artfully arranged and held with jeweled clips was swept back to fall in thick curls down her back. Smooth, honey skin begged to be caressed. Her face was exquisite, with a slender nose and vermillion-painted lips that curved into a come-hither smile and highlighted delicate cheekbones. Her green eyes were skillfully outlined in kohl, enhancing their exotic shape. She had a body to make a man's mouth water, small-boned and generously curved. A plethora of sheer, brightly colored scarves draped her form. Except for her height and dainty build, she was Martise's complete antithesis. And she must have cost him a fortune.

The *houri* bowed, her small hands clasped together as if in prayer. "It is an honor to be summoned to serve you, Master of Neith." She had a pretty voice, high and sweet.

A strangled sound reached his ears. When he looked, Martise was busy clearing the dishes away from the table, her head bowed and face turned away. The grace she usually exhibited had deserted her, and she stacked bowls with a clumsy rattle. He looked to Gurn whose withering stare threatened to immolate him on the spot.

Silhara nodded to the *houri* in greeting and motioned for Gurn to join him in a far corner of the room.

"Have you lost your mind?" he snapped in a low voice. "I sent you to the Temple of the Moon for a *houri* who wouldn't have the pox. What did you do, ask for the most expensive prostitute in the brothel?"

Gurn's snide smile confirmed his suspicion.

Silhara saw red. "You insolent bastard. I'm tempted to load her in the wagon and make you take her back. But that's what you want, isn't it? Well, tonight you can just sit in this kitchen and chew on the idea that I'm upstairs fucking away two months worth of food for us."

He didn't think it possible to sign sewage-sucking-excuse-of-a-baseborn-bilge-rat but somehow Gurn managed. Silhara was interrupted from further snarling by Martise addressing the *houri*.

"I am Martise, *adané,* servant and apprentice here. If you'll follow me, I'll show you to the room I've prepared for your stay."

Silhara's gut burned, both at her polite address to the *houri* and the fact she'd cleaned that room not knowing its intended use. Gurn's low growl highlighted his disgust. He stalked past the women and out of the kitchen. The *houri* smiled and inclined her head at Silhara as Martise led her to the stairs. Martise never looked at him.

Left alone in the kitchen and feeling lower than a maggot, he fled to the grove and vented his frustration on the wasp nests sheltered in the trees, freezing or burning them with spells that made his head ache when he finished.

When dinner was called, he sat at the table and stared at the culinary horror on his plate. Only his meal was a disaster, a nearly inedible concoction of pork burned to a slab of black coal and watery grain mush with all the taste of a stick of furniture. Gurn sat as far from him on the bench as he could without falling off the edge and glared at him as if he was an insect he'd like to smash under his shoe and smear across the floor for good measure. Martise refused to look up from her plate. She ate methodically, asked their guest about her trip to Neith and then fell silent.

Only the *houri*, who'd introduced herself as Anya, didn't treat Silhara as a pariah. She smiled, complimented him on Neith's ancient beauty, the comforts of her room and the solicitousness of his servants.

Silhara shoved the mess around on his plate with his knife before finally giving up. He stood and met Anya's gaze. "When you're finished, go to your room. I'll meet you there."

Back in his chamber, he prepared the *huqqah* and smoked the bowl down to its dregs. Martise. The smiling woman who'd emerged from a cocoon of cautious passivity to laugh and joke with him, touch his arm and offer the fire of her kiss was gone. In her place, a shard of ice had sat across from him and eaten her dinner as if the world beyond her plate had ceased to exist. She hadn't raised her eyes long enough to see the pity in Gurn's gaze, but he had, and his chest tightened.

"You are Conclave," he muttered around a ribbon of smoke. "You serve the will of the priests. I am your mentor. You are my apprentice. Nothing more." If he said it enough, he might begin to believe it.

He shed his clothes, bathed and changed into a loose tunic. Barefoot, he made his way to the guest chamber Martise prepared. The *houri* smiled when she saw him. Draped in her transparent silks, she reclined on the bed in a pose contrived to show her considerable charms to their best advantage. She rose, her hips swaying seductively as she came up against him and draped her slender arms over his shoulders.

"What would you have of me? I am yours tonight."

She was soft and supple in his arms. Despite his disquiet and the resounding disapproval of his actions from the rest of his small household, desire rose within him. He embraced her, running his hands down her back to cup her rounded buttocks.

The unexpected scent of kohl and vermillion struck his nostrils. He'd expected orange flower and soap. He paused. Anya's long hair brushed his hands, and he imagined it russet instead of black. She stirred in his embrace, bumping his groin gently, widening her stance so that his cock nestled against the silk covering her cunnus. A low moan hung trapped in his throat when her small hand slid between them to cup him. Nimble fingers played over his erection, his bollocks, caressing him through the long tunic.

He nuzzled her neck, trailing kisses down the side of her jaw. Her bottom filled his hands, rounded and firm. She was lush curves, soft breasts and skilled hands. Still, a chill thread ran through him—a detachment, as if his mind acted independent of his body and watched their play with amused boredom. His cock wanted her. His mind did not.

Frustrated, seeking the fire that licked at his limbs when he held another in his arms, Silhara pulled away. An idea came to him, one that might have the *houri* looking strangely at him. No matter. She was paid to please him, whatever his pleasure.

The cracked mirror leaning against the opposite wall was enormous, a luxury bought by a previous master of Neith generations earlier. Despite the damage, it was still an impressive piece and reflected the candlelight in its clear face. He ignored Anya's puzzled expression and turned her to face the mirror.

They made a striking pair, both dark-haired and flushed by the heat of their embrace. He loomed behind her, tall and austere. By contrast, she was small and sensually beautiful. She reminded him of the fragrant flowers blooming at the coast in shades of pink, orange and brilliant magenta. That puzzled look changed to one of trepidation when Silhara gestured and the air rippled around her.

He placed his hands on her shoulders. "I mean you no harm. This is only temporary. Watch."

His hand passed over her face, leaving a silver aura in its wake. The aura shimmered around her, transforming, lightening Anya's hair to russet, altering her features until her beauty was gone, and she looked oddly out of place in her colorful silks. The *houri* touched her face. Her eyes, now copper instead of emerald, widened in panic. She whimpered.

Silhara caressed her hair. "Peace, woman. This is nothing more than a mask. An illusion. It will fade in a few hours or sooner if I break the spell."

Her shoulders sagged in relief, and her changed eyes closed for a moment. When she opened them and smiled, all his pent-up hunger broke free. She was Martise. Silhara slid his arms around her slim waist and brought her back against him. His hands splayed dark over her jeweled bodice, and he itched to rip the contraption off her.

Anya's eyes met his in the mirror. "She doesn't know, does she? That you desire her? Want her above all others."

She faced him, and he put a finger to her lips. "Shhh. Don't speak. There are things of beauty even my magic cannot recreate."

She arched in his arms, sinuous and graceful while he removed her silks and allowed her to peel off his tunic. Her hands were practiced at touching just the right places, in just the right ways to bring the greatest pleasure. He stroked her breasts, her buttock, and slid his fingers over the smooth curve of her shaved cunnus. He didn't kiss her mouth, nor she his. He knew the way of hourin. They might use their mouths in ways that defied or horrified the imagination, but they never kissed the men—or women—they serviced on the mouth.

He guided her to the bed and lay down. She rose above him, bent and plied tongue and hands to his body, stroking and licking. For several minutes he bore her touch and watched her long brown hair flow over his belly and thighs as she kissed a path to his cock. That first burn of desire, when he'd transformed her features, had guttered. He was a fair illusionist, but it wasn't enough. The *houri* might wear Martise's face for a brief time, but she wasn't Martise. She smelled different, felt different, moved different. Even staying silent didn't help, and the fantasy he tried to play out in this room crumbled.

Silhara drew up his knees and gently pushed Anya's head away from his softening erection. "Enough," he said and drew her up so that she lay against his side. "I am undone."

Frustration, lust, need; they all ran high in his blood, but not for the woman sharing the bed with him. He stared at the ceiling, wondering if Gurn had locked away his already decimated bottle of Peleta's Fire. If he couldn't find surcease in a prostitute's willing body, he'd find it in the oblivion of another bout of drunkenness.

He glanced at Anya when she rose on one elbow and hovered over him. The longer he gazed, the less she looked like Martise, and the spell was still firmly in place. Her eyes were sympathetic, but the soul behind them was not Martise's.

"May I speak?"

He nodded.

She took his hand, pressed his palm against her cheek. "She is more than this face. You crave what no sorcery nor *hourin* trick can create. Your illusions and my skills are for naught. I'm not the woman you want."

Her words brought home the depth of his yearning. He closed his eyes, fighting down sheer terror. She kissed his hand. He opened his eyes and laid a finger across her perfect lips.

"If you say anything, I'll cut out your tongue." His words lacked any bite, though he meant every word of his threat. Martise had unmanned him before a houri, and she wasn't even here. He'd be damned and Anya dead before he let such humiliation become fuel for snickering gossip at the marketplaces.

Anya's eyebrows arched in amusement. "I wouldn't be the *Houri Prime* at the Temple if I told tales of the bedchamber."

If the fiasco of his thwarted desire hadn't already killed his erection, her statement regarding her status would have done so. Silhara groaned in agony.

"Ah gods, how much did you cost me?"

She told him, and he groaned louder. Rising, he dressed, revoked the illusion and instructed her to dress as well. She waited for him at the door while he snuffed candles and doused one of the lanterns. He took the remaining lit one and guided her into the corridor and down the stairs to the first floor. Standing before the closed door of the chamber off the side of the kitchen, he rapped sharply and waited. The door opened. Gurn, wide-eyed, naked and holding a cudgel in one hand, greeted them.

Silhara smirked. "Well, aren't you a sight? And here I thought it was me and my reputation that chased visitors away from Neith." He didn't give Gurn time to digest his sudden appearance at his door. Instead he pulled Anya in front of him and nudged her across the threshold.

Gurn's eyes went round and wide as dinner plates. Anya whistled, her admiring gaze noting all his endowments.

Silhara hid his amusement behind a frown. "You best enjoy her. She's your dinner for the next two months." His eyes narrowed. "And if you ever serve me slop like you served tonight, I'll hang your carcass from the biggest orange tree and let the crows strip you to the bone."

He strode back toward the kitchen, smiling faintly. At least one of them would enjoy so costly a gift. The smile died. *He* intended to spend a lonely night in his room, burning a bowl of tobacco and cursing the apprentice who'd brought him low before a prostitute.

He looked up, into the blackness of the third floor stairwell and wondered if she slept. Shadows clotted behind him, trailed his feet as he continued up the stairs and down the hall to his room.

CHAPTER FOURTEEN

Martise tucked a stray strand of hair into her braid and braced herself for breakfast downstairs. She hoped her swollen eyes wouldn't attract attention. Then again, she expected to find only Gurn and Cael joining her in the kitchen this morning. The master of the house was otherwise occupied.

Outside, the sky was gray and the air heavy with the scent of rain. Any other day, she'd rejoice over the coming storm. Neith and the surrounding farms and orchards were parched, desperate for a deluge. But today the weather reflected her mood, and she closed the shutters against the gloomy sky.

Her stomach knotted, and her chest ached. "He's nothing more than a path to freedom," she muttered. A repeat of the words she'd chanted to herself the previous night while she lay in her bed and wept quiet tears. She'd been lulled into believing the Master of Crows didn't quite deserve his reputation. She was wrong. His subtle cruelty was breathtaking, reminding her of Cumbria's warning when they'd first arrived at Neith.

"He possesses a sharp tongue and has eviscerated more than one hapless opponent in a conversation. You'd be no match."

The bishop was right after a fashion. Silhara had wielded the knife that gutted her, but he'd never said a word. Even Balian's crass insults paled in comparison to the mage's silent contempt.

He'd kissed her as if starved for her. Not a gentle kiss that coaxed and questioned but one that possessed and demanded reciprocal passion. She'd given it to him gladly, arched into his lean body, spread her thighs to feel the weight of him against her. She'd fit into every angular space, as if the gods had made her specifically for him. He tasted of sweet wine and smelled of summer oranges. All her senses drowned in the heat of his closeness and the feel of his callused hands on her.

At first Martise blamed it on the power of her Gift and the strange, intense connection Silhara drew from it. He believed as she did, instructing her to rein in her overly enthusiastic talent. She'd changed her mind when they tried to heal his hand. Her Gift's connection was broken, its power bound by her growing control, and still Silhara's black eyes burned as he rested his bloody palm against her chest. His fingers twitched, drifting down a fraction as if to cup her breast.

Martise, hardly daring to believe the Master of Crows might find her desirable without the blessing of her Gift, held her breath and waited. He'd fled.

She was torn between admonishing herself for not seizing the moment and pathetically grateful she hadn't. Silhara of Neith might have been moved to feel some fleeting desire for her. But he'd rejected her in the end—and driven home his point in the most devastating way. He'd rather pay for the pleasures of a woman endowed with a striking beauty than take what Martise freely offered.

Or he might not have thought of her at all.

That brought her up short. Silhara was more than capable of doling out enigmatic insults and sly innuendo, silent or otherwise.

But in her experience he usually preferred a more straightforward approach. If he didn't want her because he found her lacking, wouldn't he have simply told her? And in terms that left no room for doubt or question? Had he sent for the *houri* because he wanted a woman and saw Martise as nothing more than an additional pair of hands to labor in his grove?

Anger incinerated her melancholy. She didn't know which infuriated her more—the idea that he rejected her because she didn't meet his standards, or the notion she was no more notable than a bench or a chair and therefore never considered in his decision.

She growled, straightened her skirts with a snap and raised her chin. He wasn't worth her tears and certainly not her affections. His actions reminded her why she was at Neith in the first place, and it wasn't to become his lover.

She strode into the kitchen, indifferent to the aroma of frying ham and buttered eggs, and stopped.

Gurn, bearing the unmistakable look of a man very content with the world, sat at the table with the *houri* next to him. His big hand caressed invisible spirals over Anya's back, sometimes pausing to play with her thick hair as it cascaded over his fingers. She was as exquisite in the harsher morning light as she was in evening's candle glow. She smiled and ran her hand over Gurn's ribs and abdomen, sliding lower. Caught up in each other, neither noted another presence.

Martise, stunned by what she witnessed, cleared her throat. The two jumped apart like adolescents caught in a hallway alcove. Gurn reddened when he saw Martise, but Anya only grinned and waved her to the table.

"Martise! Good morning. Come sit with me. Gurn is good with his hands, but I still can't understand him." She winked and laughed when he blushed even more at her innuendo and rose to lift a pan of sizzling bacon from the fire.

Despite her dark mood, Martise smiled. The *houri* was a friendly, lighthearted spirit, her only artifice the crimson paint on her lips and the kohl under her eyes. While the image of Silhara naked in this woman's arms made her stomach churn with jealousy, Martise couldn't dislike her. She was paid to provide a service. Emotion didn't enter into the transaction. But beyond that, Anya seemed a kind woman, one who'd smiled gently and bowed in respect as if Martise were the mistress of the house instead of another servant.

So why would the *houri*, paid to spend the evening with Silhara, be in the kitchen groping Gurn?

Anya patted the spot Gurn vacated in invitation.

Martise nodded. "Let me help Gurn first."

Gurn handed her a cup and waved her away. She took his seat while Anya poured tea and refilled her own cup. She looked to where the servant crouched by the hearth, filling plates with his fragrant cooking.

"I think I might visit Neith again, of my own accord. If the smell from those plates is anything to judge by, Gurn is as good a cook as he is a lover. I think maybe I should pay him for such a fine evening."

Confounded by the confirmation that Anya had spent the night with Gurn instead of Silhara, Martise stared at her owl-eyed. "But I thought Sil...the master brought you to pleasure him."

Anya's eyes were measuring as she gazed at Martise over the rim of her cup. "So it would seem. But sometimes this," she waved a hand down her face and over her bodice, "isn't enough, or even what's truly wanted."

Considering the houri's breathtaking appearance, Martise found that unlikely, but a thwapping noise at the door leading to the bailey stopped her from asking Anya more. Gurn placed their plates on the table. He opened the door, and Cael sauntered in. The mage-finder ignored Anya and crawled under the table to find his customary place beneath Martise's feet. Gurn peered outside, shaking his head. He signed to Martise.

"Oh no."

Anya stared at Gurn, then at her. "What's wrong? What did he say?"

"The clouds are starting to clear and move off. If it rains, it won't be here."

A bellowed "No!" made all three people and the mage-finder jump.

Martise and Anya abandoned their seats to chase Gurn as he raced into the great hall. A rapid thudding sounded on the ceiling above them. Silhara, dressed only in trousers and looking wild-eyed and enraged, tore down the stairs. He cleared the last few steps, swinging over the railing and landing nimbly on his feet. He sprinted down the hall leading to the grove. The small entourage followed after him with Cael leading the way.

Outside, Silhara skidded to a stop. Above him the storm clouds were slowly rolling back, thinning in spots to reveal a wide and merciless blue sky. Martise stood with Gurn and Anya nearby. She glanced at Cael. The mage-finder's eyes glowed red.

Silhara raised his fist to the sky. "You are mine!"

He searched the ground, kicking twigs out of the way until he found a long sturdy stick.

"What is he doing?" Anya's tremulous voice echoed the unease in her wide eyes as she sought Martise's gaze.

Martise didn't answer, only watched Silhara as he drew a wide circle around him with the stick. A barrier ward. The mage meant to call down dangerous magic, the kind that could strike down its summoner. The man played with his own life as carelessly as children played with toys.

"Gurn, we need to move back to the house."

Alerted by her tone, the servant ushered both women to stand in the shelter of the doorway's overhang.

A subtle wind swirled from the clouds, lifting Silhara's hair until it wrapped around his body and obscured his face in snaking black tendrils. Standing in the circle's center, he raised his arms, palms curved upward in a summoner's position. The barrier circle lit around him in a ring of white fire. Martise sucked in a hard breath, her Gift awakening within her.

Obsidian clouds, swollen with rain and fractured by lightning, boiled in the east. The wind strengthened and bore down on the grove in a shrieking tempest. Orange trees bowed in its wake, supplicants before an ill-tempered god.

"What is he doing?" Anya's words were snatched away in the rising maelstrom. She huddled behind Gurn, kohl-lined eyes round and frightened. Cael howled, snapping at Martise's braid as it whipped over her shoulder.

Martise clutched Anya's arm, as much to stay upright as to reassure. "He's summoning the storm!" Her shouted reply was no more than a whisper in the wind's wail. "It will kill him, Gurn!"

He clutched her elbow in an unyielding grip. Martise didn't fight him. Despite her words, she knew it to be a useless endeavor to try and stop Silhara. Interrupting him in mid-summons was as dangerous as his attempts to force the storm in their direction.

Her stomach churned. He was powerful. She'd witnessed the strength of his Gift and the iron will he used to control it, but only god-like power could harness the force and unpredictability of weather. The few great mages who'd successfully bent Nature to their will for a brief time were legendary, and all save one had suffered gruesome deaths in the event.

"Please," she whispered, and prayed to whatever god might listen that she and Gurn wouldn't have to bury Silhara's obliterated remains in the grove he risked his life to save.

Dust blew upwards in a gritty fog, shrouding the grove and all of Neith. Martise almost lost sight of Silhara amidst the choking cloud. His lips moved, reciting ancient words unheard but felt in the earth anchoring him in place. The ground rumbled, echoing the thunder, and the wind smelled sharp with the scent of the coming deluge.

He clapped his hands together. Indigo light shot out of the spaces between his fingers and arced skyward. Martise gasped and covered her ears as the air around her compressed with a sudden punishing silence. Like her, Gurn and Anya held their hands over their ears, and the *houri* screamed. The light hurtled toward the storm line, clasped the thunderhead in a splintered embrace and wrenched it toward the grove. Clouds collapsed in on themselves, struggling against the relentless pull of Silhara's summoning spell.

Forking ever closer to the grove, lightning struck the ground in white and crimson spears. Grass, parched by the long drought, burst into flame in their path. An orange tree split beneath a lightning bolt, erupting into a column of fire.

Thunder cracked above them as the clouds began to rotate, spinning ever closer to Neith until they hung over the house and grove like a widow's veil, with the wind keening a protest over Silhara's dominance. A burst of sheet lightning shot across the underbelly of the storm and the sky opened.

The grove, bent to the wind, was instantly doused in gray sheets of rain. Parched and cracked from months of baking in the merciless sun, the thirsty ground ran rivers of water. Indigo light slowly faded into the dark clouds, a last remnant of the summoning spell. Martise watched, her heart in her throat, as Silhara lowered his arms. Rain streamed off his bare chest and shoulders as he crashed to his knees in the mud, head hanging low.

"He did it." Anya's voice was faint.

Martise bolted into the downpour with Gurn and Cael hot on her heels. Gurn overtook her and reached Silhara first. The servant placed a tentative hand on the mage's shoulder and squeezed. Silhara raised his head, and Martise took a shuddering breath. She prayed the falling rain hid her tears as she stood in front of him and met his black gaze. His face was drawn, glistening with rain. He smelled of brimstone, and his hair stuck to his cheeks and neck in wet strands, but his expression was almost blissful.

Martise wanted to scream at him, shout that he was an idiot, and a stand of trees wasn't worth his life, that she loved him and didn't want to grieve for a man who'd stolen her most guarded possession—her heart.

Instead, she held out her hand. "Will you come in from the rain, Master?" Her voice was soft, almost lost in the rain's drumming. "There is tea this morning, a warm fire in the kitchen's hearth, and those who celebrate and thank Bursin you live." Gurn's hand flexed on his master's shoulder at her words, and Cael whined.

Silhara stared at her hand for a moment before wrapping cold fingers around hers. He clambered to his feet. Gurn hovered close until the mage waved him back. "And you, apprentice? What do you thank the winged god for?"

For a moment his eyes bore the storm's lightning. He looked to Anya who still hovered beneath the door's canopy, then back at Martise.

She hesitated, unsure of his question. Did he not think she was as relieved as Gurn that he wasn't some smoking husk torched by the lightning? Or had he sensed her burgeoning hope that it was Gurn, instead of him, whom Anya pleasured the night before?

She sidestepped his unspoken question. "You are well and whole, and your grove has water."

His mouth curved in a humorless smile at her answer. They walked side by side back to the house, led by Gurn and Cael. Silhara paused once to look back at the now charred ruin of the burnt tree.

Anya stepped away from the threshold to allow them room. She stared at Silhara in wonder. "I've heard the tales. You're known as one of the greatest mages ever born. But this?" She shook her head. "A summoner of lightning?" She bowed low, as subject to a king.

Silhara wiped his wet hair from his face and made her straighten. "You make too much of it, *adané*. It's like coaxing a woman, nothing more."

Martise disagreed, trying not to stare at him with the same awe-struck expression as the *houri*. Twice he'd invoked powerful spells known to kill their users and survived both times. Despite his drenched clothing and mud-caked knees, he was majestic standing before them. The residual power of his Gift, mixed with the fury of the storm, shimmered around him, casting him in pale radiance. Even Gurn watched him with an almost reverent expression.

Silhara glowered at their dumbstruck silence. "Well? Get out of the way. I want out of these wet breeches. And my apprentice has promised me tea."

A clumsy scuffle in the narrow hallway, with Anya trying to avoid being smashed between wet people and wet dog, and they dispersed. Gurn made his way to the kitchen with Anya and Cael close behind him. Silhara followed Martise to the stairwell. She paused, waiting for him to overtake her so she could follow him. He waved her on with an impatient hand, dripping puddles of water and looking more irritated by the moment.

Martise climbed the stairs, her shoes making squishing noise on each tread. Her back prickled. Silhara climbed close behind her, close enough she smelled magic on him, along with the lingering scent of brimstone mixed with tobacco.

At the second floor landing, she widened the space between them, climbing the stairs to the third floor. His voice halted her in midstep.

"Martise." His eyes shone in the gloom. She caught her breath at the tone in his voice. "Dry your hair by the kitchen fire."

They stared at each other, and Martise sank into a midnight gaze with no stars, pulled in by the seductive power of his presence. She nodded. "As you wish." Her own voice was hoarse. She continued up the stairs, his gaze heavy on her back as she climbed.

Her fingers trembled as she peeled off her drenched clothes and dropped them into a sodden heap at the foot of her bed. He'd devoured her in that look on the stairs, his black eyes smoldering. Had Gurn been the only one to benefit from Anya's skills? Unlike his servant, Silhara almost thrummed with a frustrated tension and wore the look of a man who hadn't slept for days.

"Dry your hair by the kitchen fire."

She worked fast to loosen the wet locks of hair from her tight braid. That had not been a request. Had he asked her to shed her clothes on the stairs, she wouldn't have hesitated.

The kitchen was almost crowded when she returned, dressed and with her hair loose and damp on her shoulders. Hunched on the bench, with his elbows on the table, Silhara sipped tea and packed tobacco into the bowl of his pipe with meticulous care. He glanced at her, noted her hair and returned to his task. He'd dressed in his usual finery of worn white shirt and gray trews that had once been black. Gurn, dried and changed, puttered around the kitchen, building the fire in the hearth and clearing away their cold breakfast. Anya leaned against the door frame and watched the rain drench the bailey in a steady sheet of gray.

Martise stood by the fire and shook her head when Gurn motioned he'd reheat her meal. Her stomach was doing somersaults beneath her ribs. Food was the last thing she wanted.

Silhara turned his attention to the *houri*. "Anya, is it?"

"Yes."

He rose and came to stand next to Martise. He bent to the fire, set a piece of straw to the flame and used it to light his pipe. The crackle of burning tobacco joined with the sounds in the hearth as he drew on the pipe. The spicy aroma of matal filled the kitchen.

"This rain may last through the day. I can't afford you another night. So either Gurn loads you onto my horse and takes you back to Eastern Prime in the downpour, or you stay and consider this night nothing more than a 'friendly visit.'"

His eyebrows lowered, features severe. Unruffled by his frown, Anya gave him a friendly smile and Gurn a more seductive one.

"I'll stay. My house would consider it a favor if you sheltered me in this weather. She grinned at Gurn, who blushed. "I'd like your servant to teach me more of the language of his hands."

Martise suppressed a smile and met Silhara's amused glance.

"He's a man of many talents and speaks eloquently when he's of a mind."

Dishes rattled in the dry sink as Gurn turned away to hide his embarrassment.

Humor softened the hard look in Silhara's eyes and deepened the creases that cut from his nose to the corners of his mouth.

"Leave the dishes, Gurn," he said. "You can deal with them later."

Gurn paused in rattling the dishes, his blue eyes hopeful. Silhara looked meaningfully at Anya. "I suggest you make good use of the weather and Anya's company."

The kitchen grew quiet when they left, the only sounds Cael's snoring beneath the table, the popping fire in the hearth, and the steady drum of rain outside. Martise hazarded a glance at Silhara from beneath her lashes. He watched her, his expression enigmatic behind the haze of pipe smoke.

She cleared her throat. "You're good to Gurn. Anya is very beautiful. And kind."

He inclined his head. "And expensive. Gurn may starve for her, as will I, but I owe my servant something."

She remembered Anya's remark about Silhara's generosity. Hope warred with reproach. He was forbidden to her, a deadly distraction from her purpose at Neith and her ultimate goal. The heart didn't always obey, and she couldn't help but hope he'd not found succor between Anya's thighs the previous night.

Pipe smoke teased her nostrils as she stared at the comb in her hand and flipped it nervously in her palm. "I thought he brought her for you."

"He did." His eyes held a thousand dark secrets. "Your hair's still wet."

Understanding he would say no more about Anya, she raised her comb to show she'd complied with his command and sat down cross-legged by the fire to comb out her hair. Outside, the rain fell, and the air in the kitchen cooled.

The light enveloping him when he first walked into the house had faded. The man dressed in shabby clothes and smoking a pipe might be any poor farmer taking a rare day to rest and wait out the weather's moods, except this farmer wielded uncommon power and frightened the suspicious priests who sought to bring him under their control—or kill him if necessary.

"You will be legendary after this. Anya will return to Eastern Prime and tell everyone who'll listen what she saw here. The word will spread and grow."

Silhara's disgusted sigh joined the kitchen's comforting sounds. "Oh yes. From wrestling a storm to earth, I will be portrayed as battling a celestial army single-handedly to save some rust-covered treasure I couldn't sell at market if I wanted." His mocking smile wasn't directed at her for once. "Saving lost treasure from greedy gods is so much more interesting than saving orange trees from a drought."

He bent to empty the ashes from the pipe bowl into the hearth. His damp hair spilled in black tangles across her knees. Her fingers itched to touch the strands mingling with hers.

"It could be worse," he said. "I could have brought her to Neith in the fall during hog slaughtering. If you were still here, I'd enlist your help. We'd send Gurn's beautiful *houri* home with tales of me reveling in some blood ritual that involved sacrificing a sow and tupping my concubine-apprentice."

Martise laughed, euphoria singing through her. He'd called Anya Gurn's *houri*. Cheered by that revelation, she couldn't resist teasing him. "Likely, they'd have you sacrificing the concubine and tupping the sow."

His laughter echoed hers, a throaty, seductive sound. He returned to the table and raised his tea cup to her in appreciation of her wit. "You know them well." He sat, straddling the bench so that he partially faced her.

She finished combing out her hair, splitting the locks into three thick skeins so she could bind them into her customary braid. She paused at his command.

"Don't." His ruined voice was huskier than usual, and he stared at her with the same hungry look he'd had on the stairs. "Leave it unbound."

She dropped her hands. Her hair pooled in her lap in waves. She offered him the comb. "Would you like to use this?"

He looked at the comb, then at her. "You do it for me." His unspoken challenge hung between them. *If you dare.*

If he only knew he offered her one of her greatest desires—to touch him, feel that silky swath of hair beneath her palms. She left her place by the fire to sit on the bench behind him. Parting the tangles gently, she combed through the worst of the knots, careful not to pull too hard. He sat quietly beneath her ministrations, reminding her of a sleeping lion basking in the sun.

Once his hair was smooth and free of mats, Martise ran the comb through it for sheer pleasure. He had beautiful hair, straight and black and falling to his waist. It spread across a strong back and wide shoulders, dampening his shirt to a transparent thinness. She slid her hand under its weight and caressed his nape with light strokes of the comb.

His shoulders slumped, and he lowered his head in mute invitation for her to continue. He breathed deep, relaxing under her touch. Martise was anything but relaxed. She was on fire, recalling those moments in the library when he'd given her a taste of the passion burning within him. He was her dreams manifested, a bright and volatile star in a winter sky.

The silence in the kitchen was the calm before another storm. Even Cael no longer snored beneath the table. She lay the comb on the table and rose from the bench. Silhara didn't move, and she thought he might have fallen asleep sitting up. She reached for the teapot and caught the heavy-lidded stare he gave her.

"I'll get you more tea," she said.

She almost dropped the teapot when his hand shot out and trapped her wrist. "Say my name."

She stared at the slender fingers shackling her wrist. "Master?"

"No. Not the address of servant to master. *My name*." Dark heat laced his ruined voice.

Desire coursed through her. Bursin's wings, she wanted this man. They were connected only by the clasp of his hand, yet it seemed as if all her emotions—her passion—centered in her narrow wrist, fanning out in ever widening circles until they encompassed her entire body. He was the storm. As lethal as the lightning and just as unpredictable. She stood before him utterly enthralled.

Not once had she said his name, neither to him nor Gurn. Not even to herself. Addressing him as Master was the last barrier she'd erected between them—the only one still standing, and he commanded her to lower it. She didn't hesitate and infused her voice with all the strength of her desire.

"Silhara."

He clamped down harder on her wrist. His eyes slid shut, and for the first time she noted how thick his lashes were against his cheeks.

"I gave her your face." He spoke the words through tight lips, as if the admission pained him.

The empty teapot clattered on the table. She gaped at him. "What?"

His grip tightened, loosening just as suddenly at her pained gasp. "Gurn brought me a woman I didn't want. For a moment I changed her, gave her the face of my desire." His eyes opened, revealing his need. "It wasn't enough."

Her knees buckled. She collapsed on the bench next to him, stunned. "Master..." She shook her head. "Silhara..."

"Lie with me."

The silence stretched, relieved only by the drumming harmony of the rain outside. Silhara gripped his teacup with his other hand so hard, his knuckles turned white. The basking lion had awakened and watched her as if she were prey in the tall grass.

There were cliffs with chasms so deep and wide, a person could fall for eternity. Martise blithely stepped off the tallest one. "Yes," she said.

He breathed in audibly, a sound of triumph. His brown fingers slid off her wrist, swept across the back of her hand to interlace with her paler ones. He pulled her up with him so that she stood within the circle of his loose embrace.

Cael whuffed softly at them as they left the kitchen. Silhara stroked her palm with his thumb as he led her up the stairs to the second floor. Gentle and reassuring, it did nothing to calm the flutters dancing madly in her belly, like panicked birds trapped in too-small cages.

The flutters turned to nausea as she followed him down the second floor corridor. *"Please,"* she prayed silently. *"Not Anya's room."* He could take her in the kitchen, the library, even the muddied grove under the bleak sky, and she would welcome him eagerly. But not there.

She almost walked into his back when he halted outside his chambers. She swallowed hard. His bedchamber. A bastion of privacy that welcomed no one save Gurn, and then only to clean and bring water or dinner. The servant had given her free run of the manor, with the exception of the master's private room. That was forbidden, and Gurn would punish her himself if she broke that rule. His blue eyes had been icy when he'd laid down the stricture. It was the only time Martise ever feared the servant, and she'd yet to test that boundary despite her mission.

Like her unbending formality in addressing him, this was Silhara's barrier against her.

It fell when he opened the door.

Cool and damp from the air that seeped in through the gaps in the window frame, the chamber smelled of rain and spice, of old silk and the arousing scent unique to Neith's master. Standing at the threshold, she saw nothing in the chamber's gloom beyond the vague outlines of a bed and table.

"Come in, Martise." Silhara's voice was almost sibilant in the darkness as he tugged on her hand. "There are no soul eaters here."

No, she thought. Only heart thieves.

She let him guide her into the room. The floor was cushioned beneath her feet, and her shoe scraped over the pile of a rug. Silhara released her hand and murmured a spell. The coals in a brazier set in a far corner lit with a hiss. Their fire brightened, illuminating the room in a warm amber glow. The soft light revealed a sanctuary of worn splendor and scholarly clutter. Rugs, frayed at the ends and worn to the fibers in patches, covered the floor and draped the stone walls, their once-bright colors faded by sun and time, their threads chewed by moths. Haphazardly furnished, the room sported a table and chair piled high with scrolls and grimoires. A large chest and the brazier stood on one side of the room, along with a magnificent, ornately decorated water pipe. Near the balcony entrance, a large rumpled bed and a wash stand with basin and pitcher took up most of the space.

The door closed behind her with a decisive click. Silhara's eyes reflected pinpoints of firelight as he faced her. His calloused palms stroked her arms. "The door is neither locked nor warded."

He'd been forthright in his need for her. No flowery words or gentle coaxing. He'd seduced her with his bluntness and now with his reassurance he wouldn't stop her if she chose to leave. It was wholly symbolic. He could force her to stay with little effort, even with the door wide open.

Martise swept a finger across his lips, their tantalizing softness a temptation to capture them in a kiss. There was time enough for that and more. She wanted to savor these moments, this intimacy with the man reviled by Conclave and loved by their spy.

His tongue flicked out, tasted her fingertips. He stood still beneath her questing touch, his only reaction to her wandering hands a tightening of his grip on her arms. She caressed his jaw and neck, exploring the shallow dip between his shoulder and clavicle before moving over the broad planes of his chest. His small nipples made points beneath his shirt when she rubbed her thumbs over their sensitive tips.

He was sublime under her hands, a study in wiry strength and smooth skin, smoky heat and virility. She scrutinized his hard face, made more austere by the play of shadows along his jaw and aquiline nose.

"I don't mind if you make it darker." She found it difficult to meet his gaze. He wasn't Balian. Silhara of Neith had more character in his little finger than Balian did in his entire body, but she offered the suggestion just the same. He'd chosen her over a *houri* blessed with an uncommon beauty, yet she wanted to be sure he understood that even in the softer, more flattering light emitted by the brazier's hot coals, she was still plain, unassuming Martise.

He stared down his nose at her in a way that made her blush. "You have a clever way of insulting me, Martise."

She drew in a sharp breath. "No, that isn't my intention. I only…"

He placed a finger over her lips. She held her breath when he clasped one of her hands, slid it down his chest and over his taut stomach before curving her fingers over the bulge in his trews. They both moaned when she rubbed her palm gently over his hard shaft and stroked his bollocks with her fingers. He was hot in her hands, a tempting combination of hard and soft.

"I know what I see," he breathed into her ear and thrust against her palm. "Know what I hold. This is what you do to me."

She would have fallen had he not held her up with an arm wrapped around her back. She sought his mouth, touched her lips to his. He opened to her seeking tongue, allowing her to delve inside and stroke his mouth. His tongue twined with hers, giving back as much as he took. He tasted better than summer wine, better than the first harvest fruits of spring.

The kiss deepened, a mating of tongues that mimicked the slow thrust of his hips. His hands wandered over her body, sliding down her back, cupping her buttocks. They left trails of fire in their wake, and Martise moaned in his mouth.

His fingers worked the ties of her tunic, tugging until he grew frustrated and pulled away from her. In the half-light, his sharp cheekbones were flushed, and his mouth swollen from her kiss. "I've a mind to see all of you, Martise, and not much patience to wait. How badly do you want to save this garb?"

If she wasn't down to this and her newly sewn skirt and tunic, she'd help him rip it off her. Instead, she smiled and blushed and unlaced ties with impressive speed. The skirt fell to the floor. Her shoes skidded to a corner, and Silhara helped her pull the tunic over her head. She was left standing covered only by her unbound hair and warm fire glow.

She didn't think it possible, but his eyes darkened even more. He lifted a lock of her hair and brushed it over her shoulder, revealing her breast and the gentle curve of her waist. He said nothing, but his gaze, black and smoldering as it traveled from the top of her head to her toes, spoke volumes. She glanced at the front of his trousers, saw the curve of his erection pressed hard against the fabric.

In a show of courage, she swept the rest of her hair back, giving him full view of her. She raised her hands, palms up. "Sorry," she teased. "No third breast."

He blinked, then laughed at her reminder of their encounter in the stillroom. She grinned, pleased she'd once again made him laugh outright, even now in this moment of intense intimacy. His laughter changed to a seductive smile. Martise caught her breath when he closed the small gap between them. His fingers traced a path over her collarbones, lingered at the hollow of her throat before sketching a line between her breasts. Her nipples drew tight in anticipation of his touch.

"I'm more impressed with quality than quantity." At that, even his smile faded. He circled the outline of each breast with his fingers, finally cupping them in his hands. She arched into his warm palms. "You are beautiful beyond measure," he whispered against her mouth.

This kiss was unlike the one they just shared. Fiercer, harder, it demanded she yield to his desire, slake the need coursing through him. He caressed her breasts, sliding the rough pads of his thumbs across her nipples over and over, until she writhed in his arms and moaned into his mouth. He delved into her mouth, sucking on her tongue. His hands left her breasts, tracked the curve of her waist and slid over her hips to pull her hard against him. She whimpered as his cock rocked against her cunnus. A wave of heat spiraled out from the center of her body. She wanted him inside her, needed him naked against her.

Her hands clawed at his shirt as she kissed him. They broke apart, panting. "How badly do you want to save this shirt?" she asked.

Silhara grinned and whipped the shirt over his head, again treating her to the sight of his chest and stomach. The breeches followed, and he stood before her, burnished in gold and amber.

He was sleek and taut, darkened by the sun and muscled by the demands of the grove. The proof of his desire for her rose from the nest of dark curls between his legs.

"Like what you see?"

"Oh yes," she sighed and fell into a feverish sea when he crushed her against him, skin against skin.

He played havoc with her senses and her body. Hands and tongue, the silky brush of his hair against her nipples, a long finger sliding deep into her wet cunnus, the low, harsh groans emanating from his throat. His cock pressed along the inside of her thigh, and she parted her legs, eager to bring him close.

"The bed," she whispered between hard kisses.

"Is too far away." He bent, sucked a nipple in his mouth and drove her to madness with the play of his tongue across its tip.

Her knees gave way a second time, and this time he followed her down to the rug, stroking and learning her contours with his tongue until she stretched out beneath him. Despite the cool, rain-laden air in the room, she was sweltering. Sweat trickled between her breasts, and he licked it away before plying his mouth to each breast.

She groaned, so aroused by his seductive touch, she squirmed across the carpet. Silhara held her down, navigating a path across her midriff, pausing to dip his tongue in the shallow pool of her navel. When he reached her thighs, he stopped.

"Open for me, Martise." His tongue swept his lower lip in a lascivious motion. "I crave the taste of you."

Somewhere, in the part of her mind still capable of thought, she wondered if half the countryside could hear her cries and moans. Silhara tortured her with his tongue, his fingers, seeking the heart of her passion, sucking gently on the spot that made her mewl and buck against him.

He only quickened his pace when her back arched off the floor. The heat concentrated between her thighs, under Silhara's stroking mouth, and spread throughout her body. Blood coursed through her veins, hot and bubbling. Her fingers dug into his sweat-slick shoulders, and her legs convulsed. She cried out as sensation burst within her, and she crooned his name.

Shattered by her climax, she could only pant when he suddenly loomed over her, arms braced on either side of her head. Black hair shrouded her in a silken curtain. Silhara's mouth glistened, and his eyes blazed. His voice was guttural, hoarse. "The door is still unlocked."

She stared at him, stunned. Even now, with his lips glistening from her orgasm and his cock thrusting gently against her cunnus, he offered her the chance to stop and douse the fire between them.

She ran her hands over his quivering arms, the sculpted biceps and muscular forearms. One hand spread over his hip while the other wrapped around his cock. It pulsed in her grip. A trickle of his seed wet her fingers, and she circled the tip, coating the smooth head. He inhaled sharply.

"And the bed is still too far away," she said, pulling him down to her. Her legs rose, slid over his hips until her ankles locked at his back and anchored him.

It was all the coaxing he needed. He mounted her, sinking deep on a low moan until his bollocks rested against the curve of her bottom. Martise echoed his sounds, savoring the swell of him within her, the slide and stretching, the flex of inner muscles as she gripped his cock and tightened. He filled her as if he'd been made for her, touching every sensitive spot until she thought she would burn beneath him.

He set a rapid pace, taking her hard enough to scoot her across the rug with his thrusts. Martise held on, hips lifting to bring him deeper. Her teeth clicked against his in a savage kiss, and she tasted blood.

He broke the kiss. "Say my name, Martise."

He snarled the command, but she wasn't afraid. His hips rocked against hers, and she was impaled on his cock, reveling in his fierce possession. For a few brief hours, he was as much hers as she was his, and she could tell him how much he meant to her in a softly spoken name.

Every desire, every craving, every forbidden wish—she infused into her voice. "Silhara."

He gasped, a tortured sound, and his eyes rolled back. Martise clutched him to her as he shuddered, felt the sudden pulse of his shaft, his release followed by a wet heat as he came inside her.

He hunched over her, chest heaving as he strove to breathe. She clasped his hips with her legs to maintain their connection, reluctant to give him up. He slowly lowered his weight onto her, careful not to crush her.

His hair fell in front of his eyes, and she pushed it away with gentle fingers. His eyes were closed, and his breathing slowed to a steady rhythm.

"Is the door still unlocked?" she teased.

He didn't open his eyes, but rolled to his side, bringing her with him. His hand swept over her hip and cupped her buttocks to pull her closer. "Yes. And the bed is definitely too far away."

Martise caressed his arm, delighting in the feel of him pressed against her from shoulder to ankle. They were both slippery with sweat. She chuckled, then winced at the stinging pain blossoming on her lower back. She reached back and touched the spot. "Ouch!"

He eyed her, surprised by her exclamation. "What's wrong?"

She hissed as the stinging grew more intense. "Kurman carpets aren't nearly as soft as they're touted."

He shifted so she rested atop him and levered himself to look over her shoulder. When he lay back, he wore a sheepish smile. "You've an impressive rug burn back there."

Her eyes widened. "Truly? I never felt it happening."

His smile turned smug. "Didn't you?" He swatted her lightly on the bottom, careful to avoid her abrasion. "Lie down on the unreachable bed. I've an unguent that will ease the sting and help it heal."

He slid slowly out of her as she lifted herself off him, leaving behind a pearlescent trickle on her thigh. She knocked her knees together. "The linens. If I rest there now…"

He rose and stared at her with a mix of annoyance and amusement. "Martise, that bed and all its linens will be utterly destroyed by morning."

A pleasurable heat suffused her. He wasn't through with her. She smiled. Good. She wasn't through with him either. Even now, with her thighs wet with his seed and her insides still throbbing, she ached for him. Wanted him inside her, in her mouth, taking and giving.

He padded to the chest by the bed and opened the lid. The slow burn of desire washed her skin as she watched him. Long legs and small, taut buttocks were complimented by a slim waist and wide shoulders. The look he shot her over his shoulder let her know he'd caught her admiring his nude body. "Are you going to stand there all day?"

She shuffled to the bed and stretched out on her stomach. The frame creaked under his weight when he sat down on the edge and placed a small jar on the table holding the basin. Martise rested her head on her folded arms.

"I'm sorry," she said.

He dipped his fingers in the unguent. "More apologies. What for now?"

She giggled at his exasperation and sucked in a breath when the cold salve touched her sore back. The discomfort only lasted a moment, replaced by a warmth that eased the pain as Silhara spread the salve over her abrasion. His hands were magic in more ways than one.

"What are you sorry for?" he asked.

She hid a yawn behind her hand, lulled by the caressing circles he drew on her back. "This sore. I can't lie on my back now."

The circular stroking halted. Silhara snorted. "First, that scrape is my doing, not yours. Second, your Balian, for all his bragging, obviously lacked imagination as well as intelligence when he taught you the pleasures of the flesh." She raised her buttocks automatically when his hand slipped between her thighs and cupped her cunnus. He kissed her shoulder while his fingers teased her. "I don't need you on your back for anything, Martise, unless you want to go star-gazing with me."

CHAPTER FIFTEEN

Silhara positioned the ladder against the bookshelves and cursed as a rain of dust cascaded on his head. He squinted and waved the cloud away from his face. "Martise is right," he muttered. "We're drowning in dust."

He climbed the ladder to the topmost shelf and swiped at the intricately spun spider webs covering the line of grimoires. The library at Neith contained books and scrolls Conclave refused to archive. He and his predecessor had no such reservations. Manuscripts that told of the magery of the Waste were shelved next to books on the proper protocol for sacrificing a victim and calling up a demon.

Today he searched for tomes on the black arcana, forbidden spells and invocations, curses and possessions. Despite Conclave's assumptions and his reputation, he merely dabbled in the darker spells. The curse magic lingering over the oaks at Neith's entrance and the deadly enchantments surrounding the grove's stone enclosure were the only things he'd ever pulled from these dusty books and employed for his use. And they sucked the strength out of him. Dark spells, powerful and effective, demanded a high and constant price.

His fingers traced the spines of the books, skin tingling as he touched the leather-bound pages. The covers were smooth and faded, worn by time and made of hides whose origins he didn't want to guess. Finding the one he wanted, he climbed down the ladder and found a place by the window to read. Somewhere, in those cryptic passages, was the answer to the puzzle of Martise's Gift.

There was nothing dark about her talents. He had never felt more alive or cleansed than when she shared her Gift with him. Nor as powerful. The last had given him his first inkling of where he might find information about the nature of her Gift. Something that strong was coveted and not always by benevolent forces.

Sunlight streamed through the windows, and clouds drifted in a cerulean sky. No hint of the storm he'd called down two days before remained. Even the mud in the shaded bailey was drying. Silhara stared, unseeing, at the books before him, lost in the seductive memories of the hours spent in his bedchamber with Martise while the rain fell.

Bedding her had only increased his hunger for her, and even now, he grew hard at the recollections of her body bathed in candlelight and the feel of her surrounding him. The scrape on her back didn't stop him from taking her time and again through the day and into the night. She was adept at making him gasp in mindless ecstasy when she mounted and rode him hard.

When they rested together, panting and sweating from a bout of lovemaking, he'd tucked her against his side and satisfied his curiosity about her life at Asher.

He raised her hand and ran a finger over the toughened skin of her palm. "This isn't the hand of a pampered woman. And you didn't earn these calluses at Neith. Cumbria doesn't think much of his less fortunate relations, does he?"

She followed the path of his fingers with her eyes and shrugged. "He didn't pay much attention, and he was more often at Conclave than Asher. He sometimes called me back to Conclave if he wanted me to translate something private, but that wasn't often. His wife saw to my care when I was at Asher."

He imagined just what kind of "care" the mad Dela-fé doled out to those subjected to her will. He also imagined pinning the woman to his bailey fence with a few well-planted daggers. "I'm sure she did. I'm surprised you have no whip marks on your back. Even the most obedient servant couldn't escape that woman's malice."

"She was skilled with the switch and could draw blood without scarring."

"A talent I'm sure she bragged about to all her aristo friends."

Her bottom was smooth beneath his palm, and he spread his hand over the rounded curve. "What did you do at Asher?"

Only the faintest stiffening hinted at her unease at his question. Her voice was uninflected, and she even smiled a little.

"Much as I do here at Neith. I cleaned, laundered, made soap, took care of livestock, harvested olives, worked in the presses and served at formal dinners. I also acted as the bishop's scribe."

She wasn't telling him something. Cumbria might not have cared how Martise managed at Asher, but she was of value to him—beyond the mundane labor of a servant.

"How old were you when you became a novitiate of Conclave?"

She caressed him as he did her, running her hand along the length of his leg and over his hip. He savored her touch. She felt good—right—in his arms. "I was twelve," she said. "A high priest visited Asher and brought a mage-finder with him. The dog snapped his leash trying to get to me."

Her fingers tickled where she ran her hand along his jaw before resting it against his cheek. "They never spoke of you at Conclave. Neither the priests nor the students. At least not by name. There were rumors of a student banished on threat of death from the canonry. Was that you?" Her copper eyes reflected the glow of the brazier's dimming light.

"What? They aren't singing my praises at dawn prayers?" His lip curled. "They considered me too dangerous to let loose so they sent me here to Neith, to the Master of Crows."

"You mentioned a first Master of Crows once. Did you inherit the title?"

"The title, the reputation and Neith itself." He pressed his cheek against her hand. "Make no mistake. I've lived down to the insult and its notoriety. Conclave thought they sent me to a carrion mage who'd use me as demon bait. My mentor had other plans."

Her eyes closed for a moment. When she gazed at him again, a deep-seated anger, tempered with sympathy, sparked in her eyes. "I see why you hate them—the priests."

If she only knew just how deep that hatred ran. He banished the dark thoughts and contented himself with caressing her warm body. By rights, he should despise her as well. She was an instrument of Conclave, sent to Neith to spy on him, and she might well succeed in her endeavor, but he didn't despise her. Far from it, and the emotion welling within made him shy away from those thoughts quicker than his ruminations over the god.

Her lips parted beneath his, supple and yielding. She wasn't the beauty the houri Anya was, but she was brave and witty, learned and exceptionally observant. She fit in his arms like no other. Long after she returned to Neith, he'd remember her—and yearn for her.

He growled into her mouth and rolled over so that she sat astride him. Her hair curtained him in fragrant waves. A quick lift of her hips and he was inside her, sinking slowly into a tight, welcoming heat.

Martise's eyes gleamed, and her voice was breathless. "Can you star-gaze now, Silhara of Neith?"

He gripped her hips in his hands as she rode him, letting her set the pace until he was maddened with need. He brought her down to him, kissed her until they were both breathless and shaking. He plunged into her over and over, desperate to get closer, desperate to possess. So intense was his desire that his Gift rose of its own accord, summoned not by the working of a spell but by the ferocity of his passion. And hers answered.

Her Gift, unhampered by her developing control, surged forth. The tell-tale amber light surrounded them, and he breathed it in. Her very spirit filled him. She was strength through endurance, resolve and compassion, all overlaid by a faint melancholy—and love for him. His climax struck him like a storm tide, coursing through him in a hot river until he arched and groaned, almost bucking Martise off him. She held on and followed after him, her softer cries fading with his as she collapsed on his chest.

His limbs shook beneath her, convulsive shudders accompanied by black spots that danced in his vision. He raised his hand, saw the corona of light shimmer around his fingers and pressed them to her back. His softly murmured spell was lost in her hair. She twitched and raised her head to stare at him.

"What did you do?"

He rubbed his thumb over the smooth skin where her abrasion had been. "I healed your back."

She reached behind her, touched the spot he caressed. Her eyes widened and she gave him a beatific smile. "You're amazing. Thank you." Her eyes darkened for a moment. "I envy you, you know. Not so much for the power you possess, but that you can command it at will. I wish my Gift would do that."

Silhara said nothing, only stroked her hair when she laid her head on his shoulder and fell asleep with him still inside her. He held her tightly.

He was exhausted. Even the force of her Gift couldn't fully replenish the strength the storm and the hours of lovemaking had taken out of him. He needed to sleep. He needed to possess her again, and when she drained him enough to shave a decade off his lifespan, he'd go to the library to verify a terrible truth. His suspicion regarding the nature of her Gift had become a surety. He knew what she was. Martise's Gift wasn't a blessing; it was a curse.

A loud crack against one of the library windows snapped Silhara out of his musings. He looked in time to see a spiraling flutter of wings as a crow fell to earth. He shook his head. "Cael will enjoy that one."

The book he'd taken from the high shelf sat unopened on the table. Runes decorated the leather, mysterious symbols that stung Silhara's fingers when he traced their outlines. Yellowed pages crackled as he opened the book and began to read. It didn't take him long to find the passages he sought, and he read them in bitter triumph.

"Ah Cumbria, you have no idea what you've turned over to me, do you?"

Such information would devastate Martise. He ran a hand through his hair and sighed.

He found her working in a corner of the bailey with Gurn, hanging newly laundered clothes and linen on lines to dry. Partially concealed by the flap of damp blankets, she was unaware of his presence until he spoke.

"Apprentice, I need you in the hall."

She straightened on a gasp. "You surprised me." Her tentative smile faded at his somber expression. She nodded and dried her damp hands on her skirts.

Painted in pale light and dust motes, she faced him in the great hall, her features set as she waited for his commands. He read the grim resolve in her eyes. She expected some unpleasant lesson from him. Regret twisted his stomach into more knots. He'd practiced a calculated cruelty on her in this hall when she first arrived. His attempts at frightening her away had failed, but the fear he'd instilled in her remained, even beyond the intimacy they now shared.

He didn't know how to reassure her, especially when his purpose in bringing her was to offer up a bleak truth.

"Summon your Gift, Martise."

Her eyebrows rose, but she did as he asked. He could watch her call up her Gift a thousand times and still not grow tired of the spectacle. He'd never seen a Gift manifest in such a way—a shimmering radiance that encompassed her and lured him to her.

"And now?" Even her voice changed, resonating with the sensuality that sent heat licking down his spine.

"Now, I want you to break the glass in these windows." He gestured to the tall panes of glass, frosted with years of dirt. "You know this spell. Conclave always teaches it to the beginners."

She frowned. "Are you sure?"

Her question spoke of her confusion.

"I'm sure."

The spell was simple, a harmless exercise used to introduce very young novitiates to the art of control and manipulation and familiarize them with their own power. But even that proved beyond her ability to execute. She recited the spell twice without so much as a single spider-crack appearing in a window pane. Her shoulders hunched in defeat.

"This is futile. It's like before. The spells don't work with my Gift."

Silhara circled her, the click of his boot heels echoing in the room. "They work, just not in the way we thought." He recited the same spell and the glass cracked in three windows. "A simple breakage spell. Good for creating mischief and not much else."

He took her hand. Her Gift rushed through him, drawing down her essence so that it sang in his veins. He was swamped with power, by the force that made his own Gift hum in response. He dropped her hand before he fell to her allure and began to feed off her Gift and her soul.

"Watch."

Silhara recited the spell once more. Martise covered her ears as a concussion wave twisted the air around them. An explosion of sound followed as every window in the hall shattered, blasting outward toward the courtyard in a shower of splintered shards. Broken rainbows caught on the jagged pieces of glass still attached to the window frames, and sunlight flooded the hall. Outside, Cael howled, and Silhara heard the door to the kitchen fly open. Martise stared at him as if he'd gone mad.

He clapped his hands twice and uttered one sharp word. Gurn raced into the hall just in time to see glass fly up, snap together and hold to the window frames. The windows looked untouched save for the dirt caked on their surface. The hall returned to its gloomy state.

"Gurn." The servant stood beside him, staring up at the repaired windows. He glanced at Silhara. "Go back to the bailey. I have something to tell Martise. Alone."

Gurn hesitated for a moment, glanced at Martise's shocked expression, then bowed and left. Martise's fingers were laced together, the knuckles white against her dark skirts. A blank look, at odds with those tense hands, settled over her features.

"This," he waved a hand to encompass the windows, "shouldn't have happened. At least not how you saw it."

Her brow furrowed. "I don't understand. You're very powerful. That didn't seem beyond your reach."

"It isn't. But that particular shatter spell should have done nothing more than crack the glass. Its very nature limits the effects, no matter the power of the mage. The second spell was harder. Repairing is always more difficult than destroying. The spell should have made me bleed. I didn't." He raised his hands so she could see the shimmer of her Gift still on them. "The power of your Gift, channeled through me, transformed those spells."

She blinked at him, raised her hands which no longer glowed as his did. "My Gift lent you power?"

Silhara gut turned at the rekindled hope in her eyes. "Your Gift is rare, Martise. The last recorded Gifted with your talent was born more than fourteen hundred years ago to a coastal woman. The Kurmans call such Gifted *bide jiana*. Life-givers. That life-giver met a bad end at the hands of his lover, a crow mage who once lived not far from here."

Martise frowned. Silhara could almost hear her mentally searching the many archives she'd read and translated, the histories of Conclave and the varied talents born to the Gifted.

"I've never heard or read of a—what did you call it?—a *bide jiana*. The priests never taught us of them."

"They're legendary, so rare that many believe their existence only myth. Conclave has never had a life-giver join the priestly ranks." He smirked. "And what Conclave doesn't know or recognize is either fabrication or simply unimportant."

He kept his voice even, revealing nothing of the growing turmoil inside him. "Your Gift is no blessing, Martise. Not to you. The spells you've learned and memorized will never work for you." Her shocked gasp punctuated his statement, but he continued, relentless with the truth and determined to protect her, no matter how much she might suffer from his honesty.

"You're a vessel, nothing more. A source to be used by mages like me. Your power strengthens the magic of others."

Martise's mouth thinned to a tight line, and her eyes darkened. "How did you learn this?" she whispered.

She aged before his eyes, made haggard by his words. "I searched the library. I have several tomes of the black arcana.

Two tell of crow wizards who enslaved *bide jiana* and fed on their power like leeches on blood. One was the soul eater of Iwehvenn."

Her face went white, and she swayed. Silhara reached out to steady her, but she jerked away from his touch.

Stiffer than a rake handle, she buried her hands in her skirt and breathed slowly. She stared at the floor and then at him. "I'm going to be sick," she said flatly and rushed past him to the kitchen.

Standing alone in the great hall, he wondered why he didn't feel like celebrating his triumph over Conclave and Cumbria in particular. His spy had witnessed nothing yet that would condemn him as a traitor or a heretic. And now it mattered little if she did. Corruption could drink tea with him in the kitchen and discuss how they intended to remake the world in their preference—starting with the slow torture and death of every Conclave priest. He now held the key to her silence. Whatever prize Cumbria dangled before her for turning Silhara over to them, he doubted it was worth the sacrifice of her soul.

Out in the bailey Gurn stood by his washtub and peered at a spot behind one corner of the house. The unmistakable sound of violent retching overrode the squawks, bleats and snorts of the livestock milling about the enclosure. Silhara came to stand next to Gurn and answered his frantically signed question.

"Leave her be, Gurn. She's just learned a cruel truth."

Both men waited until Martise reappeared around the corner. Her pallor gave her eyes a sunken appearance. She met Silhara's gaze bleakly. "What will you tell the bishop?"

Silhara held her gaze. "Gurn, where's that wine we bought at market?"

Gurn signed, and Silhara took Martise's hand. Her fingers were cold in the summer heat. In the kitchen, Silhara opened the cold cellar and returned with a small jar.

"Wouldn't the Fire be better?" She was calm, but her sensual voice carried a shrill note.

"It might." He lifted the bottle of Peleta's Fire from the cupboard shelf and handed it to her. "Use it to rinse your mouth, but don't drink. I need you coherent and thinking. The wine will do well enough."

He waited while she rinsed with a combination of water and Fire and spat in the slop bucket by the door. Just a taste of the strong drink brought a hint of color back to her cheeks, and she stood straighter. They climbed to his chamber. He motioned for her to sit on the bed while he poured wine into goblets and gave her one. She drained it in two gulps and held out the cup for more.

Eyebrows raised, he refilled the cup. He dragged the only chair across the room and sat across from her, holding his own goblet. Martise eyed him warily, much as she did when she first met him. They were adversaries again.

"There are many things I plan to tell Cumbria of Asher. None should be uttered in polite company." She smiled faintly at that. "Enslaving and using another mage for the purpose of gaining power is one of the darkest arcana. By Conclave law, any mage caught performing such a practice is subject to death." He leaned forward, resting his elbows on his thighs. The little color that had returned to her cheeks faded once more.

"A bondage like no other."

"It is. And a compulsion for the mage who controls the *jiana*. A taste of it is more than tempting." His eyes narrowed when she swallowed and looked away. "For a powerful mage like me or Cumbria, your talent is worth more than a ship loaded to the waterline with gold."

He chuckled dryly. "All this time serving his household, training with Conclave, and he never knew."

"But you'll tell him, or keep me for yourself." Bitterness sharpened her words.

There were many reasons why he might like to keep Martise for himself. Her Gift wasn't one of them. With Corruption's star hanging in the sky outside his window and the god's voice promising him a power that could bring kingdoms to their knees, her Gift held only a small temptation.

"While enticing, I don't have need of such a Gift, but Cumbria would. With you empowering him, he could control Conclave. He wouldn't have to wait for the Luminary to die or the Holy See to meet and elect the next Luminary. He'd simply usurp and rule. I doubt Conclave's laws or any imaginary morality would stop him from leeching you." His lip curled into a sneer. "The man who reviles crow mages would become the epitome of all such failed men."

Martise rose and walked to the window. Framed in the curved arch and backlit by sunlight, her features were cast in shadow. "What now then?"

He frowned at the dull note in her voice, as if something more than the hope of her Gift had died within her.

"I have Conclave up my nose enough as it is, and that's with a Luminary who is reasonable and doesn't bear me ill will. I'd be a fool to help the bishop rise to greater prominence." He drained his wine and rose. She didn't back away when he approached her. "I can teach you to hide your Gift. Not just control it, but submerge it. Deep enough that the priests will never sense its presence. And I am a good liar. It won't take much to convince Conclave that I failed in finding your talent."

Martise's empty gaze raked him. "You can use me, and I can't stop you."

Her hair was soft as he stroked her braid. "How is this different from any other day?"

She closed her eyes. "I'm scared."

He caressed her cheek. He hated her fear, but it would keep her alive. "You should be. The *bide jiana* enslaved had their Gifts taken from them by force. Sex, torture, whatever their masters found necessary to make that power manifest and use it to their advantage."

Hollow laughter, edged with hysteria, escaped her. Tears spilled down her cheeks, and she covered her mouth. The laughter turned to agonized groans. Silhara wrapped his arms around her, driven by an unfamiliar urge to hold and comfort. He rubbed her back and let her tears bleed on his chest. She felt good in his arms, even in her grief.

He couldn't remember the last time he'd wept for anything, but he understood her tears. They were made of anger and broken dreams, frustration and powerlessness. He held her in silence until she hiccupped and straightened away from him.

She wiped away the remaining tears with shaking hands "Surely, the gods laugh."

Gods were nothing more to him than a convenient means by which he cursed the daily annoyances of life. Only Corruption had risen above that philosophy, and Silhara loathed his seducer. "They don't do much else, apprentice. None are worth a single genuflection from any of us." Her bottom lip quivered under his thumb. "Let me give you the means to protect yourself, Martise."

A gentle kiss on his thumb and she sighed. "Many would say I'd be a fool to trust you."

"And many would be right. I lie well, and I lie often."

Amusement lightened her somber face. "You've never lied to me."

"Haven't I?"

"Not in those things that count."

Desire rose in him. Not fierce as before, but just as strong, just as deep. Save for Gurn and Cael, and his mother so long ago, he'd not been moved to care for anyone—until now.

He led her to the bed and made slow love to her, telling her with his hands what he was too frightened to recognize in the deepest part of his heart. Afterward, he spooned against her and nestled his face in her fragrant hair. Outside, the crows screeched and flapped in the trees, and Gurn hummed an off-key chant as he swept the back stoop. Silhara had wasted the day away in here with Martise and regretted none of it.

Their lessons would be in earnest now. He'd be damned if he saw her broken on the wheel of slavery, even more damned if he gave Cumbria the chance to rise to greater power. He'd hand his soul over to Corruption with a smile if necessary to stop the bishop.

The crows' discordant songs faded, and he drifted on the edge of sleep, content to savor Martise's warmth. She stirred, slid her foot along his calf. Her voice, cool and faintly challenging, brought him fully awake.

"What will protect me from you?"

He pulled her hard against him and nipped her shoulder. "Nothing."

CHAPTER SIXTEEN

Her time here had been a spectacular failure. Martise sat on a milking stool in the bailey, milking one of the new nanny goats and wondering what she would do now. Gurn sat nearby, repairing a section of Gnat's bridle. Silhara had sequestered himself in the stillroom to bottle one of the many perfumes he made from orange flowers.

She had three more weeks at Neith with no true purpose other than continue her translations for Silhara, and that had always been a flimsy reason. Cumbria's crow had never answered her call, and she'd sung in secret three more times. Not that any message meant much. All she had to report was their trip to Iwehvenn, which was neither a secret nor a crime. If Silhara worked to betray Conclave in any way, he'd kept his machinations well-hidden.

She paused in her milking. The Master of Crows had insured her silence with his knowledge of her Gift. She shuddered at the idea of her talent revealed to others. Her current bondage was nothing compared to its potential.

Silhara had offered her the means to effectively hide what she now thought of as her curse. Each morning, instead of coaxing her talent for spell work, they strove to suppress it, push it back to the deep recesses it occupied prior to the lich's attack at Iwehvenn. Silhara's altruism cloaked a more personal motivation. Conclave,

253

under Cumbria's rule, would turn on him without hesitation. The present Luminary was a fair man, an adherent to the rule of law who insisted on justice by proof and trial. He might suspect Silhara of nefarious activities, but he wouldn't condemn him without evidence. Cumbria would not be bound by such strictures.

Martise regretted coming to Neith. Enslaved for most of her life, she'd grown accustomed to her role, but she never lost the yearning to be a free woman, to control her own life and regain that small part of her spirit locked away in a glittering jewel.

At the time she'd made her accord with Cumbria, her purpose was clear, or so she imagined. A small sob lodged in the back of her throat. Betraying Silhara might have been easy at first. Not now. Even without his knowledge of her Gift, she couldn't turn him over. She might be nothing more to him than a convenient bed mate while she stayed at Neith, but he was far more to her. The rebellious mage, who refused to wear Conclave's yoke and lived as an outcast pauper for it, had frightened her, mentored her, defended her and saw her as something more than a pair of useful, obedient hands. When he took her to his bed, he might as well have placed Cumbria's shackles on her wrists. He'd never know she'd fallen in love with him, and she'd leave Neith never saying it aloud. Her freedom wasn't worth his death.

A tug on her braid made her look up from staring blindly at the ground. The nanny goat chewed contentedly on the end. Martise yanked the braid away and flipped it over her shoulder. "No you don't, my girl. You've already chewed holes in two of Gurn's blankets. You'll not be gnawing on me today."

The air suddenly warped around her, followed by a blast of cold wind from the Solaris wood. Cael barked a warning, and the goat bleated and scampered away to take shelter under one of the bailey's overhangs.

Martise rose from her stool. "What was that?"

Gurn shrugged, looking surprised but unconcerned.

The door to the stillroom flew open, and Silhara strode out, wiping his hands on a cloth. His dark hair was restrained in a tight queue, giving his eyes a more narrow shape.

He peered past the bailey wall. "We have visitors." Gurn caught the cloth he tossed him. "Gurn, they'll have their ponies with them. You'll need to lead them in."

Martise wanted to ask who "they" were but held her tongue.

Silhara issued more instructions as he headed for the kitchen. "Set a blanket and whatever pillows you can find out in the courtyard. We'll eat our midday there." He crooked a finger at Martise. "Come with me."

Once in the kitchen he pinned her with a curious gaze. "Can you brew a pot of strong tea?"

"Yes, why?"

"Good. Brew several and bring them outside to where Gurn will set up for lunch." His eyes narrowed. "What do you know of Kurmanji customs?"

Ah, the identity of their visitors.

"A little. Asher's cook was a Kurman woman." She ticked off items on her fingers. "Don't eat with the left hand, be sure to touch your heart when you thank someone, and if you're a woman, don't meet a man's gaze directly unless you want him to know you're interested."

He arched an eyebrow. "Good. You're familiar with the important things. Especially the last. These men who visit know the ways of the plains and coastal folk are different from theirs. But I'd rather be cautious. I don't fancy another fight just to prove you're mine. And unlike your Balian, Kurmans are very good with their daggers."

He left her in the kitchen, and she watched him go, stunned and warmed by his comment.

"You're mine."

He might only mean it in the sense she was a servant of his household, and he wouldn't give her up to an amorous tribesman. Nor did she think any challenge would be issued. She wasn't Anya. Still, she clung to the hope his possessive statement was more primal than practical. Martise chastised herself for entertaining such thoughts. Whatever he meant, it mattered little.

While Gurn was gone, she managed to brew three large pots of black tea, gather several loaves of bread, salted mutton, cheese, olives and oranges. She used the remaining time to race to her room, wash her face and hands and rebraid her hair.

Gurn met her in the kitchen on his return, and between the two of them, they gathered up the food and drink, along with two large blankets and several dusty cushions. Out in the courtyard, she spotted Silhara talking with two men dressed in the typical Kurman garb of dun-colored trousers and shirt, brightened by colorful beaded vests and pointed-toe shoes. They were shorter than Silhara and stocky, with swarthy-complected faces that sported neatly trimmed beards. The hair and eyes were the same, just as black, and they both had the same prominent noses and cheekbones. If Silhara didn't have some Kurman in him, she'd eat one of her shoes.

The shadow cast by the broken walls offered a wide expanse of cool shade. Gurn laid out the blankets and set the cushions near each other while Martise placed the food in the center and sliced the bread. She watched Silhara with the Kurmans from the corner of her eye. She recognized the older of the men as one she'd seen Silhara talking to in Eastern Prime's market.

He levered a wrapped parcel off his shoulder and set it on the ground. Carefully pulling back the cloth that bound it, he lifted a crossbow and handed it to Silhara. From her vantage point, Martise saw it was a finely made weapon. Silhara must have ordered one from market to replace the one he lost at Iwehvenn. Likely paid for with the bishop's money. She smiled at the idea.

Snatches of conversation floated to her on the breeze as she waited with Gurn by the blankets. Bendewin, Asher's cook, had taught her some Kurmanji. A more guttural language than the clipped plains speech, Kurmanji was a difficult language to learn and had never been put into script. The two Kurmans spoke with a mix of rapid-fire words and flamboyant hand gestures. Obviously fluent, Silhara answered them with ease.

He broke away from their little knot, carrying the crossbow with him. Gurn eyed it with an admiring gaze.

Silhara handed the bow to the servant. "Beautiful work, isn't it? When you're through serving, take it to my chambers. I'll test-fire it later. And bring down the *huqqah*." His features sobered. "Martise, Gurn will serve the men. You serve me and me alone. And look me in the eye. They'll know you're my concubine as well as a servant."

"As you wish, but I don't think they'll notice…" She stopped, surprising herself. She'd never argued with him or questioned his instruction before. A quick glance confirmed he was as surprised as she.

"Well, well," he said, but didn't admonish her. "Rank in a Kurman tribe is based on the number of sheep you own, the wives you have and the children you've sired. Younger men have to work hard to gain a Kurman wife. Some prefer to pursue one outside the tribe."

He stepped closer but didn't touch her. Their visitors observed their interaction with interest. "Don't underestimate your presence, Martise," he said in a low voice. "You may have been faceless at Asher. You aren't at Neith. If at all possible, try not to speak."

He returned to the men and led them back to the shaded place she and Gurn had prepared for their meal. They sat in a semi-circle against the cushions and broke bread between them. Martise followed Kurman protocol, not meeting anyone's eyes save Silhara's. She hovered at his side, pouring tea and filling his plate. She was in her element and had done this very thing for Cumbria dozens of times. Only now she wasn't ignored. The Kurmans watched her as she attended their host, and the younger of the men tried to catch her eye.

Martise pretended not to understand when he remarked on her to Silhara.

"Your woman serves you well. She wasn't here the last time we traded at Neith."

Silhara popped an olive into his mouth and chewed before answering. "Martise came to Neith in the beginning of summer. Sent by Conclave."

A surprised silence met his statement before the older Kurman spoke. "You are at peace with the priests then?"

Silhara gave a short laugh. "I am never at peace with the priests. However, we've agreed to work together to rid the land of the god. Martise helps me with that. And other things." He ran his fingers lightly over her calf and handed her his cup for a refill. Both men nodded in recognition of his silent claim. The older one spoke again.

"The Brecken Falls still cascade with blood. They are rank with the smell of rotting fish. People are frightened."

Martise could only imagine the horrific scene he described. Even if the non-Gifted couldn't see its star, Corruption was making itself known throughout the far lands.

Silhara's fingers caressed hers as she handed him his full teacup. "It will only grow worse. There are plagues as well, and fertile fields have gone suddenly fallow."

Quiet reigned as the three men ate and quaffed the black tea. Again the older Kurman spoke. "The *sarsin* has extended an invitation for you to visit him. He has something for you that might help you in your quest to vanquish the god."

Silhara's eyebrows rose in interest. "I'm honored by his invitation. It's been too long since Karduk and I have shared a smoke."

Martise tried not to gape at him. Silhara, the hermit, had never before shown any pleasure in visiting with anyone, at Neith or anywhere else. Yet his voice was warm with genuine pleasure, even eagerness, at the idea of visiting this Karduk.

"You can accompany us home today." The Kurman glanced at Martise. "Bring your woman if you wish, or Karduk will be pleased to offer you one of his concubines for a night or two."

She prayed her face didn't betray her thoughts. Silhara was not hers, and despite this little play for the benefit for the Kurmans, she wasn't his. Still, she hoped he wouldn't leave her behind and find succor with one of his host's women.

He didn't reply either way to the suggestion. "Today is good. I'll have my servant ready supplies and load my horse."

They drank the last of the tea and shared a smoke from Silhara's *huqqah*. Seated behind Silhara, Martise gave silent thanks when they finished their smoke and he offered to give them a tour of the grove and show them samples of his perfumes. Her stomach rumbled. She was starved. Gurn's smile revealed he'd heard her belly's protest.

Just before the three men left for the stillroom, Silhara turned to her. "How much of that did you understand?" he asked softly.

"Most of it. I'll help Gurn with the packing." She wouldn't ask if he'd take her. She had some pride.

"Leave Gurn to it. I'll tell him what's needed. Pack for yourself, and bring something warm. It's cold in the Dramorins, even in the height of summer."

Martise struggled to suppress the pleased smile threatening to curve her lips. "It won't take me long. I can still help Gurn."

His gaze touched on her hair, her eyes and her mouth. "You are very good at assuming a role with very little instruction. I think you were more Kurman than some Kurman women at our meal." A shrewd gleam entered his eyes. "Mezdar and Peyan approved of your attentions to me, and I suspect Peyan may offer me dower-price for you."

A cold tendril of dread circled Martise's spine. She didn't know which of the men was Mezdar or Peyan, and she didn't care. She stared at Silhara, trying to discern his expression. He could be ruthless when he wanted and showed no hesitation in exercising that trait. But to try and sell her? He couldn't do it if he wanted, but to stop him, she'd have to reveal her bondage to Cumbria.

Amusement softened his hard features. He ran a finger down her neck. She tilted her head in an unconscious invitation for him to do more. He smiled. "You obviously think more poorly of me than Gurn does." His touch left hot trails on her skin. "You're not mine to sell, Martise. And even if you were... well, let's just say I have no need of sheep or carpets."

He stepped back abruptly, and Martise stopped short of reaching out to bring him back to her. "Go. You've much to do before we leave."

Flustered by his caress and the words he almost said, Martise bowed formally and turned away to help Gurn clean up the remnants of lunch. She took a few minutes in the kitchen to eat before running upstairs.

She was curious about the Kurmans. A semi-nomadic people, they lived most of the year in the high passes of the Dramorin Mountains, descending down to the plains to trade during harvest season and when the weather grew too harsh in the mountain passes. Asher's cook had been an exiled Kurman woman, though her outcast status never seemed to bother her. She'd kept those customs that benefited her and discarded those that didn't. Martise had her to thank for teaching her some of the language.

She folded and stuffed her heaviest tunic and skirts in her satchel, along with her shawl and woolen stockings she hadn't worn since her first day at Neith. She wished for a heavier wrap and hoped Gurn would pack plenty of blankets.

An odd silence broke her concentration. The endless jabber and screeching of the crows perched in the orange trees had become such a regular facet of life at Neith, she no longer noticed the noise. Now she noticed its absence. Afternoon sunlight streamed in through her open window, and she shielded her eyes from the glare with her hand. At first glance, the grove looked as it did any other day, green and full and basking in the heat. A second closer look, and Martise's heart leapt into her throat.

The ground ran red with blood. Scarlet rivers flowed down the trunks of the orange trees and pooled at their bases. Meandering streams trickled in curving patterns over the earth, drawing macabre patterns that widened and stretched to the house. It looked as if a massacre had taken place in the grove.

"Bursin's wings." She raced out of the room and nearly ran Gurn down as she tore through the kitchen. "Gurn, is Silhara in the stillroom with the Kurmans?"

She was through the door and halfway across the bailey before he could nod. The stillroom was dim and cool, redolent with the scent of orange flower and the tobacco smoke lingering on the men's clothing.

Silhara eyed her in surprise. She gave a clumsy bow.

"Martise?" His tone was more concerned than annoyed.

"Master," she nearly panted. "The grove. You'd best come now."

She flattened against the doorway as Silhara strode past her, face set in grim lines. The Kurmans stared at each other and then at Silhara's back in surprise. Martise addressed them in slow Kurmanji, careful not to look at either of them directly.

"If you will follow me, I will take you where the master has gone."

They followed without question. Outside, Silhara and Gurn stood together, surveying the grove weeping blood. Behind Martise, the Kurmans gasped and chattered in Kurmanji. Silhara turned, arms akimbo. A cold fire burned in his narrowed eyes. He addressed the Kurmans through clenched teeth.

"I look forward to seeing what Karduk has so I may destroy this vermin."

As they crowded back into the hall, Gurn motioned to Silhara. Silhara slammed the door behind him.

"There's nothing to do about it. The trees are undamaged. The god is simply making his presence known. He's frightened off the birds, which isn't a bad thing in itself. Unfortunately, the smell will draw every predator for miles. I'll lay a spell over the grove to dampen the scent, but keep Cael inside tonight. I don't want him fighting every scavenger that manages to scale the walls looking for a carcass. Put the livestock in the great hall. We'll deal with the mess later."

He ushered the Kurmans through the kitchen to the stillroom, falling back into the guttural mountain tongue to discuss additional trade for his perfumes. Even with the god ravaging the grove, there were still negotiations to be made.

Martise returned to her room to finish packing. Unnerved by the sight and odor wafting off the grove, she lit a lantern and closed the shutters on her view of the bleeding trees. She returned to the bailey and helped Gurn load Gnat with supplies, including Silhara's new crossbow. Between the two of them, they were ready by the time Silhara wanted to leave.

The grand avenue's gloom hemmed them in as they trod the path to Neith's entrance. Martise sympathized with the Kurmans. Like her, they were uneasy beneath the gnarled canopy of Solaris oaks, and constantly peered into the forest for a better look at the sinuous shapes lurking there. She almost heard Silhara's faint smile when she and the tribesmen breathed a collective sigh of relief at the end of the road.

Two sturdy ponies with shaggy coats grazed freely nearby. Mezdar or Peyan—she still didn't know who was who—whistled, and the ponies trotted to where they waited. Next to Gnat, they looked like toys, and she marveled at how easily they carried grown men through winding mountain paths.

They set off for the Dramorins with Martise riding silent behind Silhara on Gnat. She was content to remain quiet and listen to the men talk. She'd spent much of her life in such a role and learned a great deal. Silhara, grim and distracted by the god's cryptic message in the grove, became more affable as he chatted with the Kurmans. He was familiar with those they spoke of— who was cousin to whom, who fathered another child, whose parent died of some illness, who married a woman from another tribe.

At dusk they made camp near the base of the mountains. The younger Kurman disappeared into the brush with his quarrels and crossbow. Martise helped Silhara and the remaining Kurman prepare camp. She gathered wood from the surrounding area and at one point came upon Silhara hobbling Gnat amidst a patch of tender grass shoots.

"Where did the younger one go?"

Silhara peered into the brush. "Peyan? To hunt. If he doesn't come back with anything, I'll try my hand at it, but I suspect we'll eat well tonight."

She loaded more sticks onto the pile and gasped when Silhara scooped half the firewood out of her arms.

She tried to snatch it back. "Wait! Don't the Kurman think gathering wood is woman's work?"

He snagged two more pieces of wood from her load for good measure. "Martise, bearing children is woman's work. Gurn and I would be sitting in the dark every night if we waited for some wandering female to pick up sticks for us."

"But..."

"Do you truly think those two men will challenge me over how I deal with my woman?"

His woman. She liked the sound of that too much. "I thought we were supposed to follow their custom."

"We are, and we will. But I'll be happy to point out their idiocy if they'd rather wait and freeze their balls off while you get enough wood for a decent fire."

He had a point, and he was more familiar with these people than she. "Thank you, Master."

"We're alone here, Martise."

"Thank you, Silhara."

He nodded his approval and motioned her to follow him. They returned to camp to find Peyan dressing a brace of rabbits for cooking. They soon had a fire going, with the rabbits spitted and roasting over the flame. Mezdar built a small side fire, letting it burn low until the coals glowed. He set a small sheet of metal over the coals and made flat cakes from a grainy mush he'd stirred in a nearby bowl.

Sitting beside Silhara, Martise's mouth watered. Enjita bread. She'd watched Bendewin make enjita many times in Asher's kitchens. The servants lined up eagerly, plates in hand when the Kurman woman made her bread.

Silhara leaned closer. "When you drink your tea, place your hand over the cup so that others don't see you drink."

"I didn't see you do that earlier at Neith."

"Only the women cover their cups."

Eat last, drink on the sly, don't speak often. Martise was familiar with some of those strictures in her role as a slave. Being a Kurman woman didn't seem all that different from what she could tell.

In many ways, their dinner reminded her of the ones at Asher. This one was nothing like the lavish meals Cumbria held for his fellow priests or visiting dignitaries, but she occupied a similar spot. She stayed silent, listened and learned. She might have even gone unnoticed as she had at Asher save for the steady stroke of Silhara's fingers on the tip of her braid as he conversed, ate and drank tea with his companions. She was grateful they didn't linger at their meal. The smell of the roasted meat and warm bread had her stomach gnawing on her backbone, and she forced herself to go slowly once she could eat.

Mezdar stoked the fire, and all three men prepared pipes for an evening smoke. She hid a yawn behind her hand and huddled in her shawl. Despite the fire's warmth, the air had grown chilly.

Silhara, at ease in the Kurmans' company didn't look up from packing his pipe bowl.

"Find your bed, Martise. I'll be up for some time. This is bandit country, and we'll each take a watch. Put your blankets with mine. We'll stay warmer that way. And keep your shoes on. I'll join you soon."

She'd grown used to him curled against her in sleep. Even the light snores purred into her ear comforted her, and there was always the possibility that when he awakened, he'd want her beneath him. Or atop him. Martise blushed at the sensual images playing in her mind.

She prepared their bed as he instructed, crawled under the blankets—with her shoes on—and fell asleep. She woke when Silhara slid beneath the blankets and spooned against her. He laid his arm across her waist and wedged his leg between hers through her heavy skirts. His sigh tickled her ear.

"Far better if you were bare, but this will do."

They rose before dawn. Peyan, who'd taken the last watch, had already brewed tea and reheated the leftover enjita for their breakfast. The sun was just peeping over the horizon when they set off for the Kurman village.

The air grew colder and thinner as they rode through the mountain passes. The sun was high and bright, but Martise wrapped her shawl tightly around her and pressed against Silhara's back. Gnat kept a steady pace, breathing harder in the thin air. Unlike him, the mountain ponies suffered no effects from the rising elevation and clipped ahead at a swift pace. Patches of snow spilled from embankments onto the rutted paths. A brisk wind moaned a soft dirge as it whipped through the towering evergreens cloaking the mountainside.

Silhara called a sudden halt. Martise peered around his arm, expecting to see some obstacle in their path. The way was clear, with only the Kurmans watching them curiously.

"What's wrong?"

"You're quaking hard enough to make *my* teeth rattle." He moved his leg back and untied one of the packs strapped to the saddle. "Get down."

She slid off Gnat's back. Silhara followed and pulled one of their blankets from the packet. "Here. Wrap this around you."

She had only pulled the blanket over her shoulders when he picked her up and tossed her onto Gnat's back once more, this time in the front of the flat saddle. She clutched the horse's mane with one hand and held on to her blanket with the other. Silhara vaulted up behind her, scooted her back against him and took up the reins.

"Better," he said and whistled to the waiting Kurmans he was ready.

Martise couldn't agree more. The blanket's warmth and Silhara's body heat soaked through her clothing and into her bones. She leaned into his chest. "This is nice."

An amused rumble vibrated near her ear. "So glad you approve." His hand slipped under the blanket, wandered over her belly and cupped her breast. Martise sucked in a breath as his fingers teased her nipple through her shawl and tunic. The heat surrounding her turned scorching. "I agree," he murmured in her ear. "This is nice."

He stopped his teasing when she squirmed hard enough in the saddle to nearly unseat them both but left his hand on her breast, content to just hold her. Martise was ready to toss off the blanket and her shawl. Silhara's touch had left her with a throbbing ache between her thighs. She smiled a little at the feel of him hard against her back. She wasn't the only one affected by his teasing.

He rubbed the top of her head with his chin. "There will be a feast tonight. Kurmans look for any reason to have a celebration. Visitors to their camp is as good as any. The men eat separate from the women, so you won't sit with me."

Again, a separation of not only roles but proximity. "Are Kurman women such pariahs among their own people?"

"Don't be so quick to judge. It may seem that way to an outsider, but Kurman women are well-respected. They own property independent of their husbands. A man's dower-gift for a new bride is bought from his mother and given to the bride's mother. She owns the flocks, the carpets, even the houses. The women also elect the *sarsin*."

Martise, stunned by his revelations, twisted in the saddle to look at him. "I've never heard of such a thing. They own property?" She didn't bother to hide her envy. What was eating second compared to having something of your own, not tied to either a father or a husband?

Silhara's tone was sardonic. "The plains folk could learn something from these mountain savages, wouldn't you say?"

She faced forward and stared at the Kurmans riding ahead of them. Even the most elevated aristo woman couldn't lay claim to land or holdings. Ownership always passed to the closest living male relative. Maybe, she thought, it would be a fine thing to be Kurman.

"Who will serve you since we'll sit separately?"

"If I were a tribesman, one of my wives would serve. Since I'm a guest, one of the matriarchs will. You're a guest as well. While a matriarch won't tend you, you aren't expected to serve in the festivities."

"I'm more comfortable with attending, not being attended to."

Lingering amusement colored his voice. "Spoken like a servant born." His voice was more guarded when he next spoke. "These are my father's kinsmen."

Martise stared down at his hands. They held the reins in a tight grip. "I thought they might be. When I first met you, I wondered if you had Kurman blood in your veins. Will he be here?"

"No. He died while my mother still carried me. His people didn't even know of me until I'd reached my twentieth season. They came to trade at Neith with my mentor. A few saw the resemblance between us, asked the right questions. Hard to miss the Kurman nose and cheekbones."

She ran her thumb across his knuckles. "I'm sorry."

He shrugged against her back. "It was long ago. You don't miss what you never knew."

They lapsed into a comfortable silence, and she dozed at short intervals, wrapped in a cocoon of blanket and Silhara's swaying warmth. She was awake when they finally entered the outskirts of the Kurman village. Nestled high in the mountains and surrounded by a sheltering stand of pines, the village sprawled across a flat clearing. Black tents sporting bright banners in shades of red and yellow shared space with more permanent dwellings built of rough stone and roofed with woven branches mixed with sun-dried mud. The roofs were unique, built into a dome shape with a hole in a center from which smoke escaped in lazy spirals.

A few sheep milled about the village's center, and children competed with dogs to see who could chase squawking chickens the fastest. They were accompanied by parental reprimands from colorfully dressed women tending cooking fires or sitting at looms outside their doorways.

Peyan kicked his pony into a trot and alerted the village of their arrival with a loud "Aiyee!"

As a single entity, the entire village surged forward to greet them. Gnat stood patiently as many hands patted his neck and traced his withers. Silhara dismounted and helped Martise down. He was patted too, and amidst the excited chatter, she heard the word *"kurr"* several times, an endearment she recognized for "son."

Like Peyan and Mezdar, the Kurmans were swarthy-complected, darker than Silhara but with the same black hair and eyes. Their faces were broader and the eyes more almond-shaped. Many had the same aquiline nose as his and the same prominent cheekbones, but not his height. Silhara towered over the tallest villager in the crowd.

The women wore similar vests as the men, but their shirts were brighter, and their skirts draped in an array of azure, saffron and scarlet. Their dark hair was arranged in intricate braids and decorated with painted beads. All eyes suddenly focused on her.

Unused to so much attention, she blushed and gave a clumsy bow. At least she didn't stutter her Kurmanji greeting. "A fair moon above you. I am honored to break bread."

More chatter followed her greeting, along with a few admiring "ooohs." One young girl in the crowd exclaimed, "Such a beautiful voice! Do you sing?"

Silhara blanched. Martise tried not to laugh at his horrified expression. "No, I'm sorry. I don't sing well at all."

A round of disappointed protests echoed from the crowd, and Silhara gave an audible sigh of relief. He grinned at the indignant frown she shot him.

They were escorted into the heart of the village by the entire population. There was much excited talk about a welcome celebration that night and calls for Silhara to give them news of the plains. A sudden hush descended on the villagers, and the crowd parted.

A stately figure approached them. Garbed much like the other Kurman men in embroidered vest and dun trousers, he stood out amongst the crowd. His tall hat added height to his diminutive frame and sported a ruby the size of a robin's egg. Life and sun had carved fissures into a dusky face half-obscured by a white beard that touched his knees. Martise was struck by his presence, the quiet power and authority.

Silhara met him half way and bowed low with his hands clasped together as if in prayer. "I am honored, *Sarsin*."

The *sarsin* harrumphed. His dark eyes crinkled at the corner, and his mouth, almost hidden by the beard, turned up in a smile. "Good to have you here, *kurr*." He glanced at Martise. "You've brought your woman?"

"I have. She serves me well and is fine comfort on a cold night."

Martise stiffened. She'd done more for Silhara than act as tea pourer and bed warmer. Just as quickly she relaxed. Bendewin had sometimes mentioned the high value placed on a Kurman wife who tended her mate and pleased him between the sheets. While Martise judged her worth by her learning, in Kurman eyes Silhara had just paid her a high compliment.

The two men clasped hands, and the *sarsin* led him away from the crowd. Silhara spoke to Martise over his shoulder. "Go with the women. They'll show you the village and take you to the house we'll share. I'll see you later this evening."

Martise watched him go, nervous but determined to make a good impression on his kinsmen. She stood within a circle of women and children who asked her numerous questions. The Kurmanji flew so fast, she had to ask them to repeat themselves. At a lull in the conversation, a Kurman woman with white-streaked hair pushed her way to the front of the crowd.

"That's enough for now. They've traveled far and will want to rest and bathe." She looked at Martise who nodded enthusiastically.

The dwelling the woman led her to was one of the large stone houses in the village. Martise followed her inside and was instantly awash in warmth. The house was a single large room, lit by the fire dancing merrily in a pit in the center of the floor. Rugs covered the floor, providing soft footing. Rows of jars and chests were pushed against the walls, and several sheep skins made up a bed. Smoke from the fire rose to the ceiling and disappeared through the hole that allowed a column of sunlight to filter down.

She stepped over numerous pillows and walked past strings of garlic and dried peppers hung from the rafters.

Her escort pointed at the fire. She spoke in accented Plains instead of Kurmanji. "Someone will return with tea and water for a bath. Have you eaten?"

"Not yet."

The woman moved around the room, straightening the blankets on the bed and checking the contents of some of the jars. She returned to Martise and appraised her with that same measuring gaze. "I am Dercima, Karduk's fourth consort. My brother was Silhara's father."

Martise hid her surprise with another bow. "I'm Martise of Asher." She paused. How did she introduce herself? Silhara had already called her his woman, but that was more a claim than an official title. She settled on something applicable to the moment. "I serve Neith."

Dercima's gaze was shrewd, and though no taller than Martise, she still managed to look down the length of her nose at her. Martise immediately recognized the expression. "You aren't what I'd expect from my nephew."

How many times had she heard similar words in her life? "I surprise people sometimes."

Dercima's somber features relaxed with a hint of amusement. "I suspect you surprised him." She straightened a pillow before walking to the door. "Rest for now. Silhara will return later. My husband will want to talk with him, and Karduk can be long-winded."

"Does Silhara look like his father?"

Her question made Dercima pause. She turned back. Firelight reflected in her still gaze. "Yes, but Silhara's eyes are far older than Terlan's ever were. He's a harder man, a darker one. You embrace shadow." She crouched and swept out of the short doorway before Martise could ask her more.

She wasn't left alone for long. Three young women knocked and entered the house carrying supplies for a bath, a plate heaped with food, a sturdy cauldron of water and a tea kettle. Martise murmured her thanks as they left. Alone in the house, she set the tea and cauldron to heat and helped herself to the food. There were no Kurman here to reprimand her for eating before Silhara returned.

The food was a hash of ground lamb, lentils and peppers. She used the flat enjita bread as a spoon and drank half the kettle of tea to cool the spicy fire of the peppers on her tongue. Afterward, she tested the cauldron's water, undid her braid and stripped for a quick bath. Outside, the brisk air smelled of snow, but inside the house it was warm, and Martise took her time in soaping and rinsing the dust of the road off her body.

"To be greeted by such a sight each time I walk in a house."

She spied Silhara at the entrance, an admiring gleam in his dark eyes. Martise lowered her arms to her side and gave him an unobstructed view of her body.

"Raised in a brothel, I'd think such a sight common for you."

He approached her slowly, his gaze caressing her as he drew close. "True." He drew a delicate pattern over her bare breasts and midriff. "But you aren't common, even if you do only have two breasts."

He coaxed a chuckle out of her, even as he heated her blood with his nearness and his touch. "You've spoken with the *sarsin*?" She gasped and arched when he bent, took her nipple in his mouth and suckled. Martise buried her wet hands in his hair and moaned, uncaring that she was likely soaking the front of his tunic.

Silhara placed a last kiss on the tip of her nipple before stepping away. Light from the fire emphasized the color on his sharp cheekbones, and his eyes blazed. "For now. It's more a formal greeting than anything. He'll want to talk again tonight. Karduk is long-winded."

She giggled. "That's what your aunt said."

"You've spoken with Dercima? Now there is a woman to challenge a god. She is the fourth of six consorts, and the most powerful in Karduk's household. She rules them all."

He spoke of her with fondness and great respect. Martise liked seeing this side of him, a man free of the usual scorn. She dropped the wet cloth on the edge of the cauldron and reached for another to dry herself off. Silhara took the cloth from her.

"No. Finish your bath."

"But there's food…"

One black eyebrow arched. "And I'll eat it while you bathe."

The look he slanted her seduced her, and she answered his unspoken challenge. In the privacy of the Kurman house, she was not servant, nor was he master. It pleased him simply to watch her. It pleased her to have him do so.

The rest of her bath was slow and languorous. Silhara sat cross-legged against one of the cushions and ate the rest of the food on the plate. She hid her grin when, too distracted by following the path of the wash cloth over her hip, he almost put his hand in the fire instead of on the tea kettle's handle. She was plain Martise, but in those moments she felt more beautiful and sensual than all the Anyas in the world. She reveled in the decadence of tempting him. He was the *sarsin* here and she the consort performing for his pleasure.

His features tensed as she ran the drying cloth up the inside of her thigh, almost to her cunnus. He tossed his empty teacup aside and reached for her, wrapping a hand around her calf. Martise dropped the cloth and waited. He stood swiftly, resting his hands on her hips.

She played with the lacings on his tunic. "Do Kurman women bathe their men?"

Callused hands stroked a path from her hips to her waist, to the outer curve of her breasts. "Sometimes. A man's consort may choose to do so. The privilege of marriage." Silhara's smile was puzzled.

One of the laces unfurled between her fingers. "I want to bathe you."

He lost the smile. "Why?"

Such a guarded man despite his bluntness. Her heart ached within her chest, even as her body burned with desire. She would grieve him when she left Neith. One fingertip followed the arched bridge of his nose. "Because you are a pleasure to touch, a pleasure to look upon. A man who does this..." She placed his hand on her breast, let him feel the sensitive peak of her nipple. "And this..." She guided that same hand between her legs and opened her thighs so that his fingers slipped into the dampness there.

Silhara's eyes closed, and he groaned. Those wondrous fingers worked their own magic on her, sliding into her to stroke and tease. His tongue mimicked his fingers as he tilted her head back and kissed her.

For several minutes, Martise was lost to his touch before she regained her thoughts and pushed his hand away. Silhara growled in protest but didn't stop her. They were both short of breath. "I do not ask for much," she panted.

His gaze stripped her to her soul. "You ask for everything." He continued to stare at her, shadows swirling within the depths of his eyes. His shoulders lifted in a deep breath. "As you wish."

Euphoria entwined with desire. Martise divested him of his garments, casting them aside with such enthusiasm, he laughed. She paused when he stood nude before her, clothed only in the flickering light of the hearth's low flame. Burnished skin that paled below the slim waist, wide shoulders and long legs. He was beautiful, and her fingers tingled in eagerness to pay homage to that masculine beauty.

The remaining water in the cauldron was still warm, and she wet a new cloth. Silhara stood still for her slow ministrations, sucking in an audible breath when the cloth glided between his thighs and passed over his testicles in a light caress. She took her time, reveling in the sight of his skin glistening with water droplets. He swayed on his feet when she soaped him and ran her slick hands down his ribs, the indentation of his spine, and his tight buttocks. A pleased sigh escaped him when she curled slippery fingers around his cock and stroked.

Silhara's hands curled into fists at his side. His face, flushed by the heat from the fire and the heat Martise ignited in him, was drawn into sharp angles. His voice was a harsh rasp. "Finish soon, or there will be soap on the bed."

She laughed softly and trickled water over him to clean away the soap. He was wet and glistening and aroused. Martise dropped the cloth into the cauldron. Her lips fluttered against his chin. "The bed is too far away."

His breathing quickened even more as she learned his body with her mouth, lips and tongue playing on his nipples, passing across his stomach, the prominent angle of his hipbone, down to the slim, muscular thighs. Silhara buried his hands in her hair and massaged her scalp with trembling fingers. On her knees before him, Martise met his dark gaze and closed her mouth over the tip of his cock. He was the first to break their stare, throwing his head back to gasp his pleasure when she took him fully, down to the hilt.

He was endowed as any other man, but fit her mouth as perfectly as he fit within her cunnus, as if made for her and her alone. Martise savored him, the tight skin of his shaft against her tongue, the sensitive ridge running its length. His scent, of soap and musk, filled her nostrils as he thrust gently into her mouth. The muscles in his long thighs quivered beneath her hands, their shaking escalating when she reached under him to caress his bollocks.

Deep groans poured from him. Following the subtle pressure of his hands on her head, Martise sucked him harder, swirled her tongue faster over his shaft and the head of his cock. She let him almost slip out of her mouth before taking him to the hilt over and over. His throat worked with incoherent noises, and his hands gripped her hair. Two deep pulses along the length of his shaft and he filled her mouth.

Martise drank him, tasting salt on the back of her tongue. She continued to suck, draining him until his softened cock slipped out of her mouth and his knees buckled. He collapsed in front of her, head lowered, gasping harder than a winded horse. He moved enough to rest his forehead on her shoulder. Residual shudders shook him. Martise ran her hands through his silky hair, dampened at the temples with sweat.

"Did I please you?"

Silhara raised his head slowly to stare at her. High color flagged his cheekbones. His pupils swallowed the lighter black of his eyes. "Please me? You've vanquished me."

He staggered to his feet and pulled her with him to the bed. They stretched out on the soft skins. "You'll keep me warm," he said and brought her down on top of him. Martise stretched over his body, running her toes along his calves and spreading her thighs to nestle his cock against her cunnus. She wanted him. Her thighs were slick with the want, but she could wait. He was spent from her attentions, and it was a pleasure to lie with him, kissing the strong column of his throat and tasting his mouth on hers. His tongue circled hers in languid play, teeth nipping gently at her bottom lip.

"You're wet for me," he murmured against her mouth.

"How can I not be?" She flicked the corner of his mouth with her tongue. "You are beautiful to touch and taste." She was undiminished by her honest passion for him. He was her lover, and she desired him above all things.

A soft thrust against her cunnus let her know her words affected him. He rolled her onto her back and crouched over her. "I've a taste for you as well, and time enough to indulge."

He took her as she'd taken him, using his lips and tongue to drive her to madness. She came apart in his arms, keening his name as she clawed his shoulders and clamped her legs against his ribs. The throbbing between her legs didn't subside when he rose above her, turned her on her stomach, and raised her to her hands and knees. He said nothing, only spread her thighs with his knees and gripped the back of her neck with one hand.

Martise moaned, arching her back in encouragement. He mounted her in silence, his stiff cock plunging into her until he was hard against her. She reveled in the sensation—a fullness, a stretching as his cock pumped in and out of her. Inner muscles gripped him, attempting to hold him within her, and Silhara growled. His grip tightened on her neck, and he thrust faster within her, deeper until Martise thought she might feel him on the back of her throat. Stripped of courtship and the rituals of men and women, this was a claiming, a male's primal possession of a willing female.

A last thrust, and he groaned his triumph. A stream of heat pulsed deep within her. The hand holding the back of her neck loosened, slid over her shoulder in a slow caress. Silhara maneuvered them carefully to their sides, maintaining the intimate connection as he curved against her. His heart beat strong at her back.

"If we weren't the guests of honor, we wouldn't attend tonight's festivities." His words were staccato while he caught his breath.

Martise, content to lie there and enjoy the feel of him in and around her, agreed. "I'd be very happy to stay like this and let them celebrate without us. But they will want us there. Especially you."

Silhara ran his hand over the curve of her hip to cup her breast. He nuzzled the top of her head. "There'll be food and good company, ale thick enough to strain between your teeth and much dancing. They'll wonder why I can do nothing more than crawl on my hands and knees. You've drained the life out of me."

Martise chuckled. "As much noise as we both made, I doubt they'll question why you won't be leaping around the village fire."

He laughed and patted her on the hip before rolling away. A gush of wet warmth bathed her thighs when he slipped out of her, and she thanked him when he tossed her one of the dry cloths. By the time one of the Kurman came to summon them for the celebration, they were dressed, and Martise had just finished braiding Silhara's hair.

The village gathered around two large fires, the men at one, the women at another. Silhara nodded once to her before being shepherded off by the men. The women willingly took her into their fold. Martise was glad she knew some Kurman and soon joined the conversations that inevitably centered on men, children and village gossip. New to her was the talk of properties and the speculations of politics. Because Kurman women owned land and housing and elected the village *sarsin*, such things were discussed amongst them. Martise was fascinated and envious.

The night was clear and cold, and her breath swirled in front of her in a cloud, but the food was good, the ale thick as Silhara warned and the dancing wild. She was dizzy from learning the steps and clasping hands with the women as they danced in a wide circle around the fire. She caught glimpses of Silhara, graceful as always as he danced with the men. He met her gaze across the fire, and his eyes smoldered with a look that promised more of their play later in the evening. She wished the night might last forever. Here, in the high mountains, surrounded by a foreign people, she was simply Martise. Not of Asher, but of Neith. The stigma of slavery didn't exist, and Silhara's kinsmen accepted her as a woman bound willingly to him.

By the time the celebration wound down, she was hot in her clothes and tipsy from too much ale. Silhara came to her as she said goodnight to her companions.

"Karduk wants to talk to me again. He may have something that will help us in defeating Corruption." His face was somber. "Kurmans take forever to get through a conversation. There's usually a ritual pipe sharing, more ale, more smoking and even more ale." He smiled faintly. "I'll be lucky to see our bed by dawn. You go back and get some sleep. We leave tomorrow, and I want one of us rested."

Martise wanted to touch him, but there were too many watching, and Kurmans didn't show public affection except to their children. She settled for bowing instead. "I'll be waiting."

She watched him leave before finding her way to their house. She banked the coals in the fire pit, shed her clothes, and crawled beneath the blankets Silhara had tossed aside earlier. She was asleep in moments.

A strong scent of tobacco roused her from a deep slumber. Martise, groggy from sleep and the residual effects of too much ale, rolled to her side. Silhara's tall form was silhouetted in firelight as he sat near her, smoking a pipe.

"You're back," she said. "What hour is it?"

Embers in the pipe crackled as he drew in a mouth full of smoke. She made out only the sharp outline of his features, but his eyes gleamed bestial red in the fire's glow.

"The darkest hour. Go back to sleep. I'll join you soon."

Martise frowned, wondering if the ale had truly addled her senses. Silhara's voice was an echo of Corruption's, as hollow and cold as a crypt.

CHAPTER SEVENTEEN

"You must be well into your cups. What sober man sits outside in the cold dark while his woman sleeps alone in a warm house?" Dercima stood over him, casting a long shadow across his feet. With the bright moon behind her, Silhara couldn't see her expression, but her tone was quizzical and faintly mocking. "How much *shimiin arkhi* have you had tonight?"

"Not nearly enough." He patted the ground beside him in invitation. "Care to sit, aunt? Share a pipe?" He held up a skin pouch and a cup. "There's even enough *arkhi* here to numb us both." His voice was barely a rasp, hoarsened by too much smoke and the chaos raging within him.

Dercima accepted his invitation and plopped down next to him. She nodded her thanks when Silhara passed her his pipe. With the moonlight full on her strong-boned features, he could see the shrewd appraisal in her gaze, even through the haze of smoke she puffed from the pipe. "What troubles you, nephew? I'd expect you to be taking your pleasure between Martise's thighs right now. Did she bar you from your bed?"

He drained the *arkhi* in his cup, no longer wincing at the sour taste, and poured a refill from the skin pouch. Fermented mare's milk wasn't Peleta's Fire, but it would do. "Martise has never denied me."

"And if she did?"

Silhara grinned into his cup. His formidable aunt would strangle him with his own braid if he gave the wrong answer. "I've no interest in taking by force what I can purchase or have given to me freely."

Smoke swirled in a turbid crown around her head. "Then why are you out here?"

"I could ask the same of you."

She shrugged. "Karduk is currently occupied with his first consort, so I am free until dawn."

He hid his amusement behind another swallow of *arkhi*. She might be fourth consort to the *sarsin*, but Silhara suspected Dercima was the one who determined if and when Karduk enjoyed her favors. He traded her the cup for the pipe.

"I don't like regrets or remorse," he said.

Dercima gave him an arch smile. "And how does this make you different from the rest of us?"

Unused to his own brand of mockery leveled at him, Silhara's eyebrows rose. "Are you always so blunt?"

She chuckled and sipped from the cup. "You didn't get that trait from your father." Her gaze held him in place. "Now tell me, what are you doing here? And don't bother hiding it. Karduk will tell me if I ask."

No surprise there. Silhara shrugged. "Thinking of godhood, destruction and sacrifice."

He patted her on the back when she choked on her drink. She stared at him with watering eyes and swatted his arm away. "Stop that."

"My apologies." He puffed leisurely on the pipe and met her gaze.

"Most men ponder what pony they'll sell, what bride they'll take or what dice game they'll join."

Silhara tilted his head and stared at the star-filled sky. Corruption's star had followed him, hovering high above the trees in its halo of sullen light. Above it, within the blanket of twinkling lights, the al Zafira constellation shone bright and mocked him from on high. "I am not most men."

"No, you're not, though I've watched you dice with the best of them." Dercima winked.

Even when he was at his most melancholy, Dercima could still make him laugh. "If there's time tomorrow before I leave, I'll play a game or two. I'm always in need of coin."

"You're avoiding my question, *kurr*."

Yes, he was, and for good reason. The information Karduk had given rubbed a raw spot on his soul. He had choices to make. None of them good. He puffed twice more on the pipe before answering. "I thought Berdikhan was nothing more than a Kurmanji demon." Dercima sketched a protective sign at his mention of the name.

"By the time he died, he was. Any Kurman who would sacrifice his wives and children to gain more magic is a demon. The tribes didn't exile him soon enough. And truth be told, they should have killed him instead."

Dercima reached for the pipe. "Why does this bother you? Berdikhan and his foul deeds are almost forgotten by the people. Is this what has brought you outside?"

Silhara considered how much to tell his aunt. Dercima was close-lipped. And strong-willed. Nothing short of torture would make her talk, and he wasn't sure she'd do it then. Still, another depended on his discretion, had placed her faith in his promise of secrecy.

"Martise and I recovered manuscripts from Iwehvenn."

Her eyes rounded. "Are you witless? What were you doing in a lich's hall? And dragging that girl with you?" Dercima stared down her nose in disapproval.

"Do you want to hear the rest or not?"

Her mouth thinned but she held her tongue. Silhara watched as her jaw tightened around the pipe stem. He'd be at the *sarsin's* door at dawn demanding payment if his stubborn aunt broke his favorite pipe between her teeth.

"I took Martise with me so she could translate. The manuscripts were written in ancient Helenese. I don't read it. She does." He finished the cup of *arkhi* and set it aside. His stomach churned, and he didn't want what he'd imbibed to curdle anymore than it already had. "We came across several passages describing the death of an ancient god named Amunsa. He was trapped and destroyed by a gathering of northern mage-kings. They were helped by a 'king of the south.' A man they called Birdixan." He used the Helenese pronunciation, elongating the word and putting emphasis on the first syllable.

"And you think this was Berdikhan?" She sketched her ward in the air once more.

"I'm sure of it. The far lands had no kings at that time, only chiefs and *sarsins*. But a *sarsin* who ruled several tribes like Berdikhan would be seen as a king by the northern lords. And the names are similar enough to note."

"So Karduk told you nothing you didn't already know?" Dercima snorted. "Old windbag. He probably just wanted an excuse for you to visit."

Silhara smiled. Dercima might complain about her husband, but he heard affection for him in her voice.

"I may have discovered it with time and Martise's help. But time isn't on our side. Corruption grows stronger. Conclave grows impatient." And the god breathed its avarice into his dreams almost nightly now. "Karduk showed me I'd missed the obvious." He sketched the mysterious symbol that appeared next to Berdikhan's name in the manuscripts. "Zafira."

Dercima looked to the sky, and Silhara followed her gaze. They both stared at the constellation, etched in the night's blackness in a maze pattern of stars bisected by two more paths of stars—a match to the symbol in the Helenese papers.

"Poor Zafira." She handed the pipe back to Silhara. "Here. You smoke the last. I've had enough." Her skirt flapped as she dusted her hands on the folds of fabric. "Now there's a tragic tale. I like to think she loved him and willingly gave him her power. But the lot of a *bide jiana* has always been one of force, not consent. I suspect Berdikhan sacrificed her the same way he sacrificed his other consorts."

Pipe smoke filled his mouth, acrid now instead of spicy. The *arkhi* bubbled threateningly in his belly. Berdikhan had used his life-giver wife to try and harness a god and rule a world. History might well repeat itself.

"What will you tell the priests when you return to Neith?"

Nothing if he could get away with it, but that was unlikely. As much as both parties might detest the idea, he would need their help, and they his to defeat Corruption. The question was whether he was willing to die for the effort or sacrifice another for the chance to live. He imagined Martise sleeping peacefully in the house behind him, awaiting a lover who contemplated destroying her.

If Dercima could read his thoughts at the moment, she'd gut him with her eating knife.

"Your thoughts are grim. This knowledge you have now troubles you greatly. Is it not good to know of a way to defeat the fallen god?"

"It's useful knowledge. Now I have to decide what to do with the information."

"Do you consider yourself an intelligent man?" Dercima's dark eyes reflected starlight.

"Yes."

"Are you true?"

He chuckled at her question. "That depends. True to whom?"

"Yourself."

"Always." He grew more curious at her line of questioning.

She rose, and he stood as well. "A man with clear sight into his own soul will always make a wise decision."

Silhara touched her arm briefly. "I'm less concerned with wise than I am with beneficial—to me."

She wrapped her fingers over his knuckles. "And the woman you brought with you? Is she merely a night's pleasure or something more?"

Martise. Spy and lover, servant and keeper of a vast, untapped power, she was once nothing more than a nuisance. Now, she was the linchpin upon which his most fateful choices would be made.

"She's more than that, and less."

"That isn't much of an answer, nephew."

"And you ask too many questions, aunt."

Dercima smiled. "I'm off to bed." Her breath fogged in front of her. "It's cold, and I feel it more in my bones these days." She tapped him on the arm. "Don't stay out here too long. Others may awaken and see you. I don't want people asking me why my nephew is an idiot."

He smiled and bowed. "Good night, aunt."

Her soft chuckle faded as she made her way across the open common area and disappeared into the largest of the stone houses. Silhara stared after her a few moments before returning to the house he shared with Martise.

She lay as he'd left her, sprawled on her back with one arm flung across the space where he'd sleep. Her hair spread in waves over the fleece, a few strands drifting across her cheeks and down her neck.

He hadn't meant to wake her earlier. His conversation with Karduk had left him with trembling hands and a need to see her. While he'd been silent, the scent of pipe smoke had awakened her. Flushed from sleep and the heat of the fire, she'd turned to him with a dreamy gaze. He'd almost looked away and was thankful when she turned over and fell back asleep. He'd fled outside after that.

His thoughts whirled as he cleaned his pipe and undressed. The fire burned low in the pit, and he stoked the coals enough to bring more warmth in the cooling room. Birdixan of the Helenese chronicles had been no hero, only a man consumed by a need for power who saw a chance at attaining it, no matter the cost.

Berdikhan of the Kurmans had traveled north, not for the purpose of helping the mage-kings, but of taking Amunsa's power for himself. He'd brought one of his wives with him, a life-giver and a sacrifice to his all-consuming avarice. He'd failed in his attempt to both control the god and turn on the kings. And Amunsa had been destroyed.

Silhara dwelt hard on the last. Berdikhan's actions, self-seeking though they were, had been the key to the kings' triumph. A powerful mage, made even stronger by a *bide jiana's* sacrifice, had trapped Amunsa long enough for the kings to destroy the god. The idea had worked once. It could work again. But at the same price?

Naked and cold, he crouched next to Martise, admiring the way her usually pale cheeks were rosied by the heat of the nearby fire. He'd once seen her as plain. No longer. In the red-rimmed shadows cast by the low flames, she was more beautiful than anything he'd ever beheld.

The memory of her voice when she'd summoned him back from the brink of death at Iwehvenn echoed in his mind. *"Stay with me."* That plea had called to some inner need, promised a taste of something he'd never experienced. She'd pulled him back from the abyss with the temptation of her affection. He was tempted to repay her with betrayal.

He lifted a skein of her soft hair, letting it fall through his fingers in a cascade of russet waves. "You should have let me die."

CHAPTER EIGHTEEN

At the first hint of the morning sunlight gilding the tops of Silhara's orange trees, Martise rose quietly from his bed to dress. Still warmed from his body heat, she inhaled sharply at the sudden shock of cool air on her bare skin. The blankets whispered against her legs as she stretched a thigh over his hip and crawled off the bed. The movement made her wince. He'd had a voracious appetite for her the previous night. He hadn't hurt her, but his rough attentions left their mark on her hips and a reminder in her muscles.

She gazed at his outline beneath the blankets. He lay on his stomach, face partially concealed by the crook of his arm. It was still too dark to make out his features. She imagined them pinched and scowling, even in slumber. Since their return from the Kurman village, he'd been a cauldron of quietly bubbling emotion, unleashed only in the dark when she lay beneath him.

Exhausted from loving her throughout the night, he'd dragged her on top of him and promptly fallen asleep. His rest wasn't peaceful. Violent dreams made him flail in the bed, and twice Martise narrowly avoided a blow when he lashed out, battling some invisible demon. She considered retreating to her room where she could sleep without being pummeled but abandoned the idea. Whatever dark thoughts plagued the Master of Crows in his nightmares, she wouldn't leave him alone with them.

He finally quieted, his stillness interrupted by an occasional muttered curse and the soft rhythm of snoring. Martise had sighed her relief and curled against his side. Sleep didn't come easily for her. She'd mulled over Silhara's restlessness, the subtle shift in his behavior since they'd returned to Neith.

She'd noted the change the morning they packed their gear and said their farewells to the Kurmans. She hadn't asked what the *sarsin* discussed with him, and he held his silence on the matter. That silence lasted almost the entire trip back to Neith. Never jovial in the best of moods, he was even more distant. The few times he spoke to remark on their lunch or instruct her on how to set up their camp for the most protection, he'd been remote, barely acknowledging her presence.

Martise was used to others ignoring her. But not him. His actions might have hurt save for the fact he touched her constantly on the return trip. She rode in front of him, and he kept a tight grip on her as he guided Gnat home. The one night they spent on the open plain, he held watch while she slept. She'd awakened to find him running his thumb and finger over her braid as if it were a strand of prayer beads.

They'd been back at Neith for a day, and he remained taciturn and distracted. Even when he'd taken her so passionately the previous night, he said little, though his dark eyes burned when he gazed upon her. He slept now, oblivious to her movements. Or so she thought.

"You needn't tiptoe. I'm awake."

The leine slipped from her fingers at his voice. She bent to retrieve it, wincing again. "Forgive me. I tried to be quiet."

"I hurt you."

She paused. Had he seen her flinch in the dark? His eyesight was exceptional. He moved sure-footed through Neith's lightless corridors, but she'd thought it nothing more than a natural grace combined with the familiarity of his domain. Those shrewd black eyes missed very little.

She smiled and shrugged the thin leine over her head. "I didn't notice at the time. And I probably left a bruise or two on you as well."

"Come here." His voice was no less commanding for its quiet raspiness. Blankets rustled, and he sat up.

Standing patiently between his splayed knees, Martise studied his austere face in the pallid light slowly filling the room. Dark circles ringed his eyes, revealing a lassitude that went deeper than muscle and bone. His warm fingers tugged at her leine, lifting the hem until her legs were once more exposed to the chilly air. She gasped softly at his touch, the trickle of heat fluttering over her skin as he caressed the bluish marks on her hipbones and inner thighs.

"I didn't mean these."

Reawakened desire raced through her when he placed a light kiss where thigh curved into hip. "I know."

He leaned his forehead into her belly. "Say my name."

Martise swallowed down the knot lodged in her throat. Something was horribly wrong. The volatile sorcerer who captured a storm, ridiculed a god and spat in Conclave's collective face, now sat before her, a weary pilgrim seeking succor in her embrace.

"Silhara." His hair slipped through her fingers in an inky cascade as she stroked his head. His name slid off her tongue, and she savored the feel. She loved his name, the grace of it in her mouth, the sound of it on her ears. In old Coastal, his name meant Unconquered, and the man who bore the name lived up to it in every sense.

She cupped his jaw, tilting his face so she could look in his eyes. His cheeks were rough with a day's growth of beard, and his lips were still swollen from her enthusiastic kisses the night before. He sighed when she ran her thumbs lightly over his cheekbones. "You slept poorly and chased demons in your dreams. What troubles you?"

A faint smile curved his mouth and was gone. "I don't have to sleep to chase demons, Martise." Long fingers drifted gently over the back of her thighs. "You worry over nothing. I've had more than my share of bad nights." He dropped the hem of her leine.

Not like this. At least not since she'd come to share his bed. He didn't sleep many hours, but when he did, he slept hard and was as still as death in her arms. Last night was far different, and Martise sensed the *sarsin's* words, whatever they were, weighed heavily on Silhara's thoughts. The warning gleam in his eyes told her not to pursue it further.

She stood in his loose embrace for several moments, content to simply stroke his hair while he pressed his cheek against her stomach. The clatter of pans and the bang of the bailey door downstairs signaled Gurn's arrival in the kitchens.

"I have to go downstairs and help Gurn. He burned his hand on a hot pot yesterday and will be clumsy for a few days with his bandages. Do you need anything from me?" She was reluctant to leave him.

The folds of her leine muffled his chuckle. "Can you give me salvation?"

The strange question sent another bolt of dread through her. "No."

"Then tea will do." He pulled away from her, swatting her lightly on the bottom. A grim humor hardened his smile. "I'll see you and Gurn in the kitchen. And tell him I'll want a look at that burn."

She and Gurn were almost finished with breakfast when Silhara finally made an appearance. Clean-shaven but still haggard, he sat at his customary place and proceeded to drink three pots of tea without saying a word. A sidelong glance from Gurn, and Martise shook her head. Silhara had been pensive in the privacy of his chamber. Now he was dour with storm clouds gathering in his eyes. The oranges sat untouched in their bowl, another oddity. Only once had she seen him forego the ritual of eating his two oranges, and that was due to a stomach still roiling from the effect of Peleta's Fire.

"Do you not want the oranges this morning?"

His black gaze glittered. "Not today." He looked to Gurn, busy at the hearth stoking the fire. "Gurn, show me your hand."

After inspecting the burn and reciting a spell to ease the pain, Silhara pronounced the wound on the mend. He was rewrapping it when Martise interrupted him.

"You can use me to heal him, can't you?" She caught Gurn's puzzled expression.

"No."

Stunned, she stared at him wide-eyed. He lied outright. They both knew the combination of her Gift and his skill could heal Gurn's hand. Why would he not help his most trusted servant?

"But…"

"Martise!" His voice, ruined by the garroting, managed to boom in the kitchen. "You forget yourself. I said no."

Outrage at his surprising callous treatment toward Gurn almost overrode twenty-two years of servitude. She clenched her teeth against the words rushing to her lips and finally bit out "Forgive me, Master."

Her lungs burned with the need to shout at him. Martise kept her gaze firmly on the floor, assuming the long-standing posture of servant to master. The kitchen's quiet pounded in her ears, tense and humming with a silent anger. She jumped when Silhara suddenly grasped her arm and yanked her toward the door leading to the great hall.

"The library. Now."

He hauled her up the stairs and down the hall, his grip unyielding on her wrist. Martise hurried to keep up with his long strides. The library door banged against the opposite wall and Silhara thrust her inside. A cold fire flickered in his gaze as he slammed the door behind him.

"Your Gift is a danger to everyone here, Martise. If Gurn knows of your particular talent, my willingness to remain silent about it means nothing. Conclave will do whatever it has to in order to get the information it wants." He paced in front of her. "I can withstand any seer-bonding a Conclave priest might subject me to. They'll learn nothing and may well kill us both for the effort. Gurn, however, isn't Gifted and doesn't have the means to resist a bonding. Do you think if they can't interrogate the master, they won't interrogate the servant? Being mute will not guard all his secrets. And where will you be if they learn of yours?"

Her face heated. All this time living with Silhara and Gurn, she should have realized Silhara would have good reason to let his servant and friend suffer his wound. "I'm sorry, Silhara."

His expression softened. "No need to apologize. I don't fault you for your compassion, only your indiscretion." He walked to the table where her notes were neatly stacked next to the old pages they rescued from Iwehvenn. "If Conclave were to seer-bond with Gurn, it would be to glean information about me, not you. But if they discover some hint of your talent in his memories, they'll pursue it." The look he gave her from the corner of his eye was amused. "You have no reason to suspect Conclave the way I do. I'd wonder at your caution if you did."

Martise's shoulders sagged in relief. "I'm more concerned about Gurn. I'd never deliberately hurt him."

"I know."

Ancient parchment crackled under his fingers as he flipped them gently over and stared at the writing. "The Helenese make heroes of those who would make them fools."

She came to stand beside him, bemused by his cryptic remark. The Helenese script was burned on the back of her eyelids by now. She'd read the documents dozens of times, searching for something more in the story of Amunsa that might be applied to defeating Corruption. "I don't know that these papers have helped. The ancient Conclave who first exiled Corruption used a very similar ritual, but it wasn't enough to kill him. Maybe the kings were able to destroy Amunsa because he wasn't as strong."

Silhara's next statement surprised Martise. "Without these papers, Karduk's information would be useless." He smiled faintly at her wide-eyed stare. "When the Kurman were greater in number and more powerful, they were ruled by a single *sarsin*. One who claimed his place through fratricide instead of election."

Martise waited, intrigued. She knew little of Kurman history but found it fascinating, even without its ties to the Helenese documents.

Silhara continued. "The *sarsin* was powerful and united the tribes for a short time under his rule. He was also a sorcerer, as skilled as any Conclave bishop in the ways of magery and unafraid to invoke the dark arcana. But such gifts weren't enough. He sought more through any means, sent spies far and wide to find the secrets of other peoples. He even sacrificed two of his consorts and a half dozen of his children to gain more power."

"Gods." She shuddered at the thought of such monstrous acts.

Silhara flipped more of the parchment, stopping at the last page describing Amunsa's death. A long finger traced the mysterious symbol next to Birdixan's name. "That was his goal. To be a god. He was no different from the lich of Iwehvenn except he was moved by a craving to rule a world. The soul eater was moved by a fear of death and embraced something far worse."

"Then why would he help the northern kings defeat Amunsa?"

"There was nothing left for him. The tribes rose against him, banishing him and his remaining wives from Kurman territory. They had no place to go but north. The one thing he'd sought most of his life he found in exile and by accident."

Martise rubbed the chills on her arms. "The Kurman should have killed him instead of exiling him."

Silhara gave a dark, humorless chuckle. "You're not alone in your opinion. His name was Berdikhan, and he fooled the kings into thinking he was a pilgrim traveler, a man of great power who sought their good will by helping them destroy Amunsa."

Martise gasped and snatched the stack of parchment from Silhara. She shifted through the pages and laid out those with Birdixan's name mentioned. "Berdikhan. Birdixan. I missed it. The Helenese have no equivalent for the hard sound in his name. For example, Cumbria would be written as 'Xumbria.' I should have seen it."

He shrugged. "I don't see how. You can flounder your way through a sentence when speaking Kurmanji, but how would you know to make such a connection? The Kurmans have never put their language in script. You had nothing to compare."

She appreciated his support but still cursed her folly. One document made her pause. "This piece says he swallowed the god. I can only think that's willing possession."

"It is. Berdikhan believed himself strong enough to not only harness the god long enough for the kings to entrap him, but also to take the god's power for his own."

"Become the god and destroy the kings."

"Yes. But he overestimated his strength in that regard and his cleverness. The kings knew what he intended."

"Still, they remember him as a hero in these passages, not a traitor. Why?"

Silhara lips curved into a faint smile. "People are less inclined to praise you if they know someone almost made a fool of you."

Martise met his gaze, impressed. Silhara was an astute observer of human nature. That talent alone made him formidable, even without his magic to strengthen him. She flipped back through the parchment to the last one showing the symbol next to Birdixan's name. "Did Karduk know anything about this symbol?"

"No."

She paused to stare at him. Nothing in his demeanor betrayed him. He met her eyes calmly, kept his body turned to hers, wide shoulders relaxed. But her instincts fluttered their disquiet. Silhara was lying. He knew something about that symbol and chose to keep it from her.

She kept her suspicions to herself for the moment. "What will you tell Conclave?"

A subtle shift in his stance signaled his relief when she abandoned the subject of the symbol. "Everything I've just told you. As repulsive as we may all view it, I need the priests, and they need me if they want to defeat Corruption."

Conclave could definitely use Silhara in ritual. Not only was he talented, he was young and physically strong. Magic and strength depended on each other in ritual spells. However, she didn't believe Conclave trusted him enough to invite him to a god-killing.

"They'll refuse your help."

"No, they won't."

She helped him stack the parchment together, musing aloud on the ritual. "The strongest priest would have to act as Berdikhan to hold Corruption so the others might destroy him." She shook her head, puzzled. "Some of the younger bishops are powerful enough to do it, but I know of none willing to martyr themselves."

Silhara's eyebrows rose. "Don't be so sure. There's always some idiot willing to sacrifice himself for fame and glory. Immortality through martyrdom isn't all that unusual."

He placed his hand over hers as she continued to fiddle with the parchment. "Enough for now. I need to write a letter to the Luminary. I'm sure Gurn can keep you occupied until midday?"

The strange disquiet wouldn't leave her. He held something from her. She heard it in his voice, felt it in the tension of his body next to hers. "Silhara..."

"Later, Martise."

He swept out of the library, leaving her to trail after him, sick with a sense of dread.

Distracted by thoughts of her conversation with Silhara, she said little to Gurn as she spent the morning helping him with chores. Her stomach continued churning with unease. Silhara hated Conclave, had made no secret of his loathing for the priesthood. If she were honest, she sympathized with his enmity. But what if he wanted to take on the role of Berdikhan? Suds dripped from her hands as she clutched a dirty dish and stared, unseeing, at the soapy water. Silhara's survival instincts were honed too sharp for him to willingly give his life for such a cause, but he might well succumb to the temptation of vengeance. He might not die for a world, but would he do so for his own hatred?

"Ah, gods," she murmured. "What are you up to, Silhara?" She'd come to Neith for the purpose of betraying him, to send him to a different death. But that had been when the temptation of her freedom overrode the morality of her soul, and when Silhara of Neith was nothing more than a means to an end. Everything had changed since then. Even if he'd never discovered her Gift or she'd witnessed a hundred traitorous acts on his part, she wouldn't betray him. Dour and scornful, yet generous and loyal to his own, he'd taken her heart and made her love him. "You must live for me," she said softly. "Don't make my sacrifice an empty one."

She'd talk to him, beg him if necessary if such were his plans. Her hope lay with the priests. Silhara might offer to act as Berdikhan, but the priests weren't like the northern kings. They didn't trust the Master of Crows. The idea that they might allow him to participate in the ritual at all was far-fetched. Allowing him to act as the key player was out of the question.

At midday, Martise and Gurn ate their lunch in the kitchen without Silhara. Shut in the downstairs study since morning, he hadn't emerged at the tempting fragrance of Gurn's soup. Gurn loaded a tray with a deep bowl filled with broth, two loaves of bread and a pitcher of wine. Martise, desperate to speak with Silhara once more, quickly volunteered to take the tray to him.

The study door was open partway, allowing strands of light to ripple along the corridor's dark walls. Martise balanced the tray of food on one shoulder and rapped on the door to announce her presence before crossing the threshold. She saw Silhara, not at the desk writing, but standing near the small window that looked out onto the grove. A dry zephyr wind, smelling of dust and orange blossom, swept inside. It spun through the room, shuffled parchments on the desk with unseen hands and played with Silhara's dark hair before fading to a gentle sigh.

Martise might have thought nothing of it, save for the welcome warmth it brought. The chamber was icy with a sepulchral chill that reminded her of the Conclave cemetery or worse–those brief moments before a summoner brought forth a demon. Fear scuttled down her spine.

From somewhere in the house's labyrinth of corridors and rooms, Cael set up a howl loud enough to raise the dead. Silhara remained at the window, ominously still. Martise tried to swallow and found her mouth dry as chaff. Every instinct screamed at her to run, to drop the tray and race for sanctuary. Sweat dotted her upper lip despite the numbing cold pouring through the doorway. She prayed he didn't know she was there, dreaded what she might see when he finally turned and faced her.

She eased back toward the hall's shadows one step at a time. Gurn. She had to warn Gurn. Of what, she didn't know, only that they were all in imminent danger, and the master of Neith had somehow become the greatest threat to their safety.

Her cry echoed down the hall when an invisible force suddenly struck her in the back, shoving her farther into the room. She managed to twist away just in time to keep from shattering her nose against the door's edge. The tray she carried flew out of her hand, tilting end over end, sending a shower of soup and wine splattering across every surface. Martise pitched forward, staggering until her hip struck the work table. She gripped its edges in an attempt to keep her footing on the now slick floor.

The unseen hand abruptly ceased pushing her forward. Martise ran for the door, terror giving her feet wings. The crack of wood slamming against the frame buffeted her ears. She skidded in a puddle and fell against the door's carved face. When she turned to face her adversary, Silhara had abandoned his place at the window and walked slowly toward her. Backlit by the sun's red rays, he was no more than a lithe, sinister shadow.

"We meet again, servant."

Martise gasped. Sweat ran in rivulets down her ribs despite the brutal cold glazing her skin. He was no longer hoarse. The rasp normally characterizing his speech gave way to a deep timbre as smooth as a silk strangling scarf. Whoever or whatever spoke to her was not Silhara of Neith.

"Silhara?" The question fading on a choked breath as he drew closer, and she got a good look at his features.

Still the hard face she knew and loved, all sharp planes and unforgiving angles, it had taken on a skeletal cast. His prominent cheekbones stood out in high relief, accentuating the sunken hollows beneath his eyes. He looked starved, drained of life and spirit. His eyes made her shrink against the door and edge her way along the wall. The whites of his eyes were gone, replaced by a solid black stare from which something inhuman and ancient gazed back at her.

Silhara, or the thing inhabiting his body, looked upon her with unblinking curiosity, much as a viper waiting to strike. Her teeth chattered, and a faint whimper escaped her lips. He cocked his head, nostrils flaring as if to catch the scent of her terror. His actions reminded her of the way Corruption acted when it first entered her room as a white and faceless abomination.

He kept pace with her as she slid along the back wall in a futile attempt to keep distance between them. "He craves you." Long fingers reached out to skate along her collarbone. She flinched at the touch. "Why? You have no beauty to speak of." He leaned into her, drawing a deep breath against her neck. "Still, there is something within you—unique, appetizing. Something unafraid."

Horror nearly blotted out all reason, and she lunged away from him—or tried to, only to be held fast in place. Her Gift, buried within the deep recesses of her soul, twisted and turned in reaction. The power that had thrust her into the chamber now shackled her to the wall. Her heart thumped against her ribs. Over Silhara's bent shoulder she glimpsed the window, the orange grove beyond etched in the shadow of a summer sun, and the dull star drawing ever closer on the horizon.

Corruption had taken him, possessed the man whose ambitions and desires coincided with the will of the fallen god. Martise wanted to vomit. Her notions of slavery had been burned to ash more than once here at Neith. But this trumped them all. She had never known this form of bondage, singular and nightmarish. Her voice, thin and unsteady, begged for mercy. "Please. Release him. He won't serve you willingly."

The god laughed softly in her ear, the dulcet tones raising the fine hairs at her nape. "I disagree. Silhara of Neith is willful and stubborn, but he is also ambitious. All those things he wishes for—power, respect, control—I can give him. He knows this. In time, he shall turn fully to me."

Martise did her best to melt into the stone wall against her back as Silhara straightened. His gaunt face filled her vision once more. The intense, passionate lover who had arched beneath her caressing hands the night before was gone, overwhelmed by an evil whose smile never reached the dead black eyes. He swept a hand down his body. "As you can see, he is nearly mine already."

Revulsion curdled the food in her stomach. "Your price for such rewards is too high."

"Not for him. He will have dominion over the world through me, wealth and immortality. And I will have the greatest avatar ever born, stronger than those before him. One who will lead my armies and conquer all before me."

Martise's terror mingled with shock. Bursin's wings! Silhara, the reborn avatar. And he knew. Surely, he knew. Tears of despair and rage made her vision swim. A lesser man might well serve Corruption, but not the Master of Crows. A man who refused to bow to Conclave would not submit as puppet to a god.

Her lip curled as she stared into the god's dead eyes. This was no creature worthy of deification, only a parasite with no greater wish than to yoke a world to serve its petty whims.

"You're mistaken." She found some small measure of strength in the renewed steadiness in her voice. "He will not surrender to you. You've fed his temptation and turned him for a moment, but it won't last." She met the dark, reptilian gaze unflinchingly. "Release him. You are false and unworthy of either worship or Silhara's servitude."

A flicker of something—uncertainty, doubt—chased a whirl of shadows in Silhara's possessed gaze. He lashed out, fingers curving around her throat as he straight-armed her off the floor. There wasn't even time to scream. She dangled in midair, choking and clawing at the hand slowly crushing the breath out of her.

He was preternaturally strong, holding her aloft with ease, oblivious to her nails digging bloodied furrows into his hand. Her feet kicked in a desperate bid to find some purchase as black spots danced in her vision. Her struggles were rewarded when her foot connected with something soft. Silhara's calculating expression never changed. The force of her blow, which should have brought him to his knees, had no effect, filled as he was with the god's power.

He tightened his hold slowly, his mouth curving into another brittle, calculating smile. "You will have the honor of being my first condemned heretic."

Her vision grayed. Her air-starved lungs burned in her chest. Somewhere, in the fading threads of her consciousness, she heard the sound of running feet, the frantic barking of a dog. The wall behind her vibrated as the door shook on its hinges from a relentless pounding. Gurn and Cael come to save them both. Too late, her mind whispered. Too late.

"Please," she prayed in choked silence. "Help me."

A god didn't answer, but her Gift did. Released from her control, it surged out of her, bathing her and Silhara in amber light. A powerful wrench snapped her head against the wall as Silhara lost his grip. Invisible hands lifted him off his feet and slammed him across the room. He crashed into the desk, hard enough to overturn it.

Martise hit the floor in a gasping, gagging heap. She struggled to take one, two precious gulps of air before rolling to her back. The ceiling spun above her in a shimmering sea, and the pounding at the door was a monstrous heartbeat in her ears. She turned on her side and saw Silhara.

Slumped against the overturned desk, he looked like a broken doll. His head was lowered, shoulders sagging as if Corruption had suddenly cut the strings that held him a prisoner puppet. Blood streaked from his nose and down his mouth. Drops splashed on his hands, mingling with the blood seeping from the wounds she'd gouged into his skin.

She sucked in a pained breath and crawled to him, terrified that Corruption still held sway but desperate to reach him. Her sigh of relief scorched her throat when Silhara raised his head and blinked slowly. His eyes, bloodshot and nearly crossed, were human again. Tears dripped from her cheeks, mingling with the blood on his hands. Martise touched his nose, his mouth and kissed his forehead. She tried to speak, to thank more merciful gods that he was whole again, but she was mute, her voice lost from his strangle hold.

Silhara stared at her, dazed. His lips parted. Suddenly, what little color he still retained drained from his skin. His mouth opened in a rictus of pain, and he clutched the place between his legs. Martise backed away when he keeled onto his side and curled into a fetal position, gasping in wordless agony.

CHAPTER NINETEEN

Black pain roared through his body, swiping at him with claws that dug deep into his ribs, his skull, and especially into his groin and back. Martise's pinched features swam in his vision. Silhara found it hard to reconcile that the woman who now stroked his sweating face with gentle fingers was the same woman who practically kicked his balls into his throat.

"Get away from me, demon," he wheezed.

Her shoulders sagged in relief at his reprimand. Tears painted luminous trails on her pallid cheeks, and the red marks left by his fingers circled her neck in a ghastly collar. Still, she'd found the courage to come near him after what he'd just done to her.

The pounding on the door continued until the mage-ward faded. Gurn, wielding his cudgel, and Cael, red-eyed and bristling, burst into the room ready to do battle. The dog crept toward Silhara, teeth bared. Any recognition of his master had fled, and his wide nostrils twitched at Corruption's scent in the air.

Too injured to dodge a possible attack, Silhara snapped at Gurn. "Get him out of here before he decides to sink his teeth into me."

Gurn hauled Cael back, careful to stay clear of the snapping jaws as the dog resisted his efforts to toss him out the door. The moment Gurn closed the door on him, Cael set up a howling racket that had Silhara wincing.

Content to lie on his side and let the pain ebb and flow through his body, he stared at Martise. She sat next to him, a mix of fear and compassion in her gaze. Gurn crouched beside him, shaking his head. His big hands were gentle as he prodded Silhara for injuries.

Silhara shrugged off his touch. "I'll be fine in a moment. See to Martise. I just tried to kill her."

Gurn's eyes rounded at her disheveled appearance and the darkening bruises on her neck. She gave him a brief smile and tried to speak. The resulting croak made everyone flinch. Gurn clucked in sympathy. He signed he'd return with drinks for them both and something for Silhara to wash away the blood. He rose and offered his hand to help Martise stand. She declined with a quick shake of her head. Silhara's eyebrows rose when she used the same hand motions as Gurn, who grinned and bowed before leaving the room.

Silhara, as pleased as Gurn, smiled through the residual pain thrumming through his muscles. "You could have demonstrated no greater friendship to him than that. Not even if you saved his life." She blushed and signed to him that she was very fond of Gurn.

He levered himself into a sitting position and wiped the blood from his nose and mouth with a trembling hand. The metallic taste on the back of his throat made his stomach turn, and he spat on the floor to rid himself of the taste. Martise scooted to sit in front of him and signed an apology.

Silhara grumbled and shielded his groin with one hand. "Who could guess that such a small woman would make so formidable an opponent?" He winced. "I'm lucky you didn't break a rib or two. Do you often toss your lovers around the room like that?"

Martise tried to laugh and stopped. She rubbed her throat.

Silhara reached out to run a light finger over one of the marks on the side of her neck. "It's I who should beg your forgiveness. I've thieved and murdered in my lifetime and regret little of those actions. But if I've destroyed that wondrous voice..."

He'd been harsh with her. Deadly as well. He'd marked her when loving her, and again when he tried to strangle her. Two sides to a tarnished coin. A hard knot settled under his ribs. Her time at Neith was finished. So was Gurn's. The god's newest attack and subsequent possession—the worst and longest so far—solidified the decision he'd pondered over the last two days. For their protection, he'd send Martise back to the bishop before her scheduled time and order Gurn to Eastern Prime.

Martise knew his secret now, and it didn't matter if she told the world. He'd won his battles against Conclave and ultimately lost the war—and the woman he'd grown to love.

She touched his hand, entwined her fingers with his. He stared down at her chafed knuckles, the pink nails rimmed with his blood. History might see him as a hero, like Berdikhan. None would know he'd martyred himself, not for a world, but for this woman.

He tugged on her hand. "Come closer."

She hesitated for a brief moment then inched closer until she was almost in his lap.

He caressed her neck. "I can heal these with your help. But we'll do it now before Gurn returns."

After what her Gift just did to him, he took a risk in asking her to recall her magic. He hoped the near-sentient entity had reacted to Corruption's presence within him and not to him alone. Martise nodded once and closed her eyes. Within moments the air around her shimmered with amber light. Serpentine tendrils wrapped around his wrists in a lover's clasp, so different from the combative force that had swatted him across the room earlier. Power, cleansing and redeeming, flowed into his hands and spread throughout his body. The strength of her Gift washed away Corruption's taint and filled him with Martise's essence—a steady flame that burned low but strong and enveloped his soul in a soft embrace.

Bewitched by the seductive sensation of living power, Silhara reveled in the deep bonding. Martise sat still before him, her eyelids at half-mast as she met his gaze. His tongue felt thick as he recited a simple healing spell, one that did nothing more than heal a scrape. With her Gift's power, the spell worked a greater magic. The bruises faded from her skin, and the swelling muscles and tendons beneath his fingers softened.

"Enough," he said, and withdrew his hands.

Martise breathed deep and closed her eyes once more. The amber light unwound from Silhara's arms and wrists, undulating away from him to coalesce into a pinpoint of light centered at Martise's chest. It pulsed twice before disappearing into the fabric of her tunic.

Silhara nodded in approval. She had a good command of her stubborn talent now and suppressed it with less effort. With continued practice, she'd have no difficulty hiding it from the priests so they'd never suspect her Gift had manifested.

Without the comforting force of her power running in his blood, the pain of his injuries returned. He shifted and cursed when that small movement sent a sharp pain through his side. Martise reached for him, but he waved her away.

"Let's see if that spell did any good for your voice. Try to speak."

"Thank you," she said and grinned when the words came out in something more than an incoherent croak. Her voice remained a little hoarse, but no worse than it might sound if she was ill with a cold.

"You sing badly enough as it is," he teased. "I'd never be redeemed if I made you sound like me."

Her soft laughter soothed him. She didn't hate or fear him, even now after he'd almost killed her. Despair threatened to consume him. He would mourn her, even beyond his death. Were circumstances different, he'd fight to keep her, kill Cumbria if necessary to wrest her from him and face the wrath of Conclave for slaughtering their most powerful bishop. But fate played a diabolical joke on him. He would be no better than Berdikhan or even Corruption if he sacrificed his own *bide jiana* for the chance of living through the god-killing ritual. A scathing anger filled him. He wasn't noble, only heart-bound, and surely the second was more pathetic than the first. He'd give Martise up freely and destroy himself to save her. What had she once said? The gods laughed. Indeed they did.

He banished his self-recriminations. No need to dwell on what a weak fool he'd become. Martise held out a hand once more when he clambered unsteadily to his feet. Again, he waved her off.

"Don't. I've gained a healthy respect for your feet. As soon as I'm sure you haven't completely emasculated me, you can help."

She blushed. "Can't you heal yourself the same way you healed my throat?"

The idea of her hand, heated by the magic of her Gift, cupping his balls would normally have him erect. Now, with the steady ache in his groin fanning out to his back and down his legs, he found the notion less than appealing.

"Your trust in me is greater than mine in you. As much as I might usually enjoy it, I think it best you keep your hands off my cock for now, Martise."

His blunt statement took the sting out of his refusal. A small smile flickered across her lips before fading.

"Are you well, Silhara?" Dark memories shadowed her eyes. "The god... your eyes..."

A rising bile, mixed with the remnants of blood, burned the back of his throat. He raised his hands and frowned at their trembling. "Now you know why the star hovers at Neith."

Martise clasped her hands in front of her. Her white knuckles contrasted with her calm voice. "You're the avatar reborn."

"Yes."

Gurn's return prevented him from saying more. The servant carried a tray with two steaming cups and a stack of wet towels. He handed one cup to Martise and another to Silhara, along with a towel.

Martise snatched the towel out of Silhara's hand. "Will you trust me enough to bathe your face? I promise no kicking."

She set her cup on the floor when he nodded and proceeded to wipe away the blood. The cloth was cool on his cheeks and her touch soothing. Silhara stood passive beneath her ministrations, never looking away as she rubbed smears of dried blood from his nose and chin. The towel hovered at the corner of his mouth. Silhara, attuned to her every breath, bent toward her as she stood on tip-toe and kissed the spot.

"No one should suffer such bondage," she whispered against his mouth. "I would take this burden if I could."

Lightning shot through his soul. Such devotion. Martise was a compassionate woman, but this went far beyond sympathy. Did she love him as he did her? See him as something other than the threat Conclave saw? Would she grieve their separation in the same silence? The anguish in her eyes answered his question.

He stroked her temple with his thumb. "That is a debt I cannot and will not repay." The same thumb pressed against her lips when she tried to argue. "There is always a cost, Martise."

He took the towel from her and gingerly cleaned his hands before giving it back. "Don't forget your cup. My spell has done most of the work, but I can assure you Gurn's draught will heal you completely."

His cup was filled with a tea brewed blacker than ink and sweetened heavily with honey. A simple but effective restorative. Silhara raised the cup in salute to Gurn. The dull pain in his chest grew. He would soon lose Gurn as well, and that hurt almost as much as losing Martise.

Gurn, pleased his patients drank his brews, began cleaning the study. He tried unsuccessfully to shoo Martise away when she set to helping him. Silhara, still too sore to do more than watch, limped to the other side of the overturned desk. Parchment lay scattered across the floor, much of it splattered in ink. He picked up one page, his letter to the Luminary of Conclave. A black stain smeared the bottom of the letter, but it was still readable.

Eminence, I offer you the opportunity to kill me and destroy Corruption in one act. Are you interested?

Silhara, Master of Neith

The letter was dry, grains of sand still trapped on the paper. He shook it off and rolled the parchment into a tight scroll. Gurn motioned to him when he stepped over the puddles of wine and soup and made his way to the door.

"I'm well enough, though I doubt I'll sire children now." He smiled slightly at Martise's blush.

Like Gurn, she wore a worried expression. "Corruption…"

"Will bide its time. I doubt you'll see it again." He'd make certain she was back at Asher the next time Corruption paid him a visit.

He paused at the door. "I'll be in my chambers. When you and Gurn are finished here, one of you bring me a cup of the Fire."

Martise held one of Gurn's towels, now stained with wine. "Will you be all right alone?"

Silhara snorted. "I'm not a child, Martise. I haven't needed my mother for many years."

He left them in the study and limped to his room. Once inside, he groaned and cupped his groin once more. "Bursin's wings, woman. I hadn't thought to die a eunuch."

For a moment he regretted refusing the offer of her Gift to heal his own aches and pains and settled on a simple spell that numbed the soreness between his legs. His shirt was ruined, blood-stained across the chest and torn in places from Martise's clawing hands. He stripped it off and tossed it on the bed. His injured hands still shook, lingering signs of the god's brutal control. Silhara growled and strode out to his balcony. Against the blue sky, Corruption's star shone a bright white now.

"Pleased with yourself, Corruption?"

The god remained silent for once, but the star pulsed in triumph. Silhara scowled. Corruption grew stronger every day. For all his strength and skill, he didn't think he could resist much longer. If he didn't go to the god willingly, Corruption would eventually take him by force. If, however, he allowed the god possession, he might still retain some control of himself and Corruption for a short time — long enough to perform the ritual that would trap the god, killing it and him in the bargain.

Cumbria would see him dead at last, but not as he might wish. Instead of a criminal executed for treachery or heresy, Silhara would die a martyred hero.

He didn't care about heroism or martyrdom or foiling Cumbria's plans. He wanted to live, to harvest his oranges, to live at Neith without Conclave up his nose and keep Martise by his side until he died of old age instead of this cursed nobility suddenly afflicting him.

But none of this would be his fate if he stood by and watched Corruption swell with power until it consumed him and the world it sought to conquer. Despite what others might think or how history might record it, Silhara was self-serving. Corruption was no different than the lich of Iwehvenn, and Silhara chose to die with his soul intact rather than live a shell of a man who'd lost his humanity.

A sly inner voice whispered to him. *"You might live. You swive a bide jiana every night. Use her for what she is made."*

Weeks earlier, he might have done so without a second thought, when Martise was nothing more than an instrument of Conclave whose purpose was to betray him. Things had changed.

"I am pathetic," he muttered. "I condemn myself and risk a world for a woman."

He returned to his room. The letter to the Luminary lay on his bed, half unfurled next to his stained shirt. Silhara reread the short missive before rolling it and transforming it into a sphere of light no bigger than a thimble. Back out on the balcony he summoned a crow from one of the trees and placed the sphere under the ensorcelled bird's wing. The glossy black feathers were smooth as he stroked the crow's back.

"Conclave," he said. "The Luminary."

The bird cawed once before taking flight, winging its way toward the coast and Conclave's stronghold.

He expected the priests to be on his doorstep in a matter of days. The Luminary might not bother to reply; just appear with his entourage in tow to discuss his plans with Silhara.

Behind him, a soft knock sounded against his door. Martise's voice drifted to the balcony.

"Silhara?"

"For now. I'm on the balcony."

Her light footfalls drew closer. Disheveled and flushed from helping Gurn downstairs, she smiled and passed him a goblet. "How are…"

"My bollocks? Sore, but at least I'm no longer choking on them. How's your throat?"

She touched her neck. "Good. Gurn had me drink a little of the Fire, and it helped."

Silhara tipped the goblet and drained half the contents. The drink scorched his insides, leaving a pleasant euphoria in its wake. He breathed hard and rubbed his watering eyes. "Nothing can kill pain or cause it like Dragon Piss." He set the cup on the balcony railing. "Did you know soldiers use Peleta's Fire to keep battle wounds from poisoning?"

He motioned her closer and drew her against him. Her back was warm, and she smelled of orange flowers. He nuzzled her neck.

"You now have something to tell the bishop."

Martise stiffened.

"Surely, you knew I'd guessed your purpose here the day you arrived?" He kissed her temple.

Her voice was steady. "Yes, but I wouldn't have admitted it had you confronted me earlier." She turned in his arms, copper eyes guarded as she met his gaze. "And I have nothing to tell the bishop."

Silhara stroked her back and ran her long braid through his fingers. "It wouldn't matter if you did, Martise. Only you and I will know of your Gift. Your secret is safe."

She pressed against him, her breasts soft beneath her tunic. Summer sun caressed her upturned face. "Even if I had no secret to protect, I wouldn't tell the bishop what I saw today."

A declaration of loyalties changed. Silhara closed his eyes and embraced her. He should feel triumphant. He'd won over the spy and defeated Cumbria at his little game. But he'd lost the woman in the bargain.

He peered down at her. "What reward are you forfeiting for your silence?"

Her gaze slid away. "Nothing worth a man's life."

Silhara chuckled. "My fair innocent. Men sacrifice other men for power and wealth, food and sometimes just for entertainment."

She looked at him with those somber eyes. "What do we sacrifice ourselves for?"

Her question caught him off guard. He didn't answer, only kissed her forehead.

"What does the symbol mean, Silhara?"

More tenacious than a mage-finder with a kill, she refused to give up on the notion he knew about the symbol next to Berdikhan's name. Thank Bursin they weren't having this discussion at night. He might not resist the temptation to stare at Zafira's constellation as he'd done so many times since their return from the Kurman camp.

"I don't know."

Her eyes narrowed. "You're lying."

Silhara chuckled. He very much liked when she displayed such ferocity. He lowered his mouth to hers, ran his tongue along her bottom lip. "Prove it," he whispered.

She sank into him as he kissed her. He savored the feel of her in his arms. If he wasn't still recovering from Corruption's possession and her effective defense, he'd take her to bed and make love to her for the remainder of the afternoon and into the night.

He groaned when she pulled away and gave him a piercing look. "Wait. What do you mean it doesn't matter if I tell the bishop you're the avatar?"

He raised his eyes to the heavens. "So much for my powers of seduction." Martise didn't crack a smile. "Conclave's first attempt to destroy Corruption only resulted in a long exile. This time, they must rely on the avatar to defeat the god."

Realization struck her, swift and hard. Her eyes darkened until they were nearly as black as his. "No!" She clutched his arms. "Let someone else be Berdikhan. The Luminary or Cumbria. They are as strong as you. As powerful. This is Conclave's purpose, not yours!"

Silhara shrugged her off. "But it is my redemption." He raised her hand to his lips and kissed her knuckles. "What did you see when you looked into my face an hour ago?"

Her hand trembled in his grip. "Something soulless."

He inclined his head. "An apt description. Conclave has accused me of such failings many times. Now, they'd be right." He released her hand. "I've no wish to be reduced to a cipher, Martise. I'll die before that happens, and I'll take Corruption down with me."

She bowed her head. "I wish you loved me," she said in a small voice. "Maybe then I could make you halt this madness."

Her statement almost brought him to his knees. It was because he loved her that he followed this path, but telling her so would only make her protest harder or worse, do something foolish that might compromise them both. He closed his eyes for a moment and told his greatest lie.

"I don't love you. You are an admirable woman, more so than any other person I've known save Gurn. But that has little bearing here."

The faintest moan hovered between them before the afternoon breeze snatched it away. Martise clasped her hands together.

"Would it matter at all if I said I loved you?"

A part of Silhara, the smallest part that remembered his humanity and his ability to love, shuddered. "No."

He raised her head with a fingertip under her chin. Tears coursed down her wan cheeks and dripped onto his hand. He fancied they burned. "Ready your things. I'm returning you to your true master."

He kissed her again, hard. He'd take the memory of her taste with him to his death.

She returned his kiss briefly before fleeing the balcony. Once the door closed behind her he entered his chamber with the half-finished goblet of Peleta's Fire, donned a new shirt and prepared his *huqqah*.

The tobacco's smooth taste dampened the alcohol's harshness, and Silhara smoked from the *huqqah* in long draws. He exhaled a cloud of smoke in a slow breath, murmuring arcane words as he did. The smoke swirled and spun in purposeful patterns, shaping itself into a misty replica of Martise's face. The ghostly image hung in the air before him, and he traced its outline.

"My own Zafira. You have condemned me."

CHAPTER TWENTY

"How do we know we can trust you?"

Cumbria's question lashed across the clatter of tea cups and the whisper of robes.

Silhara, dressed in his red robe and at ease in his library amongst a gathering of Conclave bishops, reclined in his chair and smirked. "You don't."

Steam from the hot tea kettle scalded Martise's fingers as she refilled their cups. The contingent of priests, including the all-powerful Luminary, had been here less than two hours, and already the bishop and the mage postured and prepared to engage in combat.

Cumbria turned to the short, balding priest next to him. Younger than Cumbria and not nearly as imposing, he had a round, jovial face and sharp eyes that burned holes through a person with their stare. Martise had only been this close to the Luminary once before, and she remained suitably awed.

The bishop touched his forehead in deference. "Eminence, you would rest the fate of the world on this outcast and the mythology of those savages whose blood he shares?"

Silhara's eyebrows rose. He ran a lazy fingertip around the rim of his teacup. "I share your blood, Uncle. Are you a savage?"

Stifled gasps from the other priests punctuated Silhara's question. Martise almost dropped the half empty teapot into a lesser bishop's lap. At the makeshift sideboard hastily prepared for this meeting, Gurn calmly buttered bread slices and smiled.

"Never call me that!" His bony hands curled into fists, Cumbria leaned across the table as if to leap at Silhara and pummel him.

"Cumbria! This isn't the time for family squabbles." The Luminary's command snapped everyone to attention, including Silhara who straightened from his indolent slouch.

Martise took one of the plates of bread from Gurn with a distracted nod. Her thoughts spun. The bishop was Silhara's uncle? She doubted she'd be more shocked if he said Cumbria was actually a woman.

They were blood kin and hated each other with a ferocity reserved for born enemies. She understood a little of Silhara's animosity. He'd been treated badly at Conclave, more so than most initiates, and Cumbria had been the culprit in each abuse.

Silhara had only hinted at the bishop's motivation for bullying a novitiate, and she'd found the behavior odd. Twenty-two years of slavery to the house of Asher, and she'd never seen nor been subjected to such cruelty by her master. Cumbria was fair in his manner, harsh when necessary, uninterested in his servants most times. Why he'd act so viciously toward another, especially a relative, baffled her.

She circled the table with Gurn, placing the food in the center for easy reach. More tea was poured, and the tension in the library slowly ebbed. She was at ease in this familiar role. Hardly seen and never heard, she could observe every action, hear every word said and remember it all. Cumbria would interrogate her once they were alone, make her recite each sentence uttered by any person contributing to the conversation.

The Luminary helped himself to the bread. He pointed a piece of crust at Silhara. "I've known you since you were a boy, Silhara. An uncontrolled, rebellious, strong-willed boy with a honed instinct for survival. The man is much the same, save for the control. You're quite good at that now. The ritual of the northern kings could work, especially with a willing martyr at its center. What I want to know is why you choose to be that martyr?"

Silhara shoved his cup away and met the Luminary's sharp gaze with one of his own. "I'm the avatar reborn."

Smothering a faint moan of despair, Martise closed her eyes. He'd damned himself with that admission.

Cumbria slapped his hands on the table. "I knew it!" His voice rang triumphant. "How many times, Eminence, did I say he was the one? We took a viper into our midst, and now he's betrayed us."

Silhara rolled his eyes. "Tell me, Uncle," he emphasized the address and smiled when Cumbria's eyes sparked. "How have I betrayed Conclave? I came to you for an apprentice so that I might find a way to kill the god." For the first time Martise saw a resemblance between the two men in Silhara's overt disdain. "Martise makes a far better translator than she does a spy. You're wasting her talents." She looked away when he glanced at her. "Together, we found you a ritual that will work and an idiot ready and willing to act the sacrificial offering.

"He's lying," Cumbria snapped.

"Believe what you want. Use the ritual or don't. Use me in it or don't, but make up your mind so I'll know if I should prepare to die or prepare to harvest. I'll have orange flowers ready for picking soon."

Martise shook her head. No wonder Conclave gnashed its collective teeth. He showed no deference, offered no obsequiousness. Pragmatic to a fault, even before the most powerful men in the far lands. The fact that these same men had gathered at Neith instead of summoning him to Conclave Redoubt spoke a great deal of their acceptance to deal with the Master of Crows on his terms.

"Are you certain you're the avatar?" The Luminary's intense scrutiny might have set Silhara's robes on fire.

Silhara didn't cower. "If I'm not, then Corruption has wasted time courting the wrong puppet. Four days ago the god took full possession of me, and I almost killed the bishop's ward." Martise blushed when a dozen pairs of eyes suddenly turned to her. "He wants me, and has himself named me his avatar."

Cumbria rubbed his temples. "Eminence, he will turn on us in the ritual."

"I can turn on you now, and you can't stop me."

The bishop ignored him. "Use someone else."

The leader of Conclave looked to his bishop with a frustrated sigh. "Who, Cumbria? Are you volunteering?" He raised an eyebrow when Cumbria paled.

Silhara laughed. "Your Grace, You've tried to nail or hang my carcass from the nearest tree for more than twenty years. Now, when I offer myself on a plate, you refuse? Hoping for a little more blood sport?"

The Luminary laced his fingers together and looked to each of the priests sitting before him. "Like it or not, Silhara is the key to the ritual. Just like Berdikhan before him. He's powerful enough to trap the god within him long enough for us to do our work and physically strong enough to withstand our attack until the god is dead. Most of all, Corruption *wants* Silhara. No effort has to be made in luring the god to him."

Cumbria still resisted. "We should take this to the Holy See."

"We don't have time, and half the See is here already. We cast our vote now. If yes, then we plan at Eastern Prime and meet again at Ferrin's Tor in two days' time." He gazed at Silhara. "Can you fend off Corruption that long? Or do I need to bewitch you into unconsciousness?"

The mage chuckled. "A day or two is nothing. A month, and I might need that rest."

The Luminary raised his hand. "Cast your vote. Aye for the ritual. Nay against. I say aye."

A chorus of "aye" followed his declaration, even Cumbria, who uttered his sullen agreement last.

Martise stared at her feet. She wanted to retch. Silhara had drafted his own death warrant, and the priests had signed it. How ironic that the one man who most wanted to see him dead had been the most reluctant to give his approval.

Two days. If only two days encompassed eternity.

She looked up and found Silhara watching her, those dark eyes so deep, so filled with secrets and shadows. "Please," she mouthed to him. He shook his head before rising with the rest of the priests when the Luminary stood. He glanced at her a final time before walking out with the Luminary by his side.

Cumbria stayed behind, cornering her near the windows. Gurn hovered nearby, ostensibly to clean the table and clear away the remains of their refreshments. The bishop wore no ornamentation to dress his gray silk robes except her spirit stone on its silver chain. A terrible yearning rose within her, followed by despair. She'd given up her chance to live as a free woman, to regain the part of herself taken from her as a child. Given the opportunity, she'd do it again if it meant protecting Silhara from Conclave, but the realization didn't lessen the pain.

"You failed."

Martise dragged her gaze from the blue jewel to Cumbria's face. "Yes, Your Grace." She had no excuses, made no apologies.

His mouth turned down. "Did you even try?"

She had. At first. "Yes. I sang to your crow. He never came. I witnessed the possession, but Sil…" She paused at his narrowed look. "The mage sent a message to the Luminary before I could send one to you."

The motion of his fingers caressing the stone hypnotized her. Martise didn't hide her longing. They both knew how much that stone meant to her. Cumbria's gaunt face softened, and he let his hand fall to his side. "Nothing has turned out as I'd hoped. For you either, I expect."

"No," she said simply. Her loss was nothing compared to what Silhara faced.

"It doesn't surprise me that Silhara knew your purpose here. I am surprised he let you stay as long as you have." One gray eyebrow rose as he eyed her with a speculative gaze. "And you're none the worse for your sojourn. A bit thinner, a bit darker from the sun."

Her body was fine; her heart was shattered. She plucked at the folds of her skirt. "I was of some use with the Helenese tomes. And I helped with the harvest."

Cumbria wrapped his robes more closely about him. "Conclave will reward you for your discovery, but I won't free you." Martise keened inside but kept her expression blank. "I need your skills. And Silhara's death was never meant to be that of a hero. Make ready. We leave for Eastern Prime in an hour."

She watched him go and gasped when a heavy weight descended on her shoulder. Gurn stood next to her, sympathy deepening the blue of his eyes. So focused on Cumbria and the crushing confirmation of her continued bondage, she'd forgotten he still lingered in the room with them. He patted her shoulder in a comforting gesture.

His hands drew patterns in the air, his lips moving in soundless words. Martise chuckled despite her gloom. "Killing him won't help either of us, Gurn. Conclave justice is quick and merciless. You'd be dead, and I'd likely be sold to someone worse." She shrugged. "He isn't so bad. The lot of a slave is never easy, but mine has been far easier than most."

She patted his hand. "I have to get my things." She'd miss Gurn and Cael. They, like Silhara, had become her family. The lump in her throat made it hard to talk. She managed to croak out a question. "Will you escort us to the gates?"

He nodded and patted her arm once more. Martise left him to finish straightening the library and returned to her chamber.

The door had barely clicked shut when Silhara emerged from a shadowed corner of her room. A ripple of air flowed from his fingers, fanned out until it encompassed the chamber and lapped against the walls. Her ears popped in protest. He'd invoked a silencing ward. No one outside the door would hear a thing, not even a scream.

His eyes blazed in a face gone white with fury. "I knew you weren't Cumbria's ward." The words, icy and sharp, sent chills down Martise's arms. She retreated as he stalked her. "A servant, yes. A unique and educated one. But a slave?" He lashed out, kicked the only stool across the room so that it smashed into the opposite wall. Two of the legs split with a loud crack. "Why didn't you tell me?" he snarled. The cords in his neck tightened, skin flushing so that the circlet of scar tissue stood out in a pale band.

Martise stared, stunned at his anger. Why should her status matter now? "I saw no reason..."

"No reason?" She winced at the cutting scorn in his tone. "There was every reason."

He backed her against the wall nearest the window. Martise, heartsick at knowing she had only these few minutes with him, was unafraid. She touched his face with gentle fingers. "Why are you angry?"

Her caress worked its own magic. Silhara closed his eyes and leaned his forehead against hers. The thick fan of his lashes rested against his cheeks. She stroked the hard line of his jaw, trailed her fingers down his neck to the white garroting scar.

He straightened and opened his eyes but didn't back away from her. "He offered you your freedom, didn't he?" His eyes narrowed to slits. "You're neither greedy nor ambitious. Nor are you cold blooded. But you are enslaved. What else could motivate a quiet, gentle woman to turn a man over to his enemies?"

He didn't give her a chance to respond. "You couldn't take your gaze off that bauble he sported; he couldn't resist throwing your failure in your face." Again, his voice turned clipped and cold. "I know what that bit of jewelry is. A soul shackle."

"Yes."

She stayed against the wall when he stepped away and began pacing. "Martise, I told you my silence regarding your Gift was freely given." He stopped, flung his arms wide in frustration. "Why didn't you tell him something? Anything? I'd have held off sending my letter to the Luminary, given you time to send a letter of your own to Cumbria."

Martise scrubbed at her eyes with the heels of her palms. "I didn't know you planned to write the Luminary and spill your secrets." He frowned when she raised her hands to plead her reasoning. "I want to sleep at night, Silhara. I cannot, in good conscience, bargain a man's life at any price."

He closed the distance between them. Martise leaned into the warm hands clasping her waist. His breath tickled her throat. "Any man?" he whispered in her ear.

Her eyes closed, and she slid her arms around him, gathered him close so she felt every tense muscle. "Especially you. You more than anyone." His hair was silk against her fingers, and she breathed the scent of oranges. "You don't love me, but I love you. I will never betray you."

Silhara kissed her, tongue teasing and coaxing. He tasted of desperation and Gurn's blackberry tea. Warm hands skated over her back and across her buttocks. Martise moaned in protest when he broke the kiss. One hand rose to her face, long fingers caressing her cheeks, the bridge of her nose.

"Were I a rich man, I'd buy you from him."

His bleak smile mirrored her equally bleak thoughts.

"Cumbria of Asher wouldn't sell you a tattered blanket if he thought you wanted it, even were you the wealthiest man in the world."

"Does the High Bishop even own tattered blankets?"

"I don't think so." His heart beat strong beneath her hand—the heart of a beggar king. "Why didn't you tell me the bishop was your uncle?"

He went rigid, and his seductive mouth compressed into a tight line. "Because I never think of him as such. He was my mother's estranged brother, nothing more."

Martise disagreed. Silhara might lay claim to only a surface recognition of his relative, but there was far more between them—things dark and painful. "Why do you hate each other?"

Silhara gazed over her head. "We both blame the other for her death. He hates me because I'm the reason he wouldn't allow her back into the family embrace. She married a Kurman savage against their wishes and shamed the Asher name. I hate him because his pride forced her to live a short and brutal life." His lip curled. "Of course, that is but first in a long list of reasons why I loathe Cumbria of Asher."

He moaned softly when she pressed her lips to the puckered skin of his scar. "Cumbria was one of the priests who watched as you were garroted, wasn't he?"

"Yes."

She reeled inwardly at such heartlessness. That a man could stand by and watch as the child of a once-beloved sister struggled against an executioner's hands bewildered her. Life sometimes dictated harsh choices. Her own mother had sold her into slavery, but out of desperation and a need to feed six other children. Cumbria, wealthy beyond measure, suffered no such hardship. No wonder Silhara hated him.

His black eyes gleamed triumphantly when she told him "You have trumped him at every turn." That light dimmed when she continued. "And yet you will ultimately give him what he most wants."

Her fingers dug into Silhara's arms. The carved angles of his face blurred. "Please, I beg you, do not sacrifice yourself." She kissed his unyielding mouth, and her voice shook. "I'd rather have the god in the world than you gone from it."

"Sweet woman, I'm dead already."

Silhara lifted her off her feet, enfolding her in an embrace that threatened to break her ribs. He kissed her eyes, her nose, her mouth—heedless of her tears that made his lips glisten. Martise tried to summon her Gift, offer a last connection and take something of him for herself. The swell of power rose within her, and the back of her eyelids tingled with the warmth of the eldritch light flowing through her body.

Silhara set her down, grabbed her wrists, and pulled her hands from his face, abruptly severing the connection to her Gift. "No."

Martise started, surprised at the vehemence of his denial. He softened it with a wistful smile. "And don't think I'm not tempted to take what you're offering. But you can never summon your

Gift for any reason—not if you want to keep it secret from your master and his masters."

He kissed her palm reverently. "I'm sending Gurn to Eastern Prime. He'll be a day or so behind you. If you need him, go to the Temple of the Moon." Her eyebrows rose. Silhara chuckled. "The beautiful Anya was kind enough, and quite eager, to offer him temporary shelter."

"He won't leave willingly."

Silhara shrugged. "But he will leave, even if I have to break both his legs and throw him onto Gnat myself. He can return to Neith in a week's time if he wishes." His dark gaze bore into her. "You could return as well if you were free."

Martise smeared the tears from her cheeks. "Free or not, there will be nothing here for me in a week." She clutched his scarlet robe, the worn threads shredding under her hands. "I will beg you on my knees. Don't do this."

He peeled her fingers off the robe and brushed his lips across hers. A kiss of farewell. "Your master awaits you in the courtyard. I won't see you off." He turned away and strode to her door, pausing when she held out a supplicating hand and called his name.

"Silhara…"

His broad shoulders remained stiff, nor did he turn back to her. "Fortune favor you, apprentice." The door closed with a final click.

CHAPTER TWENTY-ONE

Silence hovered over Neith, mingling with the last streamers of light as afternoon gave way to evening. Silhara strolled across the courtyard, skirting the graveyard of broken stone and scrubgrass. Dried twigs and shards of rock crunched under his boots as he passed the iron gates. They hailed him in a thin wail of squeaking hinges, swaying gently in the hot breeze rolling off the surrounding plains. His cloak fluttered behind him, the ragged ends caressing the rails and stiles of a splintered staircase as he passed.

For as long as he resided here, this part of Neith had always been quiet. The ghosts of her builders rested peacefully, untroubled by the march of time and fate that had turned her into a crumbling ruin. Ruin or not, Neith was home. With her curse-laden wood, broken walls and an orange grove filled with battling crows, the manor and her lands were a haven to him, far from the teeming filth and misery of Eastern Prime's wharves and the bleak cruelty of Conclave's ancient seaside fortress. His spirit always calmed at Neith, the jagged edges of his bitterness blunted by her windblown isolation. Until now.

Silhara stopped to gaze at the shadowed oak wood and the sliver of road that cut a straight scar through its heart to the wide plain beyond. Gurn was well on his way to Eastern Prime, guiding Gnat and a wagon loaded with livestock—Neith's only true wealth—through a swaying ocean of giant dropseed grass. He pictured Cael, his scruffy coat decorated in grass seed, the tip of his whip-like tail snapping back and forth as he trotted next to the rolling wagon.

He hadn't resorted to crippling Gurn to make him leave, but he'd come close. The servant's melancholy at Martise's departure turned to confusion when Silhara ordered him to pack anything of value and ride for Eastern Prime. The confusion gave way to disbelief and fury when he questioned what Silhara's real plans for the priests entailed.

The two men sat across from each other at the kitchen table. Silhara sipped a cup of Peleta's Fire, welcoming the slow burn licking his throat and ribs. "You've already heard the real plans, Gurn. I'm to meet Conclave at Ferrin's Tor in two days. We destroy the god and save the world." He shrugged and drained the last of the Fire. Eyes watering from the spirits' effects, he raised the now empty cup to his servant. "And I die a hero," he wheezed.

Gurn clutched his cup of tea in a large hand. Tension fractures blossomed across the cup's surface beneath his tightening grip. His free hand slashed the air in sharp motion, and his face turned red.

Silhara shoved his cup and the bottle of Fire to the far end of the table. "*We'll* do nothing more than load the wagon and harness Gnat. You'll drive it to the city. Take Cael. I've already made arrangements for you to stay with your *houri* friend Anya for a week, or longer if you wish it." He smiled at Gurn's flushed features. "You must possess considerable skills beneath the blankets. She's sent a message expressing her eagerness for your visit."

Gurn didn't return the smile, only slammed his large hands on the table hard enough to make it rock, and signed frantically.

The numbness swelling in Silhara's heart since Martise rode off with the priests worsened. The Fire bubbled in his belly. He'd lost the woman he loved and now the friend he admired. Gurn had been more companion than servant—one who understood a need for solitude but helped keep years of loneliness at bay with his quiet presence. Silhara appreciated his loyalty, was grateful for it. How had he, a wharf rat, managed to engender such faith in a servant turned friend?

"You can't stay, and you can't help. Not here. If you're my friend as you say, you will do me this last favor. When you reach Eastern Prime, find Martise. See that she's well."

More angry hand-waving, and Gurn's face paled and turned pleading before Silhara's implacable will.

Silhara frowned. His words came out harsher than he intended. "I'm strong, Gurn but not invincible. And I'm only a man. You didn't see what I subjected Martise to under the god's influence. The question isn't if Corruption will possess me, but when. I'm no better than lich bait, and I won't live as a puppet. I want you gone by sundown."

Gurn's mulish resistance surprised him, and Silhara was finally forced to lay a geas on him to make him leave. Tears of frustrated rage and sorrow streamed down the giant's cheeks as he stood by the loaded wagon and faced his master and friend a final time.

Silhara clenched his jaw, finding it difficult to speak. "I've said it countless times. You're a piss-poor servant." He gripped Gurn's forearm as much in farewell as to stave off an embrace that might crush his ribs. "Live long, my friend. Live well."

As with Martise earlier, he didn't watch Gurn leave but retreated to his chamber and studied the afternoon shadows as they stretched across the orange grove. He'd burned down two bowls from the *huqqah* before emerging to walk Neith's inner boundaries.

A vast surge of power rushed through him when he lifted the curse wards off the wood. The dark magic, no longer a steady drain on his strength, beat like storm tide in his blood. Staggering against the sudden influx of power, Silhara breathed hard. Black lightning shot from his fingers, singeing the dry scrub grass at his feet.

The wood, free of the warping curse that kept visitors at bay, brightened with waning sunlight. Whatever darkness filled it in an hour's time was of the sun's descent, nothing more. Silhara curled his hands into fists, tamping down the residual waves of magic. He needed every bit of strength he could muster. If such means included leaving Neith's front entrance unguarded, so be it.

He left the courtyard and returned to the house, striding through the empty corridors until he reached the door leading out to the grove. Ghostly echoes followed him—Martise's alluring voice, the clatter of pots and pans as Gurn puttered in the kitchen, the staccato click of Cael's claws on the floor as he patrolled the house. Silhara paused a moment and listened. Silence.

He sighed and made his way to the grove. Like the woods at Neith's entrance, he'd warded the orchard walls with powerful spells. Again, Silhara absorbed the heady swell of power when he lifted the enchantments. Entire tribes of thieves could scale those walls now and pick his trees clean. Anger shot through him at the thought before he smothered the emotion.

The house welcomed him back with its cool shadows and pervading isolation. Silhara closed the door to his chamber and made his way to the balcony. Hanging low in the deepening indigo of encroaching twilight, Corruption's star shone its brightest since it first appeared. Silhara stared at the god's celestial manifestation and turned his magic inward. His thoughts, his emotions, every aspect of his spirit were locked down, shoved behind an ethereal door of warded strap hinges and mage-born locks.

Corruption would break through, but not before Silhara had him imprisoned within the shell of his body and bound to the priests who meant to destroy him. Martise's pale features rose in his mind's eye. At the edge of the night horizon the al Zafira constellation made her steady climb with her sister stars. He smiled. He'd done the right thing by not telling her of the symbol. He'd be honored for sacrificing himself for a world. None would know he'd done it for himself and one plain, enslaved woman.

The god's star pulsed in recognition of his regard. Silhara spread his arms wide and faced his chosen destiny. "Shall I whore for you now, Corruption?" he whispered.

He knew little else beyond those words save a wrenching agony, as if a massive hand broke every bone in his body and ground the remains beneath a boot heel. Darkness exploded in his vision, and he went blind to the world around him. An ancient malice, bred of a thousand years of sleeping hate, filled him, pounding at the door guarding his soul.

Silhara blinked and saw before him not his orange grove or the indigo sky, but the bleak landscape of a familiar nightmare. He was back on the black shores of a dead world, facing an equally lifeless ocean. In the spill of silver-capped waves, the rise and fall of a massive dark shape, edged against a moonless night, surfed the water. It drew ever closer to lure him into the waves.

He answered its silent summons, wading into the surf. The tepid waves swirled sluggishly against his legs, and he struggled against their push and pull as if he swam through blood instead of water. A whisper of sound from behind made him turn, and he trod the water, sensing the approaching leviathan at his back.

A wraith in a white leine stood on a strand of ash and burnt bone and raised a beckoning hand. Above the dull rhythm of waves lapping against his face, her voice called out—entreating, spun of vanquished starlight.

"Come ashore, my love."

Silhara wanted to answer, wanted to swim back, but the pull of the tide drew him steadily out, away from the shore and that last pale remnant of hope. Water closed over his head, drawing him down, down into the yawning maw of the creature awaiting him.

Caught in a vortex of madness, he closed his eyes only to open them immediately. This time he was back on his balcony, facing a landscape strange and warped. He saw layers of motion and color, movement and time as if through a filter of dirty water. His vision, altered by the god's possession, showed him the warmth of summer stripped of its vibrancy. Golds were faded yellows, greens only dull ash. The twilight sky was nothing more than shades of gray dotted by the sickly gleam of dying stars.

Corruption's sweetly poisonous greeting echoed within him. *"Welcome, avatar. I have waited a long time for you."*

Silhara, his voice clear and free of the scarring rasp, inhuman in its clarity, answered. "I've come willingly. The priests of Conclave seek to destroy us at Ferrin's Tor."

The god laughed. *"Then we shall play their game. They fooled me a thousand years ago. Not this time."*

Silhara watched his crows flutter and settle in his trees for the night. Corruption stilled inside him, and he sensed the god's measure.

"I will reward you, avatar. A world at your feet, kingdoms under your rule, immortality beyond your imaginings." A shocking cold burned Silhara's veins. *"But first, a punishment for defying me."*

As if pulled by strings, Silhara's arms rose. Magic, more powerful than anything he'd ever wielded, roared through him. White fire arced from his palms, spilling in cascades that raced across the ground and shot through the trees. His grove, proof of his triumph over a lifetime of obstacles and recipient of his greatest care, burst into an inferno of charring trees and screaming birds. Behind the protective door, Silhara's broken soul wailed in anguish.

CHAPTER TWENTY-TWO

"I won't mourn for a man not yet dead."

Martise scrubbed at her swollen eyes. Despite her declaration, she'd spent the night alternating between weeping and pacing the floor. She was desperate for an idea, a solution, even a miracle that might release Silhara from the trap he'd knowingly sprung on himself. By the time dawn edged the tiny window of her attic room, she was half mad with frustration.

Those priests selected to participate in the ritual at Ferrin's Tor had left Eastern Prime before first light. Cumbria had volunteered before he was even chosen. Martise knew his intentions were neither noble nor brave. A chance to watch his nephew and lifelong adversary die by Conclave's hands was worth the risk of facing Corruption.

The sun climbed higher, glazing the tile rooftops of neighboring houses in fiery shades of red and orange. The sliver of sea seen from her window reflected the same bands of bright crimson on the face of the waters. Dawn was her favorite hour of the day, and another time Martise might have paused to admire the light's beauty. But today she had a horse to steal, a journey to make, and a man to save.

Cumbria had denied her request to join those who followed him to Ferrin's Tor. "I need you here. Should we fail, you're to present yourself to the Luminary at Conclave. He will be the last barrier against the god. Your time at Neith may help him." He'd peered at her, suspicion drawing down his thin-lipped mouth into a frown. "Do you ask because you pine for the bastard mage?"

That bastard mage had just willingly given himself up as a sacrifice. While Cumbria had chosen to participate in the ritual, she doubted he'd be as willing as Silhara were he faced with the same circumstance.

"No," she said, proud her voice remained cool and expressionless. "It's only a matter of curiosity." If she could help it, the bishop would never know of her bond with Silhara or his discovery of her Gift. She owed it to him as much as herself. His soul would rage through eternity if Cumbria managed to usurp power from the Luminary through her.

She straightened her cyrtel, slipped on her shoes and took a deep breath for courage. A beating waited for her once Cumbria discovered she'd not only openly defied his command to remain in Eastern Prime, but also "borrowed" one of his valuable horses. But she'd bow before the lash and suffer every stroke if she could help Silhara in some way.

The house was quiet, kept by a minimum staff of town servants unused to the master's presence. Nearly all the Asher servants had followed him to Ferrin's Tor. None would notice if she slipped out and disappeared for a day or two.

Much smaller than his manor at Asher, Cumbria's town house was no less opulent. Martise traveled through rooms and halls decorated and maintained with exquisite care. A far cry from the ramshackle shabbiness of Neith, but if given a choice, she'd much rather be at Neith, negotiating a treacherous path of spider webs and holes in the floor to reach Gurn's welcoming kitchen.

She strode through the kitchen on her way to the stables. Bendewin hailed her with a flour-dusted hand and a scowl. A tall woman and thin as a rake, she bore the hallmark features of a Kurman tribeswoman. Black hair streaked with gray and equally dark eyes set off an aquiline nose and high cheekbones. "And who set fire to your skirts at this early hour?"

Martise paused. "I have errands to run. I'll be gone all day. Do you need me?"

The cook made to answer but was interrupted by a knock on the door leading to the back garden. A towheaded child peeked inside. "Sorry, mim. Saldin sent me. You have a visitor."

Bendewin's eyes widened. She glanced at Martise who shrugged. She followed the boy to the garden with an order for Martise. "Stay here. I want to know what you're up to."

The cook stayed on the doorstep, blocking the exit leading to the stables. Martise tapped her fingers impatiently on the worktable, sending up small clouds of flour. She was tempted to shove the woman out of the way and run, but it wouldn't do to antagonize the cook. Bendewin would keep her secrets and might even aid her.

Her fingers drew meandering lines in the scatter of flour, and she was startled to see she'd traced the enigmatic symbol next to Berdikhan's name in the Helenese scrolls. "What does this mean, Silhara?" she whispered.

So engrossed in trying to unravel the puzzle of Silhara's stubborn silence, Martise didn't hear Bendewin return until she spoke next to her.

"Foolish girl. Are you trying to give yourself bad luck?" Bendewin reached over her shoulder and quickly erased the symbol. "I heard the Master of Crows had Kurman blood, but you'd think he'd teach you something better than that about his people."

The bottom of Martise's stomach dropped out at her words, and her heart began to pound. A cautious hope rose in her. "You know this symbol?"

The cook shrugged. "I'm Kurman-raised; of course I know it." She signed a hasty protection ward in the air. "A pattern of stars. The plains people don't see the night sky the way the Kurmans do. To you, the Curl constellation is part of the Bull and the Serpent. To us, it stands alone. In Kurmanji, we call it al Zafira."

Martise sucked in a breath. Her view of the stars had been shaped by Conclave's teachings, and Conclave didn't teach the ways of the mountain tribes. Without Bendewin's knowledge, she would have never seen al Zafira.

She retraced the pattern in the flour. "What does it mean?"

Bendewin shrugged. "Nothing save a bit of bad luck. The consort of an ancient *sarsin* was named after those stars. Her husband was a mage, like the priests. Zafira met a bad end at his hands. She was what we call a *bide jiana*."

"A life-giver." Martise's voice was breathless.

The cook's eyes widened a fraction. "Yes. The old tales say he tried to gain the power of a god and used her to do it. They both died. No Kurman woman names her girl-child Zafira these days." Bendewin scowled and laid a heavy hand on Martise's shoulder. "You best sit down. You've gone whiter than milk."

Martise shook her off. Her throat closed against another bout of weeping, only these were angry tears, frustrated tears. If she could climb to the rooftop and scream her rage, she would.

Silhara's words whispered in her mind. *"I don't love you."*

Her hands curled into fists. Damn him! He'd looked her in the eye with that cool, sardonic gaze and turned his back on the chance of survival with those words.

"Liar," she snapped and raced through the door.

Bendewin's cry of "Wait!" went unheeded. Martise sprinted across the garden toward the nearby stables. She stumbled at the sight of a servant leading a familiar figure across the dusty cart road to the back gate.

"Gurn!" she cried.

Thank the gods. In her misery over Silhara's chosen fate, she'd forgotten he planned to send his faithful servant to Eastern Prime for safety. Gurn met her halfway as she flew toward him. Martise thought he'd squeeze the breath out of her and struggled until he loosened his hold. He looked haggard, his eyes sunken and dull in a face pale with grief. She suspected she looked the same.

Gurn still held her in one arm while motioning frantically with the other. Martise caught his fingers, stopping his frenetic signing.

"I'm well, Gurn." She cupped his broad face in her hands and smiled. "I'm glad to see Silhara didn't break your legs to get you to leave Neith."

Gurn's mournful expression angered. He growled low in his throat while he signed.

Martise sighed. A geas was almost as bad. Bound by the force of magery and resisting every step of the way, Gurn had left Neith with Cael in tow. A thought occurred to her. "Did Silhara only lay the geas forbidding you from returning to Neith?"

He nodded, blue eyes gleaming with curiosity.

She lowered her voice so the nearby servant wouldn't hear. "I think I can save Silhara, but I need to steal a horse."

The words were barely out of her mouth before he yanked her toward the stables.

She matched Gurn's ground-eating stride. When they reached the stable doors, she tugged on his arm. He paused, eyes bright with hopeful fires. "The stable master or one of the stable boys may be in there. You'll have to distract them while I get the horse. I suspect your size will be distraction enough, and such a talent has never been mine."

They entered the stables, startling pigeons that fluttered to the shadowy rafters in a frantic flap of wings. Inside, the air was warm and pungent with the scent of horse and feed, oiled leather and horse dung. All but three stalls stood empty, and two of the horses stretched their necks over the gates for a closer look at their visitors. One wuffled in greeting, and Martise recognized the piebald mare that first carried her to Neith from Asher.

Light pierced the interior gloom from the open door but didn't penetrate the darkness of the loft or the stalls at the far end of the stable row. Martise peered into the closest corners and listened. "Hello?" she called. Only the piebald answered her with another wuffle. She glanced at Gurn, radiant in a shimmering column of swirling dust lit by the morning sun. He watched the door and the loft by turns.

"Our luck is holding. It's just us. Cumbria rode out before first light. I wouldn't be surprised if the stable master returned home to enjoy his breakfast. Watch the door while I saddle the mare."

The horse was a friendly creature and solid mount. Her long legs would cover a lot of ground in a short time. She shoved her nose into Martise's arm, snorting with pleasure when the action earned her a quick scratch behind the ears. Martise had her bridled and saddled and was leading her out of the stall when the creak of the stable door sounded a warning.

Martise froze and peered under the mare's neck. The stable master, a wiry, grizzled man with a shock of white hair and bits of egg in his beard, stared at her accusingly. He had time for a single breath before a giant hand shot out of the dark and cuffed him. The man went down with a thud amidst a cloud of dust and straw. Martise stared at Gurn as he emerged from his hidden corner and bent to place his fingers against the fallen man's throat.

Gurn's idea of distraction wasn't as subtle as hers. Martise winced. "Is he dead?" she called in a loud whisper and breathed a sigh of relief when Gurn shook his head.

He signed to her to get moving and heaved the unconscious man over his shoulder as if he were nothing more than a half-empty grain sack. Martise swung onto the mare's back and trotted her to the entrance. She reached for Gurn and briefly clasped his outstretched hand.

"Bind and gag him if you have to, then get out of here. Did you ride Gnat to Eastern Prime?" He nodded. "Good. I'll be riding this mare hard. Gnat won't be able to keep up, but you can meet me at Ferrin's Tor later." Gurn scowled, and his hand slashed the air. Martise shook her head. "No, Silhara only laid the geas against you for Neith. There's no magery preventing you from going to the tor."

His eyes brightened. He grinned and slapped the mare on the rump. Martise grasped a handful of reins and coarse mane and held on as the animal galloped out of the stable.

They made it through the gate and into the heart of the city without incident. Martise slowed the horse to a walk, guiding her through winding track of narrow streets slick with slime and littered with refuse.

Despite the mare's eagerness to stretch her legs into a dead run, Martise kept her in check once they left the city for the open plains. She quelled the urge to give in to the horse's impatience, frantic to reach the tor. Riding hard didn't mean running her horse into the ground, and it wouldn't get her far. She wouldn't be of much use to Silhara if the mare collapsed from exhaustion, leaving her to foot it the rest of the way to the tor or wait for Gurn and Gnat.

Miles of tall grass flew past them as they cantered west toward the sacred mound. She stopped twice to rest the mare and drink from the streams that carved shaded paths from the snow-capped Dramorin peaks to the southern coast and picked a handful of fruit from a plum tree. She recalled another hot summer day when she'd rested beneath the shade of a leafy plum and admired the kiss of the sun on Silhara's bronzed skin.

Martise knew she was near the tor even before she spotted its steep slopes in the distance. Obsidian light knifed across the sky, leaving jagged wounds in the blue and splattering the clouds in an oily luminescence. As she rode closer, the mare began to shake. Her hooves struck the ground in protest, and she reared when Martise tapped her heels into her sides to coax her onward.

Closer to the tor the sky had darkened into false night. Black clouds, fey and menacing, loomed above, blotting out the sun's crimson disk as it sailed lower on the western horizon. A high, keening wind raced across the plain, bowing the grass as it barreled toward them. The horse tossed her head, squealing in panic. Martise struggled to hold her seat as the reins snapped out of her hands, and the mare bolted.

The sky tilted, obscured by her skirts and the whiplash snap of bluestem grass. Martise tumbled from the saddle, hitting the dusty ground hard enough to rattle her teeth. A stinging pain accompanied the iron taste of blood where she bit her tongue. The mare's hooves beat a fading tattoo as she raced for safety.

"Damn, damn, damn!" Martise staggered to her feet, sore from the fall and the long ride. She spat blood and dusted her skirts. The wind howled its rage, and she wanted to howl with it. So close. The tor was within sight—mere minutes on horseback, a good half hour on foot. The fear of dying was a moot point now. If she managed to survive the ritual with Silhara, Cumbria would kill her for losing his horse.

She struck out for the tor, buffeted by the magic storm blasting off its peak. The wind tore at her clothes, dried her eyes. At the base, she discovered the retainers and their horses huddled together within the protective bounds of a warding circle. None looked her way, their terrified gazes locked on the spinning column of jet light erupting from the tor's crown.

She circled away from the servants, careful not to draw attention to herself while she trekked up the hill.

The climb was steeper than it appeared and far more treacherous. The magic streaming from the top froze the surrounding turf, turning the face of the tor into a slippery pitch of ice and mud. Martise shrieked curses as she lost her footing twice and slid down the incline. Wiping mud from her cheeks, she clawed her way up on numb hands and wet knees.

Breathless and shuddering with cold, she reached the top and collapsed against a standing stone. The tableau before her sent her scrambling behind the stone.

The stones, ancient sentinels raised by the not quite human hands of a vanished race, encircled the tor's peak in a granite coronet. Within their ring, a dozen Conclave priests confronted the black tornado at its center. Reduced to pale, hollow-eyed wraiths, they swayed in the howling maelstrom, spears of crimson light shooting from their raised palms to tether them to Corruption's earthly manifestation. Cumbria stood among them, eyes wide and glazed white from the ritual's magic.

Martise covered her mouth and moaned. Thirteen mages battled Corruption on this high and ancient place, twelve within the circle, one within the storm itself. Silhara stood inside the whirlwind's center. She saw only flashes of his harsh face, cloaked by the spin of clouds, gaunt and stripped of its humanity by the god's full possession. He seemed taller than before, equaling Gurn's height, and his eyes were the same reptilian-black they'd been when he'd attacked her at Neith. The wind didn't touch him, and he watched the priests' efforts with an icy half smile of triumph. The Master of Crows had wholly become Corruption's vessel.

Despair and anger mingled with fear, lessened it so that she abandoned the safety of the stone and stepped inside the perimeter of the ritual gathering. Her Gift surged inside her, hostile, desperate to engage the malevolent force filling the space inside the ring of stones.

Martise slowly approached one of the priests, a woman she recognized from her years at Conclave. The bishop didn't even twitch when she touched her arm. Lightning bolts of magery shot through Martise's fingers, hot and sharp. Her Gift roiled in response, beating against her will. She held on, running her hand over the woman's forearm until she reached the cascade of scarlet light spilling from her palm.

The light binding the priests to the god was the path to Silhara. Martise took a shuddering breath, glanced at her lover trapped in the whirlwind, and touched the crimson stream.

Her Gift punched through the barrier of her control, buried ethereal claws in the mage-bind and wrenched her soul along as it raced toward a pilaster of shimmering obsidian.

Colors—emerald and nacreous yellow, silver and rust—collapsed in on themselves in a mad kaleidoscope. Martise gasped at the rush of wind, the agonized jolt of her spirit splitting from her body as her Gift struck the black spire and shattered the wall of the world.

She hit something soft with a muffled thud. No pain juddered up her arm or down her back. She rolled and leapt to her feet. The cold mud smeared on her face and clothes was gone. She stood on a beach, but a beach unlike any existing in the living world. Gray sand drifted over her feet, light as ash and smelling of funeral pyres. Behind her, cliffs hewn of tortured rock reached toward an endless night brightened only by twelve red stars. An ocean stretched before her, black waves tumbling toward the silent shore.

This was a dead place, a prison of vanished memories and unlife, of eternity that passed without the measure of days. A soulless quiet that devoured itself as a serpent swallowing its tail. She was in the belly of the god, and somewhere in this wretched prison Silhara waited.

Above her, the twelve points of light brightened in the moonless sky. The flat sea rolling in from a vanishing horizon suddenly split into churning waves. Martise caught a glimpse of an arching shape and a massive dorsal fin taller than a temple spire before it sank into the depths. Something swam in the dead waters, something titanic that thrashed with fury. Waves heaved, higher than castle walls. The chant of ancient spells filled the heavy air and was answered by shrieking laughter.

From the corner of her eye she glimpsed an outcropping of rock rising from the water, not far from the shore. A figure, silhouetted in red starlight, sat on the rock and watched the waves lap at his feet.

"Silhara!" Martise bellowed his name and jumped as the ghostly echo of her voice bounced off the jet cliffs behind her. She caught her breath when the water suddenly churned, leaving a wake of white peaks as the thing in the water sped for the outcropping.

She raced along the shore's edge, following the leviathan's waterborn path until she faced Silhara's rocky perch from the shore's sanctuary. He didn't look at her, but instead stared at the far horizon.

"Silhara!" she shouted once more, and he turned long enough to give her a bored glance. Martise motioned frantically. "Swim to shore, Master!"

This Silhara was the soul of the man yet unclaimed by the god. He watched her with human eyes, eyes filled with a hard resolve and an acceptance of his own death. The bitter smile he bestowed on her was poignantly familiar.

"Was it not enough that you burned my grove to the ground, Corruption? You would torture me with this illusion?" Like Martise's, his voice echoed in the vault of the god's prison. He turned away from her.

Martise closed her eyes for a moment, a sympathetic ache lodged in her chest. Willing possession wasn't enough. The god had punished him by destroying the thing that meant the most to Silhara—his trees. Such petty cruelty spoke of lesser beings unworthy of a prayer, much less worship. Hatred for Corruption rocked her.

Terrified to her bones by what her immediate future held, she was still glad to be here with the man who'd chosen her life above his own. She loved him. He was worth dying for.

"Master," she called. "I'm no illusion."

Silhara ignored her. Martise clenched her hands into fists and growled her frustration. Damn the stubborn bastard, he'd make her swim to him.

She kicked off her shoes and tucked the hem of her cyrtel into her belt. The water lapped at her feet, neither cold nor warm. She had only a sense of oily wetness, as if the tide lapped blood instead of water on the shore. This sea didn't smell of sun or salt or fish, had likely never tossed a ship on its waters or had anything other than the leviathan swim in the depths. Taking a breath, Martise waded in, certain she walked into a liquid sarcophagus.

Black waves struck her face as she swam for the rock. She kept her mouth tightly shut against the water, fearful of somehow swallowing the god's essence and tainting her soul forever.

Something vast moved below her, stirring the underwater current. Martise sensed its presence, a colossal entity that watched her from the black deep. She swam harder. In this unnatural world, she didn't tire from the exertion and soon reached the outcropping on which Silhara sat, arms braced casually over his knees.

"Silhara, help me up." She stretched out a hand. He glanced at her, annoyed.

"What do you want of me, Corruption?"

Martise slapped her hand against the slippery rock. "Stop being so thick-headed! I'm not the god or an illusion." She scrabbled harder to find a solid grip, sure the monster with its towering fin was even now rushing up from the depths, its great mouth, razored with rows of sharp teeth, opened wide to swallow her. "Damn it, Silhara. I'm Zafira."

The sucking grasp of the water pulled at her legs as Silhara yanked her out of the lifeless sea. He glared at her, the first vibrant emotion she'd seen in his face since she'd fallen into this alternate place.

He dropped her hand as if scorched by her touch. "I've poor luck. You discovered the symbol's meaning too soon."

Heedless of her drenched state and his sharp reception, Martise threw her arms around him, hugging him fiercely. Like the waters and shore, he smelled of a funeral pyre. She could see her hands through his back and shuddered. In this world, his soul had taken physical form like hers, but it was fading. Like the priests, he was becoming a wraith, drained by the god and holding onto life with an ever-weakening grasp.

Still, Martise felt the weight of his arms as he embraced her, the ferocity of his kiss. He didn't taste of oranges or tea, but of a terrible despair. Her Gift, quieted once it slung her through the barrier of realities, awakened. Martise held it down, hoarded its strength. She captured Silhara's mouth in a kiss of her own, savoring the feel of him in her arms.

"Foolish woman," he whispered against her lips. "You have made this meaningless."

"The apprentice returns." Corruption's voice, mocking and filled with malice, thundered over the waves.

"Not meaningless," she said. "Survivable." She meant to say more, but Silhara suddenly seized in her embrace, convulsing as a spear of red light from the distant stars struck him. His eyes rolled back in his head, mouth opening on a silent scream. Martise cried out with him, scrambling to hold him upright when his knees buckled. The shadowy creature surfing beneath the waves slapped an enormous fin against the rock, and Corruption's enraged howl deafened her.

Martise lowered Silhara to the wet ground, holding him like a child. Bursin! The strength of the priests and their spells. They'd attacked as one, throwing all their force against Corruption and the mage who held him in a body growing fragile with the strain.

Had this world and time allowed it, she would have cried when Silhara opened his eyes. All the stars missing from the false night glittered in his black gaze.

"I cursed the day you came to Neith." He turned his face into her hand, kissing her palm. "And cursed the day you left."

"Let me help you." She stroked a lock of hair from his cheek, loving him with her eyes, her touch. "I don't want your nobility, Silhara. It doesn't suit you."

He stared at her for a long moment. "You may well die here with me. Neither Berdikhan nor Zafira survived."

She shrugged, doing her best to conceal her terror, knowing he saw it in her eyes. "There are worse deaths."

Silhara pulled her down and kissed her again. This time Martise tasted the bitter essence of battle magic. The priests would continue to decimate him. As long as he trapped the god and was trapped by him, Conclave would attack until Corruption fell and his avatar fell with him.

"I didn't give you up to death at Iwehvenn," she said. "I won't do so now."

His sensual mouth, thinned with pain, curved into a shallow smile. "What happened to that sad mouse of a woman who first came to Neith and leapt at her own shadow?"

"I didn't love you then." Martise stroked his cheek. "And I still leap at my own shadow."

Crimson light rained down on the sea. The outcropping shuddered beneath Martise and Silhara as the water beast slammed against the rock in agitation. Silhara struggled in her arms. Martise helped him stand, shouldering his weight as he staggered.

"I'm dying," he rasped.

Martise wrapped her arms around his waist and stared into his drawn features. His dark eyes, alight with stars moments earlier, were dull.

"Then make it stop," she beseeched him. "Use me. Use my Gift. I didn't make your sacrifice futile. Don't make mine wasteful." She curved her palm against his cheek. "Let me love you for this moment. It will be enough."

Silhara laughed, a deep, hollow sound. "No, Martise of Asher." A nimbus of bloody light bathed him in macabre radiance. His hands on her shoulders tightened. "I am a greedy man. We could live a thousand years more than this twisted god, and still it will not be enough."

He bent to her, teased her lips with his. "Open for me, *bide jiana*. Let me in."

Martise shook with fright and laughed with joy. Her Gift, smashing against the gates of her will, broke free, rushed toward the man in her arms in a surge of living amber light. She fell into darkness.

CHAPTER TWENTY-THREE

She would die in his arms and by his hand. Silhara gathered Martise close and claimed her willing soul, hoarded it within his own fragile spirit and raged against the god for his actions. This wasn't a mating, but a possession, vile and parasitic. The god's control over him was limited, and the most powerful part of his being remained untouched. Silhara not only possessed Martise, he consumed her. He almost dropped her, recoiling at the thought of what he was doing to the woman who had saved him, not once but twice.

This plain, unassuming girl held a Gift more powerful than a hundred suns, a Gift rushing through him like a vast, undammed river. He'd taken what she offered because she'd offered something no other person had ever given him—hope. His Gift rallied beneath the buoyed strength of hers, filling his soul so that he no longer saw sea and rock through his own hands. No longer suffered the bludgeoning force of the god's possession or the single-minded hatred of the priests.

The waters raged around them as the creature in the depths flailed the rock, sending broken stones tumbling into the waves. The stars above, manifestations of the priests, brightened, converging their magic in preparation for attacking the god once more.

Silhara stared at Martise's peaceful face, her closed eyes. In this foul place, she burned softly, haloed in amber light. He loved her to the point of madness, to obsession and even sacrifice. He wasn't Berdikhan, and he wouldn't make her Zafira. He'd rob her of her Gift, but she'd live. If he had to destroy Corruption, Conclave and himself, she'd live.

He drew on her Gift as a starved man at a feast. The sudden agony ripping up his spine made him cry out. The priests hurled their combined might against him, and through him, to the god. Despite the agony, Silhara grasped their power, channeled it, fortified it and honed it until the magic pulsed in his hand, a blazing javelin. He flung the spear into the waves, harpooning the black shadow undulating just below the surface. Corruption's shock, its sudden terror, lashed him as hard as the priests' attack. A spray of glutinous water shot skyward as the creature launched out of the waves in a convulsive arc. A great eel-like thing with dark, slick scales, its eyeless head towered over them. The gaping mouth, pierced by the mage-spear Silhara crafted, was wide enough to swallow the moon.

Corruption twisted in the air as it hurtled back toward Silhara. The mage invoked a shield spell, using the residual strength of Conclave's magic and the ceaseless flow of Martise's Gift. The eel slammed against the mage ward before falling into the water, sending a tidal wave high as a tor toward the lifeless shore.

The god shrieked its anger. *"I am betrayed!"*

Conclave's priests flooded the ocean in crimson light. Silhara, triumphant and riddled with pain, laughed. "You are disbelieved," he shouted.

The leviathan churned the waters in rising panic. *"You are my avatar!"*

Silhara smiled a grim smile. "I am your ruin and your executioner."

A sudden silence fell around them, and the sea flattened to a glassy stillness. Corruption's voice whispered comprehension and malice. *"The apprentice."*

Silhara hugged Martise's limp body, shuddering at her lightness, the translucence of her skin as her life force faded with the diminishing of her Gift. He could no longer wait. The god now knew the source of his greatest strength. "My woman," he whispered. "My weapon."

More of the priestly light shone down, and Silhara seized it, weaving an unbreakable web as he not only drained Martise but the priests as well. A nebulous darkness billowed out from the vanished horizon and surged over the ocean's surface toward him. Silhara braced himself, knowing the god had turned all its will and power on him. To destroy Martise, destroy him and free itself from the prison of its own possession.

Silhara clenched his teeth when the blackness smashed into him. Invisible claws raked his skin. He could see nothing, only hear the cacophony of shrieks and demon howls as Corruption strove to obliterate him. Silhara fought back, bound the god in ethereal chains and bled the darkness dry. A last beseeching screech blasted his ears before the black cloud fractured like glass and exploded in a shower of obsidian splinters. The Master of Crows collapsed.

He awakened flat on his back with a close-up view of Gurn's blunt face and tear-filled eyes staring at him. A wet coldness seeped into his back and legs. The broken moans of suffering and distress serenaded him into full consciousness. He tried to speak but only managed to cough up a mouthful of blood. Gurn rolled him gently to his side so he could spit.

"Martise." He struggled to breathe. "Gurn, find Martise."

The giant stroked the damp hair away from Silhara's temple and signed before he left. Silhara remained on his side. The uncomfortable damp was the grass beneath him, muddied and brittle with melting frost. From where he huddled, he saw battered white shapes sprawled on the ground. The priests lay around him, their once pristine robes stained with dirt and blood. Some twitched and moaned. Others were ominously still.

His vision blurred, and he squinted, desperate to see another shape—small and dressed in brown wool—among the gathering. "Please," he prayed sincerely for the first time in his life. "Let her be alive."

His prayer was answered when a pair of mud-encrusted shoes and a dirty hem filled his vision. Martise fell to her knees beside him. As filthy and bloodied as he, she stared at him as Gurn had, eyes wide and full of tears, but exultant.

"You did it," she said. Her hand drifted over his face in a feather-light caress. "You defeated a god, Silhara."

He pulled her down and rolled so that she rested on top of him. Every muscle and bone in his body screamed in protest, but he ignored the pain. She was freezing, muddy and blessedly alive. He cupped her face in his palms and kissed her deeply, uncaring that he tasted of blood. So did she, and she returned his kiss with a desperate fervor, sweeping her tongue into his mouth and sucking on his lower lip.

Tears painted silver tracks on her dirty cheeks when they finally separated. "I will give tribute to the gods every day at temple. You're a hero, not a martyr."

He snorted his disdain. "I'm neither, and want to stay that way. Take your credit. Without you, I would not have lived to sing of Corruption's defeat."

Martise wiped a trickle of blood from beneath her nose. "I'm just glad it's over."

Silhara couldn't agree more. "Can you summon your Gift?"

She frowned, closed her eyes for a moment, then opened them. Her wry smile told its tale. "No. It's gone."

They both knew such would be the outcome, and in the case of her unique magic, that outcome was a blessing. Still, he remembered the excitement in her eyes when her Gift first manifested and sorrowed for its loss. He stroked her back. "Would you believe me if I said I'm sorry?"

Martise ran her finger over his lip before kissing the spot she'd caressed. No condemnation clouded her gaze. "Yes. But why be sorry? My sacrifice is no greater than yours. I'm free of another yoke, and I've lived my life until now without such power. I'll do so again. And you're here. Whole and unconquered. I'm happy with that." She kissed him again, her gaze holding a grief like his. "I heard you on the beach. I'm sorry about your grove. Corruption exacted a terrible punishment."

Anguish rose within him, despite his present fortuitous circumstances. His grove. The heart of Neith, once the heart of him. Until Martise. The thought eased his sorrow. He rubbed the tip of her braid between thumb and forefinger. "He didn't take what means most to me."

Her eyes glittered, almost as dark as his in the shadows of true night. "I love you," she whispered.

He embraced her, kissed her and inhaled her scent, almost hidden beneath the pungent odors of wet wool and blood. Corruption hadn't taken her from him, but Cumbria would. Not for long. Not if he had a say in it.

Gurn loomed over them, conspicuously occupying himself with stargazing. He looked down when Silhara raised a hand. The servant helped them stand. His eyes were glassy with tears, but he bestowed a beatific smile on Silhara and signed.

The world tilted on its axis as Silhara tottered. His stomach roiled; he wanted to retch, and his clothes were sodden and cold. All those things paled before Gurn's obvious happiness. He slapped the giant on the arm and gave him a mock scowl. "Piss-poor, disobedient servant as always. I thought I laid a geas against you."

More signing, and Martise blinked innocently when Gurn pointed to her. "Your geas prevented him from returning to Neith, not the tor."

This time Silhara's scowl was genuine. "I'm not usually so careless."

Servant and apprentice both shrugged. "You were distracted," she said.

More groans from the surviving priests, along with the whinny of horses and the rattle of carts as Conclave retainers began their climb up the tor to help their masters.

He was out of time. Even with her Gift now extinct, Conclave could never know Martise was here. No lie, no matter how skillfully told, would convince the priests she'd come as a spectator if they saw her standing with him. They'd sensed the change in his strength, the signature feel of a powerful magic not his own. He despised the clerics, but he never underestimated them.

He ached with the need to keep Martise close, to steal her away. Back to Neith where he ruled unchallenged and could defend his right to keep her. But even he couldn't break the chain that bound her to Cumbria. She had to return.

"Get out of here, Martise," he said in a harsh voice.

Bewildered by his sudden turn in mood, she gaped at him.

"They can't find you here. None can know you participated in the ritual. The priests sensed the strengthening of my magic, but they don't know why. If you stay, they will."

She shook her head, backing away as if to prevent him from physically forcing her down the hillside. "I can't leave you here. What if the priests..."

"I have Gurn for protection, and they're no stronger than I am at the moment. I can defend myself if I must. Thanks to you." He turned to his servant, avoiding his sympathetic gaze. "Get her down there and don't let the servants see her either. If you have to kill one of them to steal a horse, do it." Gurn nodded and touched a dagger in the sheath at his belt.

Martise stood before him, hands buried in her skirts, her mouth trembling. "Please," she mouthed.

He didn't dare comfort her, didn't dare get too close. If he did, he wouldn't let her go. His next words cut him like knives, and he bled inside. "You aren't mine," he said in a soft voice. "Go home, Martise...of Asher."

CHAPTER TWENTY-FOUR

"I've sold you."

The words seemed to thunder in Martise's ears. She gaped at Cumbria sitting across from her, enthroned behind his desk. The short two months following Corruption's defeat had not been kind. The tall, haughty bishop she'd served nearly all her life was stooped these days, weaker in both body and spirit. But his eyes were as glass-hard and emotionless as ever.

Martise's heart thudded against her ribs. She'd been summoned here by a bored servant and thought nothing of it. Cumbria often summoned her when assigning tasks of transcription or minor spying on the priests who came to visit him. He'd pole-axed her with his declaration.

She clasped her hands behind her to hide their trembling. "I'm sorry, Your Grace," she said softly. "I don't understand."

The scratching of a busy quill sharpened the silence as Cumbria went back to scribbling at a stack of documents before him. He didn't look up when he answered. "What is there not to understand? I've been offered a good price for you. One I can't refuse." He said the last in acid tones. "You'll pack your things and leave today. One of my retainers will escort you to Ivenyi. A caravan will take you the rest of the way. Your spirit stone is already with your new master."

Martise fell to her knees. Somewhere out there, her spirit stone rested in the hands of an unknown master. She'd wished to be free of bondage to Cumbria but not like this.

Her voice quavered. "Please, Master. I beg you, let me stay. Asher is my home. Surely I am still of use to you."

Cumbria dipped his quill in a small inkpot, unmoved by her entreaty. "You have another home now, and I can always find someone with skills similar to yours. Maybe not as good, but adequate enough to serve my purposes." He finally glanced at her, annoyance stamped on his craggy face. "I'm busy, Martise. Gather your possessions and leave."

Stumbling to her feet, Martise gave a clumsy bow and backed out of the room. Swamped with fear of an uncertain future, she made her way to the small chamber she shared with one of Delafé's handmaidens. The room was stifling. Even the breeze blowing in from the open window didn't lessen the heat pouring in from the noon sun. The gods granted her one small mercy this day. No one witnessed her silent weeping.

She sat on the edge of her narrow cot and stared unseeing at the patch of blue sky filling the window. Except for the futile years at Conclave Redoubt, Martise had lived most of her life at Asher. She knew the rhythms of the lives here, even the grand house itself; how the old rooster crowed before the sun rose and avoided Bendewin's hatchet year after year, the way the roof beams creaked and snapped in the summer afternoon as the sun went down and the air cooled, how the women chorused a singsong chant, accompanied by the wet slap of fiber as they walked wool in the bailey.

Many of the servants knew her from childhood, and while some deigned not to befriend her because of her status, they were still familiar, still understood. She'd miss them as much as those to whom she'd grown close. Even had she won her freedom, she would have asked to stay. She loved Asher; she just wanted the right to leave if she chose. Still a slave and she didn't even have the right to stay. She rose and began emptying the small chest by her bed of its contents.

The door to her room flew open and Bendewin strode in, sharp face pinched and dusted with flour. Martise gave her a quick glance and a sniffle and continued shoving her meager possessions into a worn sack.

"I just heard. Why didn't you tell me, girl?"

Martise shrugged. "I just found out myself. Who told you?"

Bendewin glared at her, arms akimbo, but a suspicious shine glazed her dark eyes. "Jarad. He's the one who'll take you to Ivenyi to meet the caravans."

Trying not to burst into tears, Martise cleared her throat and folded a leine into her pack. "Does he know where they'll take me?"

"No. They usually take the north roads this time of year, but that's all I know." The cook's face hardened. "You can run. I can help you. I still have Kurman kinsmen who owe me favors after all these years. They can offer you safe haven."

"What good would that do me, Bendewin? The bishop has already transferred my spirit stone to my new master. I am bound, soul and flesh to another owner." She paused at Bendewin's crestfallen expression and patted her arm. "Thank you, though."

The ache in her chest grew. "You've been my closest friend, even a mother when I needed one. I'll miss you most when I leave."

Bendewin patted her hand awkwardly. "Finish here and come to the kitchens. I'll have food packed for you. I don't like those caravan rests. They serve maggoty bread and rancid meat to travelers. At least you know you'll get a decent meal if I make it."

When Martise stepped into the kitchens, she found a small crowd of well-wishers waiting for her. She was hugged and cried over, blessed with protective wards and one small, foul-smelling charm. Bendewin handed her a heavy towel tied into a bag that bulged on all sides.

"There's enjita in there, along with a bit of chicken, some cheese and a few eggs. Also plums and a flask of apricot wine." Martise's eyebrows rose at the last. Bendewin sniffed. "The bishop has three casks of the stuff. He won't miss a glass or two. The old skinflint owes you that much."

Martise embraced Bendewin a final time. The woman had taken her, bloodied and half-conscious, to her room, tended her and kept the secret of her journey. She even managed to bribe the stable master not to speak of the incident in the barn, despite the hen's egg he sported on the side of his head from Gurn's blow.

Bendewin harrumphed and pushed her gently out the kitchen door. Jarad waited in the bailey with two horses, one the piebald mare. Martise smiled faintly and patted the mare on the neck. "Good to see you again, lass."

The ride to Ivenyi was short and quiet. Jarad stayed silent except to ask once if she needed water or a rest. When they reached the village, he helped her off the mare, unloaded her packs from the saddle and bid her goodbye.

Nothing more than a dusty rest stop for trade caravans, Ivenyi simmered in the afternoon heat. Martise stood outside a ramshackle rest house amidst a circle of brightly painted wagons and carts loaded with all manner of goods. The traders, a nomadic group made up of people from every clan, tribe and city mingled together, some huddled in groups to barter, others to dice while they waited for their compatriots to finish meals in the house or visit friends.

Three distinct caravans crowded the rest stop. Martise had no idea which would take her to her new home. She was set to hunt down the wagon masters and ask when the most amazing looking man approached her. Dressed in a clashing rainbow of colors, he glittered when he walked from the sunlight bouncing off the many strands of gimcrack beads he wore. Lined by time and sun, he caught Martise's wide-eyed gaze and held it with a hard, shrewd one of his own.

"Are you Martise of Asher?" She nodded. "Then you ride with my band. I'll take you to your wagon."

He didn't wait to see if she followed. Martise shouldered her pack, grabbed her lunch and hurried to catch up.

"Where will you take me?"

The faint shadow of pity in those otherwise hard eyes made her gut twist in knots. "A place few visit and none are welcome."

They wove a path through parked wagons and carts, passing knots of women crowded around campfires who paused in their conversations to watch them go by. Children raced around them, shouting and laughing in play. Martise dodged a surly dog that snapped at her heels when she walked too close.

The wagon master halted before a passenger wagon with a dapple-gray horse hitched to the front. Painted in faded colors of indigo and burgundy, the wagon was lavishly appointed by caravan standards. Wide windows allowed a cooling breeze to pass through the interior. Brocade drapes were drawn back, giving a view of thick rugs and pillows strewn about for the passenger's comfort. This was a rich person's transport.

Martise admired the wagon and glanced at the wagon master. "Why are we stopping?"

He eyed her as if she were daft. "This is your wagon."

She gaped at him and looked back at the wagon. Slaves didn't ride in such lavish accommodations. Most often they didn't ride at all. Her trip to and from Neith on horseback had been a matter of speed and convenience for Cumbria, not kindness. What manner of master spent good coin on mere property?

Martise backed away. "There must be a mistake."

Beads jangled together as the caravan's leader shrugged. "Ride in it or walk beside it. Means little to me. I've already been paid." He left her with another shrug.

Not wanting to look as foolish as he assumed, Martise opened the door and climbed the two steps gingerly. Once inside the dim interior, she was surrounded by faded opulence. The scent of some exotic perfume lingered in the air. She dropped her pack and lunch in a corner and made herself comfortable on the cushions while the caravan's traders gathered together and prepared to leave.

A rolling breeze carried the last hint of windflower and a touch of fall as it swept through the wagon's wide windows. The grasses grew taller and thicker as they traveled farther from the coast and into the interior of the far lands. In the distance, the Dramorins shadowed the horizon in a jagged silhouette. Silhara's kinsmen would have begun their descent to the plains for wintering.

These days everything reminded her of her lover. Martise missed him. Yearned for him until that yearning burned a hot fire in her heart. She'd heard nothing from him or Gurn since leaving Ferrin's Tor, nor did she expect to. Silhara was cautious, and if Cumbria ever suspected his adversary felt something for his lowly slave, the bishop would kill her. Anything to make the Master of Crows bleed.

Still, the silence from Neith weighed heavily on her mind. The weeks had dragged on slow feet. Martise wondered if Silhara thought of her as much as she thought of him. She didn't doubt he loved her. He'd been willing to sacrifice himself to protect her. Such devotion wasn't given to sudden fits and starts, and she'd learned Silhara was as constant in his loyalty and affection as he was in his hatred.

A sudden realization lightened her melancholy. She no longer belonged to Cumbria of Asher. Unless Silhara somehow managed to insult and make an enemy of her new master—and knowing Silhara, such wasn't outside the realm of possibility—she could send him a message. Something short, impartial. Something to tell him where she was if he wished to know.

Cheered by her future plan, she dug into the food Bendewin packed for her. She ate the eggs and bread and drank a little of the wine. The unchanging scenery, the rhythmic creak of wagon wheels and the potency of the wine made her lethargic. Yawning, she loosened the curtains at the window, plunging the wagon's interior into semi-darkness. The cushions were soft against her body as she curled into them and fell asleep to the memory of Silhara harvesting in his grove, the bright sun shining on his long hair, dark as a crow's wing.

Dreams plagued her. Images of dead priests sprawled across the tor's frosty ground played in her mind. Silhara on a black shore, convulsed and bowed before the priests' spells and the god's rage. Her Gift, bleeding out of her in a stream of amber blood, leaving an emptiness that went soul-deep.

The sharp rap of knuckles on her wagon door followed by an equally sharp "Woman of Asher," snapped her awake. Bewildered by the sudden wrench into wakefulness, Martise peered into the wagon's darkness. Night had descended while she slept.

"Yes?" She answered in a hoarse voice.

"Your journey's at an end. Mind your possessions and be quick about it."

Martise straightened her cyrtel, smoothed her braid as best she could and gathered her belongings. The wagon master was waiting for her when she opened her door. His dour features took on a ghastly aspect in the light of the torch he held. Behind him, the line of wagons waited. Drivers watched her from their high seats while women and children peered from behind the shelter of drapes and wagon doors.

"You'll have to walk the rest of the way. None here will travel that road. Not even the horses."

That last statement made her heartbeat speed up until it thundered in her ears. Martise stepped away from the shelter of the wagon's door. To her right, the sea of tall grass swayed in a whispering dance beneath the silver moon's light. To her left, a black forest of crippled trees squatted on the plain and sucked the moonlight into its shadows. A long, murky path shrouded in a deeper darkness cut a line through the trees.

"A place few visit and none are welcome."

Martise squeezed her satchel to her chest and tried not to shout her joy. She grinned at the caravan's leader instead, laughing when his eyebrows arched. He took a wary step back and thrust the torch at her.

"Here. You'll want this." He peered at the grand avenue's writhing shadows and signed a protective ward with his fingers. "May the gods favor you. You'll need them in this cursed place."

She took the torch with a nod of thanks and another beaming smile. "They already have."

The forest that once terrified her with its grasping trees and slinking shadows welcomed her now. Martise sensed its sibilant encouragement, its recognition of her presence the moment she set foot on the path leading to Neith. The whistles and calls, the roll of wagons and clanking of trade goods faded to silence as she followed the dark avenue to Neith. Sinuous shapes flitted through the sparse underbrush, fluid ribbons of darkness that stayed even with her pace. She no longer feared them. They were guardians now, escorts to accompany one of their own back home.

Her torch cast a corona of pale light around her and was swallowed up by the curling mist caressing her ankles. The forest smelled of damp and moss and the underlying odor of cinders.

In the distance she caught a glimpse of familiar green witchlights, like strange fireflies, moving toward her.

The lights brightened as they drew closer, revealing two familiar figures.

"Gurn! Cael!" Martise sprinted to meet them halfway, almost dropping her torch in the process.

Gurn caught her in a fierce hug. He looked the same, a giant of a man with his bald pate shining a pale moon itself and his blue eyes dark in the witchlight's spectral glow. Cael whined a greeting of his own. His whip tail snapped back and forth when Martise bent to hug him and scratch his furry ears.

She rose and wrinkled her nose. "Gods, you smell even worse since I last saw you. Is no one ever going to bathe you?"

Gurn took her satchel and lunch, giving an appreciative sniff at the contents in her food kerchief. He grasped Martise's hand, nearly dragging her down the road toward the manor in his excitement at her arrival. By the time they reached the rusted gates that closed off the courtyard, she was gasping for breath.

Aglow in the moonlight, Neith was as she remembered it, an ancient wreck, still graceful and stately in its decay. Here, the scent of ash and burnt wood lingered in the air, and Martise's happiness dimmed.

"The grove. I smell what's left of it?"

Gurn's eyes were bright with tears. His fingers moved in quick patterns.

"So much has been lost here." She nodded at Gurn's silent answer. "You're right. Much has been gained as well."

She followed him through the gates and into the manor, pausing only once for a quick glance at the great hall, a place of hard lessons and harsh revelations. Gurn ushered her toward the stairs, signing that the master awaited her in his bedchamber.

A sudden nervousness mixed with her elation, and she wiped her palms on her cyrtel before climbing the rickety steps to the second floor. The witchlights hovered before her, leading the way down the black corridor until she reached Silhara's door. It was open, and she slipped inside on silent feet.

She'd loved and been well loved in this room. Like the rest of Neith, it was a sanctuary of aging grandeur ruled by a fierce pauper king of immense power.

Silhara stood at his customary spot, facing the window leading to the balcony. He wore a new robe of rich burgundy velvet. A thin belt of silver and gemstones circled his narrow waist. Outlined in the warm shimmer of several lit candles, he was lean and tall. Martise's hands tingled with the need to touch the wide, proud shoulders.

She wasn't as silent as she thought, or he'd sensed her presence. He stretched out his arm, and her breath caught at the sight of her spirit stone swinging from the chain laced through his long fingers.

"I believe this is yours."

His ruined voice resonated in the chamber, sent gooseflesh down her arms. He'd made love to her with that voice as skillfully as he had with his hands. She followed its call like a sleepwalker, lured as much to him as to the silver-lit sapphire containing a portion of her soul.

She came up beside him, holding out her hand. The chain spilled into her palm in a gleaming waterfall, the blue jewel a warm, heavy weight against her skin. Martise gripped the necklace in tight fingers.

Silhara's profile, gilded in the moonlight shining through the window, was expressionless. He turned to her, and she stared dumbstruck, forgetting the treasure she held. Like Cumbria, he wore the trauma of the ritual on his face. The lines at the corners of his eyes had deepened, and his cheekbones were sharper, lending his austere features a gaunt appearance. But what held her gaze was his hair. A white streak ran the long length from scalp to tip.

Martise reached out and stroked the silky lock, her fingers brushing against his cheek. "When did you get this?"

His mouth curved into a faint smile. "A few weeks ago. I woke up one morning sporting this proof of my declining years. I've yet to decide if it's the result of the ritual or what Gurn served me for dinner the night before."

"It suits you. You look almost civilized," she teased.

"Kurman savage that I am," he teased back, and his smile widened.

She held up the necklace. "Cumbria said he was made an offer he couldn't refuse."

The smile transformed to a full-blown smirk of satisfaction. "The Luminary bought you. One of my rewards for saving the world and all that. The bishop wouldn't dare refuse his superior."

"He didn't know it was you."

"No. He'd have hanged you from his stable rafters before I had the chance to retrieve you if he'd known."

She shuddered. To die in the act of saving a loved one was one thing. To die for the sake of petty revenge was another.

She thrust the necklace at him gently. "Do you not want to keep it?"

He waved away her offer with a casual hand. "I warred with a god to retain my freedom, Martise. Why would I wish to have a slave of my own?"

Her fingers closed over the jewel once more, and she held it to her breast. "I can never repay you for this. I could live ten lifetimes serving you, and it wouldn't be enough."

Silhara's eyes narrowed. "There is no debt. I took your Gift from you to save myself."

"You took nothing I didn't give willingly. And you gave me my freedom in return. One has always been far greater in my eyes than the other."

Butterflies fluttered madly in her belly. He was beautiful. Standing so close, lit by candlelight and the moon's radiance, he was a fallen star—tarnished but undiminished. She felt grubby and plain in comparison.

"Please tell me Conclave gave you something other than me. Otherwise, that is poor payment for so great a risk and so great a success."

He shrugged. "I was offered another manor to the south, one that grows olives, and the barony that came with it—allied to Conclave of course." His upper lip rose a little in disdain. "I refused. Neith is my home. Oranges are my crop. I bargained for seedlings and labor to help plant them for the next two years. And a purse fat enough to keep us fed until I can begin harvesting."

Her thoughts reeled. He asked for so little. Conclave was wealthy enough and grateful enough to reward the Master of Crows with anything he asked. A great estate, ownership of a fleet of ships, a bishopric if he desired. Instead, he'd asked for an overeducated slave, field hands, orange trees and a money purse.

"I always thought you'd want to be a king."

Silhara's low chuckle caressed her. He reached behind her to pull her braid over her shoulder. Martise's eyelids fell to half-mast at the gentle tug of his fingers as he stroked her hair. "I do, but of a kingdom of my choosing, and I choose Neith."

"Won't it take years to bring the grove back to what it was?"

"A few. I disapprove of using magic to harvest a crop, but I've no qualms in employing it to coax trees to life."

His fingers wandered from her braid, danced across her collarbone with a touch so light she sighed. They trailed down the center of her chest, pausing briefly to rest against her cleavage before stopping at her hand holding the necklace. The dark of his eyes deepened.

"You are a free woman," he said. "I will give you the spell to break the stone and return that part of your soul to you. You will be able to travel the world, see those things once barred to you." His other hand rose, thumb sliding across her jawline as his fingers curved along her neck. "You're no longer property."

Martise's eyes closed, and she swayed toward him. She might not be property, but she wasn't free, and he needed no chain or spirit stone to bind her to him. She opened her eyes and met his black gaze. "What if I want to stay here? With you?"

The hand at her neck tensed, fingers pressing into her skin. His voice was almost guttural in its intensity. "You have a place here if you wish it."

He sucked in a breath when she slid her arms around his waist and drew him against her. He was wiry muscle and long bones, the soft caress of velvet and the spicy scent of matal. And he was hers—as much as she was his.

She tilted her head back and smiled at his grim, beloved features. "A place as what? A servant?"

Silhara lowered his head, and a lock of white hair, earned through harsh sacrifice and unswerving devotion, tickled her cheek.

"A companion," he whispered against her mouth. "A lover." He nibbled at her bottom lip, and his hand slid from her nape to cup the back of her head. "A beloved wife."

He teased the corner of her mouth with feathery touches and light nips. She tickled his upper lip with the tip of her tongue before pulling back enough to see his eyes.

"And will you love me for a day? A year? A lifetime?" She knew the answer but wanted to hear him say it in that beautiful, shattered voice.

"Beyond that," he whispered, eyes shining with the tempest of emotion he'd held in check until now. "Beyond the reign of false gods and meddlesome priests. Beyond al Zafira when her bright stars fade."

He kissed her then, breathed his life into her mouth, her heart, her spirit—the same way she'd breathed her Gift into him while they stood in the empty soul of a dying god.

Martise kissed him fiercely in return, holding him so tightly her arms ached, and the necklace she clutched dug into his back. When they parted, she leaned her forehead against his. "That's a long time to love someone."

Nimble fingers worked the ties of her cyrtel, unlacing them with ease. "Not long enough."

"I'd be happy with today."

Silhara parted the cyrtel's neckline, revealing her leine and the pale skin of her breasts beneath the thin fabric. A blush of desire darkened his sharp cheekbones, and his eyes glittered. The rough pad of one finger dipped into the hollow of her throat, tantalizing, teasing. "Then I'd best begin." The timbre of his voice deepened even more. "The day is dying as we speak."

Martise arched in his arms. "And the bed's too far away."

A short laugh punctuated by a gentle nip on her ear lobe made her laugh as well. "As it always is, sweet woman. As it always is."

-End-

ABOUT THE AUTHOR

Grace Draven is a fan of fantasy worlds, romance, and the anti-hero. Storytelling has been a long-standing passion of hers and a perfect excuse for not doing the laundry. She lives in Texas with her husband, three kids and big, doofus dog. You can check out her latest projects at www.gracedraven.com.

Printed in Great Britain
by Amazon